William B. (William Bower) Taylor

## A Memoir of Joseph Henry

A Sketch of His Scientific Work

William B. (William Bower) Taylor

**A Memoir of Joseph Henry**
*A Sketch of His Scientific Work*

ISBN/EAN: 9783337014360

Printed in Europe, USA, Canada, Australia, Japan

Cover: Foto ©Raphael Reischuk / pixelio.de

More available books at **www.hansebooks.com**

# A MEMOIR

OF

# JOSEPH HENRY.

## A SKETCH OF HIS SCIENTIFIC WORK.

BY

WILLIAM B. TAYLOR.

Read before the Philosophical Society of Washington,
October 26, 1878.

Second Edition.

WASHINGTON:
GOVERNMENT PRINTING OFFICE.
1880.

[ Extracted from the Henry Memorial Volume published by Order of Congress. ]

# SYNOPSIS.

## I.

## II.

# THE SCIENTIFIC WORK

OF

# JOSEPH HENRY.*

BY

## WILLIAM B. TAYLOR.

To cherish with affectionate regard the memory of the venerated dead is not more grateful to the feelings, than to recall their excellences and to retrace the stages and occasions of their intellectual conquests is instructive to the reason. Few lives within the century are more worthy of admiration, more elevating in contemplation, or more entitled to commemoration, than that of our late most honored and beloved president—JOSEPH HENRY.

Distinguished by the extent of his varied and solid learning, possessing a wide range of mental activity, so great were his modesty and self-reserve, that only by the accidental call of occasion would even an intimate friend sometimes discover with surprise the fullness of his information and the soundness of his philosophy, in some quite unsuspected direction. Remarkable for his self-control, he was no less characterized by the absence of self-assertion. Ever warmly interested in the development and advancement of the young, he was a patient listener to the trials of the disappointed, and a faithful guide to the aspirations of the ambitious. Generous without ostentation, he was always ready to assist the deserving—by services, by counsel, by active exertions in their behalf.

In his own pursuits Truth was the supreme object of his regard,—the sole interest and incentive of his investigations; and in its quest he brought to bear in just allotment qualities of a high order;—quickness and correctness of perception, inventive ingenuity in

---

* Read before the "Philosophical Society of Washington," October 26th, 1878. (*Bulletin* of the Phil. Soc. W. vol. ii. p. 230.) A large portion of the discourse (including nearly the whole of the section on the "Administration of the Smithsonian Institution") was necessarily omitted on the occasion of its delivery.

experimentation, **logical precision in deduction,** perseverance in exploration, sagacity in interpretation. *

## EARLY CAREER.

Of Henry's early struggles,—of the youthful traits which might afford us clue to his manhood's character and successes, we have but little preserved for the future biographer. Deprived of his father at an early age, he was the **sole care and the sole comfort** of his widowed mother. Carefully **nurtured in the stringent** principles **of a devout** religious faith, he adhered **through life to the** traditions **and to the** convictions derived from his honorable Scottish ancestry.

At the **age of** about seven **years, (his mother** having been induced **to** part **with him** for a time,) **he was sent by** his uncle to attend the district school **at Galway,** in **Saratoga county,** N. Y., at a distance of 36 miles from **Albany, his native city.** He remained under the care **of his** grandmother **in this village for several years,** until the **death of his uncle; when he returned to his mother at Albany.**

As a youth he was by no means precocious, as seldom have been those who have left a permanent influence on their kind. He seems to have felt no fondness for his early schools, and to have shown no special aptitude **for the** instructions they afforded. Like many **another** unpromising **lad, he** followed pretty **much his own devices, unconcerned as to the development of his latent capabilities. The books he craved were not the books his school-teachers set** before **him. The novel and the** play interested **and absorbed** the active **fancy naturally so exuberant in youth;** and the indications from his impulsive temperament and dreamy imaginative spirit were that he would probably become an actor—a dramatist—or a poet.

He was however from his childhood's years a close **observer— both of nature and** of **the** peculiarities of his fellows: and **one char-**

---

* HENRY'S tribute to Peltier, seems peculiarly applicable to himself. "He possessed in an eminent degree the mental characteristics necessary for a successful scientific discoverer; an imagination always active in suggesting hypotheses for the explanation of the phenomena under investigation, and a logical faculty never at fault in deducing consequences from the suggestions best calculated to bring them to the test of experience; an invention ever fertile in devising apparatus and other means by which the test could be applied; and finally a moral constitution which sought only the discovery of truth, and could alone be satisfied with its attainment." (Smithsonian Report for 1867, p. 158.)

acteristic early developed gave form and color to his mental disposition throughout later years,—an unflagging energy of purpose.

In 1810, or 1811, when about thirteen years of age, he was apprenticed to Mr. John F. Doty, a watch-maker and silver-smith, in Albany. He remained in this position about two years; when he was released by his employer giving up the business.

About the year 1814, while a boy of still indefinite aims and of almost as indefinite longings, having been confined to the house for a few days in consequence of an accidental injury, he took up a small volume on Natural Philosophy, casually left lying on a table by a boarder in the house. Listlessly he opened it and read. Before he reached the third page, he became profoundly interested in the statement of some of the enigmas of the great sphinx — Nature. A new world seemed opening to his inquisitive eyes. Eagerly on he read,— intent to find the hidden meanings of phenomena which hitherto covered by the "veil of familiarity" had never excited a passing wonder or a doubting question. Was it possible ever to discover the real causes of things? Here was a new Ideal — if severer, yet grander than that of art. He no longer read with the languid enjoyment of a passive recipient; he felt the new necessity of reaching out with all the faculties of a thinker, with all the activity of a co-worker.* For the first time he realized (though with no conscious expression of the thought) that there is — so to speak,—an imagination of the intellect, as well as of the emotional soul; — that *Truth* has its palaces no less gorgeous — no less wonderful than those reared by fancy in homage to the *Beautiful*.

The new impulse was not a momentary fascination. Thenceforward the novel was thrown aside, and poesy neglected; though to his latest day a sterling poem never failed to strongly impress him. As it dawned upon his reason that the foundation of the coveted

---

* "There is a great difference between *reading* and *study*, or between the indolent reception of knowledge without labor, and that effort of mind which is always necessary in order to secure an important truth and make it fully our own." J. HENRY. (*Agricultural Report* of the Patent Office for 1857, p. 421.) The book which so strongly impressed him was entitled "Lectures on Experimental Philosophy, Astronomy, and Chemistry: by G. Gregory, D. D., Vicar of West-ham." 12mo. London, 1808. The owner of the book—a young Scotchman named Robert Boyle—observing the close application of the boy, very kindly presented the book to him. Many years afterward Henry wrote in it: "It accidentally fell into my hands when I was about sixteen years old, and was the first book I ever read with attention."

knowledge must be the studies he had thought so irksome, he at once determined to repair as far as possible his loss of time by taking evening lessons from two of the professors in the Albany Academy; applying himself diligently to geometry and mechanics. And here shone out that strength of will which enabled him to rise above the harassing obstacle of the *res angusta domi*. As soon as he felt able (although yet a mere boy), he managed to procure a position as teacher in a country school, where for seven months successfully instructing boys not much younger than himself, in what he had acquired, he was enabled by rigid economy to take a regular course of instruction at the Albany Academy. Again returning to his school-teaching, he furnished himself with the means of completing his studies at the Academy; where learning that the most important key to the accurate knowledge of nature's laws is a familiarity with the logical processes of the higher mathematics, he resolutely set himself to work to master the intricacies of the differential calculus.

Having finished his academic course and passed with honor through his examinations, he then through the warm recommendation of Dr. T. Romeyn Beck — the distinguished principal of the Academy, obtained a position as private tutor in the family of General Stephen Van Rensselaer.* As this duty did not exact more than about three hours a day of his attendance, he applied his ample leisure (having in view the medical profession) — partly to the assistance of Dr. Beck in his chemical experiments, and partly to the study of anatomy and physiology, under Doctors Tully and Marsh.

His devotion to natural philosophy which had only grown and strengthened with his own growth in knowledge, led him constantly to repeat any unusual experiment as soon as reported in the foreign scientific journals; and to devise new modifications of the experiment for testing more fully the range and operation of its fundamental principles.

*Communications to the Albany Institute.*—The "Albany Institute" was organized May 5th 1824, by the union of two older

---

* Presiding officer of the original Board of Trustees of the Albany Academy.

societies; with General Stephen **Van Rensselaer as its President**:[*] and young **Henry** became **at once an active member: though with** his modest estimate of his own attainments, he preferred the part of listener and acquirer, **to that** of seeming instructor, till urged **by** those **who knew him best to add his** contributions **to** the **general** garner.

Henry's first communication **to the** Institute was read October 30th, 1824, (at the age of about twenty-six years,) and was "On the chemical and mechanical effects **of steam:** with experiments designed to illustrate the great reduction of temperature in steam of high elasticity when suddenly expanded."[†]   **From the** stop-cock **of a** strongly made copper **vessel in which steam could** be safely **generated under** considerable pressure, he **allowed an** occasional **escape; and** he showed by holding **the bulb of a thermometer in** the jet of steam, **at a** fixed distance (say of **four inches) from the** orifice, **that as the temperature and** pressure **increased within the** boiler, **the indications of the** thermometer without **grew lower;—** the **expansion and consequent** cooling of the escaping steam **under** great pressure, **increasing in a higher** ratio than the increased temperature required **for the pressure.   And** finally he exhibited the striking paradox, that the jet of saturated **steam from** a boiler will not scald the hand exposed to it, at a prescribed near distance from the try-cock, provided the steam be sufficiently hot. [‡]

Prolific and skillful in devising experiments, Henry delighted in making evident to the senses the principles he wished to impress upon the mind.   Extending the law of cooling by **expansion, from steam at high temperatures, to air at** ordinary **temperatures,** his

---

[*] The Albany Institute resulted from the fusion of "The Society for the Promotion of Useful Arts in the State of New York," organized Feb. 1791, (incorporated April 2nd, 1804,) and the "Albany Lyceum of Natural History" formed and incorporated April 23rd, 1823: of which latter society, HENRY had been a member. See "Supplement," NOTE A.

[†] *Trans. Albany Institute*, vol. 1. part 2. p. 30.

[‡] While it requires a temperature of 250° F. to generate a steam-pressure of two atmospheres (*i. e.* one additional to the existing), 25° higher will produce a pressure of three atmospheres, and 100° higher, (or 355° F.) will produce a pressure of nine atmospheres: the curve (by rectangular co-ordinates of temperature and pressure) resembling a hyperbola. The increased velocity at high pressure produces a molecular *momentum* of expansion carrying the rarefaction beyond the limit of atmospheric pressure; and in the case of the exposed hand, the injected air current doubtless adds to the cooling impression.

next communication to the Institute (made March 2nd 1825,) was "On the Production of Cold by the Rarefaction of Air." As before, he accompanied his remarks by several characteristic exhibitions.

"One of these experiments most strikingly illustrated the great reduction of temperature which takes place on the sudden rarefaction of condensed air. Half a pint of water was poured into a strong copper vessel of a globular form, and having a capacity of five gallons; a tube of one-fourth of an inch caliber with a number of holes near the lower end, and a stop-cock attached to the other extremity, was firmly screwed into the neck of the vessel; the lower end of the tube dipped into the water, but a number of holes were above the surface of the liquid, so that a jet of air mingled with water might be thrown from the fountain. The apparatus was then charged with condensed air, by means of a powerful condensing pump, until the pressure was estimated at nine atmospheres. During the condensation the vessel became sensibly warm. After suffering the apparatus to cool down to the temperature of the room, the stop-cock was opened: the air rushed out with great violence, carrying with it a quantity of water, which was instantly converted into snow. After a few seconds, the tube became filled with ice, which almost entirely stopped the current of air. The neck of the vessel was then partially unscrewed, so as to allow the condensed air to rush out around the sides of the screw: in this state the temperature of the whole interior atmosphere was so much reduced as to freeze the remaining water in the vessel." *

Although the principle on which this striking result was based was not at that time new, it must be borne in mind that this particular application, thus publicly exhibited, was long before any of the numerous patents were obtained for ice-making, not a few of which adopted substantially the same process.

*State Appointment as a Civil Engineer.*—Through the friendship and confidence of an influential judge, Henry received about this time an unexpected offer of an appointment as engineer on the survey of a route for a road through the State of New York, from

---

* *Trans. Albany Institute*, vol. 1. part 2. p. 36.

the Hudson river on the east, to lake Erie on the west, a distance of about three hundred miles. The proposal was too tempting to his natural proclivities to be refused; and being appointed, he embarked upon his new and arduous duties with the zeal and energy which were so prominent a feature of his character. "His labors in this work were exceedingly arduous and responsible. They extended far into the winter, and the operations were carried on in some instances amid deep snows in primeval forests." In connection with Professor Amos Eaton, he completed the survey with credit to himself, and to the entire satisfaction of the Commissioners of the work.

So attractive appeared the profession of engineer to his enterprising disposition, that he was about to accept the directorship in the construction of a canal in Ohio, when he was informed that the Chair of Mathematics in the Albany Academy would soon become vacant, and that his own name had already been prominently brought forward in connection with the position. At the urgent solicitation of his old friend and former teacher Dr. T. Romeyn Beck, he consented with some hesitation to signify his willingness to accept the vacant chair if appointed thereto.

*Election as Professor of Mathematics.*—In the spring of 1826, Henry was duly elected by the Trustees of the Albany Academy to the Professorship of Mathematics and Natural Philosophy in that institution. As the duties of his office did not commence till September of that year, he was allowed a practical vacation of about five months; which was partly occupied with a geological exploration in the adjoining counties, as assistant to Professor Eaton, of the Rensselaer School, and partly devoted to a conscientious preparation for his new position.

In a worldly point of view, this variety of occupation and versatility of adaptation might perhaps be regarded as unfavorable to success. As a method of culture, it was of unquestionable advantage to his intellectual powers. A hard student, with great capacity for close application, he accumulated large stores of information; and in addition to the slaking of his constant thirst for acquirement in different directions, his leisure was occupied to a considerable extent with physical and chemical investigations. On the 21st of March 1827, he delivered before the Albany Institute a lecture on "Flame," accompanied with experiments.*

*Meteorological Work.*—The Regents of the University of the State of New York, endowed by the State Legislature with supervisory functions over the public educational institutions of the State,—in 1825 established a system of meteorological observation for the State, by supplying to each of the Academies incorporated by them, a thermometer and a rain-gauge, and requiring them to keep a daily register of prescribed form, to entitle them to their portion of the literature fund of the State. In 1827, the Hon. Simeon De Witt, Chancellor of the Board of Regents, associated with himself Dr. T. Romeyn Beck and Professor Henry of the Albany Academy, to prepare and tabulate the results of these observations. The first Abstract of these collections (for the year 1828) comprised tabulations of the monthly and yearly means of temperature, wind, rain, etc. at all the stations, an account of meteorological incidents generally, and a table of "Miscellaneous Observations" on the dates of notable phases of organic phenomena connected with climatic conditions. These annual Abstracts, to which Henry devoted a considerable share of his attention, were continued through a series of years and were published in the "Annual Reports of the Regents of the University to the Legislature of the State of New York.† The third Abstract (for 1830) includes an accurate tabulation by Henry of the latitudes, longitudes, and elevations of all the meteorological stations; over forty in number.

ELECTRICAL RESEARCHES AT ALBANY: FROM 1827 TO 1832.

Of Henry's distinguished success as a lecturer and teacher, in imparting to his pupils a portion of his own zeal and earnestness in the pursuit of scientific knowledge, as well as in winning their affection and in inspiring their esteem, it is not designed here to discourse; but rather of his solitary labors outside of his professional

---

* *Trans. Albany Institute*, vol. 1. part 2. p. 59.

† *Reports of Regents, etc.* Albany, vol. 1, 1829-1835.

occupation in communicating and diffusing knowledge. Very shortly after his occupation of the academic chair of mathematics and physics, he turned his attention to the experimental study of that mysterious agency — electricity. Professor Schweigger of Halle, had improved on Oersted's galvanic indicator (of a single wire circuit) by giving the insulated wire a number of turns around an elongated frame longitudinally enclosing the compass needle; and by thus multiplying the effect of the galvanic circuits, had converted it into a real *measuring* instrument — a "galvanometer."[*] Ampère and Arago of Paris, developing Oersted's announcement of the torsional or equatorial reaction between a galvanic conductor and a magnetic needle, had found that a circulating galvanic current was capable not only of deflecting a suspended magnet, but of *generating* magnetism — permanently in sewing needles, and temporarily in pieces of iron wire, when placed within a glass tube around which the conjunctive wire of the battery had been wound in a loose helix; and had thus created the "electro-magnet."[†] The scientific world was just aroused to the close interrogation of this new marvel, each questioner eager to ascertain its most efficient conditions, and to increase its manifestations. William Sturgeon of Woolwich, England, had extended the discoveries of Ampère and Arago, by dispensing with the glass tube, constructing a "horse-shoe" bar of soft iron (after the form of the usual permanent magnet) coated with a non-conducting substance, and winding the copper conjunctive wire directly upon the horse-shoe; and had thus

---

[*] The name of GALVANI (as original discoverer of chemico-electricity) is usually retained to designate both the current and its generator; although the chemico-electric pile and battery were really first contrived by VOLTA in 1800. In the same manner OERSTED is generally accounted the discoverer of electro-magnetism, although he never devised an electro-magnet; and appears not to have been the first even to discover the directive influence of a current on a magnetic needle. Eighteen years before his announcement, GIAN DOMENICO ROMAGNOSI, a physicist of Trent, published in an Italian newspaper of that city, the *Gazzétta di Trento*, on the 3rd of August, 1802, his observation of the galvanic deflection of the needle. This important discovery was also published in Professor G. Aldini's "Essai théorique et expérimental sur le Galvanisme." 4to. Paris, 1804, p. 191; and in Professor J. Izarn's "Manuel du Galvanisme." 8vo. Paris, 1805, sect. ix. p. 120.

[†] *Annales de Chimie et de Physique*, 1820, vol. xv. pp. 93-100. VAN BEEK of Utrecht, in 1821 inverting ARAGO'S experiment, had found that an iron or steel wire coiled around a glass tube as a short helix, became magnetic on passing a charge from a Leyden jar through a straight brass wire placed within the glass tube. Communicated by Professor G. Moll. (Brewster's *Edinburgh Journal of Science*, Jan. 1822, vol. vi. p. 84.)

produced the first *efficient* electro-magnet;—capable of sustaining several pounds by its armature, when duly excited by the galvanic current.   He had also greatly improved lecture-room apparatus for illustrating the electro-magnetic reactions of rotations, etc. (where a permanent magnet is employed), by introducing stronger magnets, and had thereby succeeded in exhibiting the phenomena on a larger scale, with a considerable reduction of the battery power. *

Faraday had not yet commenced the series of researches which in after years so illumined his name, when Henry published his first contribution to electrical science, in a communication read before the Albany Institute, October 10th, 1827, "On some Modifications of the Electro-Magnetic Apparatus."   From his experimental investigations he was enabled to exhibit all the class illustrations attempted by Sturgeon, on even a still larger and more conspicuous scale, with the employment of very weak magnets (where required), and with a still further reduction of the battery power.   These quite striking and unexpected results were obtained by the simple expedient of adopting in every case where single circuits had previously been used, the manifold coil of fine wire which Schweigger had employed to increase the sensibility of the galvanometer.   He remarks :

"Mr. Sturgeon of Woolwich, who has been perhaps the most successful in these improvements, has shown that a strong galvanic power is not essentially necessary even to exhibit the experiments on the largest scale. - - - Mr. Sturgeon's suite of apparatus, though superior to any other as far as it goes, does not however form a complete set: as indeed it is plain that his principle of strong magnets cannot be introduced into every article required, and particularly into those intended to exhibit the action of the earth's magnetism on a galvanic current, or the operation of two conjunctive wires on each other.   To form therefore a set of instruments on a large scale that will illustrate all the facts belonging to

---

* *Trans. Soc. Encouragement Arts*, etc. 1825, vol. xliii. pp. 38–52.  His battery (of a single element) consisted "of two fixed hollow concentric cylinders of thin copper, having a movable cylinder of zinc placed between them.  Its superficial area is only 130 square inches, and it weighs no more than 1 lb. 5 ozs."  Mr. STURGEON was deservedly awarded the Silver Medal of the Society for the Encouragement of Arts, etc., "for his improved electro-magnetic apparatus."   Described also in *Annals of Philos.* Nov. 1826, vol. xii. new series, pp. 357–361.

this science, with the least expense of **galvanism, evidently** requires some additional modification of apparatus, and particularly in those cases in which powerful magnets cannot be applied. And such a modification appears to me to be obviously pointed out in the construction of Professor Schweigger's Galvanic Multiplier: the principles of this instrument being directly applicable to all the experiments in which Mr. Sturgeon's improvement fails to be useful." *

The coils employed in the various articles of apparatus thus improved, comprised usually about twenty turns of fine copper wire wound with silk to prevent metallic contact, the whole being closely bound together. To exhibit for example Ampère's ingenious and delicate experiment showing the directive action of the earth as a magnet on a galvanic current when its conductor is free to move, (usually a small wire frame with its extremities dipping either into mercury cups, or into mercury channels,) or its simpler modification, the "ring" of De la Rive, (usually an inch or two in diameter and made to float freely with its galvanic element in its own bath,) the effect was strikingly enhanced by Henry's method of suspending by a silk thread a large circular coil twenty inches in diameter, of many wire circuits bound together with ribbon,— the extremities of the wire protruding at the lower part of the hoop, and soldered to a pair of small galvanic plates;—when by simply placing a tumbler of acidulated water beneath, he caused the hoop at once to assume (after a few oscillations) its equatorial position transverse to the magnetic meridian. By a similar arrangement of two circular coils of different diameters, one suspended within the other, Ampère's fine discovery of the mutual action of two electric currents on each other, was as strikingly displayed. Such was the character of demonstration by which the new Professor was accustomed to make visible to his classes the principles of electro-magnetism: and it is safe to say that in simplicity, distinctness, and efficiency, such apparatus for the lecture-room was far superior to any of the kind then existing.

Should any one be disposed to conclude that this simple extension of Schweigger's multiple coil was unimportant and unmeritorious, the ready answer occurs, that talented and skillful electri-

* _Trans. Albany Institute,_ vol. I. pp. 22, 23.

cians, laboring to attain the result, had for six years failed to make
such an extension. Nor was the result by any means antecedently
assured by Schweigger's success with the galvanometer. If Sturgeon's improvement of economizing the battery size and consumption, by increasing the magnet factor (in those few cases where
available), was well deserving of reward, surely Henry's improvement of a far greater economy, by increasing the circuit factor
(entirely neglected by Sturgeon) deserved a still higher applause.

In a subsequent communication to Silliman's Journal, Henry
remarks on the results announced in October, 1827:—"Shortly
after the publication mentioned, several other applications of the
coil, besides those described in that paper, were made in order to
increase the size of electro-magnetic apparatus, and to diminish
the necessary galvanic power. The most interesting of these was
its application to a development of magnetism in soft iron, much
more extensive than to my knowledge had been previously effected
by a small galvanic element." And in another later paper, he
repeated to the same effect: "After reading an account of the galvanometer of Schweigger, the idea occurred to me that a much
nearer approximation to the theory of Ampère could be attained
by insulating the conducting-wire itself, instead of the rod to be
magnetized; and by covering the whole surface of the iron with a
series of coils in close contact."

The electro-magnet figured and described by Sturgeon (in his
communication of November, 1825,) consisted of a small bar or
stout iron wire bent into a ∩ or horse-shoe form, having a copper
wire wound loosely around it in eighteen turns, with the ends of
the wire dipping into mercury-cups connected with the respective
poles of a battery having 130 square inches of active surface.
This was probably the only electro-magnet then in existence.

In June of 1828, Henry exhibited before the Albany Institute a
small-sized electro-magnet closely wound with silk-covered copper
wire about one-thirtieth of an inch in diameter. By thus insulating the conducting wire, instead of the magnetic bar or core, he
was enabled to employ a compact coil in close juxtaposition from
one end of the horse-shoe to the other, obtaining thereby a much
larger number of circuits, and with each circuit more nearly at

right angles with the magnetic axis. The lifting power of this magnet is not stated, though it must obviously have been much more powerful than the one described by Sturgeon.

In March of 1829, Henry exhibited before the Institute a somewhat larger magnet of the same character. "A round piece of iron about one-quarter of an inch in diameter was bent into the usual form of a horse-shoe, and instead of loosely coiling around it a few feet of wire, as is usually described, it was tightly wound with 35 feet of wire covered with silk, so as to form about 400 turns; a pair of small galvanic plates which could be dipped into a tumbler of diluted acid, was soldered to the ends of the wire, and the whole mounted on a stand. With these small plates the horse-shoe became much more powerfully magnetic than another of the same size and wound in the usual manner, by the application of a battery composed of 28 plates of copper and zinc each 8 inches square." In this case the coil was wound upon itself in successive layers.

To Henry, therefore, belongs the exclusive credit of having first constructed the magnetic "spool" or "bobbin," that form of coil since universally employed for every application of electro-magnetism, of induction, or of magneto-electrics. This was his first great contribution to the science and to the art of galvanic magnetization.

In the latter part of 1829, Henry still further increased the magnetic power derived from a single galvanic pair of small size, by a new arrangement of the coil. "It consisted in using several strands of wire each covered with silk, instead of one." Employing a horse-shoe formed from a cylindrical bar of iron half an inch in diameter and about 10 inches long, wound with 30 feet of tolerably fine copper wire, he found that with a current from only two and a half square inches of zinc, the magnet held 14 pounds. Winding upon its arms a second wire of the same length (30 feet) whose ends were similarly joined to the same galvanic pair, he found that the magnet lifted 28 pounds. "With a pair of plates 4 inches by 6, it lifted 39 pounds, or more than fifty times its own weight."* On these results he remarks:

---

* It must not be forgotten that at the time when this experimental magnet was made, the strongest if not the only electro-magnet in Europe was that of STURGEON, capable of supporting 9 pounds, with 130 square inches of zinc surface in the battery.

"These experiments conclusively proved that a great development of magnetism could be effected by a very small galvanic element, and also that the power of the coil was materially increased by multiplying the number of wires, without increasing the length of each. The multiplication of the wires increases the power in two ways: first, by conducting a greater quantity of galvanism, and secondly, by giving it a more proper direction; for since the action of a galvanic current is directly at right angles to the axis of a magnetic needle, by using several shorter wires we can wind one on each inch of the length of the bar to be magnetized, so that the magnetism of each inch will be developed by a separate wire. In this way the action of each particular coil becomes directed very nearly at right angles to the axis of the bar, and consequently the effect is the greatest possible. This principle is of much greater importance when large bars are used. The advantage of a greater conducting power from using several wires might in a less degree be obtained by substituting for them one large wire of equal sectional area; but in this case the obliquity of the spiral would be much greater, and consequently the magnetic action less." *

But in the following year, 1830, Henry pressed forward his researches to still higher results. Assisted by his friend Dr. Philip Ten-Eyck, he proceeded to test the power of electro-magnetic attraction on a larger scale. "A bar of soft iron 2 inches square and 20 inches long was bent into the form of a horse-shoe 9 inches high; (the sharp edges of the bar being first a little rounded by the hammer;) it weighed 21 pounds. A piece of iron from the same bar, weighing 7 pounds, was filed perfectly flat on one surface for an armature or lifter. The extremities of the legs of the horse-shoe were also truly ground to the surface of the armature. Around this horse-shoe 540 feet of copper bell-wire were wound in nine coils of 60 feet each; these coils were not continued around the whole length of the bar, but each strand of wire (according to the principle before mentioned) occupied about two inches, and was coiled several times backward and forward over itself. The several ends of the wires

---

* Silliman's *Am. Journal of Science*, Jan. 1831, vol. xix. p. 402. The three names — ARAGO, STURGEON, and HENRY, — may well typify the infancy, the youth, and the mature manhood, of the electro-magnet.

were left projecting, and all numbered, so that the first and the last end of each strand might be readily distinguished. In this manner we formed an experimental magnet on a large scale, with which several combinations of wire could be made by merely uniting the different projecting ends. Thus if the second end of the first wire be soldered to the first end of the second wire, and so on through all the series, the whole will form a continued coil of one long wire. By soldering different ends, the whole may be formed into a double coil of half the length, or into a triple coil of one-third the length, &c. The horse-shoe was suspended in a strong rectangular wooden frame 3 feet 9 inches high and 20 inches wide."

Two of the wires (one from each extremity of the legs) when joined together by soldering, so as to form a single circuit of 120 feet, with its extreme ends connected with the battery, produced a lifting-power of 60 pounds. The same two wires being separately connected with the same battery (forming a double circuit of 60 feet each), a lifting-power of 200 pounds was obtained, or more than three times the power of the former case with the same wire. Four wires (two from each extremity of the legs) being separately connected with the battery (forming four circuits) gave a lifting-power of 500 pounds. Six wires (three from each leg) united in three pairs (forming three circuits of 180 feet each) gave a lifting-power of 290 pounds. The same six wires being separately connected with the battery in six independent circuits, produced a lifting-power of 570 pounds, or very nearly double that of the same wires in double lengths. When all the nine wires were separately attached to the battery a lifting-power of 650 pounds was evoked. In all these experiments "a small single battery was used, consisting of two concentric copper cylinders, with zinc between them; the whole amount of zinc-surface exposed to the acid from both sides of the zinc was two-fifths of a square foot; the battery required only half a pint of dilute acid for its submersion."

"In order to ascertain the effect of a very small galvanic element on this large quantity of iron, a pair of plates *exactly one inch square* was attached to all the wires; the weight lifted was 85 pounds." For the purpose of obtaining the maximum attractive power of this magnet, with its nine independent coils, "a small battery formed with a plate of zinc 12 inches long and 6 wide, and surrounded by copper, was substituted for the galvanic element used in the former experiments; the weight lifted in this case was 750 pounds."* In illustration of the feeble power of the magnetic poles when exerted separately, it was found that with precisely the same arrangements giving a holding power of 750 pounds to the double contact armature, either pole alone was capable of sustaining only 5 or 6 pounds; "and in this case we never succeeded in making it lift the armature — weighing 7 pounds. We have never seen the circumstance noticed of so great a difference between a single pole and both."

*Henry's "Quantity" Magnet compared with Moll's.*— About the same time that Henry was developing this wonderful power in the electro-magnet, Dr. Gerard Moll, Professor of Natural Philosophy in the University of Utrecht, was engaged in a similar research. In a paper published in the latter part of 1830, he states that his attention was drawn to the electro-magnet of Sturgeon in 1828, during a visit to London.† "This apparatus I saw in 1828 at Mr. Watkins's, curator of philosophical apparatus to the London University; and the horse-shoe with which he performed the experiment, became capable all at once of supporting about nine pounds.‡ I immediately determined to try the effect of a larger galvanic apparatus on a bent iron cylindrical wire, and I obtained results which appear astonishing, and are — as far as the intensity of magnetic force is concerned, altogether new. I have anxiously looked since that time into different scientific continental and English journals, without finding any further attempt to extend and improve Mr. Sturgeon's original experiment." Moll's first magnet, a horse-shoe formed of a round bar of iron about one inch thick, was about eight and one-half inches in height, and had a wrapped copper wire of about one-eighth inch diameter coiled eighty-three times around it. The weight of the horse-shoe and wire was about

---

*Silliman's *Am. Journal of Science*, Jan. 1831, vol. xix. pp. 404, 405.

†*Bibliothèque Universelle des Sciences*, etc. Sept. 1830, vol. xlv. pp. 19-35. Also *Edinburgh Journal of Science*, Oct. 1830.

‡[At the date referred to, Henry had already exhibited before the Albany Institute, a much more powerful magnet.]

five pounds; of the armature, about one and one-fourth pound; and with a single galvanic pair whose acting zinc surface was about eleven square feet, the electro-magnet supported about 50 pounds. With cautious additions, the load could be increased to 75 pounds. An additional galvanic pair of about six square feet was applied without increasing the power of the magnet. Another horse-shoe about twelve and a half inches in height, formed of a rod two and one-fourth inches in diameter, was prepared by Professor Moll, with a brass wire, one-eighth of an inch thick, wound around it in forty-four coils; the weight of the whole being about twenty-six pounds. With the galvanic element of eleven square feet, this magnet lifted 135 pounds. The largest load this magnet was afterward made to support was 154 pounds. *

As soon as the account of Moll's magnet reached this country, (late in October, or early in November,) Henry — who had obtained and had publicly exhibited nearly two years previously, considerably higher results, and who realized that there was at least one very important difference of construction between his own magnet and that of the Dutch savant, felt it a duty at once to publish the details of his own researches, in a more public form. He accordingly proceeded in the latter part of November, 1830, to write out a description of his former experiments and results, which he forwarded to Silliman's American Journal of Science, (then published only quarterly,) in time for insertion in the forthcoming number of that journal, for January, 1831; causing a copy of Professor Moll's paper, taken from Brewster's Edinburgh Journal of Science for October 1830, to be inserted in the same number. At the conclusion of his own article he remarks: "The only effect Professor Moll's paper has had over these investigations, has been to hasten their publication: the principle on which they were instituted was known to us nearly two years since, and at that time exhibited to the Albany Institute."

Comparing now Moll's results with Henry's, — we find that Henry's magnet of November or December, 1829, (a half-inch bar

---

of iron covered with several strands of wire,) excited by a galvanic pair of one-sixth of a square foot of zinc surface, sustained 39 pounds, or more than fifty times its own weight; while Moll's magnet of about double the dimensions, employing eleven square feet of battery, lifted only 75 pounds, or fifteen times its own weight. That is, Henry's magnet while about only one-seventh of the weight of Moll's (without their wrappings) supported more than half the load of the latter. Or comparing their larger magnets, — while Moll's twelve and a half inch magnet (of two and a quarter inch iron) lifted as its greatest effort 154 pounds, (a result with which the author justly felt elated,) Henry's nine and a half inch magnet (of about the same sized iron) lifted 750 pounds; or about five times its maximum load. But the most surprising contrast between the two series of experiments, resulting from their different systems, was the enormous difference of battery-power respectively applied; — Moll pushing his up to seventeen square feet, — Henry reducing his in the first case to one-sixth of a square foot, and in the latter case obtaining his five-fold duty with one-eleventh of the quantity of galvanic current. The philosopher of Utrecht, though he evidently realized with him of Albany, the importance of close-winding, employed but a single layer of coil. The latter, by means of well-considered trials had ascertained the great increase of magnetic force resulting from a considerable number of coils. On the theoretical grounds assigned by Henry therefore, Moll's single conducting wire of one-eighth inch diameter, while electrically equivalent to some half a dozen of Henry's conducting wires (of the same length and collective weight) would be magnetically inferior thereto — for equal iron cores.

Notwithstanding that Henry's successes were thus both earlier and more brilliant than those of Moll, the two names are usually associated together by European writers in treating of the development of the magnet.*

---

*FARADAY in subsequently investigating the conditions of galvanic induction, referred with approbation to the magnets of MOLL and HENRY as best calculated to produce the effects sought. In constructing his duplex helices for observing the direction of the induced current, he however adopted HENRY's method by winding twelve coils of copper wire each twenty-seven feet long — one upon the other. (*Phil. Trans. Roy. Soc.* Nov. 24, 1831, vol. cxxii. (for 1832,) pp. 126, and 138. *Experimental Researches*, etc. vol. 1. art. 6, p. 2; and art. 57, p. 15.)

*Henry's "Intensity" Magnet.*—But Henry's remarkable paper of January, 1831, contains still another original contribution to the theory and practice of electro-magnetics, no less important than his invention of the magnetic spool. While Moll had endeavored to induce strong magnetism by the use of a powerful "quantity" battery, Henry had labored to derive from a minimum galvanic power its maximum magnetizing effect: and in his varied experiments on these two factors, he discovered very curious and unsuspected relations between them. A great majority of investigators—after having definitely ascertained the striking fact of the great inferiority in magnetizing power, of a single long continuous coil, to a proportionally shortened circuit of multiple coils,— would naturally have been led to abandon all further investigation of the feebler system. Henry however recognized in this a field of instructive inquiry: and for the first time showed that the coil of short and numerous circuits, least affected by a battery of many pairs, was on the contrary most responsive to a single galvanic element; while the single extended coil, least influenced by a single pair, was most excited by a battery of numerous elements.

The illustrious Laplace had suggested to Ampère in 1820,— immediately upon the discovery of the galvanometer, that it would be desirable to test the deflection of the needle through a long circuit of conjunctive wire. The latter having made the experiment "through a very long conducting wire," (the length of which is not stated,) and having found the result "completely successful," had remarked in a paper presented to the "Royal Academy of Sciences," October 2nd, 1820, that by sending the galvanic current through long wires connecting two distant stations, the deflections of inclosed magnetic needles would constitute very simple and efficient signals for an instantaneous telegraph. *

Peter Barlow the eminent English mathematician and magnetician taking up the suggestion, had endeavored more fully to test its practicability. He has thus stated the result: "In a very early stage of electro-magnetic experiments it had been suggested that an instantaneous telegraph might be established by means of conducting wires and compasses. The details of this contrivance are so obvious, and

---

* *Annales de Chimie et de Physique,* 1820, vol. xv. pp. 72, 73.

the principle on which it **is founded so well understood, that there** was only one question which could render the **result doubtful ; and** this was,—is there any diminution of effect by lengthening **the con-** ducting wire? It had been said that the electric fluid from a common [tin-foil] **electrical** battery had been transmitted through a **wire four miles** in length without any sensible **diminution of** effect, and to every appearance instantaneously ;* **and** if this should be found **to be the case** with the **galvanic circuit, then no** question could be entertained of the practicability and utility of **the** suggestion above **adverted to.** I was therefore induced to make the trial ; but I found such a sensible diminution with only 200 **feet** of wire, as at **once** to convince me of the impracticability of the scheme. It led me how- ever to an inquiry as to the cause of this diminution, and the laws by which it is governed."†

Henry **in** his researches just referred to, (assisted by his **friend Dr. Ten-Eyck,)** employed a small electro-magnet **of** one-quarter inch iron "wound **with about 8** feet of copper **wire."** Excited with **a single** pair "composed of a **piece of** zinc plate 4 inches by **7, surrounded** with copper," (about 56 square inches of zinc sur- face,) the magnet sustained four pounds **and a** half. With about 500 **feet of** insulated copper wire (0.045 of an inch in diameter) interposed between the battery and the **magnet, its lifting power** was reduced **to two** ounces ;— or about **36 times.** With double this length of wire, or a little over 1000 **feet, interposed,** the lifting power of the magnet was only half **an ounce : thus** fully confirm- ing the results obtained **by** Barlow **with** the galvanometer. With

---

*[SALVA in 1798, had successfully worked an electric telegraph from Madrid to Aranjuez,—a distance of 26 miles. (Turnbull's *Electro-Magnetic Telegraph*, 2nd. ed. 1853, pp. 21, 22.) Frictional or mechanical electricity does not observe OHM's law of resist- ance. The only drawback to its application, is the greatly increased difficulty of insulation.]

†"On the Laws of Electro-magnetic Action." *Edinburgh Philosophical Journal,* Jan. 1825, vol. xii. pp. 105-113. In explanation and justification of this discouraging judgment from so high an authority in magnetics, it must be remembered that both in the galvanometer and in the electro-magnet, the coil **best calculated** to produce large effects, was that **of least** resistance; **which unfortunately** was not that best adapted **to a** long circuit. On the other hand, **the most efficient** magnet or galva- nometer was not found to be improved in result by increasing the number of gal- vanic elements. BARLOW in his inquiry as to the **"law of** diminution" was led (erroneously) to regard the resistance of the conducting **wire** as increasing in the ratio of *the square root* of its length. (pp. 110, 111.)

a small galvanic pair 2 inches square, acting through the same length of wire (over 1000 feet,) "the magnetism was scarcely observable in the horse-shoe." Employing next a trough battery of 25 pairs, having the same zinc surface as previously, the magnet in direct connection, (which before had supported four and a half pounds,) now lifted but seven ounces;—not quite half a pound. But with the 1060 feet of copper wire (a little more than one-fifth of a mile) suspended several times across the large room of the Academy, and placed in the galvanic circuit, the same magnet sustained eight ounces: that is to say, the current from the galvanic trough produced greater magnetic effect after traversing this length of wire, than it did without it.

"From this experiment it appears that the current from a galvanic trough is capable of producing greater magnetic effect on soft iron after traversing more than one-fifth of a mile of intervening wire than when it passes only through the wire surrounding the magnet. It is possible that the different states of the trough with respect to dryness may have exerted some influence on this remarkable result; but that the effect of a current from a trough if not increased is but slightly diminished in passing through a long wire is certain." And after speculating on this new and at the time somewhat paradoxical result, suggesting that "a current from a trough possesses more 'projectile' force (to use Professor Hare's expression,) and approximates somewhat in 'intensity' to the electricity from the common machine," Henry concludes: "But be this as it may, the fact that the magnetic action of a current from a *trough* is at least not sensibly diminished by passing through a long wire, is directly applicable to Mr. Barlow's project of forming an electro-magnetic telegraph;* and it is also of material consequence in the construction of the galvanic coil. From these experiments it is evident that in forming the coil we may either use one very long wire, or several shorter ones, as the circumstances may require: in the first case, our galvanic combination must consist of a num-

---

*[Really AMPÈRE's project, not BARLOW'S. In a subsequent paper HENRY corrected this allusion by saying, "I called it 'Barlow's project,' when I ought to have stated that Mr. Barlow's investigation merely tended to disprove the possibility of a telegraph."]

ber of plates so as to give 'projectile' force; in the second, it must be formed of a single pair." *

The importance of this discovery can hardly be overestimated. The magnetic "spool" of fine wire, of a length — tens and even hundreds of times that ever before employed for this purpose,— was in itself a gift to science, which really forms an epoch in the history of electro-magnetism. It is not too much to say that almost every advancement which has been made in this fruitful branch of physics since the time of Sturgeon's happy improvement, from the earliest researches of Faraday downward, has been directly indebted to Henry's magnets. By means of the Henry "spool" the magnet almost at a bound was developed from a feeble childhood to a vigorous manhood. And so rapidly and generally was the new form introduced abroad among experimenters, few of whom had ever seen the papers of Henry, that probably very few indeed have been aware to whom they were really indebted for this familiar and powerful instrumentality. But the historic fact remains, that prior to Henry's experiments in 1829, no one on either hemisphere had ever thought of winding the limbs of an electro-magnet on the principle of the "bobbin," and not till after the publication of Henry's method in January of 1831, was it ever employed by any European physicist. †

But in addition to this large gift to science, Henry (as we have seen) has the pre-eminent claim to popular gratitude of having first practically worked out the differing functions of two entirely different kinds of electro-magnet: the one surrounded with numerous coils of no great length, designated by him the "quantity" magnet, the other surrounded with a continuous coil of very great length, designated by him the "intensity" magnet.‡ The latter

---

* Silliman's *Am. Jour. Sci.* Jan. 1831, vol. xix. pp. 403, 404.

† HENRY's "spool" magnet appears to have been introduced into France by POUILLET in 1832. *Nouveau Bulletin des Sciences; publié par la Société Philomatique de Paris.* Séance of 23d June, 1832, p. 127. In Pouillet's *Eléments de Physique Expérimentale,* third edition, published in 1837, (vol. i. p. 572,) the date of this magnet is inadvertently given as 1831; an inaccuracy which though unimportant, is perpetuated in every subsequent edition of that popular text-book. In the second edition, published in 1832, no allusion to the magnet occurs.

‡ "In describing the results of my experiments the terms 'intensity' and 'quantity' magnets were introduced to avoid circumlocution, and were intended to be used merely in a technical sense. By the *intensity* magnet I designated a

and feebler system (requiring for its action a battery of numerous elements,) was shown to have the singular capability (never before suspected nor imagined) of subtile excitation from a distant source. Here for the first time is experimentally established the important principle that there must be a proportion between the aggregate internal resistance of the battery and the whole external resistance of the conjunctive wire or conducting circuit; with the very important practical consequence, that by combining with an "intensity" magnet of a single extended fine coil an "intensity" battery of many small pairs, its electro-motive force enables a very long conductor to be employed without sensible diminution of the effect.* This was a very important though unconscious experimental confirmation of the mathematical theory of Ohm, embodied in his formula expressing the relation between electric flow and electric resistance, which though propounded two or three years previously, failed for a long time to attract any attention from the scientific world. †

Never should it be forgotten that he who first exalted the "quantity" magnet of Sturgeon from a power of twenty pounds to a power of twenty hundred pounds, was the absolute CREATOR of the "intensity" magnet; and that the principles involved in this creation, constitute the indispensable basis of every form of the electro-

---

piece of soft iron so surrounded with wire that its magnetic power could be called into operation by an 'intensity' battery; and by a *quantity* magnet, a piece of iron so surrounded by a number of separate coils that its magnetism could be fully developed by a 'quantity' battery." (*Smithsonian Report* for 1857, p. 103.) These terms though somewhat antiquated and generally discarded by recent writers, are still very convenient designations of the two classes of action, both in the battery and in the magnet. See "Supplement," NOTE B.

* Beyond a certain maximum length there is of course, a decrease of power for each particular coil of the "intensity" magnet, proportioned to the increased resistance of a long conductor; but the magnetizing effect has not been found to be diminished in the ratio of its length. In a very long wire, the magnetizing influence (with a suitable "intensity" battery) appears to be inversely proportioned to the square of the length of the conductor.

†GEORG SIMON OHM, professor in physics at Munich, published at Berlin, in 1827, his "Galvanische Kette, mathematisch bearbeitet:" and in the following year, he published a supplementary paper entitled "Nachträge zu seiner mathematischen Bearbeitung der galvanischen Kette;" in Kastner's *Archiv für gesammte Naturlehre*: (8vo. Nürnberg:) 1828, vol. xiv. pp. 475–493. Fourteen years after the publication of the former memoir, this elaborate discussion was for the first time translated into English, by Mr. William Francis. ("The Galvanic Circuit Investigated mathematically." Taylor's *Scientific Memoirs*, etc. London, 1841, vol. ii. pp. 401–506.)

magnetic telegraph since invented. They settled satisfactorily (in Barlow's phrase) the "only question which could render the result doubtful;" and though derived from the magnet, were obviously as applicable to the galvanometer needle.* Professor Moll, the foremost of Europeans in the electro-magnetic chase, and close upon the heels of Henry in one portion of his researches, produced a powerful "quantity" magnet, but one hopelessly and radically incapacitated from any such application.

It is idle to say in disparagement of these successes, that in the competitive race of numerous distinguished investigators in the field, diligently searching into the conditions of the new-found agency, the same results would sooner or later have been reached by others. For of what discovery or invention may not the same be said? Only those who have sought in the twilight of uncertainty, can appreciate the vast economy of effort by prompt directions to the path from one who has gained an advance. Not for what might be, but for the actual bestowal, does he who first grasps a valuable truth merit the return of at least a grateful recognition.

If these results apparently so simple when announced by Henry, have never been justly appreciated either at home or abroad, no such complaint ever escaped their author. No such thought seems ever to have occurred to his artless nature. For him the one sufficient incentive and recompense was the advancement of himself and others in the knowledge of nature's laws. With the telegraph consciously within his grasp, he was well content to leave to others the glory and the emoluments of its realization.

At the beginning of the year 1831, Henry had suspended around the walls of one of the upper rooms in the Albany Academy, a mile of copper bell-wire interposed in a circuit between a small Cruickshanks battery and an "intensity" magnet of continuous fine coil. A narrow steel rod (a permanent magnet) pivoted to swing horizontally like the compass needle, was arranged so that one end remained in

* "For circuits of small resistance, galvanometers of small resistance must be used. For circuits of large resistance, galvanometers of large resistance must also be used; not that their resistance is any advantage, but because we cannot have a galvanometer adapted to indicate very small currents without having a very large number of turns in the coil, and this involves necessarily a large resistance." Professor F. Jenkin, *Electricity and Magnetism*, 12mo. London, and New York, 1873, chap. iv. sect. 8, p. 89.

contact with a leg of the soft iron core, while near the opposite end of the compass rod, a small stationary office-bell was placed. At each excitation of the electro-magnet, the compass rod or needle was repelled from one leg (by its similar magnetism) and attracted by the other leg, so that its free end tapped the bell. On a reversal of the current, the compass rod moved back to the opposite leg of the electro-magnet. This simple device the Professor was accustomed to exhibit to his classes, during the years 1831 and 1832, in illustration of the facility of transmitting signals to a distance by the swift action of electro-magnetism.*

Henry regarded his "quantity" magnet as being *scientifically* more important than his "intensity" magnet; and his success in constructing such, of almost incredible power, caused numerous requisitions on his skill. In April, 1831, Professor Silliman published in his *Journal* "An Account of a large Electro-Magnet made for the Laboratory of Yale College," under his charge. The iron horseshoe about one foot high was made from a three-inch octagonal bar 30 inches long; and was wrapped with 26 strands of copper wire each about 28 feet long. When duly excited by a single galvanic element consisting of concentric cylinders of copper and zinc, presenting about five square feet of active surface, the magnet lifted 2,300 pounds, more than a ton weight. For reversing the polarity of the magnet, a duplicate battery was oppositely connected with extensions of the ends of the coils, so that either battery could be alternately dipped. With a load of 56 pounds suspended from the armature, the poles of the magnet could be so rapidly reversed, that the weight would not fall during the interval of inversion. Professor Silliman remarks of the maker: "He has the honor of having constructed by far the most powerful magnets that have ever been known; and his last, weighing (armature and all) but $82\frac{1}{2}$ pounds, sustains over a ton;—which is eight times more powerful than any magnet hitherto known in Europe."† And Sturgeon

---

* For an account of HENRY'S relation to the electro-magnetic Telegraph, see "Supplement," NOTE C.

† Silliman's *Am. Jour. Sci.* April, 1831, vol. xx. p. 201. *Relatively,* some of HENRY'S smaller magnets were many times more powerful than this. A miniature one made by Dr. Ten-Eyck under his direction, sustained 200 times its own weight; and one still smaller, sustained more than 400 times its own weight! (Sill. *Am. Jour. Sci.* vol. xix. p. 407.)

(the true foster-father of the magnet) thus heralds the **Yale College** triumph: "By dividing about 800 feet of conducting wire into **26** strands and forming it into as many separate coils around a **bar of** soft **iron about** 60 pounds in weight and properly bent into a horse-shoe **form,** Professor Henry **has** been enabled to produce **a** magnetic force which completely eclipses every other in the whole annals of magnetism; and **no parallel is to be** found since the miraculous suspension of the celebrated oriental impostor in his iron **coffin."** *

*The first Electro-magnetic Engine.*—Among his ingenious applications of the new power, Henry's invention of the Electro-magnetic Engine should here be noticed. In a letter to his friend Professor Silliman, **he says: "I** have lately succeeded in producing motion in a little machine, by a power which **I believe** has never before been applied **in** mechanics, — by magnetic **attraction and repulsion."** The **device consisted of a** horizontal **soft iron bar,** about seven inches long, **pivoted** at its middle to **oscillate vertically, and** closely wrapped **with three strands of** insulated copper wire, whose ends **were made by** suitable extensions to project and bend downward at **either end of the beam** in reversed pairs, so as conveniently to dip **into mercury thimbles** in connection with the plates of **the battery.** Two **upright permanent magnets** having **the same polarity, were** secured **immediately under the two** ends **of the oscillating bar,** but **separated from them by about an inch.** So soon as the circuit **was** completed by the depression **of one end of the** oscillating electro-magnetic **bar, a** repulsion **at this** end co-operating with an attraction at the **opposite** end, caused immediately a contrary dip of the bar, which **by** reversing the polarity of this magnetic beam, thus **pro-**duced a constant reciprocating action and movement. The **engine** beam oscillated **at** the rate of 75 vibrations per minute **for** more than **an** hour, or as long as the battery current was maintained.†
This **simple but** original device comprised **the** first automatic pole-

* *Philosoph. Magazine; and Annals,* March, 1832, vol. xi. p. 199. HENRY'S "quantity" magnet was at once adopted by FARADAY in his researches, as well as by the continental electricians; and his device of multiple coils is still recognized as the system best adapted for powerful magnetization. See "Supplement," NOTE D.

†Silliman's *Am. Jour. Sci.* July, 1831, vol. xx. pp. 340–343.

changer or commutator ever applied to the galvanic battery,—an essential element not merely in **every variety of the** electro-magnetic machine, but in every variety of magneto-electric apparatus, **and in** every variety of the highly useful induction apparatus.

In an interesting "Historical Sketch of the rise and progress of Electro-magnetic Engines for propelling machinery;" by the distinguished philosopher James P. Joule, he remarks: "Mr. Sturgeon's discovery of magnetizing bars of soft iron to a considerable power, and rapidly changing their polarity by miniature voltaic batteries, and the subsequent improved plan by Professor **Henry of** *raising* the magnetic action **of soft** iron,—developed **new and** inexhaustible **sources of force which** appeared easily and **extensively available as a mechanical agent; and it is to** the ingen-**ious American** philosopher **above named, that we are** indebted for **the first form** of a working **model of an engine upon the** principle **of reciprocating polarity of soft iron by electro-dynamic agency."** *

**In Henry's deliberate** contemplation of his **own achievement,** his **remarkable sagacity and** sobriety of judgment **were conspicu-**ously displayed. **Unperturbed by** the enthusiasm **so natural to the** successful inventor, **he carefully scanned the capabilities of this new** dynamic agent. Considering the **source of the power, he arrived** at the conclusion that the de-oxidation **of metal** necessary for the battery, would require the expenditure of at least as much power as its combustion in the battery could refund; and that the coal consumed in such de-oxidation could be much more economically employed directly in the work to be done.† As the battery con-**sumption moreover was** found **to increase more** rapidly than the **magnetic power produced, he was at once convinced that it** could

* Sturgeon's *Annals of Electricity*, etc. March, 1839, vol. iii. p. 430. STURGEON himself the first **to devise a** *rotary* **electro-magnetic** engine, deserves honorable mention for correcting **the statement of an American writer,** and declining his mistaken award by **frankly recognizing** HENRY's right to priority. (*Annals of Electricity*, April, 1839, vol. iii. p. 554.)

† These considerations **have been** more than justified **by later** comparative investigations. RANKINE estimates that the consumption **of one** pound of zinc will not produce more than one-tenth the energy that one pound of coal **will;** and that though in the efficient utilization of this energy it is four times superior, its useful work is therefore less than half that of coal; while its cost is from forty to fifty times greater. (*The Steam Engine and other Prime Movers*. By W. J. M. Rankine. London and Glasgow, 1859, part iv, art. 395, p. 544.)

never supersede or compete with steam.*    He believed however that the engine had a useful future in many minor applications where economy was not the most important consideration.

When sometime afterward, a friend urged him to secure patents on his inventions,—the "intensity" electro-magnet with its combinations, and the magnetic engine with its automatic pole-changer, earnestly assuring him that either one with proper management would secure an ample fortune to its owner, he firmly resisted every importunity; declaring that he would feel humilitated by any attempt at monopolizing the fruits of science, which he thought belonged to the world.   And this aversion to self-aggrandizement by researches undertaken for truth, was carried with him through life. †

While such disinterestedness cannot fail to excite our admiration, it may perhaps be questioned whether in these cases it did not from a practical point of view, amount to an over-fastidiousness:— whether such legal establishment of ownership, shielding the possessor from the occasional depreciations of the envious, and securing by its more tangible remunerations the leisure and the means for more extended researches, would not have been to science more than a compensation for the supposed sacrifice of dignity by the philosopher.‡

Nor did this repugnance to patenting arise (as it sometimes does) from any theoretical disapproval of the system.   On the contrary,

---

* JAMES P. JOULE (himself an inventor of an electro-magnetic engine) in a letter dated May 28, 1839, said: " I can scarcely doubt that electro-magnetism will eventually be substituted for steam in propelling machinery." (Sturgeon's *Annals of Electricity*, vol. iv. p. 135.)  This was some years before he commenced his investigations on the mechanical equivalent of heat and other motors.  He subsequently estimated that the consumption of a grain of zinc though forty times more costly than a grain of coal, produces only about one-eighth of the same mechanical effect.

† This trait calls to mind Faraday's avowal made nearly thirty years later, when in a letter to Messrs. Smith & Bentley, dated January 3, 1859, (declining their offer for the publication of his "Juvenile Lectures,") he said: "In fact I have always loved science more than money; and because my occupation is almost entirely personal, I cannot afford to get rich." (Bence Jones' *Life of Faraday*, vol. ii. p. 423.)

‡ Several hundred patents have since been granted in this country for ingenious modifications of—or improvements upon the electro-magnetic telegraph; and probably a hundred for equally ingenious varieties of the electro-magnetic engine; all of which would have been tributary to HENRY as an original patentee.

he frequently expressed his strong conviction that a judicious code of patent laws — if faithfully administered — furnishes the most equitable method of recompensing meritorious inventors. The institution was a good one — for others.

*The discovery of Magneto-electricity.* — From the magnetizing influence of the galvanic current, physicists were almost inevitably led to expect the converse reaction; and this anticipation appears to have been co-eval with electro-magnetism. As early as 1820, the illustrious Augustin Fresnel remarked: "It is natural to try whether a magnetic bar will not produce a galvanic current in a helical wire surrounding it;" and he made various experiments to determine a question which was supposed to involve the soundness of Ampère's theory. In November, 1820, he announced that though he at first supposed his attempt at the magneto-electric decomposition of water was partially successful, he was finally satisfied that no decisive result was obtained.*

Five years later, Faraday attempted the same experimental inquiry; and among his earliest publications gave an account of his unsuccessful trials. After describing his arrangements he says: "The magnet was then put in various positions and to different extents into the helix, and the needle of the galvanometer noticed: no effect however upon it could be observed. The circuit was made very long, very short, of wires of different metals and different diameters, down to extreme fineness, but the results were always the same. Magnets more and less powerful were used, some so strong as to bend the wire in its endeavors to pass round it. Hence it appears that however powerful the action of an electric current may be upon a magnet, the latter has no tendency by re-action to diminish or increase the intensity of the former; a fact which though of a negative kind, appears to me to be of some importance."†

Nor were American physicists discouraged by the records of repeated failures: and when the great Henry magnet was received at Yale College, Professor C. U. Shepard (chemical assistant to Professor Silliman) at once attacked the problem with this new

---

* *Annales de Chimie et de Physique*, 1820, vol. xv. pp. 219–222.

† *Quarterly Journal of Science*, etc. of the Royal Institution of Great Britain, July, 1825, vol. **xix. p.** 338. This well shows the danger of generalizing **too** broadly from **negative results.**

equipment. He remarks: "As its magnetic flow was so powerful, I had strong hopes of being able to accomplish the decomposition of water by its means. My experiment however **proved unsuccessful**. - - - **I hope however** to resume the research hereafter, **under** more favorable circumstances."*

**Henry,** unsatisfied with **past** efforts, determined to pursue the **subject in an** exhaustive series **of** experiments; and had reached some momentary indications of the galvanometer, when his experiments were temporarily interrupted. Meanwhile it was announced in May, 1832, that Faraday had secured the long sought prize; though the announcement was brief, and to those eager for particulars, somewhat disappointing. Henry was accordingly induced to publish in the following **number** of Silliman's Journal (that for July) a sketch **of** his own **trials** both before and after the announced discovery. **With reference to Faraday's** discovery he remarks: " No **detail is given of the experiments, and** it is somewhat surprising **that results so interesting, and which** certainly **form a new** era **in the** history **of electricity and** magnetism, should **not have been more** fully described before this time in some of the English publications. The only mention I have found of them is **the** following **short** account from **the** 'Annals of Philosophy' **for** April, under the head **of Proceedings** of the Royal Institution.—'**Feb. 17.** Mr. Faraday gave **an account of** the **first** two **parts of his researches** in electricity; namely **volta-electric induction,** and magneto-electric induction. - - - If **a wire connected at both** extremities with a **galvanometer, be coiled in the form of a** helix around a magnet, no current of electricity **takes place in it.** This is an experiment which has been made by various persons hundreds of times, in the hope of evolving electricity from magnetism. But if the magnet be withdrawn **from or** introduced into such a helix, a current of **electricity is produced** *while the magnet is in motion,* and is **rendered evident by the** deflection of the galvanometer. If a **single** wire be **passed by a magnetic pole,** a current of electricity **is** induced through it which **can be rendered** sensible.'†

---

* Silliman's *Am. Jour. Sci.* April, 1831, vol. **xx. p. 201,** foot-note.

† *Philosoph. Mag. and Annals of Phil.* April, 1832, vol. xi. pp. 300, 301. [Although FARADAY's first communication on galvanic induction, and on magneto-electricity, was read before the Royal Society November 24, 1831, the published Trans-

" Before having any knowledge of the method given in the above account, I had succeeded in producing electrical effects in the following manner, which differs from that employed by **Mr. Faraday,** and which appears to me to develop some new and interesting facts. A piece of copper wire about thirty feet long and covered with elastic varnish, was closely coiled around the middle of the soft iron armature of the galvanic magnet described in vol. xix of the American Journal of Science, and which when excited will readily sustain between six hundred and seven hundred pounds. The wire was wound upon itself so as to occupy only about **one inch** of the length of the armature, which is seven inches in all. The armature thus furnished with **the** wire, was placed **in its proper position** across **the ends of** the galvanic magnet, **and there fastened so that** no **motion could take place.** The **two** projecting ends of the helix were dipped into two cups of mercury, and these connected with a distant galvanometer by means of two copper wires each about forty feet long. This arrangement being completed, I stationed myself near the galvanometer **and directed** an assistant at a given **word to** immerse suddenly **in a vessel of dilute** acid, the galvanic battery attached to the magnet. At the instant of immersion the north end of the needle was deflected 30° to the west, indicating a **current of** electricity from the helix surrounding the armature. **The effect** however, appeared only as a single impulse, for the **needle after a** few oscillations resumed its former undisturbed position in the **mag-** netic meridian, although the galvanic action of the **battery, and** consequently the magnetic power still continued. **I was** however much surprised to see the needle suddenly deflected from a state of rest to about 20° to the east, or in a contrary direction, when the battery was withdrawn from the acid,—and again deflected to the west when it was re-immersed. This operation was repeated many times in succession, and uniformly with the same result, the armature the whole time remaining immovably attached to the poles of the magnet, no motion being required to produce the effect, as it appeared to take place only in consequence of the instantaneous devel-

actions for 1832, containing this memoir, did not reach this country till more than a year later: so that the meager abstract of the Royal Institution Proceedings above given, was the only notice of this important discovery, here accessible for many months,]

opment of the magnetic action in one case and the sudden cessation of it in the other. - - - From the foregoing facts it appears that a current of electricity is produced for an instant in a helix of copper wire surrounding a piece of soft iron whenever magnetism is induced in the iron; and a current in an opposite direction when the magnetic action ceases; also that an instantaneous current in one or the other direction accompanies every change in the magnetic intensity of the iron.

"Since reading the account before given of Mr. Faraday's method of producing electrical currents, I have attempted to combine the effects of motion and induction." No increase of effect was however observable. On comparing the two methods separately it was found that while the sudden introduction of the end of a magnetized bar within the helix connected with the galvanometer, deflected the needle seven degrees, the sudden magnetization of the bar when within the helix deflected the needle thirty degrees. A cylindrical iron bar was made to rotate rapidly on its axis within a stationary helix, by means of a turning lathe, but no result followed.

In the following month (June) by employing an armature of horse-shoe form (admitting longer coils), Henry succeeded in obtaining vivid sparks from the magnet. "The poles of the magnet were connected by a single rod of iron bent into the form of a horse-shoe, and its extremities filed perfectly flat so as to come in perfect contact with the faces of the poles: around the middle of the arch of this horse-shoe, two strands of copper wire were tightly coiled one over the other. A current from one of these helices deflected the needle one hundred degrees, and when both were used, the needle was deflected with such force as to make a complete circuit. But the most surprising effect was produced when instead of passing the current through the long wires to the galvanometer, the opposite ends of the helices were held nearly in contact with each other, and the magnet suddenly excited: in this case a small but vivid spark was seen to pass between the ends of the wires, and this effect was repeated as often as the state of intensity of the magnet was changed. - - - It appears from the May number of the 'Annals of Philosophy,' that I have been anticipated in this experiment of drawing sparks from the magnet by Mr. James D. Forbes of Edinburgh, who obtained a spark on the 30th of March:* my experiments being made during the last two weeks of June. A simple notification of his result is given, without any account of the experiment, which is reserved for a communication to the Royal Society of Edinburgh. My result is therefore entirely independent of his, and was undoubtedly obtained by a different process."†

Henry's gratification at the acquisition of the new insight into natural law, quite absorbed all sentiment of personal pride in its independent attainment; and his appreciation and congratulation of Faraday as the first discoverer of magneto-electricity, were hearty and unreserved. He was also particular always to assign to Faraday the first observation of the curious phenomena of momentary galvanic induction; although himself an independent discoverer of the fact.

*Discovery of the "Extra Current."*—In the course of these experiments he made a very important original observation on a peculiar case of self-induction, whereby he was enabled to convert a galvanic current of "quantity" into one of "intensity." This entirely new result seemed to contradict all previous experience. He thus concludes his paper:

"I may however mention one fact which I have not seen noticed in any work, and which appears to me to belong to the same class of phenomena as those above described. It is this:—when a small battery is moderately excited by diluted acid and its poles (which should be terminated by cups of mercury) are connected by a copper wire not more than a foot in length, no spark is perceived when the connection is either formed or broken: but if a wire thirty or forty feet long be used (instead of the short wire), though no spark will be perceptible when the connection is made, yet when it is broken by drawing one end of the wire from its cup of mercury, a vivid spark is produced. - - - The effect appears somewhat increased by coiling the wire into a helix: it seems also to depend in some measure on the length and thickness of the wire. I can

* *Philosoph. Mag. and Annals*, May, 1832, vol. xi. pp. 359, 360.
† Silliman's *Am. Jour. Sci.* July, 1832, vol. xxii. pp. 405-408.

account for these phenomena only by supposing the long wire to become charged with electricity which by its reaction on itself projects a spark when the connection is broken."* This is the earliest notice of the curious phenomenon of self-induction in an electric discharge.

*Election as Professor at Princeton.*—The Trustees of the College of New Jersey at Princeton, were about this time in search of a Professor to fill the chair of Natural Philosophy in that College, made vacant by the resignation of Professor Henry Vethake, who had accepted a Professorship of Natural Philosophy in the recently established University of the City of New York. Professor Henry had already won considerable reputation as a lecturer and teacher, no less than as an experimental physicist. Professor Benjamin Silliman of Yale College, urging his appointment, wrote: " Henry has no superior among the scientific men of the country." And Professor James Renwick of Columbia College (New York) still more emphatically added: "He has no equal."

Professor Henry was unanimously elected by the Trustees;† and he accepted the appointment: although strongly attached to his first Academy, endeared to him by early memories, by six years of successful labors, and by the warm regard of all his associates. May it not be added that his residence at the capital of the State of New York was further endeared to him by life's romance,—a most congenial and happy marriage contracted in 1830.

ELECTRICAL RESEARCHES AT PRINCETON: FROM 1833 TO 1842.

In November, 1832, Henry left the scene of his early scientific triumphs, the Albany Academy, and removed to Princeton with his family. For a year or two he gave his whole attention and exertions to the duties of exposition and instruction; and during Dr. Torrey's visit to Europe in 1833, at the Doctor's request, Professor Henry filled *ad interim* his chair of Chemistry, Mineralogy,

---

*Silliman's *Am. Jour. Sci.* July, 1832, vol. xxii. p. 408.

† Dr. MACLEAN, connected with the Faculty of the College of New Jersey at Princeton for fifty years, and for fourteen years its venerable president, in his History of the College (2 vols. 8vo. Philadelphia, 1877,) gives a very interesting account of the appointment and election of JOSEPH HENRY as Professor of Natural Philosophy in 1832, vol. ii. pp. 288-291.

and Geology. These occupations left him no leisure for the pursuit of original research. He subsequently gave lectures on Astronomy, and also on Architecture.

In 1834, Henry constructed for the Laboratory of his College an original form of galvanic battery; so arranged as to bring into action any desired number of elements, from a single pair to eighty-eight. Each zinc plate 9 inches wide and 12 inches deep was surrounded by a copper case open at top and bottom, and giving thus one and a half square feet of efficient surface. Eleven of these, in eleven separate cells, formed a sub-battery; and eight of these were grouped together by means of adjustable conductors, so as to form from the whole a single battery. By means of a crank and windlass shaft in proper connection, any one or more of the eight sub-batteries could be immersed or disengaged, and if desired, a single cell alone could be charged. By another arrangement of adjustable conductors, all the zinc plates could be directly connected together, and all the copper plates together, after the plan of Dr. Hare's "calorimotor" battery; thus giving the "quantity" effect due to a single element of 132 square feet of zinc surface, or of any smaller area desired. As the author remarks concerning its various arrangements, "they have been adopted in most cases after several experiments and much personal labor." A detailed account of this battery was given in a communication read January 16th, 1835, before the American Philosophical Society (of which he had recently been elected a member), and was published in its Transactions.*

*Electrical Self-Induction.*— Meanwhile he had been engaged in his brief intervals of relaxation from his exacting professional cares during the past year, in repeating and extending his interesting observations (commenced at Albany in 1832), on the remarkable intensifying influence of a long conductor, and especially of a spiral one, when interposed in a galvanic circuit of a single pair, or a battery of low "intensity." A verbal communication on this curious form of "induction," was made to the Society on the same occasion as the description of his battery, and was illustrated by experiments exhibited before the Society.

---

* *Trans. Am. Philos. Soc.* vol. v. (n. s.) art. ix. pp. 217-222.

Faraday in his "eighth series of Researches" (read before the Royal Society June 5th, 1834), pointed out very fully the differing actions of a single galvanic element giving a "quantity" current, and of a series of elements giving an "intensity" current: * thus entirely confirming the results obtained by Henry more than three years previously.

In the Philosophical Magazine for November, 1834, appeared a paper by Faraday, "On a peculiar condition of electric and magneto-electric Induction:" in which he notices as a remarkable fact, that while a short circuit wire from a single galvanic element, gives little or no visible spark, a long conductor gives a very sensible spark. "If the connecting wire be much lengthened, then the spark is much increased."† In his interesting research, Faraday appears to have entirely overlooked Henry's earlier labors in the same field;—as contrary to his usual custom, he makes no allusion to the same results having been obtained, and published in Silliman's Journal two years and a half before.‡

These observations were made by Faraday the subject of his "ninth series of Researches," in a communication "On the influence by induction of an electric current on itself:" read before the Royal Society January 29th, 1835. In this paper he states: "The inquiry arose out of a fact communicated to me by Mr. Jenkin,— which is as follows: If an ordinary wire of short length be used as the medium of communication between two plates of an electro-motor consisting of a single pair of metals, no management will enable the experimenter to obtain an electric shock from this wire: but if the wire which surrounds an electro-magnet be used, a shock is felt each time the contact with the electro-motor is broken." Having varied the experiment, Faraday adds: "There was no sensible spark on *making* contact, but on *breaking* contact there was a very large and bright spark, with considerable combustion of the mercury." He found a similar result with the wire helix alone,— without its magnetic core. "The power of producing these phenomena exists therefore in the simple helix, as well as in the electro-magnet,

---

* *Phil. Trans. Roy. Soc.* June 5, 1834, vol. cxxiv. arts. 990–994, pp. 455, 456. *Experimental Researches in Electricity*, vol. i. pp. 301, 302.

† *L. & E. Philosoph. Mag.* Nov. 1834, vol. v. pp. 351, 352.

‡ Silliman's *Am. Jour. Sci.* July, 1832, vol. xxii. p. 408, above quoted.

although by no means in the same high degree." With continuous straight wire of the same length, he obtained a similar effect,—"yet not so bright as that from the helix." "When a short wire is used, all these effects disappear;" although there is undoubtedly a greater "quantity" of electric current in the shorter wire; thus giving "the strange result of a diminished spark and shock from the strong current, and increased effects from the weak one."[*]

While Henry derived only satisfaction from these extended verifications of his own observations, by one whom he had accustomed himself to look up to with admiration and regard, Dr. A. Dallas Bache, his attached friend, then Professor of Natural Philosophy in the University of Pennsylvania,—more jealous than himself of his scientific fame, strongly urged and insisted that he should immediately publish an account of his later researches. Henry accordingly sent to the American Philosophical Society a memoir (comprising the details of his recent verbal communication) "On the Influence of a Spiral Conductor in increasing the Intensity of Electricity from a galvanic arrangement of a Single pair, etc.," which was read before the Society, February 6th, 1835.

After citing his former paper of July, 1832, the writer remarks that he had been able during the past year to extend his experiments on the curious phenomenon. "These though not so complete as I could wish, are now presented to the Society with the belief that they will be interesting at this time on account of the recent publication of Mr. Faraday on the same subject." He then relates that employing a single pair of his battery (comprising one and a half square feet of zinc surface), he found as in his earlier experiment in 1832, that the poles being connected by a piece of copper bell-wire five inches long, no spark was given on making or breaking contact. Fifteen feet of interposed wire gave a very feeble spark; and with successive additions of fifteen feet, the effect increased until with 120 feet the maximum spark appeared to be reached, and beyond this there was no perceptible increase; while with double this length (or 240 feet) there seemed to be a diminu-

---

[*] *Phil. Trans. Roy. Soc.* Jan. 29, 1835, vol. cxxv. articles 1061-1067, and 1073, pp. 41-45. *Experimental Researches in Electricity*, vol. i. pp. 324-328. This memoir did not reach this country, of course, till a year later.

tion of intensity. **From** various trials the inference was drawn that the length required for maximum effect varied with the size of the galvanic element. Thicker wires of the same **length produced** greater effect, depending in some degree on the size of the battery. A wire **of forty feet when** coiled into a cylindrical helix "gave a more intense spark than the same wire uncoiled." A ribbon of sheet copper about an inch wide and twenty-eight feet long, being covered with silk and coiled into a flat spiral—like a watch spring—(after the plan of Dr. Ritchie) gave a vivid spark with a loud snap. When uncoiled, it produced a much feebler spark. With the insulated copper ribbon folded in its middle, and the double thickness coiled into a flat spiral, there was no spark whatever, although the same ribbon unrolled gave a feeble spark: thus showing that the induction of the current upon itself was neutralized by flowing equally in opposite directions in the double spiral. With a larger copper ribbon one inch and a half wide, and 96 feet long (weighing 15 pounds), spirally coiled, the snap of the spark could be heard in an adjoining room with the door closed. Want of material prevented the result being pushed further, so as to ascertain the range of maximum effect with this form of conductor. With increased battery surface, the effect was also increased; so that with eight elements of his battery arranged as a single pair (of 12 square feet) the spark on breaking contact "resembled the discharge of a small Leyden jar highly charged." With the flat spiral, no increase of effect was observable on the introduction of a soft iron core into the axis of the spiral, forming a magnet. With a helical or cylindrical coil about nine inches long, enclosing an iron core, "the spark appeared a little more intense than without the iron." The inference is also drawn "from these experiments, that some of the effects heretofore attributed to magneto-electric action are chiefly due to the reaction on each other of the several spirals of the coil which surround the magnet."

In these researches it was found that when the two plates of a single pair were placed even fourteen inches apart in an open trough of diluted acid, "although the electrical intensity in this case must have been very low, yet there was but little reduction in the apparent intensity of the spark." It was also shown that "the spiral conductor produces however, little or no increase of effect when introduced into a galvanic circuit of considerable intensity." When for example an "intensity" battery of two Cruickshanks troughs, each containing fifty-six elements was employed with the larger copper spiral, "no greater effect was perceived than with a short thick wire;" in either case, only a feeble spark being given.* An abstract of the results thus announced, (and which were obtained by Henry during the summer of 1834,) was communicated by Dr. A. D. Bache, as a Secretary of the American Philosophical Society, to the Franklin Journal, in order to give these interesting facts an earlier currency.† The date of original discovery was however so well established, that this friendly effort was scarcely necessary.‡

*Combined Circuits.*—In 1835, wires had been extended across the front campus of the college grounds at Princeton from the upper story of the library building to the Philosophical Hall on the opposite side, through which signals were occasionally sent, distinguished by the number of taps of the electro-magnetic bell, as first exhibited five years previously in the hall of the Albany Academy. It has already been noticed, that contrary to all the antecedent expectations of physicists, Henry had established the fact that the most powerful form of magnet (designated by him the "quantity" magnet) is not the form best adapted to distant action through an extended circuit. The ingenious idea occurred to him that notwithstanding this fundamental fact, it would be quite easy to combine the two systems so as to enable an operator to produce the most energetic mechanical effects, at almost any required distance. It is simply necessary to employ with the distant "intensity" magnet an oscillating armature with a suitable prolongation so arranged as to open and close the short circuit of an adjoining

---

* *Trans. Am. Phil. Soc.* vol. v. (n. s.) art. x. pp. 223-231.

† *Journal of the Franklin Institute,* March, 1835, vol. xv. pp. 169, 170. See "Supplement," NOTE E.

‡ M. BECQUEREL in his elaborate Treatise on Electricity, in the chapter on "The influence of an electric current on itself by induction," says with regard to the increase of tension in a feeble current when passing through a long spiral conductor, "The effects observed in these circumstances appear to have been noticed for the first time by Professor HENRY." (*Traité expérimental de l'Électricité et du Magnétisme,* 8vo. 7 vols. Paris, 1834-1840, vol. v. art. 1261, p. 231.)

"quantity" magnet of any practicable power:—a work which indeed could be accomplished by the mere swing of the most delicate galvanometer needle. Professor Henry had constructed for his own laboratory a large electro-magnet designed to surpass the celebrated magnet made for Yale College; and with it he was enabled to exhibit to his class, by employing a small portion of his "quantity" battery, an easy lifting power of more than three thousand pounds.* Such was the mechanical agency he called into action through his telegraphic circuit, by simply lifting its galvanic wire from a mercury thimble, or by again dipping it into the same. This combination has since found an important application; its principle underlying all the various forms and uses of the "relay" magnet, and of the "receiving" magnet and local battery, since employed.

*Visit to Europe.*—In order to give Professor Henry a much-needed rest from his diligent services and close application during the last four years, the Trustees of his College liberally allowed him a year's absence with full salary: thus affording him for the first time a long coveted opportunity of visiting Europe.

In February of 1837, in company with his valued and faithful friend, Professor Bache, he arrived in England; where the two American physicists formed ready and lasting intimacies with some of the most distinguished worthies of Great Britain. Everywhere received with courteous and cordial consideration, they both ever carried with them agreeable memories of their holiday sojourn abroad.

In London, many pleasant interviews with Faraday, formed a memorable circumstance. Wheatstone, then Professor of Experimental Philosophy in King's College, was engaged in developing his system of needle telegraph, and he unfolded freely to his visitors his numerous projects; and particularly his arrangement of supplementary local circuit from an additional battery, for sounding an electro-magnetic signal, by being brought into action by a movement from the main line circuit.† Henry had then the pleasure

---

* It is said that this magnet has been made to sustain 3,500 pounds. (Turnbull's *Electro-Magnetic Telegraph*, 2nd ed. 1853, p 49.)

† This was early in April, 1837. (*Smithsonian Report* for 1857, p. 111.) Two months later, or June 12th, 1837, WHEATSTONE in conjunction with W. F. COOKE had secured a patent on his system of telegraph, including the combination of circuits.

of detailing to him his own similar combination of two electro-magnetic circuits, experimentally tried more than a year previously.*

Nearly a year was employed in foreign travel, most pleasantly and beneficially both for mind and body: the greater portion of the time however being spent in London, in Paris, (where Henry formed the acquaintance of Arago, Becquerel, De la Rive, Biot, Gay-Lussac, and other celebrities,) and in Edinburgh, where he also found a galaxy of eminent and congenial minds.

In September of the same year (1837) he attended the meeting of the British Association at Liverpool; where being invited to speak, he made a brief communication on some electrical researches in regard to the phenomenon known as the " lateral discharge :" —a study to which he had been led by some remarks of Dr. Roget on the subject. "The result of the analysis was in accordance with an opinion of Biot—that the lateral discharge is due only to the escape of the small quantity of redundant electricity which always exists on one side or the other of a jar, and not to the whole discharge." Hence we could increase or diminish the lateral action by any means which affect the quantity of free electricity : — as by "an increase of the thickness of the glass, or by substituting for the small knob of the jar, a large ball. But the arrangement which produces the greatest effect is that of a long fine copper wire insulated, — parallel to the horizon, and terminated at each end by a small ball. When sparks are thrown on this from a globe of about a foot in diameter, the wire at each discharge becomes beautifully luminous from one end to the other, even if it be a hundred feet long : rays are given off on all sides perpendicular to the axis of the wire :" — forming a continuous electrical brush. It was also stated "that the same quantity of electricity could be made to remain on the wire, if gradually communicated [by a point] ; but when thrown on in the form of a spark, it is dissipated as before described :" —as though possessing a kind of momentum. When two or more wires are arranged in parallel lines (in electrical connection), only the outer sides of the

* " I informed him that I had devised another method of producing effects somewhat similar : this consisted in opening the circuit of my large quantity magnet at Princeton, when loaded with many hundred pounds weight, by attracting upward a small piece of movable wire with a small intensity magnet connected with a long wire circuit." (HENRY'S *Deposition* in the case of O'Rielly and Morse, September 7, 1849.)

exposed wires become luminous: and "when the wire is formed into a flat spiral, the outer spiral alone exhibits the lateral discharge, but the light in this case is very brilliant: the inner spirals appear to increase the effect by induction." In like manner when a ball was attached to the middle of a vertical lightning-rod having a good earth-connection, "when sparks of about an inch and a half were thrown on the ball, corresponding lateral sparks could be drawn not only from the parts of the rod between the ground and the ball, but from the part above, even to the top of the rod." *

At the same meeting, before the section on Mechanics and Engineering, Henry gave by request an account of the great extension of the Railway and Canal systems in the United States : which was listened to with great attention and interest. He also referred to the inland or river navigation in our country, describing the improvements introduced into our large river steamboats, especially on the Hudson river in New York State; where the usual speed was fifteen miles per hour or more. †

In November, 1837, Henry returned from his foreign tour greatly invigorated, — bringing with him some new apparatus: and with increased zest he re-embarked upon the duties of his professorship. Continuing his studies of electrical action, he presented verbally to the American Philosophical Society, February 16th, 1838, a notice of further observations on the "lateral discharge" of electricity while passing along a wire, going to show that even with good earth connection, free electricity is not conducted silently to the ground. ‡

In May, 1838, he announced to the Society the production of currents by induction from ordinary or mechanical electricity, analogous to that first obtained by Faraday from galvanism in 1831: and the further curious fact that on the discharge from a Leyden jar through a good conductor, a secondary shock from a

---

* *Report of Brit. Association*, for 1837, pp. 22-24, of Abstracts.

† Same *Report*, Abstracts, p. 135. It was on this occasion that Dr. LARDNER, generalizing probably from his observations on the Thames, ventured (not very courteously) to doubt whether any such speed as fifteen miles per hour on water, could ordinarily be effected. (Sill. *Am. Jour. Sci.* Jan. 1838, vol. xxxiii, p. 296.) The same authority affirmed the futility of attempting oceanic steam navigation.

‡ *Proceedings Am. Phil. Soc.* Feb. 16, 1838, vol. i. p. 6.

perfectly insulated near conductor could be obtained — more intense than the primary shock directly from the jar. *

These investigations having in view the discovery of "inductive actions in common electricity analogous to those found in galvanism" (commenced in the spring of 1836), led to renewed examination of the secondary *galvanic* current, which since November 24th, 1831, (or for seven years,) had received no special attention. Henry's very interesting series of experiments were detailed in a somewhat elaborate memoir read before the American Philosophical Society, November 2nd, 1838. Employing five different sized annular spools of fine wire (about one-fiftieth of an inch thick) varying from one-fifth of a mile to nearly a mile in length (which might be called "intensity" helices); and six flat spiral coils of copper ribbon varying from three-quarters of an inch to one inch and a half in width, and from 60 to 93 feet in length (which might be called "quantity" coils), he was able to combine them in various ways both in connection and in parallelism. A cylindrical battery of one and three-quarters square feet of zinc surface was principally used; and the galvanic circuit was interrupted by drawing one end of the copper ribbon or wire over a rasp in good metallic contact with the other pole of the battery.

From the energetic action of the flat ribbon coil in producing the induction of a current on itself, it was inferred that the secondary current would also be best induced by it. With the single larger ribbon coil in connection with the battery, and another ribbon coil placed over it resting on an interposed glass plate, at every interruption of the primary circuit an induction spark was obtained at the rubbed ends of the second coil; though the shock was feeble. With a double wire spool (one within the other) of 2650 yards, placed above the primary coil (having about the same weight as the copper ribbon) the magnetizing effects disappeared, the sparks were much smaller, "but the shock was almost too intense to be received with impunity." The secondary current in this case was one of small "quantity" but of great "intensity." With a single break of circuit in the primary, it was passed through a circle of 56 students of his senior class, with the effect of a moderate charge from

* *Proceedings Am. Phil. Soc.* May 4, 1838, vol. I. p. 11.

a Leyden jar. From various experiments, the limit of efficient length for a given galvanic power was ascertained; beyond which the induced current was diminished. Employing a Cruickshanks battery of 60 small elements (4 inches square) he found with the ribbon coil that the induced currents were exceedingly feeble, but with the long wire helix as the primary circuit that strong indications were produced. By the alternations of the ribbon and wire coils, the fact was established "that an intensity current can induce one of quantity, and by the preceding experiments the converse has also been shown that a quantity current can induce one of intensity;" a result which has had an important bearing on the subsequent development of the electro-magnetic "Induction-Coil." With a long ribbon coil receiving the galvanic current from 35 feet of zinc surface, sensible induction shocks could be felt from a large annular coil of four feet diameter (containing five miles of wire) when placed in parallelism at a distance of four feet from the primary coil; while at the distance of one foot the shock became too severe to be taken. With this arrangement an induction shock was given from one apartment to another, through the intervening partition.

*Successive orders of Induction.*—When it is considered that the primary current in such cases has a considerable duration, while the secondary current is but momentary, being developed only at the instant of change in the primary, it could certainly not have been expected that this single instantaneous electrical impulse of reaction would be capable of acting as a primary current, and of similarly inducing an action on a third independent circuit: and during the seven years in which galvanic induction had been known, no physicist ever thought of making the trial. Theoretically it might perhaps have been inferred, if such tertiary induction had any existence, as it would be coincident not with the instantaneous secondary induction, but with the initiation and termination of such momentary current, and hence in opposite signs—separated by an inappreciable interval of time, that the whole phenomenon would probably be entirely masked by a practical neutralization.

The experiments of Henry fully established however the new and remarkable result—of a very appreciable tertiary current. By connecting the secondary coil with another at some distance from the primary so as not to be influenced by it directly, but forming with the secondary a single closed circuit, not only was the distant coil capable of producing in an insulated wire helix placed over it, a distinct current of induction at the interruption of the primary, but sensible shocks were obtained from it. The experiment was pushed still further; and inductive currents of a fourth degree were obtained. "By a similar but more extended arrangement, shocks were received from currents of a fourth and a fifth order: and with a more powerful primary current, and additional coils, a still greater number of successive inductions might be obtained. - - - It was found that with the small battery a shock could be given from the current of the third order to twenty-five persons joining hands; also shocks perceptible in the arms were obtained from a current of the fifth order." As Henry simply remarks: "The induction of currents of different orders, of sufficient intensity to give shocks, could scarcely have been anticipated from our previous knowledge of the subject." By means of the small magnetizing helix introduced into each circuit, the direction of these successive currents was found to be alternating or reversed to each other. These remarkable results were obtained in the summer of 1838. *

The concluding section of this important memoir is occupied with an account of "The production of induced currents of the different orders, from ordinary electricity." An open glass cylinder about six inches in diameter was provided with two long narrow strips of tin foil pasted around it in corresponding helical courses, the one on the outside and the other on the inside, directly opposite to each other. The inner coiled strip had its extremities connected with insulated wires which formed a circuit outside the cylinder, and included a small magnetizing helix. The outer tin foil strip was also connected with wires so that an electrical discharge from a half-gallon Leyden jar could be passed through it. The magnetization of a small needle indicated an induced current through the inner tin-foil ribbon corresponding in direction with the outer cur-

---

rent from the jar.* By means of a second glass cylinder similarly provided with **helical tin-foil** ribbons in suitable connections, a tertiary current of induction was obtained, analogous to that **derived** from galvanism. "**Also by the** addition **in** the same way **of a third cylinder, a current of** the fourth order was developed."

Similar as these successive **inductions from** an electrical discharge **were to** those previously observed **in the case of the** galvanic current, they presented one puzzling **difference in the direction of the currents of** the different orders. "**These in the** experiments with the glass cylinders, instead of exhibiting **the alternations of the galvanic currents,** were all in the same direction as the discharge from the jar, or in other words they were all *plus*. On substituting for the tinned **glass cylinders,** well insulated copper coils, "alternations were found the same as **in the** case of galvanism." The only difference apparently between the two arrangements, was **that the tin-foil** ribbons were separated only by the thin glass of the cylinders, while **the copper spiral coils were** placed an inch and **a half** apart. By **varied experiments, the** direction of the induced currents was found **to depend** notably **on** the distance between **the** conductors;—the **induction ceasing at** a certain distance, (according to the amount of the charge and the characters of the conductors,) and **the direction of the induced current** beyond this critical **distance being contrary to that of the primary current.\* "With a battery of eight half-**gallon **jars, and parallel wires** about ten **feet long, the change in the direction did not take place at a less distance than from twelve to**

---

* About **a** year later, **the** distinguished **German** electrician PETER RIESS, apparently unaware **of** HENRY's researches, **discovered the** secondary current induced from mechanical **electricity, by a** very **similar** experiment. (Poggendorff's *Annalen der Physik* **und** *Chemie*, 1839, No. 5, vol. xlvii. pp. 55–76.)

† The variation in the direction of polarization (without reference **to induction** currents) appears to have been first noticed by FELIX SAVARY, **some dozen years** before. In an important memoir communicated to the Paris Academy of **Sciences July 31,** 1826, M. Savary announced that "The direction of the magnetic polarity of **small** needles exposed to an electric current directed along a wire stretched longitudinally, varies with the distance of the wire;"—the action being found to be periodical with the distance. M. Savary observed three periods, and also the fact that the distances of maximum effect and of the nodal zeros "vary with the length and diameter of the wire, and with the intensity of the discharge." He also found that "when a helix is used for magnetizing, the distance at which the needle placed within it is from the conducting wire, is indifferent; but the direction and the degree of magnetization depends on the intensity of the discharge, and on the ratio between the length and size of the wire." (Brewster's *Edinburgh Jour. Sci.* Oct. 1826, vol. v. p. 369.)

fifteen inches, and with a still larger battery and longer conductors, no change was found although the induction was produced at the distance of several feet." With Dr. Hare's battery of 32 one-gallon jars, and a copper wire about one-tenth of an inch thick and 80 feet long stretched across the lecture-room and back on either side toward the battery, a second wire stretched parallel with the former for about 35 feet and extended to form an independent circuit, (its ends being connected with a small magnetizing helix,) was tested at varying distances beginning with a few inches until they were twelve feet apart: at which distance of the parallel wire, its induction though enfeebled, still indicated by its magnetizing power, a direction corresponding with the primary current. The form of the room did not permit a convenient separation of the two circuits to a greater distance.*

The eminent French electrician Antoine C. Becquerel, in a chapter on Induction in his lárge work, remarks: "Very recently M. Henry, Professor of Natural Philosophy in New Jersey, has extended the domain of this branch of physics: the results obtained by him are of such importance, particularly in regard to the intensity of the effects produced, that it is proper to expound them here with some detail." Twenty pages are then devoted to these researches.†

A memoir was read before the Society, June 19th, 1840, giving an account of observations on the two forms of induction occurring on the making and on the breaking of the primary galvanic circuit, the two differing in character as well as in direction. In these experiments he employed a Daniell's constant battery of 30 elements; the battery being "sometimes used as a single series with all its elements placed consecutively, and at others in two or three series, arranged collaterally, so as to vary the quantity and intensity of the electricity as the occasion might require." As the initial induction had always been found so feeble as to be scarcely perceptible, (although in quantity sufficient to affect the ordinary galvanometer

---

* Trans. Am. Phil. Soc., vol. vi. (n. s.) art. ix. pp. 303–337. In the Proceedings of the Society for November 2d, 1838, when this memoir was read, it is recorded "Professor HENRY made a verbal communication during the course of which he illustrated experimentally the phenomena developed in his paper." (Proceed. Am. Phil. Soc. Nov. 2, 1838, vol. i. pp. 54–56.)

† Traité expérimental de l' Électricité et du Magnétisme, vol. v. pp. 87–107.

as much as the terminal induction,) most of the results previously obtained (such as the detection of successive orders of currents) were derived from the strong inductions at the moment of breaking the circuit. It became therefore important to endeavor to intensify the initial induction for its more especial examination: and this it was found could be effected in two ways, — by increasing the "intensity" of the battery, and by diminishing within certain limits the length of the primary coil.

"With the current from one element, the shock at breaking the circuit was quite severe, but at making the same it was very feeble, and could be perceived in the fingers only or through the tongue. With two elements in the circuit the shock at the beginning was slightly increased: with three elements the increase was more decided, while the shock at breaking the circuit remained nearly of the same intensity as at first, or was comparatively but little increased. When the number of elements was increased to ten, the shock at making contact was found fully equal to that at breaking, and by employing a still greater number, the former was decidedly greater than the latter, the difference continually increasing until all the thirty elements were introduced into the circuit. - - - Experiments were next made to determine the influence of a variation in the length of the coil, the intensity of the battery remaining the same." For this purpose the battery consisting of a single element "was employed; and the length of the copper ribbon coil was successively reduced from 60 feet, by measures of 15 feet. With 45 feet, the initial induction was stronger than with 60 feet: with the next shorter length it was more perceptible, and increased in intensity with each diminution of the coil, until a length of about fifteen feet appeared to give a maximum result." At the same time it was found that "the intensity of the shock at the *ending* of the battery current diminishes with each diminution of the length of the coil. - - - By the foregoing results we are evidently furnished with two methods of increasing at pleasure the intensity of the induction at the beginning of a battery current, the one consisting in increasing the intensity of the source of the electricity, and the other in diminishing the resistance to conduction of the circuit while its intensity remains the same."

Having thus succeeded in exalting the initial induction, Henry proceeded in his investigation. Distinct currents of the third, fourth, and fifth orders were readily obtained from it; and as was anticipated, with their signs (or directions) the reverse of the corresponding orders derived from the terminal induction. In other respects "the series of induced currents produced at the beginning of the primary current appeared to possess all the properties belonging to those of the induction at the ending of the same current."

In the course of these investigations the idea having occurred to him "that the intense shocks given by the electric fish may possibly be from a secondary current," as it appeared to him that "this is the only way in which we can conceive of such intense electricity being produced in organs imperfectly insulated and immersed in a conducting medium," he endeavored to simulate the effect by arranging a secondary wire coil furnished with terminal handles, over a primary copper ribbon coil, the two being insulated as usual. "By immersing the apparatus in a shallow vessel of water, the handles being placed at the two extremities of the diameter of the helix, and the hands plunged into the water parallel to a line joining the two poles, a shock is felt through the arms."

The former experiment of obtaining an induction shock from one room to another through a partition, was repeated on a still larger scale. All the coils of copper ribbon having been united in a single continuous conductor of about 400 feet in length, "this was rolled into a ring of five and a half feet in diameter, and suspended vertically against the inside of the large folding doors which separate the laboratory from the lecture-room. Beyond the doors, in the lecture-room and directly opposite the coil, was placed a helix formed of upwards of a mile of copper wire, one-sixteenth of an inch in thickness, and wound into a hoop of four feet in diameter. With this arrangement, and a battery of 147 square feet of zinc surface divided into eight elements, shocks were perceptible in the tongue when the two conductors were separated to the distance of nearly seven feet. At the distance of between three and four feet, the shocks were quite severe. The exhibition was rendered more interesting by causing the induction to take place through a number of persons standing in a row between the two conductors."

The second section of the memoir is mainly occupied with details of experiments on the screening effect of conducting plates (of non-magnetic metals) when interposed between the primary and second-ary coils: showing remarkable contrasts in the "quantity" and "intensity" classes of galvanic effects. When the annular spool or helix (of nearly one mile of copper wire) was employed with the large spiral coil of copper ribbon, "the coil being connected with a battery of ten elements, the shocks both at making and breaking the circuit were very severe; and these as usual were almost entirely neutralized by the interposition of the zinc plate. But when the galvanometer instead of the body, was introduced into the circuit, its indications were the same whether the plate was interposed or not: or in other words the galvanometer indicated no screening, while under the same circumstances the shocks were neutralized. A similar effect was observed when the galvanometer and the mag-netizing helix were together introduced into the circuit. The interposition of the plate entirely neutralized the magnetizing power of the helix (in reference to tempered steel) while the deflec-tions of the galvanometer were unaffected." The induction currents of the third, fourth, and fifth orders, were found to be of consid-erable "intensity;"—magnetizing steel needles, giving shocks, not being interrupted by a drop of water placed in the circuit between the ends of the severed wire,—and yet being screened or neutral-ized by a metallic plate interposed between the coils.*

A continuation of the memoir was read before the Philosophical Society November 20th, 1840, discussing further the theoretical differences between an initial or an increasing galvanic current, and a decreasing or an arrested current, in producing the phenomena of induction. On the same occasion Henry described "an apparatus for producing a reciprocating motion by the repulsion in the consec-utive parts of a conductor through which a galvanic current is passing." About ten years before, he had devised the first electro-magnetic engine (operating by intermittent magnetic attractions and repulsions); and now he had contrived the first galvanic engine, operating by the analogous intermittent attractions and repulsions of the electric current.†

---

* *Trans. Am. Phil. Soc.* June 1840, vol. viii. (n. s.) art. 1. pp. 1-18.
† *Proceedings Am. Phil. Soc.* Nov. 20, 1840, vol. i. p. 301.

*Oscillation of Electrical Discharge.*—In June, 1842, he presented a communication to the Society recounting an investigation of some anomalies in ordinary electrical induction. While with the larger needles ("No. 3 and No. 4") subjected to the magnetizing helix, the polarity was always conformable to the direction of the discharge, he found that when very fine needles were employed, an increase in the force of the electricity produced changes of polarity. About a thousand needles were magnetized in the testing helices in these researches.

This puzzling phenomenon was finally cleared up by the important discovery that an electrical equilibrium was not instantaneously effected by the spark, but that it was attained only after several oscillations of the flow. "The discharge—whatever may be its nature, is not correctly represented by the single transfer from one side of the jar to the other: the phenomena require us to admit the existence of a principal discharge in one direction, and then several reflex actions backward and forward, each more feeble than the preceding, until the equilibrium is obtained."* In every case therefore of the electrostatic discharge, the testing needles were really subjected to an oscillating alternation of currents, and consequently to successive partial de-magnetizations and re-magnetizations. The complications produced by this residual action, satisfactorily explained for the first time, the discordant results obtained by different investigators. This singular reflux of current was ingeniously applied by Henry to explain the apparent change of inductive current with differing distances. Should the primitive discharge wave be in excess of the magnetic capacity of the needle at a given position, the return wave might be just sufficient to completely reverse its polarity, and the diminished succeeding wave insufficient to restore it to its former condition; while at a greater distance, the primitive wave might be so far reduced as to just magnetize the needle fully,

* *Proceedings Am. Phil. Soc.* June 17, 1842, vol. ii. pp. 193-196.— Prof. HERMANN L. F. HELMHOLTZ some five years later (in 1847), but quite independently, suggested "a backward and forward motion between the coatings" when the Leyden jar is discharged. (*Scientific Memoirs*, edited by Dr. J. Tyndall, 1853, vol. i. p. 143.) And still five years later (in 1852) Sir WILLIAM THOMSON made the same independent conjecture. (*L. E. D. Phil. Mag.* June, 1853, vol. v. pp. 400, 401.) To FELIX SAVARY however is due the credit of having first advanced the hypothesis of electrical oscillations, as early as 1827. See "Supplement," NOTE F.

and the second wave, being still more enfeebled, would only partially de-magnetize it, leaving still a portion of the original **polarity; and** so for the following diminished oscillations.

In the course of these extended researches the presence of inductive **action was traced** to most surprising and unimagined distances. "A **single spark** from the prime conductor of the machine, of about an inch long, thrown on the end of a circuit of wire in an upper room, produced **an** induction sufficiently powerful to magnetize needles in a parallel circuit of wire placed in the cellar beneath, at a perpendicular distance of thirty feet, with two floors and ceilings — each fourteen inches thick intervening."

"The **last** part of the series of experiments relates to induced currents **from atmospheric** electricity. By a very simple arrangement, needles are strongly magnetized in the author's study, even **when the flash is at the distance of seven or eight miles, and when the thunder is scarcely audible.** On this principle he proposes a **simple self-registering** electrometer, connected with **an** elevated **exploring rod."** For obtaining the results above alluded to, **a thick** wire was soldered to the edge of the **tin** roof of his dwelling and passed into his study through a hole **in** the window frame; while a similar wire passing out to the ground, terminated in connection with **a metal** plate in a deep well close by. **Between the wire** ends within his study, various apparatus, **including** magnetizing **helices** of different sizes and characters, **could be** attached, so as **to be within the line of conduction from the roof to the** ground. **The inductions from atmospheric discharges were found** to have the **oscillatory** character observed with **the** Leyden jar; and by interposing several magnetizing **helices** with few and with many **convolutions,** Henry was able to get from a needle in the former **the** polarity due to the direct current, and in the latter, that due to the return current; thus catching the lightning (as it were) upon **the rebound.**

In examining the "lateral discharge" from a lightning-rod **in good connection with the earth, he had** often observed that while a **spark could be obtained** sufficiently **strong to be** distinctly felt, it **scarcely affected in the slightest degree a** delicate gold-leaf electroscope. **How explain so** incongruous **a** phenomenon? Henry discovered the very simple solution, by a reference to the self-induction of the rod,—a negative wave passing, succeeded immediately by a positive wave so rapidly as to completely neutralize the effect upon the electroscope before the inertia of the gold-leaf could be overcome, while actually producing a double spark (sensibly co-incident) to and from the recipient.

A few months later, "he had succeeded in magnetizing needles by the secondary current, in a wire more than two hundred and twenty feet distant from the wire through which the primary current was passing, excited by a single spark from an electrical machine."[*] In this case the primary wire was his telegraph line stretched seven years before across the campus of the college grounds in front of Nassau Hall; the secondary or induction wire being suspended in a parallel direction across the grounds at the rear of Nassau Hall, with its ends terminating in buried metallic plates:—the large building intervening between the two wires.

This brilliant series of contributions to our knowledge of a most recondite and mysterious agent, placed Henry, by the concurrent judgment of all competent physicists, in the very front rank of original investigators. His persevering researches in the electrical paradoxes of induction, perhaps more than any similar ones, tended to strengthen the hypothesis of an ætherial dynamic agency; although he himself had for a long time been inclined to favor the material hypothesis.[†]

### INVESTIGATIONS IN GENERAL PHYSICS: FROM 1830 TO 1846.

In order to give a proper connection to the experimental inquiries undertaken by Henry in various fields, it is necessary to pause here, and to recur to some of his earlier scientific labors,—beginning again at Albany.

---

[*] *Proceedings Am. Phil. Soc.* Oct. 21, 1842, vol. ii. p. 229. It is barely possible that the *primary* current might have returned through the second wire.

[†] In a paper "On the Theory of the so-called Imponderables" published some years later, in referring to the phenomena of electrical oscillation in discharge, and of the series of inductions taking place and "extending to a surprising distance on all sides," he remarks: "As these are the results of currents in alternate directions, they must produce in surrounding space a series of *plus* and *minus* motions, analogous to—if not identical with undulations." (*Proceed. Amer. Association*, Albany, Aug. 1851, p. 89.)

*Meteorology.*—From an early date Henry took a deep interest in the study of meteorology: not only on account of its practical importance, but from its relation to cosmical physics, and because from the very complexity and irregularity of its conditions, it challenged further investigation and stood in need of larger generalizations. His early association with Dr. T. Romeyn Beck in the first development of the system of meteorological observations established in the State of New York, has already been referred to in the sketch of his "Early Career." (Page 212.) This active and zealous co-operation continued from 1827 to 1832; or as long as he resided in Albany.

In September of 1830, he commenced a series of observations for Professor Renwick of Columbia College, to determine the magnetic intensity at Albany. With the assistance of his brother-in-law, Professor Stephen Alexander, these observations were continued daily for two months.* In April, 1831, a second series of observations was commenced; in the course of which his attention was attracted by a great disturbance of the needle during the time of a conspicuous "aurora" on the 19th of April, 1831. At noon of the 19th the oscillations were found to be perfectly accordant with previous ones, but at 6 o'clock P. M. a remarkable increase of magnetic intensity was indicated. At 10 o'clock of the same evening, during the most active manifestation of the aurora, the oscillations of the needle were again examined. "Instead of still indicating as at 6 o'clock an uncommonly high degree of magnetic intensity, it now showed an intensity considerably lower than usual." Thus, designating the normal intensity at the place as unity, at 6 o'clock it had increased to 1.024, and at 10 o'clock had subsided to 0.993, which according to Hansteen's observations is the usual

---

* The needles employed in these observations were a couple received by Professor RENWICK from Capt. SABINE,—one of which had belonged to Professor HANSTEEN of Norway. "They were suspended according to the method of Hansteen in a small mahogany box, by a single fiber of raw silk. The box was furnished with a glass cover, and had a graduated arc of ivory on the bottom to mark the amplitude of the vibrations. In using this apparatus, the time of three hundred vibrations was noted by a quarter-second watch, well regulated to mean time; a register being made at the end of every tenth vibration, and a mean deduced from the whole, taken as the true time of the three hundred vibrations. Experiments carefully made with this apparatus were found susceptible of considerable accuracy;" the individual observations not differing from the mean number, ordinarily more than one-thousandth. (Silliman's *Am. Jour. Sci.* April, 1832, vol. xxii. p. 145.)

relation of magnetic disturbance by an aurora.* An account of these results was communicated by Henry to the Albany Institute, January 26, 1832; and was also published in the Report of the Regents of the New York University. A little more than a month later (to wit on March 6, 1832,) he had been able to collate the various published accounts of this aurora; and he learned " the fact of a disturbance of terrestrial magnetism being observed by Mr. Christie in England on the same evening, and at nearly the same time the disturbance was witnessed in Albany, and that too in connection with the appearance of an aurora." This circumstance led him to make a careful comparison of the notices of auroral displays given in the meteorological reports in the Annals of Philosophy for 1830 and 1831, with those of the Reports of the New York Regents for the same period. "By inspecting these two publications it was seen that from April, 1830, to April, 1831, inclusive, the aurora was remarkably frequent and brilliant both in Europe and in this country; and that most of the auroras described in the Annals for this time, particularly the brilliant ones, were seen on the same evening in England and in the State of New York." From which he argues that " these simultaneous appearances of the meteor in Europe and America would therefore seem to warrant the conclusion that the aurora borealis cannot be classed among the ordinary local meteorological phenomena, but that it must be referred to some cause connected with the general physical principles of the globe; and that the more energetic action of this cause (whatever it may be) affects simultaneously a greater portion of the northern hemisphere." †

In attempting to classify and digest the meteorological data within his reach, Henry became strongly impressed with the necessity of much more extensive, continuous, and systematic observations than any as yet undertaken: and he neglected no opportunities of directing influence upon the minds of our national

---

* Professor HANSTEEN has remarked that "A short time before the aurora borealis appears, the intensity of the magnetism of the earth is apt to rise to an uncommon height; but so soon as the aurora borealis begins, in proportion as its force increases, the intensity of the magnetism of the earth decreases, recovering its former strength by degrees, often not till the end of twenty-four hours." (*Edinburgh Philosoph. Jour.* Jan. 1825, vol. xii. p. 91.)

† Silliman's *Am. Jour. Sci.* April, 1832, vol. xxii. pp. 150-155.

legislators, to impress them with the great need—as well as the practical policy of prosecuting the subject by governmental resources. No one at that day seemed so fully awake both to the importance and to the methods of prosecuting such inquiry: and no one more effectually advanced both by direct and by indirect exertions the wide-spread interest in this study, than he.

In 1839, while at Princeton, he in conjunction with his friend Professor Bache, induced the American Philosophical Society officially to memorialize the National Government to establish stations for magnetic and meteorological observations: a movement which was partly successful, though not to the extent desired. On the subject of international systems of observation and register, he justly remarks at a later date: "In order that the science of meteorology may be founded on reliable data, and attain that rank which its importance demands, it is necessary that extended systems of co-operation should be established. In regard to climate, no part of the world is isolated: that of the smallest island in the Pacific, is governed by the general currents of the air and the waters of the ocean. To fully understand therefore the causes which influence the climate of any one country, or any one place, it will be necessary to study the conditions, as to heat, moisture, and the movements of the air, of all others. It is evident also that as far as possible, one method should be adopted, and that instruments affording the same indications under the same conditions should be employed. - - - A general plan of this kind, for observing the meteorological and magnetical changes, more extensively than had ever before been projected, was digested by the British Association in 1838, in which the principal Governments of Europe were induced to take an active part; and had that of the United States, and those of South America, joined in the enterprise, a series of watch-towers of nature would have been distributed over every part of the earth. - - - Though the Government of the United States took no part with the other nations of the earth, in the great system before described, yet it has established and supported for a number of years a partial system of observation at the different military posts of the army." *

---

* *Agricultural Report* of Commissioner of Patents, for 1855. pp. 367, 368.

A large collection of original notes of various meteorological observations,—on magnetic variations, on auroras with attempts at ascertaining their extreme height, on violent whirlwinds, on hailstones, on thunder-storms, and the deportment of lightning-rods,— unfortunately never published nor transcribed, were lost (with much other precious scientific material) by fire in 1865. The phenomena of thunder-storms were always studied by Henry with great interest and attention. A very severe one which visited Princeton on the evening of July 14, 1841, was minutely described in a communication to the American Philosophical Society, November 5th, 1841. *

On November 3d, 1843, he made a communication to the Society "in regard to the application of Melloni's thermo-electric apparatus to meterological purposes, and explained a modification of the parts connected with the pile, to which he had been led in the course of his researches. He had found the vapors near the horizon, powerful reflectors of heat; but in the case of a distant thunder-storm, he had found that the cloud was colder than the adjacent blue space." †

On June 20, 1845, he read a paper before the Society on "a simple method of protecting from lightning, buildings covered with metallic roofs;" urging the importance in such cases of having the vertical rain pipes always in good electrical connection with the earth, since "on the principle of electrical induction, houses thus covered are evidently more liable to be struck than those furnished either with shingle or tile. It is of course necessary to have the metallic roof in good metallic connection with the gutters and pipes; and the latter may conveniently have soldered to the lower end a ribbon of sheet copper two or three inches wide, continuing into the ground surrounded with charcoal and extending out from the house till it terminates in moist ground. ‡

---

* *Proceed. Am. Phil. Soc.* vol. ii. pp. 111-116.

† *Proceed. Am. Phil. Soc.* vol. iv. p. 22.

‡ *Proceed. Am. Phil. Soc.* vol. iv. p. 179. HENRY appears to have been much impressed with the conducting value of the tinned sheet-iron pipes commonly used as rain spouts, from observing that amid the strange vagaries of the circuitous path pursued by the lightning (in cases of houses struck by this destructive agent), the rain pipe was not unfrequently selected as part of the route;—marks of explosive violence being exhibited at its lower end, and sometimes at its top as well,—while the pipe itself was found to be uninjured.

In this paper he incidentally meets the much debated question whether a lightning-rod is efficient as a conductor by its solidity, or by its surface only. While he had been able to magnetize small needles placed transversely to the *edges* of broad strips of copper, through which electrical discharges were passed, he could obtain no signs of magnetism in needles when placed transversely near the *sides* of such strips about mid-way from the edges. In like manner he failed to discover any action in a small magnetizing helix placed within a section of gas-pipe and connected with it at either end, when transmitting through the system an electrical spark; while he easily obtained magnetic effects with a galvanic current passed through the same arrangement.* From these and other experiments he was led to believe that mechanical electricity tends to pass mainly along the exterior surface of a conductor, and accordingly that Ohm's law of conduction is not applicable to lightning or mechanical electricity. †

Some popular uneasiness having been excited in 1846, in consequence of telegraph poles being occasionally struck by lightning, and of the supposed danger to travellers along highways likely to result therefrom, a communication on the subject addressed to Dr. Patterson, one of the Vice-Presidents of the American Philosophical Society, was read before the Society, and referred to Professor Henry for report. This was in the very infancy of the electro-magnetic telegraph; as it had not then been in existence more than a couple of years. Henry responded in a communication read June 19th, 1846, to the effect that while telegraph wires as long conductors were eminently liable to receive discharges of atmospheric electricity both from charged clouds and from the varying electrical condition of the air at distant points along the line (as for

---

* In passing a galvanic current through an iron tube, he obtained the evidence of an induction from both the inside and the outside of the tube, but in opposite directions.

† This very important question cannot be regarded as even yet decisively settled:—eminent authorities maintaining that electricity *in flow*—of whatever origin—observes equally the ratio of proportionality to area of cross section in the conductor. Probably the law of conductivity varies with circumstances. RITCHIE remarks that "if a metallic rod be raised to a red heat, its power of conducting common electricity is increased, whilst its conducting power for voltaic electricity is considerably diminished." (*Journal of the Royal Institution of Great Britain*, Oct. 1830, vol. i. (n. s.) p. 37.)

example even by a fog or precipitation of vapor at one station) as also from induction at a distance, the danger to travellers along a telegraph road would be very slight, unless a person should be standing or passing quite close to a pole at the moment of its being struck. He however recommended that for the protection of the poles, they should be provided with conductors. "The effects of powerful discharges from the clouds may be prevented in a great degree by erecting at intervals along the line and beside the supporting poles a metallic wire connected with the earth at the lower end, and terminating above at the distance of about half an inch from the wire of the telegraph. By this arrangement, the insulation of the conductor will not be interfered with, while the greater portion of the charge will be drawn off. I think this precaution of great importance at places where the line crosses a river and is supported on high poles. Also in the vicinity of the office of the telegraph, where a discharge falling on the wire near the station might send a current into the house of sufficient quantity to produce serious accidents."* This precaution has now been largely adopted, especially on the telegraph lines of the central portion of the United States, which are more liable to the effects of lightning.†

*Molecular Physics.* — Among other inquiries many original examinations were made by Henry in the domain of molecular physics. While Professor in the College of New Jersey in 1839, his attention was attracted to a curious case of metallic capillarity. A small lead tube about eight inches long happening to be left with a bent end lying in a shallow dish of mercury, he noticed a few days afterward that the mercury had disappeared from the dish, and was spread on the shelf about the other end of the tube. On a careful examination of the tube by incision, it appeared that the mercury had not passed along the open canal of the tube, but had percolated through its solid substance. To test this, a solid rod of lead about one-fourth of an inch thick and seven inches long was bent into a siphon form, and the shorter end immersed in a small shallow vessel of mercury; a similar empty vessel being placed under the longer end.

---

* *Proceed. Am. Phil. Soc.* vol. iv. p. 266.

† Prescott. *Electricity and the Electric Telegraph,* 8vo. N. York, 1877, chap. xxiii. pp. 296 and 411.

In the course of 24 hours a globule of mercury was found at the lower end of the lead rod; and in five or six days it had all passed over excepting what appeared in the form of crystals of a lead amalgam in the upper vessel. * A long piece of thick lead wire was afterward suspended in a vertical position, with its lower end dipping into a cup of mercury. In the course of a few days, traces of the mercury were found in the rod at the height of three feet above the cup: thus showing that a metal impervious to water or oil (excepting under very great pressure) was easily penetrated to great distances by a liquid metal.

Some years later on a visit to Philadelphia he endeavored with the assistance of his friend Dr. Patterson (then Director of the United States Mint), by melting a small globule of gold on a plate of clean sheet-iron, to obtain its capillary absorption; but without effect; probably owing to the interposition of a thin film of oxide. Applying to another personal friend, Mr. Cornelius of Philadelphia, a very intelligent and ingenious manufacturer of bronzes, and plated ornaments for chandeliers, etc. to try whether a piece of silver-plated copper heated to the melting point of silver would show any absorption of that metal, he learned that it was a common experience under such circumstances to find the silver disappear; but that this had always been attributed to a volatilization of the silver, or in the workman's phrase,—to its being "burnt off." At Henry's request the experiment was tried: the heated end of a silver-plated piece of copper exhibited on cooling and cleaning, a copper surface; the other end remaining unchanged. Henry next had the copper surface slightly dissolved off by immersion for a few minutes in a solution of muriate of zinc, when as he had anticipated, the silver was again exposed, having penetrated to but a very short and tolerably uniform distance below the original surface. †

In 1844, he made some important observations on the cohesion of liquids. Notwithstanding that Dr. Young early in the century maintained that "the immediate cause of solidity as distinguished from liquidity is the *lateral adhesion* of the particles to each other," and had shown that "the resistance of ice to extension or com-

---

* *Proceed. Am. Phil. Soc.* vol. 1. p. 82.

† *Proceed. Am. Phil. Soc.* June 20, 1845, vol. 1v. p. 177.

pression is found by experiment to differ very little from that of water contained in a vessel," * all the most popular text-books on physics continued to teach that the cohesion of the liquid state is intermediate between that of the solid and the gaseous states. † It seemed therefore desirable to test the question by some more direct means than the resistance of liquids contained in closed vessels; and for this purpose Henry employed the classical soap-bubble. "The effect of dissolving the soap in the water is not as might at first appear, to increase the molecular attraction, but to diminish the mobility of the molecules." In fact the actual *tenacity* of pure water is greater than that of soap-water.

The first set of experiments was directed to determine "the quantity of water which adhered to a bubble just before it burst." The second set of experiments was devised to measure the contractile force of a soap-bubble blown on the wider end of a U-shaped glass tube half filled with water, by the barometric column sustained in the narrower stem of the tube; the difference of level being carefully observed by means of a microscope. The thickness of the soap-bubble film at its top was estimated by the last of the Newton rings shown previous to bursting. The result arrived at from both sets of experiments was that water instead of having a cohesion of 53 grains to the square inch (as was very commonly stated), has a cohesive force of several hundred pounds to the inch; or that the inter-molecular cohesion of a liquid is fully equal to that of the substance in the solid state. ‡

---

* Young's *Lectures on Nat. Philos.* Lect. 50, vol. 1. p. 627.

† "If we attempt to draw up from the surface of water a circular disk of metal say of an inch in diameter, we shall see that the water will adhere and be supported several lines above the general surface. This experiment which is frequently given in elementary books as a measure of the feeble attraction of water for itself, is improperly interpreted. It merely indicates the force of attraction of a single film of atoms around the perpendicular surface, and not of the whole column elevated." (*Agricultural Report* for 1857. p. 427.—Henry's paper on Meteorology.)

‡ *Proceed. Am. Phil. Soc.* April 5 and May 17, 1844, vol. iv. pp. 56, 57, and 84, 85. The original notes of these interesting experiments containing the numerical results obtained under a great variety of conditions, laid aside for further reductions and comparisons, were destroyed by fire in 1865. Since the density of most solid substances differs very slightly from that of their liquid state, being indeed less in many,—unless at considerably lower temperatures, (as in the case of ice, and most of the metals,) it appears quite improbable that the difference between solidity and liquidity could depend in any case on the degree of cohesion. On the contrary, the cohesion of water should be sensibly greater than that of ice, since its constituent

In 1846, he presented to the Philosophical Society an epitome of his views on the molecular constitution of matter; giving the reasons for accepting the atomic hypothesis of Newton. He pointed out that the discovery and establishment of a general scientific principle "is in almost all cases the result of deductions from a rational antecedent hypothesis, the product of the imagination; founded it is true on a clear analogy with modes of physical action, the truth of which has been established by previous investigation:" and he urged that the hope of further advancement lies in the assumption "that the same laws of force and motion which govern the phenomena of the action of matter in masses, pertains to the minutest atoms of these masses." He therefore felt "obliged to assume the existence of an ætherial medium formed of atoms which are endowed with precisely the same properties as those we have assigned to common matter."

"According to the foregoing rules we may assume with Newton, the existence of *one kind of matter* diffused throughout all space, and existing in four states, namely the ætherial, the aeriform, the liquid, and the solid."* [In referring to this postulated *fourfold state of matter*, Henry was accustomed to point out the remarkable analogy between this conception, and that of the four elements of the ancients, — fire, air, water, and earth.]

"In conclusion, it should be remembered that the legitimate use of speculations of this kind, is not to furnish plausible explanations of known phenomena, or to present old knowledge in a new and more imposing dress, but to serve the higher purpose of suggesting new experiments and new phenomena, and thus to assist in enlarging the bounds of science, and extending the power of mind over matter; and unless the hypothesis can be employed in this way, however much ingenuity may have been expended in its construction, it can only be considered as a scientific romance worse than

---

molecules are closer together. Of the nature of that "lateral *adhesion*" which resists the flow of solids (excepting under the conditions of great strain — long continued), and whose absence is marked in liquids by their almost perfect and frictionless mobility, our present science affords us no intimation.

* Two hundred years ago, NEWTON speculating on the unity of matter, ventured the suggestion, "Thus perhaps may all things be originated from æther."—Letter to the Secretary of the Royal Society—Henry Oldenburg, January, 1676. (*History of the Royal Society:* by Thomas Birch, vol. iii. p. 250.)

useless, since it tends to satisfy the mind with the semblance of truth, and thus to render truth itself less an object of desire."*

*Light and Heat.*—Henry also made important investigations on some peculiar phenomena connected with light and heat. For the purpose of experimenting on sun-light he devised in 1840, a very simple form of heliostat, based on the suggestion of Dr. Young, whereby the solar ray was received into an upper room in a direction parallel to the earth's axis, by means of a simple equatorial movement of the reflector;† which was effected by the aid of a common cheap pocket watch placed on a small hinged board set by a screw to the angle of latitude. The mirror mounted on a swivel and properly balanced, presented no sensible resistance to the running of the watch, which was arranged for the 24-hour rotation by a watchmaker of Princeton. The whole cost of the completed instrument (including the time-movement) was but sixteen dollars. If any particular direction of the ray was required, it was only necessary to place a stationary mirror in the fixed path of the ray, adjusted to the desired angle. ‡

In 1841, on repeating experiments of Becquerel and Biot on "Phosphorescence," he discovered some new characteristics in the emanation (particularly when excited by electrical light) which had not before been observed.§ These were more fully detailed in a communication made to the American Philosophical Society, in 1843, "On Phosphorogenic Emanation." This phenomenon had been first observed in the diamond, when taken into a dark room immediately after exposure to direct sunlight, or to a vivid electric spark; and was afterward observed in several other substances,— notably in the chloride of calcium — "Homberg's phosphorus."‖ It had also been shown by Becquerel that while this phosphores-

---

* *Proceed. Am. Phil. Soc.* Nov. 6, 1846, vol. iv. pp. 287–290.

† Dr. Young's *Lectures on Nat. Phil.* lect. xxxvi. vol. i. p. 426. The equatorial heliostat appears to have been first suggested by FAHRENHEIT.

‡ *Proceed. Am. Phil. Soc.* Sept. 17, 1841, vol. ii. p. 97.

§ *Proceed. Am. Phil. Soc.* April 16, 1841, vol. ii. p. 46.

‖ HOMBERG'S phosphorus is a calcium chloride prepared by melting one part of sal ammoniac (ammonic chloride) with two parts of slaked lime. CANTON'S phosphorus is a calcium sulphide formed by a mixture of three parts of sifted and calcined oyster shells, and one part of flowers of sulphur, exposed for an hour to a strong heat.

cence may be fully excited in the sensitive body by rays which
have passed through transparent sulphate of lime, or through
quartz, the effect is entirely arrested by a plate of transparent mica,
or glass.* Henry by a long series of experiments greatly extended these lists, including in them a large number of liquids.
He also subjected both the exciting rays (especially that of the electric spark), and the luminous emanation, to various treatment, by
reflection, refraction, polarization, etc. The Nicol prism was found
to obstruct this peculiar exciting ray so much as to permit scarcely
any impression ; but what was remarkable and unexpected, a pile
of thin mica plates which seemed to cut off entirely the phosphorogenic impression, was found when placed obliquely at the best
polarizing angle, to distinctly excite a surviving luminous spot.
On examination of the phosphorescence excited by polarized light,
no effect was perceived by a rotation of the analyzer: "when the
beam was transmitted through crystals in different directions with
reference to their optical axis, no difference could be observed."
The phosphorescence was completely depolarized, as if taking an
entirely new origin in the sensitive substance: a fact re-discovered
by Professor George G. Stokes some ten years later, with regard to
fluorescent emanations.

That the phosphorogenic effect does not depend on a heating of
the substance, appeared to be shown by the fact that "the lime
becomes as luminous under a plate of alum as under a plate of
rock-salt." The emanation was examined by a prism of rock-
crystal, and by one of rock-salt : — science had not then the spectro-
scope. While the impression could be readily made by a reflected
beam from a metallic mirror, it failed entirely when directed from
a looking-glass. The luminous effect on the phosphorescent substance was found to be defined in location by the form of the opening made in sheet-metal screens. Different portions of the electric
spark being tested by means of a narrow slit in the screen, the
two terminals of the spark were found to be much more active (as
measured by the subsequent duration of the phosphorescence) than
the middle portion. By a suitable arrangement of double screens

---

* That there should be such a difference between quartz and glass or mica, is certainly a remarkable circumstance.

with three slits each, he was able to make simultaneous star-like "photographs" on the substance, of the two extreme portions of the spark and of a middle point: and while the latter point "exhibited a feeble phosphorescence for two or three seconds" only, the two former "continued to glow for more than a minute;" and yet the middle of the spark appeared to the eye quite as vivid as its extremities. It was also observed that while a sensitive daguerreotype plate received no impression from the electric spark, inversely another similar plate exposed for several minutes to the direct light of the full moon received a photographic impression, while the lime similarly exposed, exhibited no phosphorescence.*

As a striking illustration of the closely allied phenomenon of fluorescence, Henry was afterward accustomed on the occurrence of a bright aurora, to expose a sheet of paper written or figured with a solution of bisulphate of quinia to the auroral light, when the characters (quite invisible by lamp-light or even by day-light) would distinctly glow with a pale blue light; — indicating the electrical nature of the meteor.

In January, 1845, in conjunction with Professor Stephen Alexander, he instituted a series of experimental observations on the relative heat-radiating power of the solar spots. On the 4th of January a large spot through which our terrestrial globe could have been freely dropped, (having been estimated at more than 10,000 miles in diameter,) favorably situated near the middle of the disk, was examined with a telescope of four inches aperture. A screen having been arranged in a dark room, with a thermo-electric apparatus behind it and having its terminal or pile just projecting through a hole in the screen, the image of the spot was received upon it, giving a clearly defined outline about two inches long and one inch and a half wide. By a slight motion of the telescope the spot could readily be thrown on or off the end of the pile as desired. A considerable number of observations indicated very clearly by the

---

* *Proceed. Am. Phil. Soc.* May 26, 1843, vol. iii. pp. 38-44. This interesting but obscure subject although apparently connected with the phenomenon of "fluorescence" has yet an entirely distinct phase in its abnormal continuance of luminosity,—similar to the familiar effect of a thermal impression. It is possible however that the conversion of wave-periodicity (wave-length), shown by Stokes to be the characteristic of fluorescence, may require time for its full development.

differing deflections of the galvanometer needle "that the spot emitted less heat than the surrounding parts of the luminous disk."[*] A brief account of the results obtained by these researches given in a letter to his friend Sir David Brewster, was read by the latter at the Cambridge Meeting of the British Association in June, 1845.[†] The determinations arrived at have been fully confirmed by the later observations of Secchi and others.[‡]

In 1845, he contributed a paper to the Princeton Review, on "Color Blindness;" which although in the modest form of a literary review of two Memoirs then recently published, (that of Sir David Brewster in the Philosophical Magazine; and that of Professor Elie Wartman, of Lausanne, in the Scientific Memoirs,) supplied original observations on this interesting department of the physiology of vision.

*Miscellaneous Contributions.*—Henry's miscellaneous contributions to physical science are so numerous and varied, that only a brief allusion to some of them can be afforded. In 1829, he published quite an elaborate "Topographical sketch of the State of New York, designed chiefly to show the general elevations and depressions of its surface."[§] And in later years he devoted much attention to physical geography. He also made some geological explorations and observations in the State of New York. He performed at various times a good deal of chemical work (chiefly of an analytical character),—first as Dr. T. Romeyn Beck's assistant,[||]

---

[*] *Proceed. Am. Phil. Soc.* June 20, 1845, vol. iv. pp. 173–176.

[†] *Report Brit. Assoc.* 1845, part ii. p. 6.

[‡] P. ANGELO SECCHI—during the years 1848 and 1849, (then a young man of thirty,) was Professor of Mathematics at the College of Georgetown, D. C. and in the preparation of his "Researches on Electrical Rheometry," published in the third volume of the *Smithsonian Contributions*, (art. ii. 60 pp.) he received from Henry the friendly assistance of apparatus and suggestions. It is interesting to refer to Henry's introduction of Professor Secchi's first researches to the attention of the Regents of the Smithsonian Institution, when the name was as yet wholly unknown to the scientific world. "Another memoir is by Professor Secchi, a young Italian of much ingenuity and learning, a member of Georgetown College. It consists of a new mathematical investigation of the reciprocal action of two galvanic currents on each other, and of the action of a current on the pole of a magnet." (*Smithsonian Report* for 1849, p. 172, S. ed. and p. 164, H. R. ed.) Professor Secchi was appointed Director of the Observatory at Rome, in 1850.

[§] *Trans. Albany Institute*, vol. i. pp. 87–112.

[||] "HENRY was then Dr. BECK's chemical assistant, and already an admirable experimentalist." Address before the Albany Institute, by Dr. O. Meads, May 25, 1871. (*Trans. Albany Institute*, vol. vii. p. 21.)

and afterward independently, as well as mediately in directing his own pupils and assistants. In 1833, he devised an improvement on Wollaston's mechanical scale of the chemical equivalents, for the benefit of his pupils in chemistry : — a contrivance which was much used and highly appreciated at the time.

The suggestion had been thrown out by more than one astronomer, that carefully timed observations on characteristic meteors or "shooting-stars" might be made available for determining differences of longitude between the stations of observation.* For many years however the proposition had been generally regarded as offering rather a speculative than a practical method of solving a problem of so great nicety. Henry in concert with his brother-in-law, Professor Alexander, and with his friend Professor Bache, determined to ascertain by actual trial the availability and value of the system. On the 25th of November, 1835, Professor Bache observing at his residence in Philadelphia (assisted by Professor J. P. Espy,) — simultaneously with Professor Henry and Professor Alexander, at the Philosophical Hall at Princeton, they obtained seven co-incidences: — the instant of disappearance of the meteor being in each case selected as the most accurately attainable epoch. These seven observations (whose greatest discrepancies amounted to but a trifle over 3 seconds) gave a mean result of 2 minutes 0.61 second (time longitude), differing only one second and two-tenths from the mean estimate of relative longitude arrived at by other methods. †

In 1840, Henry gave an account of "electricity obtained from a small ball partly filled with water, and heated by a lamp." ‡

---

* "The merit of first suggesting the use of shooting-stars and fire-balls as signals for the determination of longitudes is claimed by Dr. Olbers and the German astronomers for BENZENBERG, who published a work on the subject in 1802. Mr. Bailey however has pointed out a paper published by Dr. MASKELYNE twenty years previously, in which that illustrious astronomer calls attention to the subject, and distinctly points out this application of the phenomena." This was dated Greenwich, November 6th, 1783. (*L. E. D. Phil. Mag.* 1841, vol. xix. p. 554.)

† *Proceed. Am. Phil. Soc.* Dec. 20, 1839, vol. i. pp. 162, 163. "This appears to have been the first actual determination of a difference of longitude by meteoric observations." (*L. E. D. Phil. Mag.* 1841, vol. xix. p. 553.) Several years later (in 1838) similar meteoric observations were made between Altona and Breslau; and also between Rome and Naples.

‡ *Proceed. Am. Phil. Soc.* Dec. 18, 1840, vol. i. p. 323.

In 1843, he read a communication to the Society, "On a new method of determining the velocity of Projectiles:" for this purpose employing two screens of fine insulated wire each in circuit with a galvanometer, and at determined near distances in the path of the projectile; — whereby the galvanic currents would be successively interrupted at the instants of penetration. To record the interval, each galvanometer needle is provided at one end with a marking pen touching a horizontally revolving cylinder, which is divided by longitudinal lines into 100 equal parts, and is driven by clock-work at the rate of ten revolutions per second, giving therefore to the interval of passage between two consecutive lines, the thousandth part of a second. * Another still more ingenious method is suggested, whereby the galvanometer may be dispensed with: each circuit including an induction coil, one end of whose secondary circuit is connected with the axis, and the other end placed very nearly in contact with the surface of the graduated paper on the revolving cylinder, so as to give the induction spark through the paper at the instant of the interruption of the primary circuits by the projectile passing through the wire screens. This is really a much neater and more direct application of the electric interruption than the employment of a galvanometer needle for making the record, as it involves no material inertia. If desirable, the cylinder may be made to have a very slow longitudinal movement by a screw, so as to give a helical direction to the tracings; and different pairs of screens similarly arranged at distant points in the path of the projectile may be employed to determine the variations of velocity in its flight. †

Henry was always a watchful student of psychological and subjective phenomena. Witnessing on one occasion the performance of an athlete before a large assembly, he noticed with a curious interest the "inductive" sympathy manifested by nearly every spectator (himself included) in being swayed by a movement as of

---

* It appears that WHEATSTONE devised his ingenious electro-magnetic "chronoscope" in 1840; though he unfortunately published no account of it till 1845; or two years after the publication by HENRY. And this was called out as a reclamation, on the publication of a similar invention by L. BREGUET, of Paris, in January of the same year. See "Supplement," NOTE G.

† *Proceed. Am. Phil. Soc.* May 30, 1843, vol. iii. pp. 165–167.

assistance to the performer. In remarking the impression of being moved, while steadily watching a series of passing canal boats, he referred the impression (amounting almost to a sensation of movement on each boat reaching a certain point,) to the relative angle of vision formed by the moving body.

He made a number of experiments on the flow of water jets under varying conditions: also observations on sonorous flames when passing into a stove-pipe of eight inches diameter and about ten feet in length: on the comparative rates of evaporation from fresh and from salt water: on the slow evaporation of water from the open end of a U-shaped tube, and the much greater rapidity of evaporation when the tube is open at both ends: extended notes of which, with a great number of other researches, perished in the flames.

In 1844, he published a Syllabus of his Lectures at Princeton. In December of that year he presented to the Philosophical Society a communication of a somewhat more theoretical character than usual,—on the derivation and classification of mechanical motors. He refers these to two classes;—the first, those derived from celestial disturbance (as water, tide, and wind powers),—and the second, those derived from organic bodies or forces (as steam and other heat powers, and animal powers). The forces of gravity, cohesion, and chemical affinity are not included, since these tend speedily to stable equilibrium; and they become sources of mechanical power only as they are disturbed by some of those before mentioned. It is not the running down of the water-fall, or the clock-weight, which is the true origin of their useful work, but the lifting of them up. The same is true of the power derived from combustion. He then adds that his second class (the forces derived from the organic world) might perhaps by a similar process of reasoning be derived from the first class; (that of celestial disturbance;)—regarding "animal power as referable to the same sources as that from the combustion of fuel," and the action of the vegetative power as "a force derived from the divellent power of the sunbeam," being simply a case of solar de-oxidation. Organism—vegetable and animal, he considers as built up under the *direction* of a vital principle, which is not itself a mechanical force. Volcanic power is neglected as compara-

18

tively feeble and limited, and not practically utilized.* This interesting digest presents one of the earliest and clearest theoretical statements we have, of the correlation and transformation of the physical forces; including with these the so-called organic forces.

## ADMINISTRATION OF THE SMITHSONIAN INSTITUTION.

By an Act of Congress approved August 10, 1846, the liberal bequest to the United States, for the promotion of Science, by James Smithson of London, England, was appropriated to the foundation of the Institution bearing his name; the establishment being made to comprise the chief dignitaries of the Government as the supervising body, and a Board of Regents being created for conducting the business of the Institution after completing its organization. As the testator had bequeathed his fortune,† in simple terms "for the increase and diffusion of knowledge among men," there arose not unnaturally a great diversity of opinion both among Congressmen, and among the Regents, as to the most desirable method of executing the purpose of the Will: and the organizing Act was itself a sort of compromise, after many years of discussion and disagreement in both branches of Congress. To literary men, no instrument of knowledge could be so important as an extensive Library: — to the professional, a seat of education or public instruction — general or special — supplemented by elaborate courses of public lectures, appeared the obvious and necessary means of diffusing useful learning, — to the "practical," a large agricultural and polytechnic institute — supplemented perhaps by a museum, was the only fitting plan of developing the resources of our country: — to the artistic, extensive galleries of art were the most worthy and instructive objects of patronage. The Regents sought counsel from the distinguished and the learned: and several of them applied to Professor Henry for his opinion. He gave the subject a careful

---

* *Proceed. Am. Phil. Soc.* Dec. 20, 1844, vol. iv. pp. 127–129. This appears to be the first — as it is probably the best — analysis of physical energy, which has been proposed. Twenty years later, a similar analysis (with certainly no improvement in the classification) was adopted by Professor Tait, in an essay on "Energy;" (*North British Review*, 1864, vol. xl. art. iii. p. 191, of Am. edition:) and by Dr. Balfour Stewart, in his *Elementary Treatise on Heat*, Oxford, 1866: (book iii. chap. v. art. 388, p. 351.)

† The whole amount of the bequest was a trifle over 100,000 pounds, or about 540,000 dollars.

consideration; and announced very decided views. As Smithson was a man of scientific culture, a Fellow of the Royal Society, an expert analytical chemist, and devoted to original research, Henry held that the language of his Will must receive its most accurate and scientific and at the same time most comprehensive interpretation; that the words "increase and diffusion of knowledge among men" were deliberately and intelligently employed; and that no local or even national interests were as broad as its terms,—that no merely educational projects of whatever character, no schemes of material and practical advancement however useful, could justly be regarded as fulfilling the obvious intent—expressed by a scientific thinker and writer—first of all the *increase* of knowledge by the promotion of original research,—the addition of new truths to the existing stock of knowledge, and secondly—its widest possible diffusion among mankind.*

These wise and far-reaching views exerted a marked influence; and though hardly then in accord with the opinion of the majority, yet led to his election December 3d, 1846, as the "Secretary" and actual Director of the infant institution.† A second time was Henry called upon to sever dearly prized associations,—the prosperous and congenial pursuits of fourteen years within the classic halls of Princeton. One motive turned the wavering scale. Here was a rare occasion offered by the enlightened provision of James Smithson, to secure for abstract science and unpromising original research, a much needed encouragement and support; and an obligation imposed upon the scientific few to resist and if possible prevent the perversion of the trust to the merely popular uses of the short-sighted many. That years would be required for shaping the character and conduct of the institution as he desired, was certain;—that this could not be effected without much opposition and various obstacle, he very clearly foresaw. That during these years of active supervision and direction, he must abandon all hope of personal opportunity for original research, he as freely accepted in the expressive remark made to a trusted friend in consultation on

---

* "Programme of Organization," *Smithsonian Report* for 1847. See "Supplement," NOTE H.

† See "Supplement," NOTE I.

the occasion: "If I go, I shall probably exchange permanent fame for transient reputation."

With the assurance of the Trustees of the College of New Jersey, that should he fail to realize his programme, or should he satisfactorily accomplish his apostolic purpose, his chair should always be at his command, with a hearty welcome back, Henry, neither spurred by over-confidence, nor depressed with undue timidity, though filled with anxious solicitude for the future, accepted the appointment tendered to him. He removed with his family to Washington, December 14, 1846, and at once commenced his administration of the duties assigned to him by the Regents of the Institution.

Summoned thus to the occupancy of a new and untried field, and to the discharge of essentially executive functions, he from the first displayed a clearness and promptness of judgment, a singleness and steadiness of aim, a firmness and consistency of decision, combined with a practical sagacity and moderation in adapting his course to the exigencies of adverse conditions, which stamped him as a most able and successful administrator. Without concealment and without diplomacy, his distinctly avowed principle of action was steadily and patiently pursued. * With honest submission to the controlling Act of Congress, he made as honest avowal of his desire and of his endeavor to have that legislation modified. Hampered by provisions he deemed unwise and injurious, he yet skillfully managed to reconcile contestant interests, and to secure the entire confidence and concurrence of the Regents. Henceforth his purpose and his effort were to be directed to the unique object of encouraging and fostering the development of what has so flippantly been designated "useless knowledge;" and merging self in the community of physical inquirers and collaborators, to become the high-priest of abstract investigation;—prepared to lend all practicable assistance to that small but earnest band of nature-students, who inspired by no aims of material utility, seek from their mistress as the only reward of their devotion, a closer intimacy, a higher knowledge of truth.†

---

* See "Supplement," NOTE J.

† HENRY has finely said: "Let censure or ridicule fall elsewhere,—on those whose lives are passed without labor and without object; but let praise and honor be bestowed on him who seeks with unwearied patience to develop the order, harmony, and beauty of even the smallest part of God's creation. A life devoted

Of the two distinct objects of endowment specified by Smithson's Will, — "the *increase* — and the *diffusion* — of knowledge," **Henry** forcibly remarked: "These though frequently confounded, are very different processes, and each may exist independent **of the** other. **While we rejoice that in our** country above all others, **so much attention** is paid to the *diffusion* of knowledge, truth compels us to **say that** comparatively little encouragement is given to its *increase*.* There is another division with regard to knowledge which Smithson does not embrace **in** his design; viz. the application of knowledge to useful purposes in the arts.    **And it was not necessary** he should found an institution for this purpose.    **There are already in every** civilized country, establishments and **patent laws for the encourage-** ment of this department **of mental industry.    As soon as any branch of** science **can be** brought **to bear on the necessities, con-** veniences, or luxuries **of life, it meets with encouragement and reward.**    Not so with **the discovery of the** incipient **principles of** science.    The investigations which lead to these, receive **no fostering** care from Government, and are considered by the superficial **observer** as trifles unworthy **the** attention **of** those who place the supreme good in that which **immediately** administers to the physical needs or luxuries of life.    **If physical well-being were alone the** object of existence, every avenue **of enjoyment should be** explored to its **utmost extent.**    But he who **loves truth** for its own sake, feels that its highest claims are **lowered and its** moral influence marred by being continually summoned to **the bar of immediate and palpable** utility.    Smithson himself **had no such narrow views.†    The promi-**

exclusively to the study of a single insect, is not spent in vain. No animal how-ever insignificant is isolated; it forms a part of the great system of nature, and is governed by the same general laws which control the most prominent beings of the organic world." (*Smithsonian Report* for 1855, p. 20.)

*[SWAINSON the Naturalist, the countryman and friend of Smithson, has very pointedly marked this recognized distinction. "The constitution of the Zoological Society is of a very mixed nature, admirably adapted indeed to the reigning taste. It is more calculated however to *diffuse* than to *increase* the actual stock of scien-tific knowledge." (*Discourse on the Study of Natural History*, Cabinet Cyclopedia, 16mo. London, 1834, part iv. chap. i. sec. 221, p. 314.) And again: "It is very essential when we speak of the diffusion or extension of science, that we do not confound these stages of development with discovery or advancement; since the latter may be as different from the former as depth is from shallowness." (Same work, part iv. chap. ii. sec. 240, p. 343.)]

†[In regard to the value of scientific truth, SMITHSON in a communication dated June 10th, 1824, has forcibly expressed his strong "conviction that it is in his

nent design of his bequest is the promotion of abstract science.  In this respect the Institution holds an otherwise unoccupied place in this country; and it adopts two fundamental maxims in its policy; — first to do nothing with its funds which can be equally well done by other means; and second to produce results which as far as possible will benefit mankind in general." *

Congress — naturally with a prevailing tendency to the literary, the showy, and the popular, had (after eight years of dilatory controversy) directed in its organizing Act (sec. 5,) the erection of a building "of sufficient size, and with suitable rooms or halls for the reception and arrangement upon a liberal scale, of objects of natural history, including a geological and mineralogical cabinet, also a chemical laboratory, a library, a gallery of art, and the necessary lecture-rooms."  By the 9th section of the Act, the Board of Regents were authorized to expend the remaining income of the endowment "as they shall deem best suited for the promotion of the purpose of the testator."  Out of an annual income of some 40,000 dollars, the Regents in full accord with their Secretary (whose carefully elaborated programme they officially adopted December 13, 1847,) succeeded in creditably inaugurating all the objects specified in the charter; and at the same time in establishing the system of publication of original Memoirs, to which Henry justly attached the first importance.

An incident in itself too slight to produce a visible ripple on the current of Henry's life, is yet too characteristic to be here omitted. Dr. Robert Hare having in 1847 decided upon resigning his Professorship of Chemistry in the Medical Department of the University of Pennsylvania, (the largest and best patronized in the country,) the vacant chair was tendered by the Board of Trustees to Professor Henry.  His friend Dr. Hare himself used his influence to induce Henry to become his successor; particularly dwelling on the large amount of leisure afforded for independent investigations.

knowledge that man has found his greatness and his happiness, the high superiority which he holds over the other animals who inhabit the earth with him; and consequently that no ignorance is probably without loss to him, no error without evil."  (Thomson's *Annals of Philosophy*, 1824, vol. xxiv. or new series, vol. viii. p. 54.)]

* *Smithsonian Report* for 1853, p. 8.

The income of this professorship was more than double the salary of the Smithsonian Secretaryship. The position, tempting as it might have been under different circumstances, was however declined. Henry felt that to leave his present post before his cherished policy was fairly settled and established, would be most probably to abandon nearly all the results of the experiment: and having set before himself the one great object of directing the resources of the Smithsonian Institution as far as possible to the advancement of science, in conformity with the undoubted intention of its founder, (and as the execution therefore of a sacred trust,) he resolutely put aside every inducement that might divert him from the fulfillment of his task. *

Of the half a dozen objects of attention specified in the 5th section of the organizing Act, (the various inspiration of different partisans,) not one directly tended to further the primary requirements of the Will: — even the Laboratory being avowedly introduced simply as a utilitarian workshop for mining and agricultural analyses. Regarded as methods of *diffusing* existing knowledge they were obviously local and limited in their range: and as compared with the instrumentality of the Press, were certainly very inefficient for spreading the benefits of the endowment among men. †

Henry with a rare courage dared maintain against most powerful influence, that the interests specifically designated must all be subordinated to the fundamental requirement, the promotion of

---

* Some six years later, a somewhat similar temptation was presented. In 1853, on the resignation of President Carnahan of the College of New Jersey at Princeton, an effort was made to induce the return of Professor Henry to his academic seat, by a movement to obtain for him the Presidency of the College. Such a token of affectionate remembrance could not but be grateful and touching to his feelings; but a sense of obligation was upon him, not to be laid aside. He had undertaken a work and a responsibility which must not be left to the hazard of failure. He declined the proffered honor — with thanks; and warmly recommended Dr. Maclean to the vacant position: who thereupon was duly elected. (Maclean's *Hist. of College of New Jersey*, vol. ii. p. 336.)

† "The objects specified in the Act of Congress evidently do not come up to the idea of the testator as deduced from a critical examination of his will. A library, a museum, a gallery of arts, though important in themselves, are local in their influence. I have from the beginning advocated this opinion on all occasions, and shall continue to advocate it whenever a suitable opportunity occurs." (*Smithsonian Report* for 1853, p. 122 (of Senate edit.)—p. 117 (of H. Rep. edit.) The superficial pretext was not wanting on the part of some, that the words "increase and diffusion" were not to be taken too literally, but to be considered as the tautology of legal equivalents, applicable to the development of the individual mind; since school-boys (if not the pundits) were evidently capable of an "increase" of knowledge.

original research for increasing knowledge : and that this was amply sustained by the residuary grant of authority to the Regents (under the 9th section of the Act) "to make such disposal as they shall deem best suited *for the promotion of the purposes of the testator*, anything herein contained to the contrary notwithstanding," of any income of the Smithsonian fund "not herein appropriated, or not required for the purposes herein provided." Henry's carefully studied programme comprised two sections: the first, embracing the details of the plan for carrying out the explicit purpose of Smithson ; the second, indicating the proper steps for carrying out the provisions of the Act of Congress. The first and principal section proposed as methods of promoting research, — the stimulation of particular investigations by special premiums, — the publication of such original memoirs furnishing positive additions to knowledge by experiment and observation as should be approved by a commission of experts in each case, — the active direction of certain investigations by the provision of instruments as well as of the necessary means, the appropriations being judiciously varied in distribution from year to year, — the prosecution of experimental determinations and the solution of physical problems, — the extension of ethnology (especially American), and in general the conduct of such varied explorations as should ultimately result in a complete physical atlas of the United States. As methods of promoting the diffusion of knowledge, it was proposed to give a wide circulation to the published original memoirs or Smithsonian "Contributions to Knowledge" among domestic and foreign libraries, institutions, and scientific correspondents, to have prepared by qualified collaborators, series of careful reports on the latest progress of science in different departments, and to provide facilities for the distribution and exchange of scientific memoirs generally.

It is unnecessary here to follow closely the slow steps by which — through all the obstructions of narrow prejudice and ignorant misconstruction, of selfish interest and pretended philanthropy, of friendly remonstrance and hostile denunciation, — the policy originally marked out by the Secretary was with unwavering resolution and imperturbable equanimity steadily pursued, until it gained its assured success; the vindication and the unpretentious triumph of "the just man tenacious of purpose."

The most formidable of the specialist schemes both in Congress and elsewhere, was that of the Library faction, which prosecuted with remarkable zeal and energy, threatened by the acknowledged ability of its leading advocates to control the action of the Regents, even to the neglect and abandonment of all the other interests indicated by the statute. * In Henry's judgment the Institution should possess simply a working library, an auxiliary for those engaged in scientific research, a repertory well supplied with the published Proceedings and Transactions of learned Societies, but which so far from aiming at an encyclopædic or a literary character, should be mainly supplementary to the large National Library already established at the Capital. † "The idea ought never to be entertained that the portion of the limited income of the Smithsonian fund which can be devoted to the purchase of books will ever be sufficient to meet the wants of the American scholar. On the contrary it is the duty of this Institution to increase those wants by pointing out new fields for exploration, and by stimulating other researches than those which are now cultivated. It is a part of that duty to make the value of libraries more generally known, and their want in this country more generally felt." ‡

*Processes of Divestment.*—Henry's declaration that the moderate means at command were insufficient to support worthily either a Library, or a Museum, alone, was early justified. The Library though slowly formed of only really valuable scientific works, and this largely by exchanges with the Smithsonian publications, § in

---

* See "Supplement," NOTE K.

† "To carry on the operations of the first section a working library will be required, consisting of the past volumes of the transactions and proceedings of all the learned societies in every language. These are the original sources from which the most important principles of the positive knowledge of our day have been drawn." (*Smithsonian Report* for 1847, p. 139 of Sen. ed.—p. 131 of H. Rep. ed.)

‡ *Smithsonian Report* for 1851, p. 224 (of Sen. ed.)—p. 216 (of H. Rep. ed.)

§ "It is the intention of the Regents to render the Smithsonian library the most extensive and perfect collection of Transactions and scientific works in this country, and this it will be enabled to accomplish by means of its exchanges, which will furnish it with all the current journals and publications of societies, while the separate series may be completed in due time as opportunity and means may offer. The Institution has already more complete sets of Transactions of learned societies than are to be found in the oldest libraries in the United States." (*Smithsonian Report* for 1855, p. 29.)

the course of a dozen years amounted to about **40,000 volumes:** and the annual **cost of** binding, superintendence, and the constant enlargement of room and of cases, was becoming a serious tax upon the resources of the Institution. The propriety of transferring the **custody of this** valuable and rapidly increasing collection to the **National** Library established **by Congress, was** repeatedly urged **upon the attention of that body:** and by an **Act approved April** 5th, 1866, such transfer was at last effected.

"Congress had presented **to the Institution a** portion of the public reservation on which the building is situated. In the planting **of this with trees, nearly** 10,000 dollars of the Smithson income were expended." Ultimately however opportunity was taken **to have the** Smithsonian park included in the general appropriation **by** the Government for improving the public grounds.

The courses of Lectures which were continued from their establishment in **1849, to** 1863, were then abandoned. In conformity with **the judicious** policy entertained from **the** beginning not to **consume** unprofitably **the** limited means of **the** Institution by attempting **to do what** could be as well **or** better accomplished **by** other organizations, its herbarium comprising 30,000 botanical **specimens and other** allied objects, was transferred to the custody **of the** Agricultural Department. Its collection of **anatomical and** osteological specimens was transferred **to the Army** Medical Museum. And its Fine-Art collections **were** transferred to the custody of the "Art-Gallery" established **at W**ashington (with a larger endowment than the whole Smithsonian **fund) by** the enlightened liberality **of** Mr. W. W. Corcoran.

**Such were** the successive processes **by** which much of the early **and injudicious** legislative work **of** organization, intended for popularising the activities of the Institution, was gradually undone; greatly **to the** dissatisfaction and foreboding of many of its well-meaning friends. **"It** should be recollected" said Henry, "that **the Institution is not a** popular establishment."*

---

* *Smithsonian Report* for 1876, p. 12. A distinguished politician, now many years deceased, (an influential Member of Congress—and possible statesman,) in the confidence of friendship pointed out with emphasis, how by a few judicious expedients — involving only a moderate reduction of the income of the Institution, golden opinions might be won from the press, and the Smithsonian really be made quite

*The National Museum.*—The last heritage of misdirected legislation — the National Museum, still remains in nominal connection with the Institution; although Congress has recognized the justice of making special provision for its custody by an annual appropriation ever since its establishment in 1842,— four years before the organization of the Smithsonian Institution. The Government collection of curiosities had accumulated from the contributions of the various exploring expeditions; and Henry from the first, had objected to receiving it as a donation, foreseeing that it would prove more than "the gift of an elephant."* In his *first Report*, he ventured to say: "It is hoped that in due time other means may be found of establishing and supporting a general collection of objects of nature and art at the seat of the general Government, with funds not derived from the Smithsonian bequest."† In his third annual Report he remarked: "The formation of a Museum of objects of nature and of art requires much caution. With a given income to be appropriated to the purpose, a time must come when the cost of keeping the objects will just equal the amount of the appropriation: after this no further increase can take place. Also, the tendency of an institution of this kind unless guarded against, will be to expend its funds on a heterogeneous collection of objects of mere curiosity." Justly jealous of any dependence of the Institution, designed as a monument to its founder, upon the varying favors or caprices of a political government, or of any confusion between the National Museum, and its own special collections for scientific study rather than for popular display, he added: "If the Regents accept this Museum, it must be merged in the Smithsonian collections. It could not be the intention of Congress

---

a "popular" establishment. Unseduced by these friendly suggestions of worldly wisdom, Henry astonished his adviser by the smiling assurance that his self-imposed mission and deliberate purpose was to prevent, as far as in him lay, precisely that consummation. Had the philosopher repudiated the "breath of his nostrils" he could not have been looked upon by the politician, as more hopelessly demented.

  *His friend Professor Silliman in a letter dated December 4th 1847, wrote: "If it is within the views of the Government to bestow the National Museum upon the Smithsonian Institution, the very bequest would seem to draw after it an obligation to furnish the requisite accommodations without taxing the Smithsonian funds: otherwise the gift might be detrimental instead of beneficial."

  †*Smithsonian Report* for 1847, p. 139 (Sen. ed.)—p. 132 (H. Rep. ed.)

that an Institution founded by the liberality of a foreigner, and to which he has affixed his own name, should be charged with the keeping of a separate Museum, the property of the United States. - - - The small portion of our funds which can be devoted to a museum may be better employed in collecting new objects, such as have not yet been studied, than in preserving those from which the harvest of discovery has already been fully gathered." Nor was he reconciled to the gift by the suggestion that a suitable appropriation would be granted by the National Government, for the expense of its custody. "This would be equally objectionable; since it would annually bring the Institution before Congress as a supplicant for government patronage."*

In his Report for 1851, he forcibly stated in regard to the requirements of a general Museum, that "the whole income devoted to this object would be entirely inadequate:" and he strongly urged a National establishment of the Museum on a basis and a scale which should be an honor and a benefit to the people and their Capital city. "Though the formation of a general collection is neither within the means nor the province of the Institution, it is an object which ought to engage the attention of Congress. A general Museum appears to be a necessary establishment at the seat of government of every civilized nation. - - - An establishment of this kind can only be supported by Government; and the proposition ought never to be encouraged of putting this duty on the limited though liberal bequest of a foreigner."† This policy was urged in almost every subsequent Report. "There can be but little doubt that in due time ample provision will be made for a Library and Museum at the Capital of this Union, worthy of a Government whose perpetuity depends upon the virtue and intelligence of the people. It is therefore unwise to hamper the more important objects of this Institution by attempting to anticipate results which will be eventually produced without the expenditure of its means."‡ "The importance of a collection at the seat of government, to illustrate the physical geography, natural history,

---

* *Smithsonian Report* for 1849, pp. 181, 182 (of Sen. ed.)—pp. 173, 174 (of H. Rep. ed.)

† *Smithsonian Report* for 1851, p. 227 (of Sen. ed.)—p. 219 (of H. Rep. ed.)

‡ *Smithsonian Report* for 1852, p. 253 (of Sen. ed.)—p. 245 (of H. Rep. ed.)

and ethnology, of the United States, **cannot** be too highly estimated; but the support of such a collection ought not to be a burden **upon** the Smithsonian fund." *

The popular mind did **not** however appear to be prepared to accept these earnest presentations; and in **1858, the** National Museum was transferred by law to the custody of the Smithsonian Institution, **with** the same annual appropriation (4,000 dollars) which had been granted to **the** United States Patent Office when in charge **of** it.

So rapidly were the treasures of the Museum increased by the gathered fruits of various government explorations and surveys, as well as by the voluntary contributions of the numerous and wide-spread tributaries of the Institution, that the policy was early adopted of freely distributing duplicate specimens to other institutions where they would be most appreciated and most usefully applied. And in this way the Smithsonian became a valuable center of diffusion of the means of investigation in geology, mineralogy, botany, zoology, and archæology.† The clear foresight which announced that the Museum must very soon outgrow the entire capacity of the Smithsonian resources, has been most amply vindicated:‡ and to-day a large Government building is stored from basement to attic, with boxed up rarities of art and nature, sufficient more than twice to fill the Smithsonian halls and galleries, in addition to their present overflowing display.§ The strong desire of Henry to see established in Washington a National Museum on a scale worthy of our resources, and in which the existing overgrown collections might be so beneficially exhibited, he did not live

---

* *Smithsonian Report* for 1853, p. 11 (of Sen. ed.)—p. 9 (of H. Rep. ed.)

† See "Supplement," NOTE L.

‡ From the rapid growth of the national collection after it was transferred to the custody of the Smithsonian Institution, the annual appropriation of 4,000 dollars by Congress very soon became wholly insufficient to defray even one-half its necessary expenses. A memorial signed by the Chancellor and the Secretary, was presented to Congress May 1, 1868, in which the memorialists "beg leave to represent on behalf of the Board of Regents, that the usual annual appropriation of 4,000 dollars is wholly inadequate to the cost of preparing, preserving, and exhibiting the specimens;—the actual expenditure for that purpose, in 1867, having been over 12,000 dollars." (*Smithsonian Report* for 1867, p. 115.) It was not however till 1871 that the appropriation was raised to 10,000 dollars. In 1873, it was increased to 15,000 dollars, and in 1875, to 20,000 dollars.

§ See "Supplement," NOTE M.

to see gratified. That the realization of this beneficent project is only a question of time, is little doubtful; for it cannot be supposed that collections so valuable, and so manifestly beyond the capacities of the Institution, will be suffered to waste in uselessness. And when established, its being and its benefits will in no small degree be due to him who first realizing its necessity, and most appreciating its importance, with unwearying perseverance for twenty-five years omitted no opportunity of urging upon members of Congress its importunate claims.

*Meteorological Work.*—In the conduct of what were appropriately called the "active operations" of the Institution—under the first section of the programme (in contradistinction to the local and statical objects of the second section), a rare energy and promptness was exhibited. The very first Report of the Secretary announced not only the acceptance and preparation for publication of an elaborate work by Messrs. Squier and Davis, on explorations of "Ancient Monuments of the Mississippi Valley," but the commencement of official preparations "for instituting various lines of physical research. Among the subjects mentioned by way of example in the programme, for the application of the funds of the Institution, is terrestrial magnetism. - - - Another subject of research mentioned in the programme, and which has been urged upon the immediate attention of the Institution, is that of an extensive system of meteorological observations, particularly with reference to the phenomena of American storms. Of late years in our country more additions have been made to meteorology than to any other branch of physical science. Several important generalizations have been arrived at, and definite theories proposed, which now enable us to direct our attention with scientific precision to such points of observation as cannot fail to reward us with new and interesting results. It is proposed to organize a system of observations which shall extend as far as possible over the North American continent. - - - The present time appears to be peculiarly auspicious for commencing an enterprise of the proposed kind. The citizens of the United States are now scattered over every part of the southern and western portion of Northern America, and the extended lines of telegraph will furnish a ready means of warning the more northern and eastern observers to be on the watch for the first appearance of an advancing storm."*

An appropriation for the purpose having been made by the Regents, a large number of observers scattered over the United States and the Territories became voluntary correspondents of the Institution. Advantage was taken of the stations already established under the direction of the War, and of the Navy Departments, as well as of those provided for by a few of the States. The annual reports of the Secretary chronicled the extension and success of the system adopted; and in a few years between five and six hundred regular observers were engaged in its meteorological service. The favorite project of employing the telegraph for obtaining simultaneous results over a large area was at once organized; and in 1849, a system of telegraphic despatches was established, by which (a few years later) the information received in Washington at the Smithsonian Institution was daily plotted upon a large map of the United States by means of adjustable symbols. Espy's generalization that the principal storms and other atmospheric changes have an eastward movement,† was fully established by this rapidly gathered experience of the Institution; so that " it was often enabled to predict (sometimes a day or two in advance) the approach of any of the larger disturbances of the atmosphere."‡

Eminently efficient as the enterprise approved itself, increasing experience served to demonstrate the expanding requirements of the

---

* *Smithsonian Report* for 1847, pp. 146, 147 (of Sen. ed.)—pp. 138, 139 (of H. Rep. ed.) Professor Loomis (to whom among others "distinguished for their attainments in meteorology" letters inviting suggestions, had been addressed,) recommended that there should be at least one observing station within every hundred square miles of the United States; and he sagaciously pointed out that "When the magnetic telegraph [ then an infant three years old ] is extended from New York to New Orleans and St. Louis, it may be made subservient to the protection of our commerce." This interesting letter was published in full as "Appendix No. 2," to the *Report*. In 1848, a paper was read before the British Association by Mr. John Ball, "On rendering the Electric Telegraph subservient to Meteorological Research: in which the author suggested that simultaneous observations so collected, might reveal the direction and probable time of arrival of storms. (*Report Brit. Assoc.* Swansea, Aug. 1848. Abstracts, pp. 12, 13.)

† FRANKLIN is said to have been the first who stated the general law, that the storms of our Southern States move off to the northeastward over the Middle and Eastern States.

‡ *Smithsonian Report* for 1864, p. 44. An interesting and instructive *résumé* of results accomplished within fifteen years was given in this *Report*, pp. 42–45: and continued in the succeeding *Report* for 1865, pp. 50–59.

service; and it was seen that to prosecute the subject of meteorology over so large a territory, with the fullness necessary, would require a still larger force of observers, and a greater drain upon the resources of the Institution, than could well be spared from other objects; and as the great value of the system was fully recognized by the intelligent, the propriety of maintaining a meteorological bureau by the national support was early presented to the attention of Congress. This most important department of observation had been advanced by Henry to that position, in which a larger annual outlay than the entire income of the Institution was really required to give just efficiency to the system. In his Report for 1865, he remarked: "The present would appear to be a favorable time to urge upon Congress the importance of making provision for the reorganizing all the meteorological observations of the United States under one combined plan, in which the records should be sent to a central depot for reduction, discussion, and final publication. An appropriation of 50,000 dollars annually for this purpose would tend not only to advance the material interests of the country, but also to increase its reputation. - - - It is scarcely necessary at this day to dwell on the advantages which result from such systems of combined observations as those which the principal governments of Europe have established, and are now constantly extending."*

Five years later, in support of the proposition that the subject from its magnitude now appealed to the liberality of the nation, he briefly recapitulated the work accomplished by the limited means of the Institution. "The Smithsonian meteorological system was commenced in 1849, and has continued in operation until the present time. - - - It has done good service to the cause of meteorology; 1st, in inaugurating the system which has been in operation upward of twenty years: 2nd, in the introduction of improved instruments after discussion and experiments: 3rd, in preparing and publishing at its expense an extensive series of meteorological tables: 4th, in reducing and discussing the meteorological material which could be obtained from all the records from the first settlement of the country till within a few years: 5th, in being the first to show

---

* *Smithsonian Report* for 1865, p. 57.

the practicability of telegraphic weather signals: 6th, in publishing records and discussions made at its own expense, of the Arctic expeditions of Kane, Hayes, and McClintock: 7th, in discussing and publishing a number of series of special records embracing periods of from twenty to fifty years in different sections of the United States,—of great interest in determining secular changes of the climate: 8th, in the publication of a series of memoirs on various meteorological phenomena, embracing observations and discussions of storms, tornadoes, meteors, auroras, etc.: 9th, in a diffusion of a knowledge of meteorology through its extensive unpublished correspondence and its printed circulars. It has done all in this line which its limited means would permit; and has urged upon Congress the establishment with adequate appropriation of funds, of a meteorological department under one comprehensive plan, 'in which the records should be sent to a central depot for reduction, discussion, and final publication.'"*

In 1870, a meteorological department was established by the Government under the Signal Office of the War Department, with enlarged facilities for systematic observations: and agreeably to the settled policy of the Institution, this important field of research was in 1872, abandoned in favor of the new organization.† Of the voluminous results of nearly a quarter of a century of systematic records over a wide geographical area which have been slowly digested and laboriously discussed, only a small portion has yet been published. The publication of the series when practicable, will yet prove an inestimable boon to meteorological theory.

Although our country can boast of many able meteorologists, who have greatly promoted our knowledge of the laws of atmospheric phenomena, it is safe to say that to no single worker in the field is our nation more indebted for the advancement of this branch of science to its present standing, than to Joseph Henry. Quite as much by his incitement and encouragement of others in such researches, as by his own exertions, does he merit this award. To

---

* *Smithsonian Report* for 1870, p. 43.

† As an illustration of the popular favor in which this Signal service is held, it may be stated that the annual appropriation by Government for its support now exceeds not merely the entire Smithsonian income, but *sixteen times* that amount; or in fact its whole endowment.

him is undoubtedly due the most important step in the modern system of observation,— the installation of the telegraph in the service of meteorological signals and predictions.*  While giving however his active supervision to the extensive system he had himself inaugurated, publishing many important reductions of particular features, as well as various circulars of detailed instructions to observers, of the desiderata to be obtained by those having the opportunities of arctic, oceanic, and southern explorations, and directing the constant observations recorded at the Institution as an independent station, he made many personal investigations of allied subjects;—as of the aurora, of atmospheric electricity and thunder-storms, of the supposed influence of the moon on the weather,—and contributed a valuable series of memoirs on meteorology, embracing a wide range of physical exposition, to the successive Agricultural Reports of the Commissioner of Patents, during the years 1855, '56, '57, '58, and 1859.  Instructive articles on Magnetism and Meteorology were prepared in 1861 for the American Cyclopædia.  And one of his latest published papers comprises a minute account of the effects of lightning in two thunder-storms; one occurring in the spring of last year (1877) at a Light-house in Key West, Florida, and the other occurring in the summer of last year at New London, Connecticut.†

*Archæological Work.*—One of the earliest subjects taken up for investigation by the Institution, was that of American Archæology; the attempt by extended explorations of the existing pre-historic relics, mounds, and monuments, of the aborigines of our country, to ascertain as far as possible their primitive industrial, social and intellectual character, and any evidences of their antiquity, or of

---

* "However frequently the idea may have been suggested of utilizing our knowledge by the employment of the electric telegraph, it is to Professor Henry and his assistants in the Smithsonian Institution that the credit is due of having first actually realized this suggestion.  - - - It will thus be seen that without material aid from the Government, but through the enlightened policy of the telegraph companies, the Smithsonian Institution *first in the world* organized a comprehensive system of telegraphic meteorology, and has thus given—first to Europe and Asia, and now to the United States, that most beneficent national application of modern science—the Storm Warnings."  Article on "Weather Telegraphy" by Professor Cleveland Abbe.  (*Am. Jour. Sci.*, Aug. 1871, vol. ii. pp. 83, 85.)

† *Journal of the American Electrical Society*, 1878, vol. ii. pp. 37–44.  The communication is dated Oct. 13, 1877; though not published till during the author's last illness.

their stages of development. The first publication of "Smithsonian Contributions" comprised in a good sized quarto volume an account of extensive examinations of the mounds and earthworks found over the broad valley of the Mississippi, with elaborate illustrations of the relics and results obtained: and this volume extensively circulated by gift and by sale, attracted a wide-spread attention and interest, and gave a remarkable stimulus to the further prosecution of such researches. "Whatever relates to the nature of man is interesting to the students of every branch of knowledge; and hence ethnology affords a common ground on which the cultivators of physical science, of natural history, of archæology, of language, of history, and of literature, can all harmoniously labor. Consequently no part of the operations of this Institution has been more generally popular than that which relates to this subject."*

Special explorations inaugurated by the Institution, have supplied it with important contributions to archæological information, and with the rich spoils of collected relics; which together with much material gathered from Arctic and from Southern regions, from Europe, from Asia, and from Africa, fill now a large museum hall 200 feet long and 50 feet wide, exclusively devoted to comparative Anthropology and Ethnology. In 1868, the Secretary reported that "during the past year greater effort had been made than ever before to collect specimens to illustrate the ethnology and archæology of the North American continent:" and he dwelt upon the importance of the subject as a study connecting all portions of the habitable earth, pointing out that "it embraces not only the natural history and peculiarities of the different races of men as they now exist upon the globe, but also their affiliations, their changes in mental and moral development, and also the question of the geological epoch of the appearance of man upon the earth.  -  -  -  The ethnological specimens we have mentioned are not considered as mere curiosities collected to excite the wonder of the illiterate, but as contributions to the materials from which it will be practicable to reconstruct by analogy and strict deduction, the history of the past in its relation to the present."†

-----

* *Smithsonian Report* for 1860, p. 38.

† *Smithsonian Report* for 1868, pp. 26 and 33.

Two years later he reported: "The collection of objects to illustrate anthropology now in possession of the Institution is almost unsurpassed, especially in those which relate to the present Indians and the more ancient inhabitants of the American continent." Deprecating the frequent dissipation of small private collections of such objects at the death of their owners, he forcibly urges that "the only way in which they can become of real importance, is by making them part of a general collection, carefully preserved in some public institution, where in the course of the increasing light of science, they may be made to reveal truths beyond present anticipation." *

In his last Report — for 1877, (just published, and which he did not live to see in print,) he says: "Anthropology, or what may be considered the natural history of man, is at present the most popular branch of science. It absorbs a large share of public attention, and many original investigators are assiduously devoted to it. Its object is to reconstruct as it were the past history of man, to determine his specific peculiarities and general tendencies. It has already established the fact that a remarkable similarity exists in the archæological instruments found in all parts of the world, with those in use among tribes still in a savage or barbarous condition. The conclusion is supported by evidence which can scarcely be doubted, that by thoroughly studying the manners and customs of savages and the instruments employed by them, we obtain a knowledge of the earliest history of nations which have attained the highest civilization. It is· remarkable in how many cases, customs existing among highly civilized peoples are found to be survivals of ancient habits." He then argues from the significance thus developed of many trivial practices and unmeaning ceremonies handed down from immemorial time, the importance to a full comprehension of the customs of modern society, of a scientific study of the myths and usages of ancient peoples. "American anthropology" he remarks, "early occupied the attention of the Smithsonian Institution;" and alluding to its first published work, he says, "from the time of the publication of this volume until the present, contributions of value have been made annually by the

---

* *Smithsonian Report* for 1870, pp. 35, 36.

Institution to this branch of knowledge. - - - The collection of the archæology and ethnology of *America,* in the National Museum, is the most extensive in the world: and in order to connect it permanently with the name of Smithson, it has been thought advisable to prepare and publish at the expense of the Smithsonian fund, an exhaustive work on American anthropology, in which the various classes of specimens shall be figured and described." * This great work still remains to be perfected.

*Publications.*—To attempt the recapitulation of the various branches of original research initiated or directly fostered by the Institution, would be to write its history. The range and variety of its active operations, and the value of their fruits, are in view of the limited income, and the collateral drains of less important objects exacted from it, something quite surprising. Scarcely a department of investigation has not received either directly or indirectly liberal and efficient assistance: and a host of physicists in the successful prosecution of their diverse labors, have attested their gratitude to the Institution, and no less to the ever sympathetic encouragement of its Director.

Of the various works submitted to the Institution,—differing widely as they necessarily must in the comprehensiveness as well as in the originality of treatment of their diversified topics,—only those were accepted for publication, which had received the approval of a commission of distinguished experts in each particular field of inquiry. But even after such formal approval and acceptance, Henry ever maintained a sense of responsibility which entailed upon him a vast amount of unrecognized and little appreciated labor, in his desire to make each publication a credit to the Institution as well as to its author. In the editing of this multitudinous material, he gave a critical attention to each memoir; and there are probably few of the series which do not bear the marks of his watchful care, in the elimination of obscurities, of redundancies, or of personalities, and in the pruning of questionable metaphors, of

---

* *Smithsonian Report* for 1877, pp. 22, 23. Circulars broadly distributed by the Institution, have served to give desired direction to popular attention and activity in this field of research; and the extent of co-operation is such as probably only the "Smithsonian" could have secured, unless by a vastly greater outlay.

294

imperfect or hasty generalizations, or of incidental inaccuracies of statement or inference.

Over one hundred important original Memoirs, generally too elaborate to be published at length by any existing scientific society, issued in editions many times larger than the most liberal of any such society's issue, most of them now universally recognized as classical and original authorities on their respective topics, forming twenty-one large quarto volumes of "SMITHSONIAN CONTRIBUTIONS TO KNOWLEDGE," distributed over every portion of the civilized or colonized world, constitute a monument to the memory of the founder, James Smithson, such as never before was builded on the foundation of one hundred thousand pounds: and before which the popular Lyceums of our leading cities, with endowments averaging double this amount, are dwarfed into insignificance.

Such as these Lyceums with their local culture, admirable and invaluable in their way, but exerting no influence upon the progress of science, or outside of their own communities, and scarcely known beyond their cities' walls,—such was the type of institute which early legislators could alone imagine. Such as the "Smithsonian Institution" stands to-day,—such is the monument mainly constructed by the foresight, the wisdom, and the resolution of Henry.* All honor to the Regents, who with an enlightenment so far in advance of the ruling intelligence of former days, and against the pressures of overwhelming preponderance of even educated popular sentiment, courageously adopted the programme of the Secretary and Director they had appointed; and who throughout his career, so wisely, nobly, and steadfastly upheld his policy and his purpose.

Fifteen octavo volumes of "Smithsonian Miscellaneous Collections" of a more technical character than the "Contributions,"

* "It is not by its castellated building, nor the exhibition of the museum of the Government, that the Institution has achieved its present reputation; nor by the collection and display of material objects of any kind, that it has vindicated the intelligence and good faith of the Government in the administration of the trust. It is by its explorations, its researches, its publications, its distribution of specimens, and its exchanges, constituting it an active living organization, that it has rendered itself favorably known in every part of the civilized world; has made contributions to almost every branch of science; and brought, more than ever before, into intimate and friendly relations, the Old and the New Worlds." (Memorial to Congress, by Chancellor S. P. CHASE, and Secretary JOSEPH HENRY. Smithsonian Report for 1867, p. 114.)

(including systematic and statistical compilations, scientific summaries, and valuable accessions of tabular "constants,") form in themselves an additional series; and represent a work of which any learned Society or Institution might well be proud. And thirty octavo volumes of annual Reports, rich with the scattered thoughts and hopes and wishes of the Director, form the official journal of his administration.

*The Bibliography of Science.*—Among the needful preparations for conducting original inquiry, none is more important than ready access and direction to the existing state of research in the particular field, or its allied districts. This information is scattered in the thousands of volumes which form the transactions of learned Societies; and its acquisition involves therefore in most cases a very laborious preliminary bibliographical research. To make this vast store of observation available to scientific students, by the directory of well arranged digests, would appear to fall peculiarly within the province of an Institution specially established for promoting the increase and diffusion of knowledge among men: and was early an object of particular interest to Henry. In his Report for 1851, he remarked: "One of the most important means of facilitating the use of libraries (particularly with reference to science,) is well-digested indexes of subjects, not merely referring to volumes or books, but to memoirs, papers, and parts of scientific transactions and systematic works. As an example of this, I would refer to the admirably arranged and valuable catalogue of books relating to Natural Philosophy and the Mechanic Arts, by Dr. Young. This work comes down to 1807; and I know of no richer gift which could be bestowed upon the science of our own day, than the continuation of this catalogue to the present time. Every one who is desirous of enlarging the bounds of human knowledge, should in justice to himself as well as to the public, be acquainted with what has previously been done in the same line; and this he will only be enabled to accomplish by the use of indexes of the kind above mentioned."*

* *Smithsonian Report* for 1851, p. 225 (of Sen. ed.)—p. 217 (of H. Rep. ed.) The valuable *Repertorium commentationum a societatibus litterariis editarum,* edited by Prof. JEROM D. REUSS, and published in 16 quarto volumes at Gottingen, (1801-1821,) to a large extent supplied this desideratum, down to the end of the last century.

At the time, and for years afterward, one-half of the Smithsonian income was diverted by the requirements of Congress to the local objects of the Lyceum: and the hopelessness of attempting a work — additional to that already mapped out, which would require the united labors of a large corps of well-trained and educated assistants for many years, and the subsequent devotion of the whole available income for many years following, to complete its publication, was fully realized.  The project however was not abandoned: and in 1854, Henry conceived the plan of taking up the more limited department of *American* Scientific Bibliography; and by the persevering application of a fixed portion of the income annually for a succession of years, of finally producing a thorough subject-matter index, as well as an index of authors, for the entire range of American contributions to science from their earliest date.  Inspired with this ambition, he sought to enlist the co-operation of the British Association for the Advancement of Science, in procuring with its large resources, a similar classified index for British and European scientific literature.

The favorable reception of this project, was officially announced to Henry by the Secretary of the Association, in the transmission of the following extract from the proceedings of that body for 1855. "A communication from Professor Henry of Washington having been read, containing a proposal for the publication of a catalogue of philosophical memoirs scattered throughout the Transactions of Societies in Europe and America, with the offer of co-operation on the part of the Smithsonian Institution, to the extent of preparing and publishing in accordance with the general plan which might be adopted by the British Association, a catalogue of all the American memoirs on physical science, — the Committee approve of the suggestion, and recommend that Mr. Cayley, Mr. Grant, and Professor Stokes be appointed a committee to consider the best system of arrangement, and to report thereon to the council." [*]  The report of this committee dated 13th June, 1856, was presented to the succeeding Meeting of the British Association; in which they take occasion to say: "The Committee are desirous of expressing their sense of the great importance and increasing need of such a catalogue.  -   -

---

[*] *Report Brit. Assoc.* Glasgow, **Sept. 1855**, p. lxvi.

The catalogue should not be restricted to memoirs in Transactions of Societies, but should comprise also memoirs in the Proceedings of Societies, in mathematical and scientific journals:" etc. - - - "The catalogue should begin from the year 1800. There should be a catalogue according to the names of authors, and also a catalogue according to subjects."* The committee comprising Fellows of the Royal Society of London finally succeeded in interesting that grave body in the undertaking: and the result was that greatly to Henry's satisfaction, the entire work was ultimately assumed by the Royal Society itself.

In the course of ten years that liberal Society aided by a large grant from the British Government gave to the world its half instalment of the great work, in its admirable "Catalogue of Scientific Papers" alphabetically classified by authors, in seven or eight large quarto volumes. In the Preface to this splendid monument of industry and liberality, stands the following history of its inception. "The present undertaking may be said to have originated in a communication from Dr. Joseph Henry, Secretary of the Smithsonian Institution, to the Meeting of the British Association at Glasgow in 1855, suggesting the formation of a catalogue of Philosophical memoirs. This suggestion was favorably reported on by a Committee of the Association in the following year. - - - In March, 1857, General Sabine, the Treasurer and Vice President of the Royal Society, brought the matter before the President and Council of that body, and requested on the part of the British Association, the co-operation of the Royal Society in the project: whereupon a committee was appointed to take into further consideration the formation of such a catalogue. - - - No further step was taken by the British Association or by the Royal Society in co-operation with that body: but the President and Council of the Royal Society acting on the recommendations contained in a Report of the Library Committee dated 7th January, 1858, resolved that the preparation of a Catalogue of scientific memoirs should be undertaken by the Royal Society independently, and at the Society's own charge."†

---

* Report Brit. Assoc. Cheltenham, Aug. 1856, pp. 463, 464.

† Preface to Catalogue of Scientific Papers, (1800–1863) vol. i. 1867, pp. iii, iv. The second and most important division of this great and invaluable work,—the classified Index to Subjects,—still remains to be accomplished.

*System of Exchanges.*—For the diffusion of knowledge among men, one of the methods adopted by Henry from the very commencement of his administration was the organization of a system by which the scientific memoirs of Societies or of individuals from any portion of the United States, might be transmitted to foreign countries without expense to the senders: and by which in like manner the similar publications of scientific work abroad might be received at the Smithsonian Institution, for distribution in this country. * This privilege however is properly restricted to *bona fide* donations and exchanges of scientific memoirs; all purchased publications being carefully excluded and left to find their legitimate channels of trade. By an international courtesy — creditable to the wisdom and intelligence of the civilized Powers, — such packages to and from the Institution are permitted to pass through all custom-houses, free of duty; an invoice of authentication being forwarded in advance. When it is considered that this large work of collection and distribution (including the constant supply of the Institution's own publications, and the extensive returns therefor of journals, proceedings, and transactions, for its own library) requires the systematic records and accounts in suitable ledgers, with the accurate parcelling and labelling of packages, large and small, to every corner of the globe, it may well be conceived that no small amount of labor and expense is involved in these forwarding operations. † A recognition of the benefits conferred by this

---

* "The promotion of knowledge is much retarded by the difficulties experienced in the way of a free intercourse between scientific and literary societies in different parts of the world. In carrying on the exchange of the Smithsonian volumes, it was necessary to appoint a number of agents. These agencies being established other exchanges could be carried on through them and our means of conveyance, at the slight additional expense owing to the small increase of weight. - - - The result cannot fail to prove highly beneficial, by promoting a more ready communion between the literature and science of this country and the world abroad." (*Smithsonian Report* for 1851, p. 218, Senate ed.)

† It may be stated that the number of foreign institutions and correspondents receiving the Smithsonian publications exceeds two thousand; whose localities embrace not only the principal cities of Europe (from Iceland to Turkey), of British America, Mexico, the West Indies, Central and South America, and of Australia, but also those of New Zealand, Honolulu in the Sandwich Islands, twelve cities in India, Shanghai in China, Tokio and Yokohama in Japan, Batavia in Java, Manila in the Philippine Islands, Alexandria and Cairo in Egypt, Algiers in northern Africa, Monrovia in Liberia, and Cape Town in southern Africa. The correspondents and recipients in the United States, are probably nearly as numerous.

generous enterprise, is practically indicated by the rapid enlargement of the operations. The weight of matter sent abroad by the
Institution at the end of the first decade was 14,000 pounds for the
year 1857: the weight sent at the end of the second decade was
22,000 pounds for the year 1867: and the weight sent at the end
of the third decade was 99,000 pounds for the last year 1877.
This admirable system has been greatly encouraged and facilitated
by the most praiseworthy liberality of the great lines of ocean
steamers, and of the leading railway companies, in carrying the
Smithsonian freight in many cases free of charge, or in other cases at
greatly reduced rates: an appreciative tribute alike to the beneficent
services and reputation of the Institution, and to the personal
character and influence of its Director. *

"This part of the system of Smithsonian operations has everywhere received the commendation of those who have given it their
attention or have participated in its benefits. The Institution is
now the principal agent of scientific and literary communication
between the old world and the new.  -   -   -   The importance of
such a system with reference to the scientific character of our country, could scarcely be appreciated by those who are not familiar
with the results which flow from an easy and certain intercommu-
nication of this kind. Many of the most important contributions
to science made in America have been unheard of in Europe, or
have been so little known, or received so little attention, that they
have been republished as new discoveries or claimed as the product
of European research."† It would indeed be difficult to estimate
rightly the benefit to science in the encouragement of its cultivators,
afforded by this fostering service. Few Societies are able to incur
much expense in the distribution of their publications; and hence

---

* "The cost of this system would far exceed the means of the Institution, were
it not for important aid received from various parties interested in facilitating
international intercourse and the promotion of friendly relations between distant
parts of the civilized world. The liberal aid extended by the steamship and
other lines, mentioned in previous reports, in carrying the boxes of the Smithson exchanges free of charge, has been continued, and several other lines have
been added to the number in the course of the year." (*Smithsonian Report* for
1867, p. 39.) Notwithstanding this unprecedented generosity, the exchange system
has reached such proportions as to require for its maintenance one-fourth of the
entire income from the Smithsonian fund.

† *Smithsonian Report* for 1853, p. 25 (of Senate ed.)

their circulation is necessarily very limited. The fructifying interchange of labors and results, dependent on their own resources,
would be obstructed by the recurring expenses and delays of customs interventions, and by unconscionable exactions: and indeed
without the Smithsonian mechanism, nine-tenths of the present
scientific exchanges would be at once suppressed. Let it be hoped
that so beneficent a system will not break down from the weight of
its own inevitable growth.

*Astronomical Telegraphy.*—Analogous in principle to the system
of exchange, is that adopted for the instantaneous trans-Atlantic
communication of discoveries of a special order. In the year 1873,
in the interests of astronomy (to which Henry was ever warmly
devoted) he concluded "a very important arrangement between the
Smithsonian Institution and the Atlantic Cable Companies, by which
is guaranteed the free transmission by telegraph between Europe
and America of accounts of astronomical discoveries which for the
purpose of co-operative observation require immediate announcement."* This admirable service to science, so creditable to the
intelligence and the liberality of the Atlantic Telegraph Companies,
embraces direct reciprocal communication between the Smithsonian
Institution and the foreign Observatories of Greenwich, Paris,
Berlin, Vienna, and Pulkova. During the first year of its operation, four new planetoids were telegraphed from America, and seven
telescopic comets from Europe to this country.

"Although the discovery of planets and comets will probably
be the principal subject of the cable telegrams, yet it is not intended
to restrict the transmission of intelligence solely to that class of
observation. Any remarkable solar phenomenon presenting itself
suddenly in Europe, observations of which may be practicable in
America several hours after the sun has set to the European observer,—the sudden outburst of some variable star similar to that
which appeared in *Corona borealis* in 1866,—unexpected showers
of shooting stars, etc. would be proper subjects for transmission by
cable.

"The announcement of this arrangement has called forth the
approbation of the astronomers of the world: and in regard to it

---

* *Smithsonian Report* for 1873, p. 32.

we may quote the following passage from the fifty-fourth annual report of the **Royal Astronomical** Society of England: 'The great value of this concession on the part of the **Atlantic telegraph** and other Companies, cannot be too highly prized, and our science **must** certainly be the gainer by this disinterested act of liberality. Already **planets discovered in America** have been observed in Europe on the evening following the receipt of the telegram, or within two or three days of their discovery.'"*

*Official Correspondence.*—A vast amount of individual work having in view the diffusion of knowledge, has been performed by the correspondence of the Institution; which may be best described in the language of an extract from one of the early reports: "There is one part of the Smithsonian operations that attracts no public attention, though it is producing important results in the way of diffusing knowledge, and is attended perhaps with more labor than any other part. I allude to the scientific correspondence of the Institution. Scarcely a day passes in which communications are not received from persons in different parts of the country, containing accounts of discoveries, which are referred to the Institution, or asking questions relative to some branch of knowledge. The rule was early adopted to give respectful attention to every letter received, and this has been faithfully adhered to from the beginning up to the present time. - - - Requests are frequently made for lists of apparatus, for information as to the best books for the study of special subjects, for suggestions on the organization of local societies, etc. Applications are also made for information by persons abroad, relative to particular subjects respecting this country. When an immediate reply cannot be given to a question, the subject is referred by letter to some one of the Smithsonian co-laborers to whose line of duty it pertains, and the answer is transmitted to the inquirer, either under the name of the person who gives the

---

* *Smithsonian Report* for 1873, p. 33. In 1876, a stellar **outburst** in the "Swan" observed by Dr. Schmidt of Athens, on the 24th of November, was announced. Less brilliant than the similar **outburst** which occurred in the northern "Crown" in May, 1866, it continued to decline through the month of December, and at the close of the year, had dwindled from the third to the eighth magnitude. (This may possibly be the **same** "temporary star"—seen in *Cygnus* in 1600, and again in 1670: and having therefore a period of **variability** of about 69 years.)

information, or under that of the Institution, according to the circumstances of the case.  -  -  -  Many of those communications
are of such a character, that at first sight it might seem best to treat
them with silent neglect; but the rule has been adopted to state
candidly and respectfully the objections to such propositions, and
to endeavor to convince their authors that their ground is untenable.
Though this course is in many cases attended with no beneficial
results, still it is the only one which can be adopted with any hope
of even partial good."*

The information given to scientific inquirers has been of an exceedingly varied and highly valuable character, not unfrequently
involving a large amount of research from special experts; who
have been accustomed cheerfully to bestow a degree of attention on
difficult questions thus presented, which would have been accorded
perhaps less ungrudgingly to others than to the universally honored
Smithsonian Director.  As to the pretensions and importunities of
the unscientific,—such is the judgment pronounced after a quarter
of a century of laborious experience with them:

"'The most troublesome correspondents are persons of extensive
reading, and in some cases of considerable literary acquirements,
who in earlier life were not imbued with scientific methods, but who
not without a certain degree of mental power, imagine that they
have made great discoveries in the way of high generalizations.
Their claims not being allowed, they rank themselves among the
martyrs of science, against whom the scientific schools and the envy
of the world have arrayed themselves.  Indeed to such intensity
does this feeling arise in certain persons, that on their special subjects they are really monomaniacs, although on others they may be
not only entirely sane, but even evince abilities of a high order.
-  -  -  Two persons of this class have recently made a special
journey to Washington, from distant parts of the country, to demand
justice from the Institution in the way of recognition of their claims
to discoveries in science of great importance to humanity; and each
of them has made an appeal to his representative in Congress to
aid him in compelling the Institution to acknowledge the merits of
his speculations.  Providence vindicates in such cases the equality

of its justice in giving to such persons an undue share of self-es-
teem and an exaltation of confidence in themselves, which in a great
degree compensate for what they conceive to be the want of a just
appreciation by the public. Unless however they are men of great
benevolence of disposition, who can look with pity on what they
deem the ignorance and prejudice of leaders of science, they are apt
to indulge in a bitterness of denunciation which might be injurious
to the reputation of the Institution, were their effects not neutralized by the extravagance of the assertions themselves."*

To the projectors and propellers of Paine electric engines, and
Keely motors, eager for a marketable certificate from such an
authority, Henry would calmly reply: "We may say that science has
established the great fact — without the possibility of doubt, that
what is called power, or that which produces changes in matter, cannot be created by man, but exists in nature in a state of activity or in
a condition of neutralization; and furthermore that all the original
forces connected with our globe, as a general rule have assumed a
state of permanent equilibrium, and that the crust of the earth as
a whole (with the exception of the comparatively exceedingly small
proportion, consisting of organic matter such as coal, wood, etc.) is
as it were a burnt slag, incapable of yielding power; and that all
the motions and changes on its surface are due to actions from celestial space, principally from the sun. - - - All attempts to
substitute electricity or magnetism for coal power must be unsuccessful, since these powers tend to an equilibrium from which they
can only be disturbed by the application of another power, which
is the equivalent of that which they can subsequently exhibit.
They are however, with chemical attraction, etc. of great importance as intermediate agents in the application of the power of heat
as derived from combustion. Science does not indicate in the slightest degree, the possibility of the discovery of a new primary power
comparable with that of combustion as exhibited in the burning of
coal. Whatever unknown powers may exist in nature capable of
doing work, must be in a state of neutralization, otherwise they
would manifest themselves spontaneously; and from this state of
neutralization or equilibrium, they can be released only by the action

---

* *Smithsonian Report* for 1875, pp. 37, 38.

of an extraneous power of equivalent energy; and we therefore do not hesitate to say that all declarations of the discovery of a new power which is to supersede the use of coal as a motive-power, have their origin in ignorance or deception, and frequently in both. A man of some ingenuity in combining mechanical elements, and having some indefinite scientific knowledge, imagines it possible to obtain a certain result by a given combination of principles, and by long brooding over this subject previous to experiment, at length convinces himself of the certainty of the anticipated result. Having thus deceived himself by his sophisms, he calls upon his neighbors to accept his conclusions as verified truths; and soon acquires the notoriety of having made a discovery which is to change the civilization of the world. The shadowy reputation which he has thus acquired, is too gratifying to his vanity to be at once relinquished by the announcement of his self-deception; and in preference he applies his ingenuity in devising means by which to continue the deception of his friends and supporters, long after he himself has been convinced of the fallacy of his first assumptions. In this way what was commenced in folly, generally ends in fraud."*

In looking back upon the struggles, conflicts, and obstructions of the past, it really seems quite marvelous that so much should have been accomplished, with so limited expenditure. These large results are partly due to the admirable method of the Secretary, his clear presage of effects, and his high power of systematic distribution and appliance; partly to the intelligent zeal and sympathetic energy of the able assistants whom he had associated with him almost from the organization of the institution; and partly to the personal magic of the man,— to the surprising amount of voluntary co-operation he was able to call forth in almost every direction, by the sheer force of his own earnest industry, and the contagious influence of his own devotion to the cause of scientific advancement.

*Scientific Observatories.*—One of the objects very dear to Henry's heart, was the establishment of a physical observatory (with a physical laboratory in connection) for the systematic observation and record of important points in celestial and terrestrial physics. For

---

* *Smithsonian Report* for 1875, pp. 39, 40.

the proper maintenance of such an establishment, he thought an income as large as that of the Smithson fund, would not be too much: and on two different occasions he endeavored to enlist the interest of wealthy and public-spirited citizens in such an enterprise. One of these was Mr. McCormick of Illinois; and a letter on the subject was afterward printed (without its address) in the Report for 1870. * The other was Mr. Lick of California: who after some hesitation, decided in favor of an astronomical observatory. Another allied object of great interest to Henry, and one requiring as large an endowment, was a well-equipped chemical laboratory, in which —under judicious restrictions—those really engaged in original researches, should have liberal facilities of appliances and needed materials, furnished them. He considered that an important part of the work to be accomplished by a physical and chemical laboratory, would be the determination and tabulation of "The Constants of Nature and Art" with a much wider range of subjects, and on a scale of much greater completeness and accuracy, than had heretofore been attempted: and thus might be realized the great work or works of reference, suggested by Charles Babbage as a scientific *desideratum*. † Had the Smithsonian fund been twice as large as it is, both these great enterprises for the increase of knowledge, would undoubtedly have been successfully inaugurated by Henry.

*Loss by Fire.*—Early in the year 1865, (on the 24th day of January,) the central portion of the Smithsonian Building suffered from a disastrous fire, the effects of which were aggravated by the extreme severity of the winter cold, which greatly obstructed the efficiency of the engines brought into action. ‡ "The progress of the fire was so rapid, that but few of the contents of the upper rooms could be removed before the roof fell in. The conflagration was only stayed by the incombustible materials of the main building:" the flooring of the upper story, forming an iron and brick

---

* *Smithsonian Report* for 1870, pp. 141-144.

† Brewster's *Edinburgh Jour. Sci.* April, 1832, vol. vi. pp. 334-340.— *Smithsonian Report* for 1856, pp. 289-302.

‡ The accident resulted from the carelessness of some workmen in the upper picture gallery, who in temporarily setting up a stove, inserted the pipe through a wall-lining into a furring space (supposing it a flue), but which conducted directly under the rafters of the roof.

vaulting over the lower or principal story. Neither wing of the building was reached by the fire; and the valuable Library (not then transferred to the Capitol), and the Museum, fortunately escaped without injury. The Stanley collection of Indian portraits, comprising about 200 paintings, and estimated as worth 20,000 dollars, was entirely destroyed. A fine full-sized copy in Carrara marble, by John Gott, of the antique statue known as "The Dying Gladiator," was crumbled into a formless mass of stone.

The Secretary's office unfortunately fell within the range of the flames. "The most irreparable loss was that of the records, consisting of the official, scientific, and miscellaneous correspondence; embracing 35,000 pages of copied letters which had been sent, (at least 30,000 of which were the composition of the Secretary,) and 50,000 pages of letters received by the Institution; the receipts for publications and specimens; reports on various subjects which have been referred to the Institution; the records of experiments instituted by the Secretary for the Government; four manuscripts of original investigations, [memoirs by collaborators,] which had been adopted by the Institution for publication; a large number of papers and scientific notes of the Secretary; a series of diaries, memorandum and account books." * This truly "irreparable loss" of the original notes of many series of experiments by Henry, of varied character, running back for thirty years, kept for the purpose of reduction and discussion, or further extension (as leisure might permit), and of which but few had been published even by results, — was borne by their author with his characteristic equanimity; and was very rarely alluded to by him, unless when in answer to inquiries respecting particular points of his researches, he was compelled to excuse the absence of precise data.

The Lecture Room — a model of its class — entirely burned out by the fire, was not reconstructed: but the space it occupied on the upper floor, was with the adjacent rooms (used as the apparatus room, and the art gallery) thrown into one large hall, 200 feet long, — at present occupied as the ethnological museum. Advantage was taken of the hazard demonstrated by the fire, to induce Congress in the following year to transfer the custody of the Smith-

* *Smithsonian Report* for 1865, p. 18.

sonian collection of scientific works to the National Library: and the propriety of this change was thus defended. "The east wing of the Smithsonian building, in which the books were deposited is not fire-proof, and is liable to destruction by accident or the torch of the incendiary, while the rooms of the Capitol are of incombustible materials. This wing was moreover filled to overflowing; and a more extended and secure depository could not be obtained, except by another large draught on the accumulated funds intended to form part of the permanent capital." *

*Second Visit to Europe.*—At a meeting of the Board of Regents, held February 3rd, 1870, "General Delafield in behalf of the Executive Committee, stated that they deemed it highly important for the interests of the Institution in the promotion of science, and due to the Secretary for his long and devoted services, that he should visit Europe to consult with the savans and societies of Great Britain and the continent; and he therefore hoped that a leave of absence would be granted to Professor Henry for several months, and an allowance be made for his expenses. On motion of Dr. Maclean it was unanimously *Resolved*, That Professor Henry, Secretary of the Institution, be authorized to visit Europe in behalf of the interests of the Smithsonian Institution, and that he be granted from three to six months leave of absence, and two thousand dollars for travelling expenses for this purpose." †

It is not necessary here to recount the particulars of this second visit of Henry to Europe, more fully than in the brief account given by him in his annual Report. "Before closing this report, it is proper that I should refer to a resolution adopted by your honorable board at its last session, granting me leave of absence to visit Europe to confer with savans and societies relative to the Institution, and making provision for the payment of my expenses. The presentation of this proposition was entirely without my knowledge, but I need scarcely say that its unanimous adoption was highly gratifying to my feelings; and that I availed myself of the privilege it offered with a grateful appreciation of the kindness

---

* *Smithsonian Report* for 1866, p. 14.

† *Smithsonian Report* for 1869, p. 89.

intended. I sailed from New York on the 1st of June, returning after an absence of four and a half months, much improved in health, and with impressions as to science and education in the Old World, which may be of value in directing the affairs of the Institution. Although limited as to time, and my plans interfered with somewhat by the war, I visited England, Ireland, Scotland, Belgium, parts of Germany and France. But deferring for the present an account of my travels, and the observations connected with them, I will merely state that as your representative, I was everywhere kindly received, and was highly gratified with the commendations bestowed on the character and operations of the Institution intrusted to your care." *

*Service on the Light-House Board.*—While the whole high bent of Henry's mind was rather toward abstract than utilitarian research, there was no well devised system of practical benefit for man, that did not command his earnest sympathy or enlist his active co-operation; — no labor in such co-operation from which he shrank, if he felt that without the sacrifice of other duties, he could make such labor useful. On the establishment of the Light-House Board, in 1852, Henry was appointed one of its members; and although his valuable time was already fully occupied, he consented to serve on the Board, in the hope of aiding to benefit the interests of navigation. To the requirements of his new position, he brought his accustomed energy, skill, and eminently practical judgment; and soon made his influence felt throughout the light-house service.†

---

* *Smithsonian Report* for 1870, p. 45.

† In less than ten years from the organization of the Light-House Board, the lenticular system of AUGUSTIN JEAN FRESNEL had been introduced into all the light-houses of the United States. LEONOR FRESNEL, Secretary of the Light-House Board of France, (the brother of that distinguished physicist,) in a letter addressed to the Secretary of the United States Light-House Board, dated May 7th, 1861, says: "The prodigious development of this service within so short a time under the Light-House Board, has truly astonished me My old experience in fact enables me the better to appreciate how much energy and activity were necessary to bring to this degree of perfection, the light-house service of such a vast expanse of coast, as well on the Pacific. as on the Atlantic. without mentioning the task of succeeding in establishing against hostile prejudices the adoption of a new system." (*Report to Secretary of the Treasury*, Feb. 4, 1862. Mis. Doc. No. 61, 37th Cong. 2nd Sess. Senate, p. 16.)

When the steadily advancing cost of whale oil made it necessary to seek for some more economical illuminant, he attacked the problem with his habit of scientific method. Colza oil or rape-seed oil had been used in France with some success; and efforts were made to introduce its culture and production in this country. Lard oil had been tested by Professor J. H. Alexander of Baltimore, and pronounced by him of very inferior value as an illuminant. For accuracy of determination, Henry caused to be prepared at the Light-house Depot on Staten Island, a long dark fire-proof chamber, and had it painted black on all its interior surfaces for the purpose of photometric observations. In ordinary lamps, the colza oil was found to be about equal to whale oil in illuminating power, and lard oil inferior to it. Petroleum or mineral oil was also tried; but its quality was at that time too variable, and its use was found to be too dangerous. Experiment showed that lard oil had a greater specific gravity than sperm oil, a less capillarity or ascensional attraction in a wick, and a less perfect fluidity. The conditions were varied; and it was found that with elevation of temperature, the fluidity, and the capillarity, of the lard oil increased more rapidly than those of the sperm oil, until at about 250° F. the former surpassed the latter in these qualities. With these results, it became important to compare the oils in large lamps, such as were actually required for the lanterns of light-houses. The heat evolved by the large-sized Argand burners, would seem peculiarly to favor the lard oil: a few trials, with a proper adaptation of the lamps, established its supremacy; and conclusively demonstrated — contrary to all the laboratory trials of former experimenters, that for the purpose desired, this contemned article was for equal quantities a more brilliant illuminant than mineral kerosene oil, or vegetable colza oil, or animal sperm oil, while its market price was only about one-fourth that of the latter.* Against all the opposition of interested dealers, and prejudiced keepers, the lard oil was at once introduced into actual use in the years 1865 and 1866, in all the light-houses of the United States; with a saving of at least one dollar on every gallon of the hundred thousand in annual use; that is of 100,000 dollars per annum.

---

*See "Supplement," NOTE N.

During the progress of these useful labors, no less important investigations were commenced, on the most efficient forms of apparatus for acoustic signalling, as the substitutes for light signals during the prevalence of sea-board fogs. "Among the impediments to navigation, none perhaps are more to be dreaded than those which arise from fogs.  -  -  -  The only means at present known for obviating the difficulty, is that of employing powerful sounding instruments which may be heard at a sufficient distance through the fog, to give timely warning of impending danger." *

Gun signals were early abandoned, as inefficient, dangerous, and expensive: inefficient, because of both "the length of the intervals between the successive explosions, and the brief duration of the sound, which renders it difficult to determine with accuracy its direction." Innumerable projects eagerly pressed upon the Board by visionary inventors (some of them being rattles, gongs, or organ pipes operated by manual cranks, many of them being varieties of automatic horn or whistle operated by the winds or the waves) were impartially tested, and uniformly rejected as wholly insufficient: very few of their projectors having the slightest practical idea of the requirements of the service. Experiments on steam-whistles of large size and on horns with vibrating steel tongues or reeds, sounded by steam-power, or by hot-air engines, varied and continued for several years under wide changes of conditions, finally determined their most efficient size and character. †

In 1867, comparative trials were made at Sandy Hook (on the Jersey shore, at the entrance to Raritan Bay, and to New York Bay,) with three powerful instruments; a large steam-whistle whose cup was 8 inches in diameter, and made adjustable in pitch; a large reed trumpet 17 feet long and 38 inches in diameter at its flaring mouth, whose steel tongue was 10 inches long, $2\frac{3}{4}$ inches

---

* *Report of Light-House Board* for 1874, p. 83.

† An enterprising inventor had secured a patent for a metallic compound or alloy for steam-whistles, especially adapted to increase greatly their power as fog-signals. In vain was he assured that his "improvement" was a fallacy; that the cylindrical cup of the whistle was not a bell, but only a resonant chamber; and that its material was comparatively unimportant. He was only with difficulty convinced, when HENRY had his whistle formally tested, with a stout cord wound tightly around its cylindrical surface: when its tone under steam escape was proved to be as full, as loud, and as penetrating, as with the cord removed.

wide, and half an inch thick at its smaller vibrating end, and was blown by a hot-air engine; and lastly a large siren horn operated by steam at different pressures, the aerial vibration being produced by the intermittence of a revolving grating disk or valve in the small end of the horn, driven at high velocities by the steam engine, and its pitch regulated by the adjustable speed of the revolving disk.   The trumpet or fog-horn was provided with a series of replaceable steel tongues of different sizes, and the siren was driven at five different pitches of from 250 to 700 impulses per second, and at steam pressures varying from 20 pounds to 100 pounds per square inch.   For the purpose of accurate estimation, within short distances, a phonometer or "artificial ear" was employed, having at its smaller upturned end a horizontal drum of stretched membrane, sprinkled with sand, after the plan devised by Sondhauss. Trumpets of the same size, were made of different materials, as of brass, iron, and wood; but these differences were found to exercise little or no influence on the intensity or penetration of the sound. Trumpets were also made of different shapes, straight and curved, and square as well as round, with equal lengths and equal areas of cross section; from whose trials it appeared that the conical form gave nearly double the distance of action on the sand of the "artificial ear," that was given by the pyramidal form.   Such investigations — varied and long-continued, serve to show the conscientious earnestness with which Henry sought to give the highest efficiency to the expedients available for the protection of life and property along our extended sea coast.

The steam-whistle was found to be less powerful than the trumpet, with the same expenditures of fuel.   Steam-whistles were afterwards tried of 10 inches, 12 inches, and 18 inches in diameter. The largest size was not found to give results proportioned to its increased consumption; and the 10 or 12 inch size was regarded as practically the most efficient.   The siren was found to be the most powerful and penetrating of the instruments tested, as it admitted more advantageously the application of a higher steam expenditure.   The best result with this instrument was attained with a pressure of from 60 to 80 pounds, and at a pitch between 350 and 400 vibrations per second.   Under favorable conditions, this instrument frequently made itself heard at a distance of fifteen, and twenty miles. Henry's large experience with the occasional aerial impediments to sound propagation,* and his strong sense of the vital importance of having fog-signals recognized at a distance, under the most adverse conditions, led him to favor the introduction of the most powerful sounders attainable, without absolutely limiting the decision to their relative economy. Hence he was the first to devise improvements in the siren, and to press its adoption at important or dangerous stations, notwithstanding its higher consumption of steam or heat power. †

Partly under the stimulus given to the sale of lard oil by the striking proofs of its excellence as an illuminant under favorable conditions, furnished by Henry, this article slowly advanced in price; though probably not to an extent of more than a fourth part additional cost. Henry's energies again were called into requisition to devise a remedy. Neither gas, nor electricity, the favorite means of numerous projectors and advisers, appeared justified, on the score of economy.‡ A new series of elaborate experiments was undertaken to determine whether mineral oil (so abundant as to be easily procurable at one-third the cost of lard oil) could not be made available. The great improvements introduced into its prep-

---

* An abstract of Henry's elaborate and invaluable researches on some abnormal phenomena of Sound—the crowning labor of his life, must be reserved for a concluding section.

† Major G. H. Elliott, commissioned by the U. S. Light-House Board to make a tour of inspection of European Light-house establishments in 1873, in his Report published by the Senate in 1874, says of the British and French systems, "I saw many details of construction and administration which we can adopt to advantage, while there are many in which we excel. Our shore fog-signals particularly, are vastly superior both in number and power." (*Report on European Light-houses*, p. 12.) "To the careful and laborious investigations and experiments of the distinguished Chairman of the Light-House Board, prolonged through a series of years, and prosecuted under a great variety of conditions, is largely to be attributed the acknowledged superiority of our fog-signal service." (*Journal of Franklin Institute*, Jan. 1876, vol. lxxi. p. 43.)

‡ *Report of L. H. Board* for 1874, p. 11. No agency (for whatever purpose) has proved so enticing to the half-informed as *electricity*. For years past scarcely a month has elapsed without some new form of patent electric-light, or some marvelous application of electric-lights, being pertinaciously urged by sanguine "reformers" upon the Light-House Board for adoption; some of these ideal schemes being the mounting of electric-lights on buoys, or on the masts of light-ships, or their suspension from moored balloons. Many eminently original minds have earnestly desired to obtain contracts for supplying all the light-houses with oxy-hydrogen lime lights. In a fog, the most powerful electric-light is as useless as the cheapest kerosene lamp.

aration in later years by high distillation, seemed to justify the attempt. Not only was a laborious inquiry into the best conditions of combustion, by precise photometric measurement required, but for the security of the service, equally laborious examinations into the best practicable methods of testing, of handling, and of storing this material.* To secure a proper oxygenation in burning, a modification of the lamp was required. "It was soon apparent that the use of mineral oil would necessitate a change of lamps, and attention is now directed to the perfection of one which will produce the best results from this illuminant. It is thought that the lamps now used with lard oil can be converted at no great expense and successfully used with mineral oil. Our experiments have shown that this oil can be more readily used in the smaller lamps; and it is proposed as soon as suitable ones can be prepared, to put it into use at such stations of the fifth and sixth order, as may be thought expedient; when if it be found satisfactory, an attempt will be made to substitute it for lard oil in lamps of the higher orders."† "This change is proposed entirely with reference to economy; for it has been found by repeated experiment, that while a somewhat superior light may be obtained from a small lamp charged with kerosene, a larger lamp charged with lard oil affords the greater illuminating power. So great is this difference in lamps of the first order with five wicks, that the rates of light from kerosene and lard, are as three to four respectively. Since the safety of the keeper and the continuity of the light are essential elements in the choice of an illuminant, a thorough acquaintance with the nature of the substance is essentially necessary. With a view therefore to the introduction of kerosene, a series of experiments have been made during the last two years on the different varieties of this material found in the market."‡

---

* "It has been established that the ordinary fire-test is insufficient as usually applied, and that an explosive mixture may be formed by confining the vapors given off at a temperature in some cases twenty degrees lower than that certified to by the public inspector. That this inquiry is of great practical importance to the Light-house system, must be evident when we reflect that means must be devised for testing the oil offered for acceptance in accordance with contracts; for storing it; for transporting it to light-house stations; for preserving it in butts at the stations; and for the instruction of the keepers in its daily use." (*Report of L. H. Board*, 1877, p. 5.)

† *Report of L. H. Board*, 1875, p. 6.

‡ *Report of L. H. Board*, 1877, p. 4.

In 1871, on the resignation of Admiral Shubrick, Henry was chosen as the Chairman of the Light-House Board; and his energetic labors in behalf of the service, fully vindicated the wisdom of the choice. Punctual in his attendance on the weekly meetings of the Board, he inspired others with a portion of his own zealous devotion. Nor did he fail to urge upon the Government, the constant need and responsibility of maintaining an efficient establishment. He emphatically declared that "The character of the aids which any nation furnishes the mariner in approaching and leaving its shores, marks in a conspicuous degree its advancement in civilization. Whatever tends to facilitate navigation or to lessen its dangers, serves to increase commerce; and hence is of importance not only to the dwellers on the seaboard, but to the inhabitants of every part of the country. - - - Therefore it is of the first importance that the signals, whether of light or sound, which indicate the direction of the course, and the beacons which mark the channel, shall be of the most improved character, and that they be under the charge of intelligent, efficient, and trustworthy attendants." * And rising to a higher argument, he pointed out that "It is not alone in its economical aspect that a light-house system is to be regarded: it is a life-preserving establishment founded on the principles of Christian benevolence, of which none can so well appreciate the importance as he who after having been exposed to the perils of the ocean—it may be for months—finds himself approaching in the darkness of night a lee shore. But it is not enough to erect towers, and establish other signals: they must be maintained in an efficient state with uninterrupted constancy." † Unfailing continuity was the watch-word of his administration.

---

* *Report of L. H. Board,* 1873, pp. 3, 4. The coast line of the United States is far more extended than that of any other nation on the globe. "The magnitude of the Light-house system of the United States may be inferred from the following facts: from the St. Croix River on the boundary of Maine, to the mouth of the Rio Grande in the Gulf of Mexico, includes a distance of over 5,000 miles; on the Pacific coast, a length of about 1,500 miles; on the great northern Lakes, about 3,000 miles; and on inland rivers about 700 miles; making a total of more than 10,000 miles. Nearly every square foot of the margin of the sea throughout the whole extent of 5,000 miles along the Atlantic and Gulf coast, is more or less illuminated by light-house rays; the mariner rarely losing sight of one light until he has gained another." (p. 4, of same Report.)

† *Report of L. H. Board,* 1874, p. 5.

A formal report made to the Honorable Secretary of the Treasury by the Naval Secretary of the Light-House Board, dated May 21st, 1878, (very shortly after Henry's death,) simply detailing for information, the character of his gratuitous services to the light-house establishment during a quarter of a century, (and not intended for the public,) takes the inevitable form of eulogy. A portion of it is here quoted:

"As Chairman of this committee, Professor Henry acted as the scientific adviser of the Board. But in addition it was his duty to conduct the experiments made by the Board, not only in the matter of original investigation, and testing of the material used, but in examining and reporting on the models, plans, and theories, presented by others to the Board. The value of the services he rendered in this position is simply inestimable. He prepared the formula for testing our oils; he conducted the series of experiments resulting in the substitution of lard oil for sperm oil, which effected an immense saving in cost; and he also conducted the experiments which have resulted in making it possible to substitute mineral oil for lard oil, when another economy will be made. His original investigation into the laws of sound have resulted in giving us a fog-signal service conceded to be the best in the world. His examinations into the action of electricity, have enabled the Board to almost completely protect its stations from the effect of lightning. The result of his patient, continuous, practical experimentation is visible everywhere in the service. No subject was too vast for him to undertake; none too small for him to overlook. And while he has brought into the establishment so many practical applications of science, he has done almost as much service by keeping out what presented by others seemed plausible, but which on examination proved impracticable.

"Every theory, plan, or machine, which was pressed on the Board, as for the interests of commerce and navigation, was referred to the committee on experiments, when it was examined by its Chairman, and was formally reported upon. If it had no practical value, the report on record simply stated the inexpediency of its adoption: but the Professor often verbally pointed out to the presenter, its fallacy; and sent him away — if not satisfied — at least feeling that he had been well treated.   He thus prevented not only the adoption of impracticable plans, but avoided the enmity of their inventors.

"Professor Henry made many valuable reports, containing the results of his elaborate experiments into matters which were formally referred to him, which are spread on the records of the Board; and the reports were drawn in such form that his suggestions were capable of and received practical application.   But in addition to this, he was constantly extending his scientific researches for the benefit of the service in all directions.   His summer vacations were as a rule passed in experimentation at the laboratory of the Establishment at Staten Island, on its steamers, or at its light-stations, pushing his inquiries to their last results.   To experimentation in the interests of this service, Professor Henry seemed to give his whole heart.   It appeared as if he never lost sight of the needs of the Establishment, and as if he never neglected an opportunity to advance its interests.   In addition to his other duties, Professor Henry presided as Chairman of the Light-House Board for the last seven years at its weekly meetings, when he did much to infuse into the different members of the Board, his own spirit of labor for, and devotion to its interests." *

*Services to the National Government.*—The value of Henry's services to the various Executive Departments of our Government, faithfully and unostentatiously performed through a long series of years and a succession of Presidential Administrations, cannot be estimated, as its history can never be written.   Whatever material for it existed in the form of abstracts of inquiries, trials, and reports, prior to 1865, unfortunately perished in the fire of that year.   Whenever in any important case a scientific adviser could be useful to the proper conduct of a Bureau, Henry's reputation generally pointed him out as the most suitable expert and arbiter. On the outbreak of the great civil war, the number of such refer-

---

* *Executive Documents,* No. 94, Forty-fifth Congress, 2d Session, Senate, pp. 2, 3.   It is gratifying to know that on the presentation of his report and recommendation to Congress, by the high-minded Secretary of the Treasury, a moderate appropriation for the benefit of his bereaved family was at once passed, in slight recognition of Henry's "inestimable" services.

ences was naturally very considerably increased. The Departments of War, of the Navy, and of the Treasury, were besieged by projectors with every imaginable and impossible scheme for saving the country, and demolishing the enemy. Torpedo balloons, electric-light balloons, wonderful compounds destined to supersede gunpowder and revolutionize the art of war; cheap methods for the manufacture of Government bonds and paper-money; multitudinous expedients for the prevention of counterfeiting, by devices in the engraving, by secret markings, by anti-photographic inks, by peculiar textures of paper, (applicable to coupons, to circulating notes, to revenue stamps,)—each warranted to be infallible; such were among the agencies by which patriotic patentees and adroit adventurers were willing to serve their country and to reap their reward by the moderate royalty or percentage due to the magnificence of the public benefit. Such were among the unenviable tasks of examination and adjudication accepted by Henry, only from an intrepid sense of duty.

"The course which has been pursued of rendering the Government in its late trials, every aid which could be supplied by scientific research, has been warmly approved. As most persons are probably entirely ignorant of the services really rendered to the Government by the Institution, I may here state the fact that a large share of my time, (all indeed which could be spared from official duties,) has been devoted for the last four years to investigations required by the public exigencies. Within this period, several hundred reports, requiring many experiments, and pertaining either to proposals purporting to be of high national importance, or relating to the quality of the multifarious articles offered in fulfillment of legal contracts, have been rendered. The opinions advanced in many of these reports, not only cost much valuable time, but also involved grave responsibilities. While on the one hand the rejection of a proposition would be in contravention to the high importance claimed for it by its author, on the other the approval of it would perhaps incur the risk of the fruitless expenditures of a large amount of public money. It is not necessary, I trust, to say that the labor thus rendered was entirely gratuitous, or that in the judgment pronounced in any case, no regard was paid to the interested solicitations or personal influence of the parties concerned: on the contrary it has in some instances resulted from the examination of materials sold to the Government, that attempted fraud has been exposed, and the baffled speculator received his due reward in condemnation and punishment. These facts it is thought will be deemed a sufficient answer to those who have seemed disposed to reproach the Institution with the want of a more popular demonstration — but of a really far less useful or efficient aid in the support of the Government." *

In the performance of these troublesome and often disagreeable labors, conducted with the single aim necessitated by all his scientific habits and instincts, it of course resulted that a great majority of his judgments and recommendations were decidedly adverse to the hopes and wishes of the aspirants to fame and fortune. Having once satisfied himself of the frivolity or the chicanery of an article or project, his decision was inflexible; and although importunate appeals to the Department Secretary, abetted by a prostituted political or other influence, in one or two instances succeeded in fastening for a time upon the public Treasury a worthless or a noxious leech, the vast number of such, excluded from experimental imbibitions by Henry's critical supervision, must have been a protection to the public interests quite beyond the reach of estimation: while on the other hand, the supplies of honest contractors awarded their just commendation, and the rare proposals of real merit favorably reported upon, which from a hasty survey might have been confounded and overlaid with the mass of untried puerilities, no less served to strengthen and assist the Government during its years of greatest trial, need, and exhaustion.

From the outset of the unnatural sectional revolt, fully appreciating the vastness of the interests, the sacrifices, and the dangers involved, Henry contemplated the crisis — not with despondency, but with a profound sorrow and solicitude. While his sympathies and his hopes were all for the preservation of the national integrity of jurisdiction, he was little given to public exhibitions of his feelings. Undemonstrative — less from temperament than from the deliberate and habitual subjection of emotional expression to reason,

---

* *Smithsonian Report for* 1864, p. 15.

during those times of feverish excitement apprehension and circumspection necessarily attendant on the prevalence of a gigantic rebel-
lion, (unparalleled in incentive, in temper, and in magnitude,) many
of whose leaders had been among his personal friends, he was not
unnaturally looked upon by many as lukewarm in his patriotism,
if not disloyal in his citizenship. To the occasional inuendoes of
the press, he deigned no answers: he was the last man to accord
compliance with the urgency of a popular clamor. And yet during
the entire period of the Southern Insurrection, he was the personal
and trusted friend of President Lincoln.*

### CONTRIBUTIONS TO SCIENCE AT WASHINGTON.

In addition to what may be called the public labors of Henry so
diligently performed in various fields after his advent to the Smithsonian Institution, it is well briefly to contemplate the special scientific work he was able to accomplish in the intervals of his exacting
occupations, that some estimate may be formed of the independent
value of his later contributions, as well as of his wonderful industry. While still engaged in his difficult task of organizing and
shaping the policy of the Institution, in 1850, on taking occasion
to present before the American Association at New Haven, Conn.

---

* Early in the war (in the autumn of 1861,) a caller at the Presidential Mansion
very anxious to see the Chief Magistrate of the nation, was informed that he
could not then be seen, being engaged in an important private consultation.
The caller not to be repulsed, wrote on a piece of paper that he must see Mr.
Lincoln personally, on a matter of vital and pressing importance to the public
welfare. This of course secured his admission to the presence of Mr. Lincoln,
who was sitting with a middle-aged gentleman. Observing the hesitancy of his
visitor, the President told him he might speak freely, as only a friend was
present. Whereupon the visitor announced that for several evenings past he
had observed a light exhibited on the highest of the Smithsonian towers, for a
few minutes about nine o'clock, with mysterious movements, which he felt
satisfied were designed as signals to the rebels encamped on Munson's hill in
Virginia. Having gravely listened to this information with raised eyebrows, but
a subdued twinkle of the eye, the President turned to his companion, saying
"What do you think of that? Professor Henry." Rising with a smile, the person
addressed replied, that from the time mentioned, he presumed the mysterious
light shone from the lantern of an attendant who was required at nine o'clock
each evening to observe and record the indications of the meteorological instruments placed on the tower. The painful confusion of the officious informant, at
once appealed to Henry's sensibility; and quite unmindful of the President, he
approached the visitor, offering his hand, and with a courteous regard counselled
him never to be abashed at the issue of a conscientious discharge of duty, and
never to let the fear of ridicule interfere with its faithful execution.

a *résumé* of the electrical phenomena exhibited by the Leyden jar, and their true interpretation, he remarked that "for the last three and a half years, all his time and all his thoughts had been given to the details of the business of the Smithsonian Institution. He had been obliged to withdraw himself entirely from scientific research; but he hoped that now the Institution had got under way, and the Regents had allowed him some able assistants, that he would be enabled in part at least to return to his first love—the investigation of the phenomena of nature." *

*Thermal Telescope.*—Shortly after his establishment at Washington, he continued a series of former experiments with the "thermo-galvanic multiplicator" devised by Nobili and Melloni in 1831; and by some slight but significant modifications of the apparatus, he succeeded in imparting to it a most surprising delicacy of action. With the thermo-electric pile carefully adjusted at the focus of a suitable reflector, his "thermal telescope" when directed to the celestial vault, indicated that the heat radiated inward by our atmosphere when clear, is least at the zenith, and increases downward to the horizon; as was to have been inferred from its increasing mass: when directed to clouds, they were found to differ very widely accordingly as they were condensing or being dissipated; some even indicating a less amount of radiation than the surrounding atmosphere. When directed to a horse in a distant field, its animal heat concentrated on the pile, was distinctly made manifest on the galvanometer needle. Even the heat from a man's face at the distance of a mile could be detected; and that from the side of a house at several miles distance.† These and many similar observations demonstrated to sense the inductions of reason, that there is a constant and universal exchange by radiation in straight lines from every object in nature, following the same laws as the palpable emanation from incandescent bodies; and that even when the amplitude of the thermal vibrations (equivalent to the square root of their dynamic energy) is reduced a million fold, its existence may still be distinctly traced.

---

* *Proceed. Am. Assoc.* 4th Meeting, New Haven, Aug. 1850, p. 378.

† Silliman's *Am. Jour. Sci.* Jan. 1848, vol. v. pp. 113, 114.

Henry showed by experiment, that ice could be employed both as a convex lens for converging heat to a focus, and also as a concave mirror for the same purpose: a considerable portion of the incident rays being transmitted, a large portion reflected, and the remainder (a much smaller quantity) absorbed by the ice.

In 1849, for the purpose of estimating the effects of certain meteorological conditions of the atmosphere, he made some experiments on the lateral radiation from a current of ascending heated air at different distances above the flame; the latter being thoroughly eclipsed.

He also experimented on the radiation of heat from a hydrogen flame, which was shown to be quite small, notwithstanding the high temperature of the flame. By placing an infusible and incombustible solid in the flame, while the temperature is much reduced, the radiant light and heat are greatly increased: * — results closely analogous to those obtained by him in the differences between the audibility of vibrating tuning-forks when suspended by a soft thread, or when rigidly attached to a sounding-board. These results have also an undoubted significance with regard to celestial radiations; not only as to the differences between gaseous nebulæ and stars or clusters, but as to the differences between stars in a probably different state of condensation or of specific gravity.

A few years later, he continued his investigation of this subject of radiation, more especially with reference to Rumford's "Observations relative to the means of increasing the quantities of Heat obtained in the Combustion of Fuel:" published in Great Britain in 1802.† He found that Rumford's recommendation of the introduction of balls of clay or of fire brick (about two and a half inches in diameter) into a coal fire, was fully justified as an economic measure: more heat being thereby radiated from the fire into the room, and less being carried up the flue. He also showed however that for culinary purposes, while the incandescent or heated clay increases the *radiation*, and thereby improves the quality of the fire for *roasting*, it correspondingly expends the *temperature*, and thereby diminishes its power for *boiling*. "That a

---

* *Proceed. Am. Phil. Soc.* Oct. 19, 1849, vol. v. p. 108.
† *Journal Royal Institution*, 1802, vol. i. p. 28.

solid substance increases the radiation of the heat of a flame, is an interesting fact in connection with the nature of heat itself. It would seem to show that the vibrations of gross matter are necessary to give sufficient intensity of impulse to produce the phenomena of ordinary radiant heat." *

In 1851, he read before the American Association at Albany, a paper "On the Theory of the so-called Imponderables:" (mainly a development of his earlier discussion in 1846, of the molecular constitution of matter,) in which he forcibly criticised a frequent tendency to assume or multiply unknown and unrealizable modes of action: holding that with regard to the most subtle agencies of nature, we have no warrant by the strict scientific method, for resorting to other than the observed and established laws of matter and force, until it has been exhaustively demonstrated that these are insufficient. The fundamental laws of mechanical philosophy "are five in number; viz. the two laws of force—attraction, and repulsion, varying with some function of the distance; and secondly, the three laws of motion—the law of inertia, of the co-existence of motions, and of action and re-action. Of these laws we can give no explanation: they are at present considered as ultimate facts; to which all mechanical phenomena are referred, or from which they are deduced by logical inference. The existence of these laws as has been said, is deduced from the phenomena of the operations of matter in masses; but we apply them by analogy to the minute and invisible portions of matter which constitute the atoms or molecules of gases, and we find that the inferences from this assumption are borne out by the results of experience." He regarded the modern kinetic or dynamic theory of gases, by its predictions and verifications, as furnishing almost a complete establishment of the atomic and molecular theory of matter. Referring to the ingenious hypothesis of Boscovich, he thought that though well adapted to embrace the two static laws above mentioned, it did not appear equally well adapted to satisfy in any intelligible sense the three kinetic laws. He contended that any attempt at conforming our conception of the ultimate constitution of matter to the

* *Proceed. Am. Assoc.* Providence, Aug. 1855, pp. 112-116. "On the Effect of mingling Radiating substances with Combustible materials."

inductions of experience, would seem to conduct us directly to the atomic hypothesis of Newton. A careful study of the dynamics of the so-called "imponderables" certainly tended to their unification. Admitting the difficulty of framing an entirely satisfactory theory of the resultant transverse action of electricity, he suggested that a tangential force was not accordant with any inductions from actual experience; and was incapable of direct mechanical realization. Extending the atomic conception of matter to the ætherial medium of space, he concluded by urging "the importance in the adoption of mechanical hypotheses, of conditioning them in strict accordance with the operations of matter under the known laws of force and motion, as exhibited in time and space." *

Among the various public Addresses delivered by Henry on special occasions, reference may be here made to his excellent exposition of the nature of power, and the functions of machinery as its vehicle,—concluding with a sketch of the progress of art, pronounced at the close of the Exhibition of the Metropolitan Mechanics' Institute, in Washington, on the evening of March 19th, 1853. After representing to his hearers the close physical analogy between the human body as a moving machine, and the steam locomotive under an intelligent engineer, he remarked: "In both, the direction of power is under the influence of an immaterial, thinking, willing principle, called the soul. But this must not be confounded as it frequently is with the motive power. The soul of a man no more moves his body, than the soul of the engineer moves the locomotive and its attendant train of cars. In both cases the soul is the directing, controlling principle; not the impelling power." †

*Views of Education.*—Another address deserving of special notice (delivered the following year,) is his introductory discourse before the "Association for the Advancement of Education," as its retiring President. In this, he maintained that inasmuch as "the several faculties of the human mind are not simultaneously developed, in educating an individual we ought to follow the order of nature, and to adapt the instruction to the age and mental stature of the pupil.

---

* *Proceed. Am. Assoc.* Albany, Aug. 1851, pp. 84–91.

† *Closing Address* Metr. Mech. Inst. Washington, 1853, p. 19.

Memory, imitation, imagination, and the faculty of forming mental habits, exist in early life, while the judgment and the reasoning powers are of slower growth." Hence less attention should be given to the development of the reasoning faculties, than to those of observation: the juvenile memory should be stored rather with facts, than with principles: and he condemned as mischievous "the proposition frequently advanced, that the child should be taught nothing but what he can fully comprehend, and the endeavor in accordance with this, to invert the order of nature, and attempt to impart those things which cannot be taught at an early age, and to neglect those which at this period of life the mind is well adapted to receive. By this mode we may indeed produce remarkably intelligent children, who will become remarkably feeble men. The order of nature is that of art before science; the entire concrete first, and the entire abstract last. These two extremes should run gradually into each other, the course of instruction becoming more and more logical as the pupil advances in years."—"The cultivation of the imagination should also be considered an essential part of a liberal education: and this may be spread over the whole course of instruction, for like the reasoning faculties the imagination may continue to be improved until late in life."

Applying this same reasoning to the moral training of youth, he considered that (as in the intellectual culture) the object should be "not only to teach the pupil how to *think*, but how to *act* and to *do;* placing great stress upon the early education of the habits. - - - We are frequently required to act from the impulse of the moment, and have no time to deduce our course from the moral principles of the act. An individual can be educated to a strict regard for truth, to deeds of courage in rescuing others from danger, to acts of benevolence, generosity, and justice. - - - The future character of a child and that of the man also, is in most cases formed probably before the age of seven years. Previously to this time impressions have been made which shall survive amid the vicissitudes of life, amid all the influences to which the individual may be subjected, and which will outcrop as it were, in the last stage of his earthly existence, when the additions to his character made in later years, have been entirely swept away." Childhood (he intimated) is less the parent of manhood, than of age: the special vices of the individual child though long subdued, sometimes surviving and re-appearing in his "second childhood."

Affirming that culture is constraint,—education and direction an expenditure of force, and extending his generalization from the individual to the race, he controverted the idea so popular with some benevolent enthusiasts, that there is a spontaneous tendency in man to civilization and advancement. The origins of past civilizations—taking a comprehensive glance at far distant human populations—have been sporadic as it were, and their prevalence comparatively transitory. "It appears therefore that civilization itself may be considered as a condition of unstable equilibrium, which requires constant effort to be sustained, and a still greater effort to be advanced. It is not in my view the 'manifest destiny' of humanity to improve by the operation of an inevitable necessary law of progress: but while I believe that it is the design of Providence that man should be improved, this improvement must be the result of individual effort, or of the combined effort of many individuals animated by the same feeling and co-operating for the attainment of the same end. - - - If we sow judiciously in the present, the world will assuredly reap a beneficent harvest in the future: and he has not lived in vain, who leaves behind him as his successor, a child better educated—morally, intellectually, and physically, than himself. From this point of view, the responsibilities of life are immense. Every individual by his example and precept, whether intentionally or otherwise, does aid or oppose this important work, and leaves an impress of character upon the succeeding age, which is to mould its destiny for weal or woe, in all coming time. - - - The world however is not to be advanced by the mere application of truths already known: but we look forward (particularly in physical science) to the effect of the development of new principles. We have scarcely as yet read more than the title-page and preface of the great volume of nature, and what we do know is as nothing in comparison with that which may be yet unfolded and applied." *

---

* *Proceed. Assoc. Adv. Education*, 4th Session, Washington, Dec. 28, 1854, pp. 17-31. The pregnant thought that human civilization is an artificial and coerced condition, would seem to have a suggestive bearing on the two great theories of

*Experiments on Building-Stone.*—In 1854, a series of experiments on the strength of different kinds of building-stone, was undertaken by Henry as one of a commission appointed by the President, having reference to the marbles offered for the extension of the United States Capitol. Specimens of the different samples — accurately cut to cubical blocks one inch and a half in height, were first tried by interposing a thin sheet of lead above and below, between the block and the steel plates of the crushing dynamometer. "This was in accordance with a plan adopted by Rennie, and that which appears to have been used by most if not all of the subsequent experimenters in researches of this kind. Some doubt however was expressed as to the action of interposed lead, which induced a series of experiments to settle this question; when the remarkable fact was discovered that the yielding and approximately equable pressure of the lead caused the stone to give way at about half the pressure it would sustain without such an interposition. For example, one of the cubes precisely similar to another which withstood a pressure of upwards of 60,000 pounds when placed in immediate contact with the steel plates, gave way at about 30,000 pounds with lead interposed. This interesting fact was verified in a series of experiments embracing samples of nearly all the marbles under trial, and in no case did a single exception occur to vary the result.

"The explanation of this striking phenomenon (now that the fact is known) is not difficult. The stone tends to give way by bulging out in the centre of each of its four perpendicular faces, and to form two pyramidal figures with their apices opposed to each other at the centre of the cube, and their bases against the steel plates. In the case where rigid equable pressure is employed, as in that of the thick steel plate, all parts must give way together. But in that of a *yielding* equable pressure as in the case of inter-

---

development, and *evolution*, so generally confounded by the superficial. What may be called the radical difference between these two views of organic extension, is that the former assumes an inherent mysterious tendency to progression, whose motto is ever "excelsior;" while the latter assumes a general tendency to variation within moderate limits in indefinite directions; so that elevation is no more normal than degradation, and indeed may be regarded as rarer and more exceptional, since at every upward stage attained by the few, there are probably more further digressions downward than upward, the motto being ever "aptior."

posed lead, the stone first gives way along the outer lines or those of least resistance, and the remaining pressure must be sustained by the central portions around the vertical axis of the cube. After this important fact was clearly determined, lead and all other interposed substances were discarded, and a method devised by which the upper and lower surfaces of the cube could be ground into perfect parallelism. - - - All the specimens tested were subjected to this process, and on their exposure to pressure were found to give concordant results. The crushing force sustained was therefore much greater than that heretofore given for the same material." *

In the same communication, interesting remarks are made on the *tensile* strength of materials, particularly the metals. "According to the views presented, the difference in the tenacity in steel and lead does not consist in the attractive cohesion of the atoms, but in their capability of slipping upon each other:" that is on the difference of lateral *adhesion* of the molecules, as exemplified in ice and water. A bar of soft metal — as lead — subjected to tensile strain, by reason of the greater freedom of the exterior layers of molecules, exhibits a stretching and thinning; while the interior molecules being more confined by the surrounding pressure, are less mobile, permit less elongation of the mass, and are therefore the first to commence breaking apart. Accordingly on ultimate separation, each fragment exhibits a hollow or cup-like surface of fracture, where the interior portion of the material has first parted: the depth of the concavity being somewhat proportioned to the malleability or ductility of the substance. "With substances of greater rigidity, this effect is less apparent, but it exists even in iron, and the interior fibres of a rod of this metal may be entirely separated, while the outer surface presents no appearance of change. From this it would appear that metals should never be elongated by mere stretching, but in all cases by a process of wire-drawing, or rolling. A wire or bar must always be weakened by a force which permanently increases its length without at the same time compressing it." †

---

* *Proceed. Am. Assoc.* Providence, Aug. 1855, pp. 102-112.

† This conclusion is not at all in opposition to the ascertained fact of the increased strength imparted to an iron rod by "thermo-tension," discovered by Professor WALTER R. JOHNSON, in 1838. (*Journal of Franklin Institute*, Oct. 1839, vol. xxiv. n. s. pp. 232-236.)

*Hydrometric Experiment.*—A novel project for the rectification of spirits by the simple process of static separation of the alcohol and water by the stress of their specific gravities when exposed in long columns, produced in 1854 a considerable sensation. It was alleged in various publications by those interested in the new enterprise, that the coercitive compression exerted by the water in a long hydrostatic column greatly accelerated the displacement and separation induced by gravitation, and that only a few hours were necessary to complete the process, if the depth of the liquid were sufficiently great.*

A patent was obtained: affidavits and samples fully attested the wonderful efficiency of the process; and only the co-operation of confiding capitalists was required, to realize fabulous profits, and effect a manufacturing and commercial revolution.

Simply in the interests of truth, Henry undertook the careful investigation of this surprising pretension. One of the towers of the Smithsonian Building supplied a convenient well for the experiment, easily accessible throughout its height. "A series of stout iron tubes of about an inch and a half internal diameter formed the column; the total length of which was one hundred and six feet. Four stop-cocks were provided; one at the bottom, one about four feet from the top, and the other two to the intermediate space equally divided or nearly so." Very careful hydrometer and thermometer registers were made at increasing intervals of time, the last being that of nearly half a year: a portion of the reserved liquor being simultaneously tested. The result stated, is: "There is not the slightest indication of any difference of density between the original liquor and that from the top or bottom of the column, after the lapse of hours, days, weeks, or months. The fluid at the bottom of the tube it must be remembered was for five months exposed to the pressure of a column of fluid at least one hundred feet high."†

---

* An incidental remark in Gmelin's "Handbook of Chemistry" seemed to give some color of plausibility to the scheme. "Brandy kept in casks is said to contain a greater proportion of spirit in the upper, and of water in the lower part." Gmelin's *Handbook*, Translated by Henry Watts, London, 1841, part i. sect. 4,—vol. i. p. 112.

† *Proceed. Am. Assoc.* Providence, Aug. 1855, pp. 142, 143.

*Sulphuric-acid Barometer.*—In 1856, Henry had constructed for the Smithsonian Institution, at the suggestion of Professor George C. Schaeffer, a large sulphuric-acid barometer, whose column being more than seven times the height of the mercurial column (about $18\frac{1}{2}$ feet) gave correspondingly enlarged and sensitive indications. Water barometers with cisterns protected by oil, (as that constructed by Daniell for the Royal Society,) have always proved instable. With reference to sulphuric acid, "The advantages of this liquid are: 1st that it gives off no appreciable vapor at any atmospheric temperature; and 2nd that it does not absorb or transmit air. The objections to its use are: 1st the liability to accident from the corrosive nature of the liquid, either in the filling of the tube or in its subsequent breakage; and 2nd its affinity for moisture, which tends to produce a change in specific gravity." The latter defect was obviated by a drying apparatus consisting of a tubulated bottle containing chloride of calcium, and connected by a tube with the glass bottle forming the reservoir, which excluded all moisture from the transmitted air. "The glass tube [of the barometer] is two hundred and forty inches long, and three-fourths of an inch in diameter; and is inclosed in a cylindrical brass case of the same length, and two and a half inches in diameter. The glass tube is secured in the axis of the brass case by a number of cork collars, placed at intervals." * This barometer continued in successful and satisfactory use for many years; and had its readings constantly recorded.

Of several of Henry's courses of experiments, no details have been published; and his original notes appear to have perished. In 1861, he made a number of experiments on the effects of burning gunpowder in a vacuum, as well as in different gases.

"A series of researches was also commenced, to determine more accurately than has yet been done, the expansion produced in a bar of iron at the moment of magnetization of the metal by means of a galvanic current. The opportunity was taken with the consent of Professor Bache, of making these experiments with the delicate instruments which had previously been employed in determining

* *Proceed. Am. Assoc.* Albany, Aug. 1856, pp. 135-138.

the varying length, under different temperatures, of the measuring apparatus of the base lines of the United States Coast Survey." * This wonderfully microscopic measuring apparatus — devised by Mr. Joseph Saxton, was capable of distinguishing (by means of the light-ray index of its contact reflector,) a dimension equal to a half wave-length of average light, or the 100,000th part of an inch. The long under-ground vaults of the Smithsonian building having been selected as a suitable place for the precise verification of the residual co-efficient of compensated temperature expansion of the base rods of the Survey, the opportunity was seized by Henry, at the termination of the investigation, to apply the same delicate apparatus to the determination of the polarized or magnetic expansion. The results of these delicate and interesting investigations are lost to the world.

In less than six years from the time of these researches, he was called on to mourn the death of his life-long intimate and honored friend, who had always exhibited so brotherly a sympathy and co-operation with his own varied labors. In consequence of this event — the death of his friend Professor A. Dallas Bache in 1867, Henry was chosen in 1868, to be his successor as President of the National Academy of Sciences. At the request of that body, he prepared a eulogy of his friend the late President, which was read before the Academy April 16th, 1869. In grateful acknowledgment of the wise counsels and valuable services of Dr. Bache as one of the Smithsonian Regents, he observed: "In 1846 he had been named in the act of incorporation as one of the Regents of the Smithsonian Institution, and by successive re-election was continued by Congress in this office until his death, a period of nearly twenty years. To say that he assisted in shaping the policy of the establishment would not be enough. It was almost exclusively through his predominating influence that the policy which has given the Institution its present celebrity, was after much opposition finally adopted. - - - Professor Bache with persistent firmness tempered by his usual moderation, advocated the appropriation of the proceeds of the funds principally to the plan set forth in the first

---

* *Smithsonian Report* for 1861, p. 38.

report of the Secretary, namely of encouraging and supporting original research in the different branches of science. - - - It would be difficult for the Secretary — however unwilling to intrude anything personal on this occasion, to forbear mentioning that it was entirely due to the persuasive influence of Professor Bache, that he was induced — almost against his own better judgment, to leave the quiet pursuit of science and the congenial employment of college instruction, to assume the laborious and responsible duties of the office to which through the partiality of friendship he had been called. Nor would it be possible for him to abstain from acknowledging with heart-felt emotion, that he was from first to last supported and sustained in his difficult position by the fraternal sympathy, the prudent counsel, and the unwavering friendship of the lamented deceased." *

Many minor contributions in various fields of scientific observation, must here be omitted: but it would be inexcusable, in this place and on this occasion, to neglect a reference to the active part he took in the organization and advancement of this Society; † and the unflagging interest ever exhibited in its proceedings, from the date of its convocation, March 13th, 1871, to that of his last illness. All here, remember with what punctuality he attended the meetings — whether of the executive committee or of the society, undeterred by inclemencies of the weather which often kept away many much younger members. All here, recall with what unpretentious readiness he communicated from his rich stores of well-digested facts, observations — whether initiatory or supplementary, on almost every topic presented to our notice; how apt his illustrations and suggestions in our spontaneous discussions; and with what unfailing interest we ever listened to his words of exposition, of knowledge, and of wisdom: utterances which we shall never hear again; and which unwritten and unrecorded, have not been even reported in an abstract.

---

* *Biographical Memoirs, Nat. Acad. Sci.* vol. I. pp. 181-212. Republished in the *Smithsonian Report* for 1870, pp. 91-116. The father of Professor BACHE—Richard Bache, was a son of the only daughter of the illustrious BENJAMIN FRANKLIN.

† The Philosophical Society of Washington.

*Range of information.* — It was not alone in those physical branches of knowledge to which he had made direct original contributions, that the mental activities of Henry were familiarly exercised and conspicuously exhibited. There was scarcely a department of intellectual pursuit in which he did not feel and manifest a sympathetic interest, and in which he did not follow with appreciative grasp its leading generalizations. Holding ever to the unity of Nature as the expression and most direct illustration of the Unity of its Author, he believed that every new fact discovered in any of nature's fields, would ultimately be found to be in intimate correlation with the laws prevailing in other fields — seemingly the most distant.* To his large comprehension, nothing was insignificant, or unworthy of consideration. He ever sought however to look beyond the ascertained and isolated or classified fact, to its antecedent cause; and in opposition to the dogma of Comte, he averred that the knowledge of facts is not *science*, — that these are merely the materials from which its temple is constructed by the generalizations of sagacious and attested speculation.

Among his earlier studies, Chemistry occupied a prominent place. The youthful assistant in the laboratory of his former Instructor and ever honored friend, Dr. T. Romeyn Beck, and later, himself a teacher of the art and knowledge to others, a skillful manipulator, an acute analyst and investigator of re-actions, he seemed at first destined to become a leader in chemical research. Like Newton, he endeavored to bring the atomic combinations under the conception of physical laws; believing this essential to the development of chemistry as a true science. He always kept himself well-informed on the progress of the more recent doctrines of quantivalence, and the newer system of nomenclature.

He had also paid considerable attention to geology; with its relations to palæontology on the one side, and to physical geography on the other.

* "A proper view of the relation of science and art will enable him [the reader] to see that the one is dependent on the other; and that each branch of the study of nature is intimately connected with every other." (*Agricultural Report* for 1857, p. 419.) "The statement cannot be too often repeated, that each branch of knowledge is connected with every other, and that no light can be gained in regard to one, which is not reflected upon all." (*Smithsonian Report* for 1859, p. 15.)

As intimated in touching upon the stimulus given to "archæological work" by the Smithsonian publications, (*ante*, p. 290,) Henry ever displayed a warm sympathy with researches in Anthropology; and he would pleasantly justify this partiality by repeating the familiar "*homo sum*" of Terence." A student of the "comparative anatomy" of ethnology,—of the obscure but cumulative traces of a remote human ancestry,—and of the curious relics of social, civil, and religious customs, apparently derived from distant or from vanished races, he amassed a fund of well-digested information in these alluring fields, to be appreciated only by the specialist in such pursuits.

Familiar with the details—as well of astronomical observation as of the mathematical processes of reduction, he would have done honor to any Observatory placed under his charge. He was lenient in his judgment of the ancient star-worshippers; and was always greatly attracted by astronomical discoveries. As already mentioned (*ante*, p. 239,) he delivered in 1834, a course of Lectures on Astronomy.

Well read in the science of Political Economy, he had by observation and analysis of human nature, made its inductive principles his own, and had satisfied himself that its deductions were fully confirmed by an intelligent appreciation of the teachings of financial history. He attributed the lamentable disregard of its fundamental doctrines, by many of our so-called legislators, to a want of scientific training, and consequent want of perception and of faith in the dominion and autonomy of natural law.

A good linguist, he watched with appreciative interest the progress of comparative philology, and the ethnologic significance of its generalizations, in tracing out the affiliations of European nations. By no means neglectful of lighter literature, he enjoyed at leisure evenings, in the bosom of his cultivated family, the readings of modern writers, and the suggestive interchange of sentiment and criticism. Striking passages of poetry made a strong impression on his retentive memory; and it was not unusual to hear him embellish some graver fact, in conversation, with an unexpected but most apt quotation. With a fine æsthetic feeling, his appreciation and judgment of works of art, were delicate and discriminating.

Among the subjects to which he had given a close and critical attention, was the attractive field of Architecture, both in its historical development as a Fine-art—symbolizing devotional sentiment, and in its later manifestations as the application of antique and eclectic forms of ornamentation to utilitarian structures. His very admiration of ancient classic and gothic art, made him intolerant of the servile reproduction of Temple and Cathedral styles for purposes and uses to which they were wholly unsuited.* And he was severe in his criticisms on the too frequent practice of wasting a large portion of the funds bequeathed to scientific, educational, or charitable purposes, on showy and pretentious piles, (the inspiration and the monument of an ambitious architect,) to the permanent spoliation and restriction of the endowment intended for intellectual and moral ends.

*The Reign of Law.*—Henry held very broad and decided views as to the reign of order in the Cosmos. Defining science as the "knowledge of natural law," and law, as the "will of God," he was always accustomed to regard that orderly sequence called the "law," as being fixed and immutable as the omniscient providence of its Divine Author: admitting in no case caprice or variableness: and he would quote with expressive emphasis, Halley's classic lines,

——"Quas dum primordia rerum
Pangeret Omniparens leges violare Creator
Noluit, æternique operis fundamina fixit."

---

* "The Greek architect was untrammelled by any condition of utility. Architecture was with him in reality a *fine-art*. The temple was formed to gratify the tutelar deity. Its minutest parts were exquisitely finished, since nothing but perfection on all sides and in the smallest particulars, could satisfy an all-seeing and critical eye. It was intended for external worship, and not for internal use. - - - The uses therefore to which in modern times, buildings of this kind can be applied, are exceedingly few. - - - *Modern* architecture is not like painting or sculpture, a 'fine-art' *par excellence:* the object of these latter is to produce a moral emotion, to awaken the feelings of the sublime and the beautiful: and we egregiously err when we apply these productions to a merely utilitarian purpose. To make a fire-screen of Rubens' Madonna, or a candelabrum of the statue of the Apollo Belvidere, would be to debase these exquisite productions of genius, and do violence to the feelings of the cultivated lover of art. Modern buildings are made for other purposes than artistic effect, and in them the æsthetical must be subordinate to the useful; though the two may co-exist, and an intellectual pleasure be derived from a sense of adaptation and fitness, combined with a perception of harmony of parts, and the beauty of detail. The buildings of a country and an age should be an ethnological expression of the wants, habits, arts, and sentiments of the time in which they were erected." (*Proceed. Am. Assoc.* at Albany, Aug. 1856, part 1, pp. 120, 121, and *Smithsonian Report* for 1856, p. 222.)

The doctrine of the absolute dominion of law—so oppressive and alarming to many excellent minds, was to him accordingly but a necessary deduction from his theologic and religious faith.

The series of meteorological essays already referred to as contributed to the Agricultural Reports of the Commissioner of Patents, (ante, p. 290,) commences with this striking passage: "All the changes on the surface of the earth and all the movements of the heavenly bodies, are the immediate results of natural forces acting in accordance with established and invariable laws; and it is only by that precise knowledge of these laws, which is properly denominated science, that man is enabled to defend himself against the adverse operations of Nature, or to direct her innate powers in accordance with his will. At first sight, it might appear that meteorology was an exception to this general proposition, and that the changes of the weather and the peculiarities of climate in different portions of the earth's surface, were of all things the most uncertain and farthest removed from the dominion of law: but scientific investigation establishes the fact that no phenomenon is the result of accident, or even of fitful volition. The modern science of statistics has revealed a permanency and an order in the occurrence of events depending on conditions in which nothing of this kind could have been supposed. Even those occurrences which seem to be left to the free will, the passion, or the greater or less intelligence of men, are under the control of laws—fixed, immutable, and eternal." And after dwelling on the developments and significance of moral statistics, he adds: "The astonishing facts of this class lead us inevitably to the conclusion that all events are governed by a Supreme Intelligence who knows no change; and that under the same conditions, the same results are invariably produced." *

*Organic Dynamics.*—The contemplation of these uniformities leads naturally to the great modern generalization of the correlation of all the working energies of nature: and this to the subject of organic dynamics. "Modern science has established by a wide and careful induction, the fact that plants and animals consist princi-

---

* *Agricultural Report Com. Pat.* for 1855, pp. 357, 358.

pally of solidified air; the only portions of an earthy character which enter into their composition, being the ashes that remain after combustion." Some ten years before this, or in 1844, (as already noticed in an earlier part of this memoir,—*ante*, p. 273,) Henry had very clearly indicated the correlation between the forces exhibited by inorganic and organic bodies: arguing that from the chemical researches of Liebig, Dumas, and Boussingault, "it would appear to follow that animal power is referable to the same sources as that from the combustion of fuel:" * probably the earliest explicit announcement of the now accepted view. In the series of agricultural essays above referred to, he endeavored to frame more definitely a chemico-physical theory by which the elevation of matter to an organic combination in a higher state of power than its source, might be accounted for. Regarding "vitality" not as a mechanical force, but as an inscrutable *directing* principle resident in the minute germ — supposed to be vegetative, and inclosed in a sac of starch or other organic nutriment, he considered the case of such provisioned germ (a bean or a potato for instance) embedded in the soil, supplied with a suitable amount of warmth and moisture to give the necessary molecular mobility, soon sending a rootlet downward into the earth, and raising a stem toward the surface, furnished with incipient leaves. Supposing the planted germ to be a potato, on examination we should find its large supply of starch exhausted, and beyond the young plant, nothing remaining but the skin, containing probably a little water. What has become of the starch? "If we examine the soil which surrounded the potato, we do not find that the starch has been absorbed by it; and the answer which will therefore naturally be suggested, is that it has been transformed into the material of the new plant, and it was for this purpose originally stored away. But this though in part correct, is not the whole truth: for if we weigh a potato prior to germination, and weigh the young plant afterward, we shall find that the amount

---

* *Proceed. Am. Phil. Soc.* Dec. 1844, vol. iv. p. 129. The admirable treatise of Dr. JULIUS R. MAYER of Heilbronn, on "Organic Movement in its relation to material changes," in which for the first time he maintained the thesis that all the energies developed by animal or vegetable organisms, result from internal changes having their dynamic source in external forces, was published the following year, or in 1845. RUMFORD nearly half a century earlier, had a partial grasp of the same truth. (*Phil. Trans. R. S.* Jan. 25, 1798, vol. lxxxviii. pp. 80–102.)

of organic matter contained in the latter, is but a fraction of that which was originally contained in the former. We can account in this way for the disappearance of a *part* of the contents of the sac, which has evidently formed the pabulum of the young plant. But here we may stop to ask another question: By what power was the young plant built up of the molecules of starch? The answer would probably be, by the exertion of the vital force: but we have endeavored to show that vitality is a *directing principle*, and not a mechanical power, the expenditure of which does work. The conclusion to which we would arrive will probably now be anticipated. The portion of the organic molecules of the starch, &c. of the tuber, as yet unaccounted for, has run down into inorganic matter, or has entered again into combination with the oxygen of the air, and in this running down and union with oxygen, has evolved the power necessary to the organization of the new plant. - - - We see from this view that the starch and nitrogenous materials in which the germs of plants are imbedded, have two functions to fulfill, the one to supply the pabulum of the new plant, and the other to furnish the power by which the transformation is effected, the latter being as essential as the former. In the erection of a house, the application of mechanical power is required as much as a supply of ponderable materials." *

The less difficult problem of the building up of the plant after the consumption of the seed, under the direct action of the solar rays, is then considered; the leaves of the young plant absorbing by their moisture carbonic acid from the atmosphere, which being decomposed by solar actinism, yields the de-oxidized carbon to enter

---

* *Agricultural Report,* for 1857, pp. 410–444. In May, 1842, Dr. JULIUS R. MAYER published in Liebig's *Annalen der Chemie* etc. his first remarkable paper on "The Forces of Inorganic Nature," constituting the earliest scientific enunciation of the correlation of the physical forces; and (if we except the work of SEGUIN in 1839,) of the mechanical equivalent of heat. (*Annalen u.s.w.* vol. xlii. pp. 233–240.) In September, 1849, Dr. R. FOWLER read a short paper before the British Association at Birmingham, on "Vitality as a Force correlated with the Physical Forces." (*Report Brit. Assoc.* 1849, part ii. pp. 77, 78.) In June, 1850, Dr. W. B. CARPENTER presented to the Royal Society a much fuller memoir "On the Mutual Relations of the Vital and Physical Forces." (*Phil. Trans. R. S.* vol. cxl. pp. 727–757.) Neither of these essays accounts for the amount of building energy displayed in the development of the seed, under conditions of low and diffused heat: and the expression "Vital Force" used both by FOWLER and CARPENTER, was studiously avoided by HENRY.

22

into the structure of the organism. "All the material of which a tree is built up, (with the exception of that comparatively small portion which remains after it has been burnt, and constitutes the ash,) is derived from the atmosphere. In the decomposition of the carbonic acid by the chemical ray, a definite amount of power is expended, and this remains as it were locked up in the plant so long as it continues to grow." And thus under the expenditure of an external force, the plant (whether the annual cellular herb or the perennial fibrous tree) was shown to be built up from the simpler stable binary compounds of the inorganic world to the more complex and unstable ternary compounds of the vegetable world. " In the *germination* of the plant, a part of the organized molecules runs down into carbonic acid to furnish power for the new arrangement of the other portion. In this process no extraneous force is required: the seed contains within itself the power, and the material, for the growth of the new plant up to a certain stage of its development. Germination can therefore be carried on in the dark, and indeed the chemical ray which accompanies light retards rather than accelerates the process." This important organic principle appears to receive in these passages its earliest enunciation.

It was also pointed out that on the completion of the cycle of growth (however brief or however extended), the decay of the plant not only returns the elevated matter to its original lower plane, but equally returns the entire amount of heat energy absorbed in its elevation: an amount precisely the same, whether the slow oxidation be continued through a series of years, or a rapid combustion be completed in as many minutes. "The power which is given out in the whole descent is according to the dynamic theory, just equivalent to the power expended by the impulse from the sun in elevating the atoms to the unstable condition of the organic molecules. If this power is given out in the form of vibrations of the ætherial medium constituting heat, it will not be appreciable in the ordinary decay say of a tree, extending as it may through several years: but if the process be rapid, as in case of combustion of wood, then the same amount of power will be given out in the energetic form of heat of high intensity."

The elevation of inorganic matter (carbonic acid, water, and ammonia,) to the vegetable plane of power, introduces naturally the consideration of the still higher elevation of vegetable organic matter to the animal plane of power. "As in the case of the seed of the plant, we presume that the germ of the future animal pre-exists in the egg; and that by subjecting the mass to a degree of temperature sufficient perhaps to give greater mobility to the molecules, a process similar in its general effect to that of the germination of the seeds commences. - - - During this process, power is evolved within the shell, we cannot say in the present state of science under what particular form; but we are irresistibly constrained to believe that it is expended under the direction again of the vital principle, in re-arranging the organic molecules, in building up the complex machinery of the future animal, or developing a still higher organization, connected with which are the mysterious manifestations of thought and volition. In this case as in that of the potato, the young animal as it escapes from the shell, weighs less than the material of the egg previous to the process of incubation. The lost material in this case as in the other, has run down into an inorganic condition by combining with oxygen, and in its descent has developed the power to effect the transformation we have just described." The consumption of internal power does not however stop with the development of the young animal, as it does in the case of the young plant. "The young animal is in an entirely different condition: exposure to the light of the sun is not necessary to its growth or its existence: the chemical ray by impinging on the surface of its body does not decompose the carbonic acid which may surround it, the conditions necessary for this decomposition, not being present. It has no means by itself to elaborate organic molecules; and is indebted for these entirely to its food. It is necessary therefore that it should be supplied with food consisting of organized materials; that is of complex molecules in a state of power. - - - The power of the living animal is immediately derived from the running down of the complex organized molecules of which the body is formed, into their ultimate combination with oxygen, in the form of carbonic acid and water, and into ammonia. Hence oxygen is constantly drawn into the lungs, and carbon is constantly evolved.  -  -  -  The animal is a curiously contrived arrangement for burning carbon and hydrogen, and for the evolution and application of power.  A machine is an instrument for the application of power, and not for its creation.  The animal body is a structure of this character.  -  -  -  A comparison has been made between the work which can be done by burning a given amount of carbon in the machine — man, and an equal amount in the machine — steam-engine.  The result derived from an analysis of the food in one case, and the weight of the fuel in the other, and these compared with the quantity of water raised by each to a known elevation, gives the relative working value of the two machines.  From this comparison, made from experiments on soldiers in Germany and France, it is found that the human machine in consuming the same amount of carbon, does four and a half times the amount of work of the best Cornish engine.  -  -  -

"There is however one striking difference between the animal body and the locomotive machine, which deserves our special attention; namely the power in the body is constantly evolved by burning (as it were,) parts of the materials of the machine itself; as if the frame and other portions of the wood-work of the locomotive were burnt to produce the power, and then immediately renewed. The voluntary motion of our organs of speech, of our hands, of our feet, and of every muscle in the body, is produced not at the expense of the soul but at that of the material of the body itself. Every motion manifesting life in the individual, is the result of power derived from the death as it were of a part of his body. We are thus constantly renewed and constantly consumed; and in this consumption and renewal consists animal life." *

Seven years after the publication of this highly original and suggestive exposition, (whose topics and line of discussion had been

* *Agricultural Report* for 1857, pp. 415–449. This important essay it will be observed, antedates Prof. JOSEPH LE CONTE's paper "On the Correlation of Physical, Chemical, and **Vital Force**," read before the American Association at Springfield, Aug. 1859, (*Proceed. Am. Assoc.* pp. 187–203: and Sill. *Am. Jour. Sci.* Nov. 1859, vol. xxviii. pp. 305–319,) as well as Dr. CARPENTER's second and more mature paper "On the application of the Principle of Conservation of Force to Physiology," published in Crookes' *Quarterly Journal of Science,* for Jan. and April, 1864, (vol. i. pp. 76–87; and pp. 259–267.)

distinctly formulated and sketched out more than two years before, at the commencement of the series in 1855,) the eminent physiologist Dr. Carpenter produced his valuable memoir on the Conservation of Force in Physiology; in which for the first time he distinctly affirms the development of vegetative reproductive energy, by the partial running down of matter to its stabler compounds,— "by the retrograde metamorphosis of a portion of the organic compounds prepared by the previous nutritive operations:" and also the ultimate return by decay, of the whole amount of force as well as of matter, temporarily borrowed from nature's store. Likewise with animal powers, "these forces are developed by the retrograde metamorphosis of the organic compounds generated by the instrumentality of the plant, whereby they ultimately return to the simple binary forms (water, carbonic acid, and ammonia,) which serve as the essential food of vegetables. - - - Whilst the vegetable is constantly engaged (so to speak) in raising its component materials from a lower plane to the higher, by means of the power which it draws from the solar rays,—the animal whilst raising one portion of these to a still higher level by the descent of another portion to a lower, ultimately lets down the whole of what the plant had raised." * So little was Henry's earlier paper known abroad, that his name does not occur in Dr. Carpenter's dissertation.

*Derivation of Species.*— With regard to the great biologic question of the past fifteen years—the affiliation of specific forms, it was impossible that Henry should remain an unconcerned observer. Brought up (as it may be said) in the school of Cuvier, but slightly impressed with the brilliant previsions of his competitor, Geoffroy Saint Hilaire, accustomed to look upon the recurrent hypotheses of automatic development as barren speculations, and beside all this, ever the warmly attached personal friend of Agassiz, he approached the consideration of this controverted subject, certainly with no antecedent affirmative pre-possessions. His general acquaintance with the ascertained facts of the metamorphic development of the individual organism from its origin, as well as with the remarkable analogies and homologies disclosed by the sciences of comparative

* *Quart. Jour. Sci.* 1864, vol. I. pp. 87 and 267.

physiology and embryology, served however in some measure to prepare his mind to apprehend the significance of the indications which had been so industriously collected, and so intelligently collated: and from the very first, he accepted the problem as a purely philosophical one; employing that much abused term in no restricted sense.   With no more reserve in the expression of his views, than the avoidance of unprofitable controversies, (though no one more than he — enjoyed the calm and purely intellectual discussion of an unsettled question by its real *experts*,) he yet found no occasion to write upon the subject.   The unpublished opinions however, of one so wise and eminent, cannot be a matter of indifference to the student of nature; and their exposition cannot but assist to enlighten our estimate of the mental stature of the man, and of his breadth of apprehension and toleration.

Whatever may be the ultimate fate of the theory of natural selection, (he remarked in the freedom of oral intercourse with several naturalists,) it at least marks an epoch, — the first elevation of natural history (so-called) to the really scientific stage: it is based on induction, and correlates a large range of apparently disconnected observations, gathered from the regions of palæontology or geological successions of organisms, their geographical distribution, climatic adaptations and remarkable re-adjustments, their comparative anatomy, and even the occurrence of abnormal variations, and of rudimentary structures — seemingly so uselessly displayed as mere simulations of a "type."   It forms a good "working hypothesis" for directing the investigations of the botanist and zoologist. *   Natural selection indeed — no less than artificial, (he was accustomed to say,) is to a limited extent a fact of observation; and the practical question is to determine approximately its reach of application, and its sufficiency as an actual agency, to embrace larger series of organic changes lying beyond the scope of direct human experience.   It is for the rising generation of conscientious zoologists and botanists to attack this problem, and to ascertain if practicable its limitations or modifications.

* "In the investigation of nature, we provisionally adopt hypotheses as antecedent probabilities, which we seek to prove or disprove by subsequent observation and experiment; and it is in this way that science is most rapidly and securely advanced." (*Agricult. Report*, 1876, p. 456.)

These broad and fearless views, entertained and expressed as early as 1860, or 1861, exhibiting neither the zealous confidence of the votary, nor the jealous anxiety of the antagonist, received scarcely any modification during his subsequent years. Nor did it ever seem to occur to him that any reconstruction of his religious faith was involved in the solution of the problem. So much religious faith indeed was exercised by him in every scientific judgment, that he regarded the teachings of science but as revelations of the Divine mode of government in the natural world: to be diligently sought for and submissively accepted; with the constant recognition however of our human limitations, and the relativity of human knowledge.* Not inappropriately may be here recalled a characteristic statement of the office of hypothesis, made by him some ten years earlier: presenting a consideration well calculated to restrain dogmatism — whether in science or in theology. "It is not necessary that an hypothesis be absolutely true, in order that it may be adopted as an expression of a generalization for the purpose of explaining and predicting phenomena: it is only necessary that it should be well conditioned in accordance with known mechanical principles. - - - Man with his finite faculties cannot hope in this life to arrive at a knowledge of absolute truth: and were the true theory of the universe, or in other words the precise mode in which Divine Wisdom operates in producing the phenomena of the material world revealed to him, his mind would be unfitted for its reception. It would be too simple in its expression, and too general in its application, to be understood and applied by intellects like ours." †

## INVESTIGATIONS IN ACOUSTICS.

During the last quarter of a century, among the many interests which demanded and engaged his attention, Henry studied with

---

* With reference to the intimations of the comparative antiquity of man, HENRY quoted with sympathetic approbation the sentiment so well expressed by the Bishop of London in a Lecture at Edinburgh, that "The man of science should go on honestly, patiently, diffidently, observing and storing up his observations, and carrying his reasonings unflinchingly to their legitimate conclusions, convinced that it would be treason to the majesty at once of science and of religion, if he sought to help either by swerving ever so little from the straight line of truth." (*Smithsonian Report* for 1868, p. 33.)

† *Proceed. Am. Assoc.* Albany, Aug. 1851, pp. 85, 86, and 87.

much care various phenomena of acoustics, and added much to our practical as well as theoretical knowledge of that important agency —sound.   In 1851, he read a communication before the American Association, "On the Limit of Perceptibility of a direct and reflected Sound," in which he gave as the result of experimental observations, the subjective fact that a wall or other reflecting surface if beyond the distance of about 35 feet from the ear, or from the origin of the sound, gives a distinguishable echo from the sound; but that if the ear or the sounding agent be placed within this distance, the reflected sound appears to blend completely with the original one.   From a number of experiments, he found that under the same circumstances, this limit of perceptibility did not vary more than a single foot; but that under differing conditions the limit of distance ranged from 30 to 40 feet, (equivalent to a difference of from 60 to 80 feet of sound travel,) depending partly on the sharpness or clearness of the sound, and partly on the pitch or the length of the soniferous wave, which affected the amount of overlapping of the two series.   These results imply a duration of acoustic impression on the ear of about one-sixteenth of a second; serving to show that 16 vibrations to the second must be about the lower limit of a recognizable musical tone. *   As applied to Lecture-rooms, he pointed out that the ceiling should not be more than about thirty feet high, within which elevation, a smooth ceiling would tend to re-inforce the sound of a speaker's voice. †

Many experiments were afterward made on the resonance of different materials, by means of tuning forks.   While a tuning fork suspended by a fine thread continued to vibrate for upward of four minutes with scarcely any appreciable sound, if placed in contact with the top of a pine table, the same vibration continued but ten seconds, but gave a loud full tone.   On a marble topped table the sound was much more feeble, and the vibration continued nearly two minutes.   While the tuning fork against a brick wall gave a

---

* FELIX SAVART some twenty years previously, concluded from observations with the siren, "that sounds are distinctly perceptible, and even strong, when composed of no more than eight vibrations in a second." (*Rev. Encycl.* July, 1832. Quoted in Silliman's *Am. Jour. Sci.* for 1832, vol. xxii. p. 374.) This does not seem to agree with ordinary observations, as it is certain that intervals of one-eighth of a second would give a very appreciable rattle to almost every ear.

† *Proceed. Am. Assoc.* Cincinnati, May, 1851, pp. 42, 43.

feeble tone continuing for 88 seconds, against a lath and plaster partition it gave a sound considerably louder but continuing only 18 seconds. On a large block of soft india-rubber resting on the marble slab, the vibration was very rapidly extinguished, but without giving any sensible sound. This anomaly required an explanation. By means of a compound wire of copper and iron inserted into the piece of rubber, and having the extremities connected with a thermo-galvanometer, it was found that in this case the acoustic vibrations were converted into heat. Sheets of india-rubber therefore are among the best absorbers and destroyers of sound. A series of experiments was also made on the reflection of sound, to determine the materials least adapted, and those best adapted to this purpose. A *résumé* of these researches, having reference to the acoustic properties of public halls, was read before the American Association in August, 1856.*

In 1865, as Chairman of the Committee of Experiments of the U. S. Light-House Board, Henry commenced an extended series of observations on the conduct and intensity of sound at a distance, under varying meteorological conditions. Well aware that for the practical purposes of giving increased security to navigation, the experiments of the laboratory were of little value, he undertook a number of experimental trips on board sailing vessels, and on steamers, in order to make his observations under the actual conditions of the required service. As many of his investigations demanded intelligent co-operation, and sometimes at the distances of many miles, he associated with him at different times, among members of the Light-House Establishment, Commodore Powell, Commodore Case, Admiral Trenchard, Commander Walker, Captain Upshur, General Poe, General Barnard, General Woodruff, Mr. Lederle, and other engineers of different Light-House Districts, and outside of the establishment, Dr. Welling and others.

At the outset of his experiments, he found that sound reflectors, which play so interesting a part in lecture-room exhibitions, were practically worthless (of whatever available dimensions) for the purpose of directing or concentrating powerful sounds to any con-

* *Proceed. Am. Assoc.* Albany, Aug. 1856, pp. 128–131.

siderable distance.    At the distance of a mile or two a large steam
whistle placed in the focus of a concave reflector 10 feet in diameter
could be heard very nearly as well directly behind the reflector, as
directly in front of it.    In like manner the direction of bell-
mouths and of trumpet-mouths, was found to be of comparatively
little importance at a distance; showing the remarkable tendency
to diffusion, especially with very loud sounds.    Most of the observations made on ship-board were afterward repeated on land; and
several weeks were occupied with these important researches.

"During this series of investigations an interesting fact was discovered, namely, a sound moving against the wind, inaudible to the
ear on the deck of the schooner, was heard by ascending to the
mast-head.    This remarkable fact at first suggested the idea that
sound was more readily conveyed by the upper current of air than
the lower."    After citing observations by others apparently confirming the suggestion of some dominant influence in the upper
wind, Henry adds: "The full significance however of this idea did
not reveal itself to me until in searching the bibliography of
sound, I found an account of the hypothesis of Professor Stokes in
the Proceedings of the British Association for 1857,* in which the
effect of an upper current in deflecting the wave of sound so as to
throw it down upon the ear of the auditor, or directing it upward
far above his head, is fully explained."†    A rough attempt was
made in the course of these observations (which were undertaken
at the Light-house near New Haven, Connecticut) to compare the
velocity of the wind in the upper regions with that near the surface
of the earth.    "The only important result however was the fact
that the velocity of the shadow of a cloud passing over the ground
was much greater than that of the air at the surface, the velocity
of the latter being determined approximately by running a given
distance with such speed that a small flag was at rest along the side
of its pole.    While this velocity was not perhaps greater than six
miles per hour, that of the shadow of the cloud was apparently
equal to that of a horse at full speed."‡

* *Report Brit. Assoc.* Dublin, 1857, vol. xxvii. 2d part, pp. 22, 23.
† *Report of Light-House Board* for 1874, p. 92.
‡ This difference has since been established by a number of independent
observations.  Mr. Glaisher from his balloon ascents in 1863–1865, ascertained that

In October, 1867, a series of observations was made at Sandy Hook (New Jersey) with various instruments. A sound reflector being employed, the distance at which the sand on the phonometer drum —carried in front, ceased to move was 51 yards, as compared with a distance of 40 yards, without the reflector. At a greater distance, with a more sensitive instrument, the ratio was very much diminished. Experiments were also made on the relative distances at which the trumpet affected sensibly the drum of the phonometer in different directions, giving as their result a limiting spheroid whose reach in the forward axis of the trumpet was about double that in the rear axis, and at right angles to the axis, was about a mean proportional between the two. With greater distances, these differences were evidently very much reduced, the radii becoming more equalized. In the summer of 1871, Henry made investigations at different Light-stations, on our western coast of California.

The very important observation that a sound could best be heard at an elevation when the wind is adverse (that is when it blows from the observer towards the acoustic signal,) and that after it had even been entirely lost to the ear in such case, it might be regained in full force by simply ascending to a suitable elevation,—admitted apparently but one explanation, namely that the line of successive impulse constituting a sound-beam was deflected or bent upwards by the action of the opposing wind. If—as had already been shown to be the case sometimes, and as might therefore be expected generally,—the adverse wind were assumed to be a little stronger at the elevation than at the surface, such a result would at once follow. "The explanation of this phenomenon as suggested by the hypothesis of Professor Stokes is founded on the fact that in the case of a deep current of air the lower stratum or that next the earth is more retarded by friction than the one immediately above,

the upper currents of air are frequently five or six times more rapid than the surface currents. (*Travels in the Air*, p. 9.) Prof. Cleveland Abbe remarks: "From seven balloon ascensions made on July 4th, 1871, at different points in the United States, I have deduced the velocity of the upper currents as about four times that of the surface wind prevailing." (*Bulletin Philosoph. Soc. Washington*, Dec. 16, 1871, vol. i. p. 39.) And M. Peslin states in general terms: "It is certain according to all observations made both in mountains and in balloons, that the force of the wind increases considerably as we ascend in the atmosphere." (*Bulletin International de l'Observ. de Paris et de l'Observ. Phys. Cent. Montsouris*, July 7, 1872.)

and this again than the one above it, and so on. The effect of this diminution of velocity as we descend toward the earth is in the case of sound moving with the current, to carry the upper part of the sound waves more rapidly forward than the lower parts, thus causing them to incline toward the earth, or in other words, to be thrown down upon the ear of the observer. When the sound is in a contrary direction to the current, an opposite effect is produced, the upper portion of the sound-waves is more retarded than the lower, which advancing more rapidly in consequence, inclines the waves upward and directs them above the head of the observer." *

From several observed and reported cases where the sound of a fog-signal was exceptionally heard to a greater distance against the wind than toward the direction of the wind, Professor Henry for a while hesitated to give the hypothesis of Professor Stokes an unqualified acceptance; but forced as he was constantly to recur to it as the only plausible explanation of the ordinary influence of wind on the transmission of sound, he finally was able to satisfy himself that even the apparent exceptions to the rule were really in accord with it. Having more than once observed that when the upper current of air, as indicated by the course of the clouds, is in an opposite or different direction from the lower or sensible wind, the range of audibility is more affected and favored by the upper current, it was a natural induction to extend such a condition in imagination to other cases of abnormal behavior of sound. A large amount of subsequent labor and attention was devoted to the determination of this important question.

In 1872 it was observed from on board a steamer approaching Portland Head station in the harbor of Portland (Maine) that the fog-signal which had been distinctly heard through many miles, was lost to the ear when within two or three miles of the point, that it continued inaudible throughout the nearer distance of a mile or so, and that it was again heard as the station was neared. At Whitehead light station on a small rocky island about a mile and a half from the coast, (being some 65 miles northeast of Portland Head,) it was observed on board a steamer approaching the station during a thick fog, that the signal (a 10-inch steam whistle) though

---

* *Report of Light-House Board* for 1874, p. 106.

distinctly heard at the distance of six miles or more, and with increasing distinctness as the steamer advanced, was suddenly lost at about three miles, and was not recovered until within a quarter of a mile from the station; the wind at the time being approximately adverse to the sound. A six-inch steam whistle on board the steamer was meanwhile distinctly heard at the station during the whole time of inaudibility of the larger ten-inch whistle, which had also been sounded without any interruption. This remarkable phenomenon implied a compound flexure of the sound-beams, and accorded with previous observations made at the same points by General Duane the engineer in charge of the first and second Light-House Districts.

In 1873 observations were again made at Whitehead station, and at Cape Elizabeth light station, both on the coast of Massachusetts. At Whitehead the steam whistle was heard through a distance of 15 miles, with a light adverse wind. At Cape Elizabeth, with a stronger adverse wind, the siren was heard only about nine miles.

In 1874, observations were made at Little Gull island, (off the coast of Connecticut;) at Block island, (off the coast of Rhode Island;) and at Sandy Hook, (New Jersey.) At Little Gull island the sound of a siren was heard against a moderate wind, only three and a half miles. At Block island the siren was reported to have been heard under favoring conditions of wind through a distance of more than 25 miles. While it was frequently heard at Point Judith station, and the siren at the latter point was as frequently heard at Block Island, (the distance between the two points being 17 miles,) it was shown on comparison of records, that the two instruments had not been heard simultaneously; the wind when favorable to the one being unfavorable to the other.

At Sandy Hook, for the purpose of making simultaneous observations in different directions, three steamers (the tenders of different light-houses) were employed, with steam whistles specially adjusted to the same tone and power. The latter quality having been carefully tested by the phonometer, the three vessels steamed out abreast on trial; and their whistles sounding in regular succession "became inaudible all very nearly at the same moment." One of the vessels being then anchored at a distance from land, the two others were directed in opposite courses, one with the wind, or eastward, the other against it, or westward. In 15 minutes the whistle of the former ceased to be heard, while that of the latter was very distinctly heard; the anemometer showing a wind of about six miles per hour. About noon the vessels changed positions, but the sound from the west continued audible for about three times the distance of that from the east, though the wind had declined to nearly a calm or to about half a mile per hour. In an hour and a half the wind had changed to "within two points of an exactly opposite direction, blowing from the indications of the anemometer at the rate of ten and a half miles per hour." The vessels once more departing, one with the wind, the other against it, the sound of the whistle coming against the wind was this time heard for the greater distance, contrary to expectation. On the following day a number of small balloons having been provided, a similar series of experiments to that of the preceding day was made; a station being selected at a greater distance from land. On the first trial, with a light wind from the west of about one and a quarter miles per hour as indicated by the anemometer, a balloon was set off which continued rising and moving eastward till lost to sight. Two of the vessels taking opposite courses as before, gave the sound in the direction of the wind about double the duration of that coming against the slight wind. The vessels then changed places in their opposite courses; the wind having subsided to a calm. "A balloon let off ascended vertically until it attained an elevation of about 1,000 feet, when turning east it followed the direction of the previous one. In this case the sound of the whistle coming from the east was heard somewhat longer than the opposite one. At the third trial made after noon, the wind had changed nearly one-third of the circle, its force being about five miles per hour. The vessels once more taking their courses with the wind and against it, "several balloons set off at this time were carried by the surface wind westwardly until nearly lost to sight, when they were observed to turn east, following the direction of the wind traced in the earlier observations." In this case the sound was heard with the wind very slightly farther than against it. It was thus shown that the upper current of wind had remained constant throughout the day, while the changing surface wind was apparently a land and sea breeze "due to the heating of the land as the day advanced:" and the varying behavior of the sound-beams was easily explained by the varying differences of velocity in their wave fronts at different heights.

In 1875 Henry continued his observations at Block island, (R. I.) and at Little Gull island: (Conn.) The southern light-house on Block island standing on the edge of a perpendicular cliff 152 feet above the sea level, and being itself 52 feet high (to its focal plane) this point was selected for making investigations on the effect of altitude in modifying unfavorable conditions of audibility. Observers were accordingly stationed on the beach at the foot of the cliff, and also on the tower 200 feet above, to record simultaneously the duration of the whistle signals of two steamers proceeding in opposite directions toward the right and the left. The sound coming against the wind (of about seven miles per hour) continued audible at the upper station four times longer, (i. e. for four times greater distance) than at the lower station. The sound coming with the wind, was unexpectedly heard at the lower station for a longer period than at the upper one. Another observation (with the wind about five miles per hour) gave for the sound against the wind, rather more than twice the distance of audibility at the upper station; and for the sound favored by the wind, a slightly greater distance at the top than at the bottom station. The next observation gave as before, with the adverse wind, the advantage of more than double the distance of audibility to the upper station; meanwhile one of the observers at the foot of the cliff, after the sound was entirely lost, managed by climbing to a ledge about 30 feet above the beach, to recover the signal quite distinctly, and to hear it for some time. The sound coming with the wind continued to be heard at both the higher and the lower stations for precisely the same time, giving on this occasion no advantage to either. Observations made on board the two steamers while moving in opposite directions, gave for the sound travelling with the wind, a duration and distance more than five times that for the sound which came against the wind. Five similar experiments gave very similar results. The two vessels moving in opposite courses, each at right angles to the direction of the wind, gave a very close equality for the reciprocal durations of the sound. In the following month, similar observations were made at Little Gull island, which were very accordant with those made at the former station. As a result of plotting the ranges of audibility in different directions from a given point, producing a series of circular figures (more or less distorted) of very different sizes, Henry was inclined to believe that the whole area of audition is less in high winds than in gentle winds. These investigations as their author well remarks,— "though simple in their conception, have been difficult and laborious in their execution. To be of the greatest practical value they were required to be made on the ocean under the conditions in which the results are to be applied to the use of the mariner, and therefore they could only be conducted by means of steam vessels of sufficient power to withstand the force of rough seas, and at times when these vessels could be spared from other duty. They also required a number of intelligent assistants skilled in observation and faithful in recording results." *

In the summer of last year, 1877, with undiminished ardor, he continued his observations on sound; selecting this time Portland harbor, Monhegan island, and Whitehead light station, on the coast of Maine. At the latter station, the abnormal phenomenon of a region of inaudibility near the fog-signal, and extending outward for two or three miles, (beyond which distance the signal is again very distinctly heard,) had for several years been frequently observed. This singular effect is noticed only in the case of a southerly wind when the vessel is approaching the signal from the same quarter, and consequently with the wind adverse to the direction of the sound-beams, a condition of the wind which is the usual accompaniment of a fog. The observation showed this intermediate "belt of silence" to be well marked on board the steamer both on approaching the station and on receding from it by retracing the same line of travel. Meanwhile the intermittent signal whistle from the steamer was distinctly heard at the station on both the outward and homeward trips of the vessel, throughout its course. The next set of observations was made on the opposite

---

* Report of the Light-House Board for 1875, p. 107.

side of the small island, by directing the course of the steamer northward; and in this case the shore signal was distinctly heard throughout the trip, while the signal from the vessel passed through the "belt of silence" to the observers at the station. The hypothesis of a local sound shadow of definite extent, is excluded by the simple fact that the regions traversed were entirely unobstructed, the two points of observation — movable and stationary — being constantly in view from each other when not obscured by fog. The hypothesis of a stationary belt of acoustic opacity is equally excluded by the uninterrupted transmission of sound through the critical region in one direction; and this too whichever order of observation be selected. So that in one of the cases the powerful whistle ten inches in diameter blown by a steam pressure of 60 pounds, failed utterly to make itself heard, while the sound from a much feebler whistle only six inches in diameter and blown by a steam pressure of 25 pounds, traversed with ease and fulness the very same space. The only hypothesis left therefore is that of diacoustic refraction; by which the sound-beam from one origin is bent and lifted over the observer, while from an opposite origin the refraction is in a reversed direction; and such a quality in the moving air is referable to no other observed condition but that of its motion, that is to the influence of the wind. Observations were afterward made at Monhegan island, on some of the more normal effects of the refraction of sound by differences of wave velocity, all fully confirming the supposition which had been so variously and critically subjected to examination.

The principal conclusions summed up in the last Report for 1877, are: 1st. The audibility of sound at a distance depends primarily upon the pitch, the intensity, and the quantity of the sound: the most efficient pitch being neither a very high nor a very low one,—the intensity or loudness of sound resulting from the amplitude of the vibration, and the quantity of sound resulting from the mass of air simultaneously vibrating. 2nd. The external condition of widest transmission of sound through the air is that of stillness and perfect uniformity of density and temperature throughout. 3rd. The most serious disturbance of the audibility

23

of sound at a distance, results from its refraction by the wind, which as a general rule moving more freely and rapidly above than near the earth, tends by this difference to lift the sound-beams upward when moving against the wind, and in a downward curve when moving with it. 4th. When the upper current of air is adverse to the lower or sensible wind, or whenever from any cause the wind below has a higher velocity than that above—in the same direction, the reverse phenomenon is observed of sound being heard to greater distances in opposition to the sensible wind than it is when in the direction of the surface wind. 5th. While suitable reflectors and trumpet cones are serviceable in giving prominent direction to sounds within moderate or ordinary distances, yet from the rapid diffusibility of the sound-beams, such appliances are worthless for distances beyond a mile or two. 6th. The siren has been frequently found to have its clearest penetration through a widely extended fog, and also through a thick snow-storm of large area. 7th. Intervening obstructions produce sound shadows of greater or less extent, which however at a distance but slightly enfeeble the sound, owing to the lateral diffusion and closing in of the sound-waves. 8th. The singular phenomenon of distinct audibility of sound to a distance with a limited intermediate region of inaudibility where no optical obstruction exists, is due sometimes to a diffusion of upper sound-beams which have not suffered the upward refraction; sometimes to the lateral refraction of sound-beams or to the lateral spread of sound from directions not affected by the upward refraction; and very frequently to a double curvature of the refracted sound-beams under an adverse lower wind, by reason of the wave fronts being less retarded by the lower or surface stratum of wind than by that a short distance above, and at still greater heights being again less retarded, and finally accelerated by the superior favoring wind.

These remarkable series of acoustic investigations undertaken after the observer had considerably exceeded his three-score years,—perseveringly continued weeks at a time, and sometimes for more than a month,—extending through a period of twelve years, and pursued over a wide and extremely irregular range of sea-coast, and under great variety of both topographical and meteorological conditions, untiringly prosecuted by numberless sea trips of 10, 15, and even 20 miles in single stretches, in calm, in sunshine, in storm, with every variety of disregarded exposure,—form altogether a labor and a research, quite unequalled and unapproached by any similar ones on record. As a result of so great earnestness and thoroughness in the conduct of an enterprise of so great difficulty, Henry has advanced and enriched our knowledge by contributions to the science of acoustics, unquestionably the most important and valuable of the century. By persistent cross-examination of the bewildering anomalies of sound propagation under wide diversities of locality and condition, he has succeeded in evolving order out of apparent chaos, in reclaiming a new district, now subjected to the orderly reign of recognized law, and in raising the plausible but long neglected hypothesis of Stokes into the domain of a verified and fully established theory. Only on the subject of the ocean echo had he failed to reach a solution which entirely satisfied his judgment;* and at the ripe age of four-score years he had mapped out a further extension of his laborious search after truth, when his untiring and beneficent purposes were cut short by death.

With these great labors—(a full demand upon the energies of youthful vigor) fittingly closed the life of one whose long career had been dedicated to the service of his race,—no less by the unrecorded incitations and encouragements of others to the prosecution of original research, than by his own direct and earnest efforts on all occasions to extend the boundaries of our knowledge. Nor is it permitted us to indulge in vain regrets that thirty years of such a life were seemingly so much withdrawn from his own chosen

---

* "The question, therefore, remains to be answered: what is the cause of the aerial echo? As I have stated, it must in some way be connected with the horizon. The only explanation which suggests itself to me at present is, that the spread of the sound which fills the whole atmosphere from the zenith to the horizon with sound-waves, may continue their curvilinear direction until they strike the surface of the water at such an angle and direction as to be reflected back to the ear of the observer. In this case the echo would be heard from a perfectly flat surface of water, and as different sound-rays would reach the water at different distances and from different azimuths, they would produce the prolonged character of the echo and its angular extent along the horizon. While we do not advance this hypothesis as a final solution of the question, we shall provisionally adopt it as a means of suggesting further experiments in regard to this perplexing question at another season." (*Report of L. H. Board*, 1877, p. 70.)

ministry at the altar of science, to be occupied so largely with the drudgery and the routine of merely administrative duties. True though it be, that talents adapted to such functions are very much more common and available than those which form the successful interrogator of Nature, who that knows by what exertions Smithson's wise endowment was rescued from the wasteful dissipation of heterogeneous local agencies and objects — by what heroic constancy, and through what ordeals of remonstrance and misconception, of contumely and denunciation, the modest income of the fund (husbanded and increased by prudent management) was yearly more and more withdrawn from merely popular uses and interests, and more and more applied to its truest and highest purpose, the fostering of abstract research, the founding of a pharos for the future,— the "increasing and diffusing of knowledge among men,"— who that knows all this, can say that Henry was mistaken in his devotion, or that his ripest years were wasted in an unprofitable mission? *   But in addition to this vast work,—accomplished as probably no one of his scientific compeers would have had the fortitude and the indomitable persistence to carry through, his personal contributions to modern science (as has been shown) have throughout been neither few nor unimportant.

One remarkable circumstance relating to Henry's directorship of the Smithsonian publications (which have had so wide a distribution and influence)† must not be here passed over.   Having himself,

---

* "But it is not alone the material advantages which the world enjoys from the study of abstract science on which its claims are founded. Were all further applications of its principles to practical purposes to cease, it would still be entitled to commendation and support on account of its more important effects upon the general mind.  It offers unbounded fields of pleasurable, healthful, and ennobling exercise to the restless intellect of man, expanding his powers and enlarging his conceptions of the wisdom, the energy, and the beneficence of the great Ruler of the universe.  From these considerations then, and others of a like kind, I am fully justified in the assertion that this Institution has done good service in placing prominently before the country the importance of original research, and that its directors are entitled to commendation for having so uniformly and persistently kept in view the fact that it was not intended for educational or immediately practical purposes, but for the encouragement of the study of theoretical principles and the advancement of abstract knowledge."  (*Smithsonian Report* for 1859, p. 17.)

† "The number of copies of the Smithsonian Contributions distributed, is greater than that of the Transactions of any scientific or literary society; and therefore the Institution offers the best medium to be found for diffusing a knowledge of scientific discoveries."  (*Smithsonian Report* for 1851, p. 202.)

amidst the absorbing occupations of his position, conducted so valuable original investigations—on the strength of building materials, —on the best illuminants and their proper conditions,—and especially in his last great labor on the philosophy of sound, we should naturally expect to find them displayed in the "Smithsonian Contributions;" where in interest and importance second to none contained in that extensive and admirable series, these memoirs would have found their fitting place, and have given honor to the collection. But as if to avoid all semblance of a personal motive in his resolute policy of administration, he published nothing for himself at the expense of the Smithsonian fund; his numerous original productions being given to the public through the channel of various official reports. And thus it has occurred that his writings scattered in the different directions which seemed to him at the time most suitable, with little thought of any special publicity or perpetuity, have largely failed to reach the audience which would most appreciate them. And many of his most valuable papers— never by himself collected—must be searched for in unsuggestive volumes of Agricultural, or Light-House Board Reports. *

For him it seemed enough that what was once established, would not be willingly let die; that the medium or the occasion of communication was of comparatively little consequence, if but a new fact or principle were thrown into proper currency, and duly accepted as part of the world's wealth: and beyond all ordinary men he seemed to feel the insignificance of personal fame as compared with the infinite value of truth. The most appropriate monument of such a man would be a full collection of his writings, produced in a worthy and appropriate style of publication.

Less than a year ago, (on the evening of November 24th, 1877,) he delivered in this place before this Society his annual address, shortly after his re-election as its President;—an address which as we beheld the remarkable fulness and freshness of the speaker's

---

* Many valuable communications made to the American Association, to the National Academy of Sciences, to the Washington Philosophical Society, and to other bodies, from rough notes, which their author was prevented from writing fairly out, by the unceasing pressure of his multitudinous official and public duties, have unfortunately been published only by title.

mental and **bodily powers,**— we little thought **was in reality his** valedictory. **In it he** concisely yet lucidly portrayed for **the stimu**lation of **more youthful** physicists, the processes and **the qualities** necessary **for success** in original research ;— the awakened attention to **"the seeds of great** discoveries constantly floating around us,"— **the careful observation, the clear** perception of the actual facts **uncolored as** much as possible **by** *a priori* conceptions or expecta**tions,— the** faculty of persevering watchfulness, and the judgment **to** eliminate (with all due caution) **the conditions which** are accidental,— the importance **of a provisional** hypothesis,— the conscientious and impartial **testing of such by** every expedient that ingenuity may suggest,— the lessons taught by failure,— the firm holding of the additional facts **thus** gleaned, though adverse and disappointing,— the diligent pondering, and the logical application of deductive consequences, to be again examined, until as the reward of patient solicitation, the answer of nature is at least revealed.

"The investigator now feels amply rewarded for all his toil, and is conscious of **the pleasure of** the self-appreciation which flows from **having** been initiated into the **secrets** of nature, and allowed **the place not merely** of **an** humble worshipper in the vestibule of **the temple of** science, but an officiating **priest at the** altar. In this **sketch which I have given of a successful** investigation, it will be **observed that several faculties of** the mind are called into operation. **First, the** imagination, which **calls** forth the forms of things unseen **and gives them a local habitation, must be** active in presenting to **the mind's eye a definite conception of the** modes of operation of **the forces in nature sufficient to produce the** phenomena in question. Second, the logical power must **be trained in order to** deduce from **the assumed premises the** conclusions **necessary to test** the truth **of** the assumption in the form of an experiment; and again the ingenuity must be taxed to invent the experiment or to bring about the arrangement of apparatus adapted to test the conclusions. These faculties of mind may all be much improved and strengthened by **practice. The most important** requisite **however to** scientific **investigations of this character, is** a mind well **stored** with clear **conceptions of scientific generalizations, and** possessed of sagacity **in tracing analogies and devising hypotheses.** Without the use of hypotheses or antecedent probabilities, as a general rule no **extended** series of investigations can be made as to the approximate cause of casual phenomena. They require to be used however with **great** care, lest they become false guides which lead to error rather **than** to truth." * Who that listened could fail to perceive that the speaker was unconsciously giving us **precious glimpses into his own experience** ?

In less than two **weeks after this,** his last appearance among us, he suffered **at New York a** temporary numbness in his hands, which he feared might threaten a paralysis; **but a** subsequent swelling of his feet and hands **revealed to his physician the nature of** his inward disease **as a nephritis, which had insidiously** assailed him before **it was suspected, and had doubtless been aggravated by his unremitting scientific labors continued as usual through his last summer vacation. Only a month before he died, he thus** described the **commencement of his malady: "After an almost** uninterrupted **period of** excellent health for fifty years, I **awoke on** the 5th **of December at my** office in the Light-House **Depot in** Staten Island, finding **my right** hand in a paralytic **condition. This** was at first referred by the **medical** adviser, to an **affection of the** brain, but as the paralysis subsided in a considerable degree in the course of two days, this conclusion was doubted, and on a thorough examination through the eye, and by means of auscultation, and **chemical analysis, Dr. S. Weir** Mitchell and Dr. J. J. Woodward **pronounced the disease** an affection of **the kidneys." †**

---

* *Bulletin Phil. Soc. Washington,* Nov. 24, 1877, vol. ii. pp. 165, 166.

† Opening Address, written for the meeting of the National Academy of Sciences, April 16th, 1878. (*Proceed. Nat. Acad. Sci.,* vol. i, part 2, pp. 127, 128.) In the same address (read to the Academy by the Secretary) he remarked: "I am warned that I must devote my energies with caution, and expend no more power — physical or mental, than is commensurate with my present condition, and in consideration of this I think it advisable to curtail as much as possible, the various offices which have been pressed upon me in consideration of my residence in the city of Washington, and my association with the Smithsonian Institution. - - - I therefore beg leave to renew my request to be allowed to resign the presidency of the Academy, the resignation to take effect at the next meeting. I retain the office six months longer, in the hope that I may be restored to such a condition of health as to be able to prepare some suggestions which may be of importance for the future of the Academy." And in his closing Address at the end of the session, three days later (April 19th), in earnest words having now the solemnity of a valedictory charge, he urged that moral integrity of character is **essential** to conscientious fidelity in scientific research; and that

Aware that his illness was fatal, he yet felt lulled by that strange flattery of disease when unattended with a painful wasting, into the thought that he might probably survive the approaching warmer weather; and fully prepared for death, with the sense of life still strong within him, he planned what might yet be accomplished.

But with occasional alternations of more favorable symptoms, with the uræmia steadily increasing, his strength slowly declined: and as he lay at noon of the 13th of last May, [1878,] with growing difficulty of breathing — surrounded by loving and anguished hearts — his last feeble utterance was an inquiry which way the wind came. With intellect clear and unimpaired, calmly that pure and all unselfish spirit passed away; leaving a void all the more real, all the more felt, that the deceased had reached a good old age, and had worthily accomplished his allotted work.

## PERSONALITY AND CHARACTER.

Of Henry's personal appearance, it is sufficient to say, that his figure, above the medium height, was finely proportioned; that his mien and movement were dignified and imposing; and that on whatever occasion called upon to address an assembly,

> " With grave aspéct he rose, and in his rising seemed
> A pillar of state: deep on his front engraven
> Deliberation sat, and public care."

His head and features were of massive mould; though from the perfect proportion of his form, not too conspicuously so. His expansive brow was crowned with an abundant flow of whitened hair; his lower face always smoothly shaven, expressed a mingled gentleness and firmness; and his countenance of manly symmetry was in all its varying moods, a pleasant study of the mellowing, moulding impress of long years of generous feeling, and a worthy exponent of the fine and thoughtful spirit within: wearing in

---

it should therefore be an indispensable test of membership in an Academy strenuous in maintaining its exalted function. "It is not social position, popularity, extended authorship, or success as an instructor in science which entitles to membership, but actual new discoveries; nor are these sufficient if the reputation of the candidate is in the slightest degree tainted with injustice or want of truth. Indeed I think that immorality and great mental power exercised in the discovery of scientific truths, are incompatible with each other; and that more error is introduced from defect in moral sense than from want of intellectual capacity." (Same *Proceedings*, p. 129.)

repose a certain pensive but benignant majesty, in the abstraction of study a semblance of constrained severity, in the relaxation of friendly intercourse a genial frank and winning grace of expression. The varying shades of such expression, with the changing current of his thought, combined with a certain reserve, — or (perhaps more properly) freedom from effusiveness, — imparted to his aspect and his intercourse a singular charm.* His whole physique was in admirable harmony with his power of intellect; — the fitting vesture of the *mens sana in corpore sano.* Like his intimate personal friend Agassiz, he seemed to stand and to move among men as the very embodiment of unfailing vigorous health and physical strength; and only a year ago, he walked with as erect and elastic a carriage, with as firm and sprightly a step, as any one here present.

It is difficult to attempt even a sketch of Henry's intellectual character, without allusion to his moral attributes; so constantly did the latter dominate the former. It may be said that the most characteristic feature of his varied activities was earnestness, and this as usual, was the offspring as much of a moral as of a mental purpose.

His mind was eminently logical; and this rational power was exhibited in every department of his theoretical or his practical pursuits. He never showed or felt uneasiness at necessary deductive consequences, if the premises were well considered or appeared to be well founded; confident that all truth must ultimately be found consistent. If presented with the problem of an untried case, while avowing the necessity of reserve in predicting results, he seemed to have an almost intuitive apprehension of the operation of natural law. If confronted with an unfamiliar phenomenon, whether in the experience of others, or in his own observations, his imagination was fertile in the suggestion of test conditions for eliminating variable influences. While few have ever held the function of hypothesis in higher estimation as an instrument of research, no one ever held hypothesis in more complete subjection.

---

*Of the numerous photographic portraits of Henry taken within the past ten or twenty years, it has been often remarked that no two appear to have the same character, or to bear a very close resemblance to each other. Three or four meritorious portraits in oil (of life-size) perpetuate his likeness, with the same characteristic differences.

As a lecturer and instructor, he was always most successful. Free from all self-consciousness, thinking only of his subject, and its fittest mode of presentation, he spoke from the fullness of a ripened knowledge, — intent on communicating to others the intellectual pleasures of insight he had made his own; and without attempt at oratorical display, his expositions — in simple, direct, and conversational language, were so lucid, satisfying, and convincing, that they enlisted from the beginning and secured to the close, the attentive interest of his auditors.

His sympathy with the pursuits of the rising generation of physicists was ever manifested in a disposition to frequent consultation and interchange of views with them; as if (aware of the usual tendency to mental ossification with advancing years,) he thus sought by familiar association to drink at the fountain of perennial youth. And surely no one was ever more successful in retaining life's coveted greenness in age; — not more in the child-like simplicity of his disposition, in the geniality of his affections, and in his undimmed faith, hope, and charity, for mankind, than in his intellectual freedom from undue prejudices, and in his readiness calmly to discuss or adopt new theories.

And this leads to the reflection that in the seeming contrasts of his nature were combined qualities which formed in him a resultant of character and of temperament as rare as admirable. With this great mobility of aptitude and of circumspection, this adaptability of mental attitude, he yet possessed an unusual firmness of resolution. With a manly sturdiness of conviction he presented an unvarying equability of temper and of toleration; and with perfect candor as perfect a courtesy. With a characteristic dignity of figure of presence and of deportment, he preserved an entire freedom from any shade of arrogance. With a warm and active charity, he still displayed a shrewd perception of character; and while ever responsive to the appeals of real distress, his insight into human nature protected him from being often deceived by the wiles of the designing. Intolerant of charlatanry and imposture, he was capable of exhibiting a wonderful patience with the tedium of honest ignorance. Possessing in earlier life a natural quickness of temper, and always a high degree of native sensibility, his perfect self-control led the casual acquaintance to regard him as reserved and unimpressible. Of him it may be truly said in simple and oft-quoted words:

> " His life was gentle; and the elements
> So *mixed* in him, that Nature might stand up
> And say to all the world—This was a MAN!"

With all his broad humanity, he possessed but little of what is known as "humor." He could enjoy the ludicrous more heartily when drolly narrated by its appreciative victims, than when sarcastically recited at the expense of another. The sparkle of wit he fully appreciated, provided it were free from coarseness and from personal satire. From the subordination of his sense of humor to his native instinct of sincerity, he had no approbation — or indeed tolerance of "practical jokes," holding that the shock to the feelings or to the confidence of the dupe, is far too high a price for the momentary hilarity enjoyed by the thoughtless at a farcical situation. Newspaper hoaxes — literary or scientific, in like manner received his stern reprobation, as uncompensated injuries to popular trust and to the cause of popular enlightenment.

Strong in his unerring sense of justice and of right, he allowed no prospects of personal advantage to influence his judgment in action, in decision, or in opinion: he never availed himself of the opportunities offered by his position, of reaping gain from profitable suggestions or favorable awards: and he never willingly inflicted an injury even on the feelings of the humblest. ' This was characteristically shown in the pains taken to convince the judgment of those against whose visionary projects he was so often called upon to report in the public interests of the Smithsonian Institution, of the Light-House service, and of the General Government: — often expending an amount of valuable time and of patience which few so situated would have accorded, or could well have afforded. And yet on the other hand when himself the subject of injustice, misconstruction, or abuse, he never suffered himself to be provoked into a controversy; — as if holding life too serious, time too precious, to be wasted in mere disputation. Least of all did he ever think of resorting to retaliatory conduct or to the expression of opprobrious sentiments. He calmly put aside disturbing elements, and seemed endowed with the power of excluding from his mental vision all irritating incidents. In that benignant breast there harbored no resentments.

Great as is the loss we have sustained of "guide, philosopher, and friend," we have yet the mournful satisfaction of reflecting that his influence, powerful as it always has been for good, still survives — in his works, his high example, and his unclouded memory; — that our community, our country, the world itself, has been benefitted by his existence here; and that as time rolls on, its course will be marked by increasing circles of appreciation, reverence, and gratitude, for the teachings of his high and noble life.

# LIST OF THE

# SCIENTIFIC PAPERS OF JOSEPH HENRY.

1825. On the production of cold by the rarefaction of Air: accompanied with Experiments. (Presented Mar. 2.) Abstract, *Trans. Albany Institute.* vol. i. part ii. p. 36.

1827. On some Modifications of the Electro-magnetic Apparatus. (Read Oct. 10.) *Trans. Albany Inst.* vol. i. pp. 22–24.

1829. Topographical Sketch of the State of New York; designed chiefly to show the General Elevations and Depressions of its Surface. (Read Oct. 28.) *Trans. Albany Inst.* vol. i. pp. 87–112.

1829. First Abstract of Meteorological Records of the State of New York, for 1828. (In conjunction with Dr. T. Romeyn Beck.) *Annual Report of Regents of University*, to the Legislature of New York.—Albany, 1829.

1829. On the Mean Temperature of Twenty-seven different Places in the State of New York, for 1828. (In conjunction with Dr. T. Romeyn Beck.) Brewster's *Edinburgh Jour. Science*, Oct. 1829, vol. i. n. s. pp. 249–259.

1830. Second Abstract of Meteorological Records of the State of New York for 1829. (In conjunction with Dr. T. Romeyn Beck.) *Annual Report of Regents of University*, to the Legislature of New York.—Albany, 1830.

1831. On the Application of the Principle of the Galvanic Multiplier to Electro-magnetic Apparatus, and also to the development of great Magnetic power in soft iron, with small Galvanic Elements. Silliman's *American Jour. Science*, Jan. 1831, vol. xix. pp. 400–408. *Jour. of Roy. Institution of Gr. Brit.* May, 1831, vol. i. pp. 609, 610.

1831. Tabular Statement of the Latitudes, Longitudes, and Elevations, of 42 Meteorological Stations in New York. *Annual Report Regents of University* to Legislature N. Y. 1831.

1831. Third Abstract of Meteorological Records of State of New York for 1830. (In conjunction with Dr. T. Romeyn Beck.) *Annual Report of Regents of University*, to the Legislature of New York.—Albany, 1831.

1831. An Account of a large Electro-magnet, made for the Laboratory of Yale College. (In conjunction with Dr. Ten Eyck.) Silliman's *Am. Jour. Sci.* April, 1831, vol. xx. pp. 201–203. *Jour. of Roy. Institution of Gr. Brit.* Aug. 1831, vol. ii. p. 182.

1831. On a Reciprocating Motion produced by Magnetic attraction and repulsion. Silliman's *Am. Jour. Sci.* July, 1831, vol. xx. pp. 340–343. Sturgeon's *Annals of Electricity*, etc. vol. iii. pp. 430–432.

1832. On a Disturbance of the Earth's Magnetism in connection with the appearance of an Aurora as observed at Albany on the 19th of April, 1831. (Communicated to the Albany Institute, Jan. 26, 1832.) *Report of Regents of University*, to the Legislature of New York.—Albany, 1832. Silliman's *Am. Jour. Sci.* July, 1832, vol. xxii. pp. 143–155.

1832. Fourth Abstract of Meteorological Records of the State of New York for 1831. (In conjunction with Dr. T. Romeyn Beck.) *Annual Report of Regents of University*, to the Legislature of New York.—Albany, 1831.

1832. On the Production of Currents and Sparks of Electricity from Magnetism. Silliman's *Am. Jour. Sci.* July, 1832, vol. xxii. pp. 403–408.

1832. On the effect of a long and helical wire in increasing the intensity of a galvanic current from a single element. (Conclusion of preceding paper.) Silliman's *Am. Jour. Sci.* July, 1832, vol. xxii. p. 408. Becquerel's *Traité expérimental de l'Électricité*, etc. 1837, vol. v. pp. 231, 232.

1833. Fifth Abstract of Meteorological Records of the State of New York for 1832. (In conjunction with Dr. T. Romeyn Beck.) *Annual Report of Regents of University*, to the Legislature of New York.—Albany, 1833.

1835. Contributions to Electricity and Magnetism. No. I. Description of a Galvanic Battery for producing Electricity of different intensities. (Read Jan. 14.) *Transactions Am. Philosoph. Society*, vol. v. n. s. pp. 217–222. Sturgeon's *Annals of Electricity*, etc. vol. i. pp. 277–281.

1835. Contributions to Electricity and Magnetism. No. II. On the influence of a Spiral Conductor in increasing the intensity of Electricity from a Galvanic arrangement of a single Pair, etc. (Read Feb. 6.) *Trans. Amer. Phil. Soc.* vol. v. n. s. pp. 223–232. Sturgeon's *Annals of Electricity*, etc. vol. i. pp. 282–290. Taylor's *Scientific Memoirs*, vol. i. pp. 540–547.

1835. Facts in reference to the Spark, etc. from a long Conductor uniting the poles of a Galvanic Battery. *Journal of Franklin Institute*, Mar. 1835, vol. xv. pp. 169, 170. Silliman's *Am. Jour. Sci.* July, 1835, vol. xxviii. pp. 327–331.

1837. A Notice of Electrical Researches, particularly in regard to the "lateral discharge." (Read before the British Association at Liverpool, Sept. 1837.) *Report Brit. Assoc.* 1837. Part II. pp. 22–24. Silliman's *Am. Jour. Sci.* April, 1838, vol. xxxiv. pp. 16–19.

1838. A Letter on the production directly from ordinary Electricity of Currents by Induction, analogous to those obtained from Galvanism. (Read to Philosoph. Society, May 4.) *Proceedings Am. Phil. Soc.* vol. i. p. 14.

1838. Contributions to Electricity and Magnetism. No. III. On Electro-dynamic Induction. (Read Nov. 2.) *Trans. Am. Phil. Soc.* vol. vi. n. s. pp. 303–337. Silliman's *Am. Jour. Sci.* Jan. 1840, vol. xxxviii. pp. 209–243. Sturgeon's *Annals of Electricity*, etc. vol. iv. pp. 281–310. *L. E. D. Phil. Mag.* Mar. 1840, vol. xvi. pp. 200–210: pp. 254–265: pp. 551–562. Becquerel's *Traité expérimental de l'Électricité*, etc. vol. v. pp. 87–107. *Annales de Chimie et de Physique*, Dec. 1841, 3d series: vol. iii. pp. 394–407. Poggendorff's *Annalen der Physik und Chemie*. Supplemental vol. i. (Nach Band li.) 1842, pp. 282–312.

1839. A novel phenomenon of Capillary action: the transmission of Mercury through Lead. (Read Mar. 15.) *Proceedings Am. Phil. Soc.* vol. i. pp. 82, 83. Silliman's *Am. Jour. Sci.* Dec. 1839, vol. xxxviii. pp. 180, 181. *Biblioth. Universelle*, vol. xxix. pp. 175, 176. Liebig's *Annalen der Chemie*, etc. vol. xl. pp. 182, 183.

1839. A Letter on two distinct kinds of dynamic Induction by a Galvanic current. (Read to Phil. Soc. Oct. 18.) *Proceedings Am. Phil. Soc.* vol. i. pp. 134–136.

1839. Observations of Meteors made Nov. 25, 1835, simultaneously at Princeton and at Philadelphia, for determining their difference of Longitude. (In conjunction with Professors A. D. Bache, S. Alexander, and J. P. Espy.) *Proceedings Am. Phil. Soc.* Dec. 21, vol. i. pp. 162, 163. Silliman's *Am. Jour. Sci.* Oct. 1840, vol. xxxix. pp. 372, 373.

1840. Contributions to Electricity and Magnetism. No. IV. On Electro-dynamic Induction. (Read June 19.) *Trans. Am. Phil. Soc.* vol. viii. n. s. pp. 1–18. Silliman's *Am. Jour. Sci.* April, 1841, vol. xli. pp. 117–152. Sturgeon's *Annals Electricity*, etc. vol. vii. pp. 21–56. *L. E. D. Phil. Mag.* June, 1841, vol. xviii. pp. 482–514. *Annales de Chim. et de Phys.* Dec. 1841, 3d ser. vol. iii. pp. 407–436. Poggendorff's *Annal. der Phys. und Chem.* 1841, vol. liv. pp. 84–98.

1840. Contributions to Electricity and Magnetism. No. IV,—continued. Theoretical Considerations relating to Electro-dynamic Induction. (Read Nov. 20.) *Trans. Am. Phil. Soc.* vol. viii. n. s. pp. 18–35.

1840. On the production of a reciprocating motion by the repulsion in the consecutive parts of a conductor through which a galvanic current is passing. (Read Nov. 20.) *Proceedings Am. Phil. Soc.* vol. i. p. 301.

1840. Electricity from heated Water. (Read Dec. 18.) *Proceedings Am. Phil. Soc.* vol. i. pp. 322–324.

1841. Report of the Tenth Meeting of the British Association, etc. *Princeton Review*, Jan. 1841, vol. xiii. pp. 132–149.

1841. Description of a simple and inexpensive form of Heliostat. (Read Sept. 17.) *Proceedings Am. Phil. Soc.* vol. ii. pp. 97, 98.

1841. Observations on the effects of a Thunderstorm which visited Princeton on the evening of the 14th of July, 1841. (Read Nov. 5.) *Proceedings Am. Phil. Soc.* vol. ii. pp. 111–116.

1842. Résumé des Recherches faits sur les Courants d'Induction. *Archives de l'Electricité*, 1842, vol. ii. pp. 348–392.

1842. Contributions to Electricity and Magnetism. No. V. On Electro-dynamic Induction: and on the oscillatory discharge. (Read June 17.) *Proceedings Am. Phil. Soc.* vol. ii. pp. 193–196.

1843. On Phosphorogenic Emanation. (Read May 26.) *Proceedings Am. Phil. Soc.* vol. iii. pp. 38–44. Walker's *Electrical Magazine*, 1845, vol. i. pp. 444–450.

1843. On a new Method of determining the Velocity of Projectiles. (Read May 30.) *Proceedings Am. Phil. Soc.* vol. iii. pp. 165–167. Walker's *Electrical Magazine*, 1845, vol. i. pp. 350–352.

1843. Nouvelles Expériences sur l'Induction développée par l'Electricité ordinaire. (Translated.)   *Archives de l'Electricité*, 1843, **vol. iii. pp. 484–488.**

1843. On the application of Melloni's thermo-electric apparatus to Meteorological purposes. (Presented orally Nov. 3.)   *Proceedings Am. Phil. Soc.* vol. **iv.** p. 22.

1843. **Theory of the discharge of the Leyden jar.** (Presented Nov 3.)   *Proceedings Am. Phil. Soc.* vol. iv. pp. 22, 23.

1844. **On the Cohesion of** Liquids. **(Read April 5.)** *Proceedings Am. Phil. Soc.* vol. iv. pp. **56, 57.** Silliman's *Am. Jour. Sci.* Oct. 1844, vol. xlviii. pp. **215, 216.**

1844. **On the** Cohesion of Liquids,—continued. (Read May 17.)  *Proceedings Am. Phil. Soc.* vol. iv. pp. 84, **85.** Silliman's *Am. Jour. Sci.* Oct. 1844, vol. xlviii. pp. 216, 217. *L. E. D. Phil. Mag.* June, 1845, vol. xxvi. pp. **541–543.**

1844. **Syllabus of Lectures on** Physics. **Princeton, 8vo. 1844.** Republished in part in *Smithsonian Report*, 1856, pp. 187–220.

1844. Classification and Sources of Mechanical **Power. (Read Dec. 20.)** *Proceedings. Am. Phil. Soc.* vol. iv. pp. 127–129.

1845. On the **Coast Survey.** *Princeton Review*, April, **1845,** vol. xvii. pp. 321–344.

1845. On the relative Radiation of Heat by the Solar Spots. **(Read June** 20.) *Proceedings Am. Phil. Soc.* vol. iv. pp. 173–176. Brief Abstract in *Report Brit. Assoc.* 1845. **Part II.** p. 6. Walker's *Electrical Magazine*, 1846, vol. ii. pp. 321–324. Froriep's *Neue Notizen*, etc. No. 826, 1846, **vol. xxx**viii. col. 179–182. Poggendorff's *Annalen der Physik und Chemie*, **1846,** vol. lxviii. pp. 102–104.

1845. **On the Capillarity of Metals. (Read June 20.)** *Proceedings Am. Phil. Soc.* vol. iv. pp. 176–178. **Froriep's** *Neue Notizen*, etc. No. 855, 1846, vol. **xxxviii. col. 167–169. Poggendorff's** *Annalen der Physik und Chemie.* 2d **supplemental vol. (Nach Band lxxii.) 1848, pp.** 358–361.

1845. **On** the Protection **of Buildings** from Lightning. (Read June 20.) *Proceedings Am. Phil. Soc.* vol. iv. p. 179. Silliman's *Am. Jour. Sci.* 1846, vol. ii. pp. **405, 406.** Walker's *Electrical Magazine*, 1846, vol. ii. pp. 324-326. Froriep's *Neue Notizen*, etc. No. 823, 1846, vol. xxxviii. col. 133, 134.

1845. An account of peculiar effects **on a house struck by Lightning. (Read June** 20.) *Proceedings Am. Phil. Soc.* vol. iv. p. 180.

1845. On Color Blindness. *Princeton Review*, July, **1845,** vol. xvii. pp. 483–489. *Smithsonian Report*, 1877, pp. 196–200.

1845. On the discharge of Electricity through **a** long **wire, etc.** (Read Nov. 7.) *Proceedings Am. Phil. Soc.* vol. iv. pp. 208, 209.

1846. Repetition **of** Faraday's Experiment on the Polarization of Liquids under the influence **of a** galvanic current. (Read Jan. 16.) *Proceedings Am. Phil. Soc.* vol. iv. pp. 229, 230.

1846. Extrait d'une Lettre à M. de la **Rive, sur** les Télégraphes Electriques dans les Etats-Unis de l'Amérique. *Biblioth. Universelle. Archives,* 1846, vol. ii. p. 178.

1846. Report on the action of Electricity on the Telegraph Wires: and Telegraph-poles struck by Lightning. (Read June 19.) *Proceedings Am. Phil. Soc.* vol. iv. pp. 260–268. Silliman's *Am. Jour. Sci.* 1847, vol. iii. pp. 25–32. *L. E. D. Phil. Mag.* 1847, vol. xxx. pp. 186–194. *Agricultural Report,* Commr. Pats. 1859, pp. 509–511.

1846. On the ball supported by a water jet: also experiments in regard to the "interference" of heat. (Read Oct. 16.) *Proceedings Am. Phil. Soc.* vol. iv. p. 285.

1846. On the corpuscular hypothesis of the constitution of Matter. (Read Nov. 6.) *Proceedings Am. Phil. Soc.* vol. iv. pp. 287–290.

1846. On the Height of Auroræ. (Read Dec. 3.) *Proceedings Am. Phil. Soc.* vol. iv. p. 370.

1847. Programme of Organization of the Smithsonian Institution. (Presented to the Board of Regents, Dec. 8, 1847.) *Smithsonian Report,* 1847, pp. 120–132.

1847. Article on "Magnetism" for the Encyclopædia Americana. *Encycl. Amer.* 1847, vol. xiv. pp. 412–426.

1848. On Heat.—A Thermal Telescope. Silliman's *Am. Jour. Sci.* Jan. 1848, vol. v. pp. 113, 114.

1848. Explanations and Illustrations of the Plan of the Smithsonian Institution. Silliman's *Am. Jour. Sci.* Nov. 1848, vol. vi. pp. 305–317.

1849. On the Radiation of Heat. (Read Oct. 19.) *Proceedings Am. Phil. Soc.* vol. v. p. 108.

1850. Analysis of the dynamic phenomena of the Leyden jar. *Proceedings Amer. Association,* Aug. 1850, pp. 377, 378.

1851. On the Limit of Perceptibility of a direct and reflected Sound. *Proceedings Amer. Association,* May, 1851, pp. 42, 43.

1851. On the Theory of the so-called Imponderables. *Proceedings Amer. Association,* Aug. 1851, pp. 84–91.

1853. Address before the Metropolitan Mechanics' Institute, Washington. (Delivered March 19.) 8vo. Washington, 1853, 19 pp.

1854. Meteorological Tables of mean diurnal variations, etc.—Prepared as an Appendix to Mr. Russell's Lectures on Meteorology. *Smithsonian Report* for 1854, pp. 215–223.

1854. Thoughts on Education; an Introductory Discourse before the Association for the Advancement of Education. (Delivered Dec. 28.) *Proceedings Assoc. Adv. Education,* 4th Session, 1854, pp. 17–31. *Amer. Jour. of Education,* Aug. 1855, vol. i. pp. 17–31.

1855. On the mode of Testing Building Materials, etc. *Proceedings Am. Assoc.* Aug. 1855, pp. 102–112. Silliman's *Am. Jour. Sci.* July, 1856, vol. xxii. pp. 30–38; *Smithsonian Report,* 1856, pp. 303–310.

1855. On the effect of mingling Radiating Substances with Combustible Materials: (or incombustible bodies with fuel.) *Proceedings Am. Assoc.* Aug. 1855, pp. 112–116.

24

1855. Account of Experiments on the alleged spontaneous separation of Alcohol and Water. *Proceed. Am. Assoc.* Aug. 1855, pp. 140–144.

1855. On the Induction of Electrical Currents. (Read Sept. 11.) *Proceedings Am. Academy of Arts*, etc. vol. iii. p. 198.

1855. Note on the Gyroscope. Appendix to Lecture by Professor E. S. Snell. *Smithsonian Report*, 1855, p. 190.

1855. Remarks on Rain-fall at varying elevations. *Smithsonian Report*, 1855, pp. 213, 214.

1855. Directions for Meteorological Observations. (In conjunction with Professor A. Guyot.) *Smithsonian Report*, 1855, pp. 215–244.

1855. Circular of Inquiries relative to Earthquakes. *Smithsonian Report*, 1855, p. 245.

1855. Instructions for Observations of the Aurora. *Smithsonian Report*, 1855, pp. 247–250.

1855. On Green's Standard Barometer for the Smithsonian Institution. *Smithsonian Report*, 1855, pp. 251–258.

1855. Circular of Instructions on Registering the periodical phenomena of animal and vegetable life. *Smithsonian Report*, 1855, pp. 259–263.

1855. Meteorology in its connection with Agriculture, Part I. *Agricultural Report of Commr. Pats.* 1855, pp. 357–394.

1856. On Acoustics applied to Public Buildings. *Proceedings Am. Assoc.* Aug. 1856, pp. 119–135. *Smithsonian Report*, 1856, pp. 221–234. *Canadian Journal*, etc. Mar. 1857, vol. ii. n. s. pp. 130–140.

1856. Account of a large Sulphuric-acid Barometer in the Hall of the Smithsonian Institution Building. *Proceedings Am. Assoc.* Aug. 1856, pp. 135–138.

1856. Meteorology in its connection with Agriculture, Part II. General Atmospheric Conditions. *Agricultural Report* of Commr. Pats. 1856, pp. 455–492.

1857. Communication to the Board of Regents of the Smithsonian Institution, relative to a publication by Professor Morse. *Smithsonian Report*, 1857, pp. 85–88.

1857. Statement in relation to the history of the Electro-magnetic Telegraph. *Smithsonian Report*, 1857, pp. 99–106.

1857. Meteorology in its connection with Agriculture, Part III. Terrestrial Physics, and Temperature. *Agricultural Report* of Commr. Pats. 1857, pp. 419–506.

1858. Meteorology in its connection with Agriculture, Part IV. Atmospheric Vapor, and Currents. *Agricultural Report* of Commr. Pats. 1858, pp. 429–493.

1859. On Meteorology. *Canadian Naturalist and Geologist*, Aug. 1859, vol. iv. pp. 289–291.

1859. Application of the Telegraph to the Prediction of Changes of the Weather. (Read Aug. 9.) *Proceedings Am. Academy of Arts*, etc. vol. iv. pp. 271–275.

1859. Meteorology in its connection with Agriculture, Part V. Atmospheric Electricity. *Agricultural Report* of Commr. Pats. 1859, pp. 461–508.

1859. On the Protection of Buildings from the effects of Lightning. *Agricult. Report*, Com. Pat. 1859, pp. 511–524.

1860. On the Conservation of Force. Silliman's *Am. Jour. Sci.* July, 1860, vol. xxx. pp. 32–41.

1860. Circular to Officers of Hudson's Bay Company (April 20.) *Smithsonian Miscell. Collections*, No. 137, vol. viii. pp. 1–4.

1860. Description of Smithsonian Anemometer. *Smithsonian Report*, 1860, pp. 414–416.

1861. Letter on Aeronautics to Mr. T. S. C. Lowe. (March 11.) *Smithsonian Report*, 1860, pp. 118, 119.

1861. Article on "Magnetism" for the American Cyclopædia. Edited by Ripley and Dana. *Am. Cycl.* 1861, vol. xi. pp. 61–63.

1861. Article on "Meteorology" for the American Cyclopædia. Edited by Ripley and Dana. *Am. Cycl.* 1861, vol. xi. pp. 414–420.

1862. Report of the Light-House Board on the proposed Transfer of the Lights to the Navy Department. Exec. Docts. 37th Cong. 2d Sess. Senate, Mis. Doc. No. 61, pp. 2–18.

1863. Letter to Orlando Meads, Chairman of Committee of Trustees, etc. on the semi-centennial celebration of the Albany Academy. (Dated June 23.) *Proceedings on Semi-Centennial Anniversary*, etc. pp. 66, 67.

1863. Introduction to Memoir by Professor J. Plateau. On the Figures of Equilibrium of a Liquid Mass, etc. *Smithsonian Report*, 1863, pp. 207, 208.

1864. On Materials for Combustion in Lamps of Light-Houses. (Read Jan. 12, before the National Academy of Sciences.) [Not published in Proceedings.]

1865. Report relative to the Fire at the Smithsonian Institution, occurring Jan. 24th, 1865. (In conjunction with Mayor Richard Wallach.) Presented to the Regents February, 1865. *Smithsonian Report*, 1864, pp. 117–120.

1865. Queries relative to Tornadoes: directions to observers. *Smithsonian Miscell. Collections*, No. 190, vol. x. pp. 1–4.

1865. Remarks on the Meteorology of the United States. *Smithsonian Report*, 1865, pp. 50–59.

1865. Remarks on Ventilation: especially with reference to the U. S. Capitol. *Smithsonian Report*, 1865, pp. 67, 68.

1866. Report on the Warming and Ventilating of the U. S. Capitol. (May 4.) *Exec. Doc.* No. 100. H. of Rep. 39th Cong. 1st Sess. pp. 4–6.

1866. Report of Building Committee on Repairs to Sm. Inst. building from Fire. (In conjunction with Genl. Richard Delafield, and Mayor Richard Wallach.) Presented to Regents April 28. *Smithsonian Report*, 1865, pp. 111–114.

1866. On the aboriginal Migration of the American races. Appendix to paper by F. Von Hellwald. *Smithsonian Report*, 1866, pp. 344, 345.

1866. Remarks on Vitality. *Smithsonian Report*, 1866, pp. 386–388.

1866. Meteorological Notes. To Correspondents. *Smithsonian Report*, 1866, pp. 403–412.

1866. Investigations in regard to Sound. (Read Aug. 10, before the National Academy of Sciences.) [Not published in Proceedings.]

1867. Circular relating to Collections in Archæology and Ethnology. (Jan. 15.) Smithsonian Miscell. Collections, No. 205, vol. viii. pp. 1, 2.

1867. Circular relative to Exchanges. (May 16.) Smithsonian Report, 1867, p. 71.

1867. Suggestions relative to Objects of Scientific Investigation in Russian America. (May 27.) Smithsonian Miscell. Collections, No. 207, vol. viii. pp. 1–7.

1867. Notice of Peltier. Smithsonian Report, 1867, p. 158.

1867. Notes on Atmospheric Electricity. To Correspondents. Smithsonian Report, 1867, pp. 320–323.

1867. On the Penetration of Sound. (Read Jan. 24, before the National Academy of Sciences. [Not published in Proceedings.]

1868. Appendix to a Notice of Schœnbein. Smithsonian Report, 1868, pp. 189–192.

1868. On the Rain-fall of the United States. (Read Aug. 25, before the National Academy of Sciences.) [Not published in Proceedings.]

1869. Memoir of Alexander Dallas Bache. (Read April 16.) Biographical Memoirs of Nat. Acad. Sci. vol. i. pp. 181–212. Smithsonian Report, 1870, pp. 91–116.

1870. Letter. On a Physical Observatory. (Dec. 29.) Smithsonian Report, 1870, pp. 141–144.

1871. Observations on the Rain-fall of the United States. Proceedings California Academy of Sciences, vol. iv. p. 185.

1871. Instructions for Observations of Thunder Storms. Smithsonian Miscell. Collections, No. 235, vol. x. p. 1.

1871. Circular relative to Heights. For a topographic chart of N. America. Smithsonian Miscell. Collections, No. 236, vol. x. p. 1.

1871. Directions for constructing Lightning-Rods. Smithsonian Miscell. Collections, No. 237, vol. x. pp. 1–3. Silliman's Am. Jour. Sci. Nov. 1871, vol. ii. pp. 344–346.

1871. Letter to Capt. C. F. Hall, in regard to the Scientific Operations of the Expedition toward the North Pole. (June 9.) Smithsonian Report, 1871, pp. 364–366.

1871. Suggestions as to Meteorological Observations; during the Expedition toward the North Pole. Smithsonian Report, 1871, pp. 372–379.

1871. Meteorological Notes and Remarks. Smithsonian Report, 1871, pp. 452, 455, 456, 459, 461.

1871. Effect of the Moon on the Weather. Smithsonian Report, 1871, pp. 460, 461.

1871. Anniversary Address as President of the Philosophical Society of Washington. (Delivered Nov. 18.) Bulletin Phil. Soc. Washington, vol. i. pp. 5–14.

1872. Remarks on Cosmical Theories of Electricity and Magnetism: an Appendix to a Memoir by Professor G. B. Donati. Smithsonian Report, 1872, pp. 307–309.

1872. On certain Abnormal Phenomena of Sound, in connection with Fog-signals. (Read Dec. 11.) *Bulletin Phil. Soc. Washington*, vol. i. p. 65, and Appendix ix. 8 pp.

1873. Letter to John C. Green, Esq. of New York, on his establishment of the "Henry Chair of Physics" in the College of New Jersey. *Washington Daily Chronicle*, Mar. 21, 1873.

1873. On Telegraphic Announcements of Astronomical Discoveries. (May.) *Smithsonian Miscell. Collections*, No. 263, vol. xii. pp. 1–4.

1873. Remarks on the Light-House Service. *Report of Light-House Board*, 1873, pp. 3–7.

1874. Report of Investigations relative to Fog-Signals, and certain abnormal phenomena of Sound. *Report of Light-House Board*, 1874. Appendix, pp. 83–117.

1874. Memoir of Joseph Saxton. (Read Oct. 4.) *Biographical Memoirs of Nat. Acad. Sci.* vol. i. pp. 287–316.

1874. Remarks on Recent Earthquakes in North Carolina. *Smithsonian Report*, 1874, pp. 259, 260.

1875. Remarks on the Light-House Service. *Report of Light-House Board*, 1875, pp. 5–8.

1875. An account of investigations relative to Illuminating Materials. *Report of Light-House Board*, 1875. Appendix, pp. 86–103.

1875. Investigations relative to Sound. *Report of Light-House Board*, 1875. Appendix, pp. 104–126.

1875. On the Organization of Local Scientific Societies. *Smithsonian Report*, 1875, pp. 217–219.

1876. Article on "Fog," for Johnson's Universal Cyclopædia. Edited by Dr. Barnard. *J. Univ. Cycl.* vol. ii. pp. 187, 188.

1876. Article on "Fog-Signals" for Johnson's Universal Cyclopædia. Edited by Dr. Barnard. *J. Univ. Cycl.* vol. ii. pp. 188–190.

1876. Article on "Hygrometry" for Johnson's Universal Cyclopædia. Edited by Dr. Barnard. *J. Univ. Cycl.* vol. ii. pp. 1072–1074.

1876. Letter to Rev. S. B. Dod; on researches made at Princeton. (Dated Dec. 4.) *Princeton Memorial*, May 19, 1878, 8vo. N. Y. pp. 51–70.

1877. Article on "Lightning" for Johnson's Universal Cyclopædia. Edited by Dr. Barnard. *J. Univ. Cycl.* vol. iii. pp. 32–36.

1877. Article on "Lightning-Rods" for Johnson's Universal Cyclopædia. Edited by Dr. Barnard. *J. Univ. Cycl.* vol. iii. pp. 36, 37.

1877. Remarks on the Light-House Service. *Report of Light-House Board*, 1877, pp. 3–7.

1877. Report of Operations relative to Fog-Signals. *Report of Light-House Board*, 1877. Appendix, pp. 61–72.

1877. Address before the Philosophical Society of Washington. *Bulletin Phil. Soc. Washington*, vol. ii. pp. 162–174.

1878. On Thunder Storms.    (Letter Oct. 13.)    *Journal Am. Electrical Society*, 1878, vol. ii. pp. 37–44.

1878. Letter to Joseph Patterson, Esq. of Philadelphia, on the "Joseph Henry Fund." (Dated Jan. 10.)    *Public Ledger and Transcript*, May 14, 1878. *The Press :* of Philadelphia, May 14, 1878.

1878. Report on the Ventilation of the Hall of the House of Representatives.  (Jan. 26.)   45th Cong. 2nd Sess. H. R. Report, No. 119, pp. 1–6.

1878. Report on the Use of the Polariscope in Saccharimetry.  (Feb. 5.)   Mis. Doc. 45th Cong. 2nd Sess. H. R.

1878. Opening Address before the National Academy of Sciences.   (Read April 16.) *Proceedings Nat. Acad. Sci.* vol. i. part 2, pp. 127, 128.

1878. Closing Address before the National Academy of Sciences.   (Read April 19.) *Proceedings Nat. Acad. Sci.* vol. i. part 2, pp. 129, 130.

Eng.ª by S

# SUPPLEMENT.

---

# SUPPLEMENTARY NOTES.

### *Note A.  (From p. 209.)*

#### HENRY'S FIRST EXPERIMENTS.

From the time of leaving the Albany Academy young Henry exhibited a great fondness for chemical experimentation. The wonderful transformations of familiar substances under the magic spell of decomposing re-actions and combining affinities, seemed to his ardent imagination to offer a possible clue to the mystery of matter and of force. His mental activity sought an outlet in assisting to establish the "Albany Lyceum."

Orlando Meads, LL.D. in the "Annual Address" read before the Albany Institute, May 25, 1871, thus records his early reminiscences:

"When a boy in the Albany Academy in 1823 and 1824, it was my pleasure and privilege, when released from recitations, to resort to the chemical laboratory and lecture room. There might be found from day to day through the winter, earnestly engaged in experiments upon steam and upon a small steam-engine, and in chemical and other scientific investigations, two young men — both active members of the 'Lyceum,' then very different in their external circumstances and prospects in life, but of kindred tastes and sympathies; the one was Richard Varick DeWitt, the other was Joseph Henry, as yet unknown to fame, but already giving promise of those rare qualities of mind and character which have since raised him to the very first rank among the experimental philosophers of his time. Chemistry at that time was exciting great interest, and Dr. Beck's courses of chemical lectures, conducted every winter in the lecture room of the Academy, were attended not only by the students, but by all that was most intelligent and fashionable in the city. Henry, who had been formerly a pupil in the Academy, was then Dr. Beck's chemical assistant, and already an admirable experimentalist, and he availed himself to the utmost of the advantages thus afforded, of prosecuting his investigations in chemistry, electricity, and galvanism." *

---

* *Transactions of Albany Institute*, 1872, vol. vii. pp. 20, 21.

## Note B.   (*From p. 227.*)

### "INTENSITY" AND "QUANTITY" CURRENTS.

Early in the century, the eminent chemist Dr. **Thomas** Thomson endeavored to express the difference between mechanical electricity and chemical electricity, by characterizing the former as possessing "intensity," and the latter as possessing "quantity." From the increase of electrical effects with the multiplication of galvanic pairs in a pile or battery, Volta a short time before had designated such action as "electromotor" force. Dr. Robert Hare in 1816 devising a galvanic battery in which all the positive elements were directly connected together, as were all the negative elements, (thus constituting it virtually a battery of a single pair,) from the heating effects obtained, designated the action as "calorimotor" force. It appeared quite natural afterward to distinguish these classes of effects by the old terms — "intensity" for electromotive force, and "quantity" for calorimotive force. There is obviously a close analogy between these differences of condition or resultant, and the more strongly contrasted conditions of mechanical and chemical electricity: and indeed the whole may be said to lie in a continuous series, from the highest "intensity" with minimum quantity, to the greatest "quantity" with minimum intensity.

Peltier in 1836 published a paper entitled "Definition of the terms electric *Quantity* and *Intensity*, derived from direct experiment:" in which he showed that "if we form a voltaic pair of two fine wires, zinc and copper, immersed in pure water, and connected by a circuit of copper wire 300 metres (328 yards) long, although there is as we know a continuous current in this closed circuit, the copper wire if placed immediately over a magnetic needle, will not deflect it from the magnetic meridian. But if the needle be surrounded by a "multiplicator" formed of 100 or 200 coils of the long wire, there will be at once a notable deviation; and if the number of coils be increased to 2,000 the deviation may extend to 60 degrees." In this experiment, as the primitive current has not been changed, but a "factitious quantity" only has been produced by conducting it 2,000 times around the magnetic needle, Peltier inferred that it is by the *quantity* (and by no other modification) that the action has been thus enhanced; and that it is therefore through its *quantity* that a current acts on the magnetic needle.

"Taking now a thermo-electric pair, zinc and copper, of five square millimetres, (the 129th part of a square inch,) and heating one of the solderings to 40 degrees, (104° F.) we find that with the same closed circuit and multiplicator of 2,000 coils, the needle will not be deflected; the electricity will not pass. But if we retrench

1,800 coils, (shortening the conductor to this extent,) the galvanometer now of 200 coils will begin to give notable deviations. If we reduce it to 10 coils, the deflection will be considerably augmented. Finally, if we reduce it to a single coil formed of a strip of copper containing as much substance as the 200 coils, the deflection of the needle may amount to even 60 degrees. The quantity of electricity produced in this experiment by the thermo-electric pair is therefore evidently 2,000 times greater than that of the above hydro-electric pair, since we obtain the same deviation with a single coil as with the factitious quantity given by the reduplication of the coils. On the other hand, in the first experiment the length of the conducting wire was easily traversed by the hydro-electric current; the inertia of the matter was overcome without difficulty and without appreciable loss of the current: in the second experiment this inertia could not be overcome; the power of action was insufficient and it was necessary to reduce the circuit to a very small length for the electricity to be able to traverse it." From these phenomena, Peltier argued that two very distinct conditions were presented, which should not be confounded; an action of *quantity* without resistance, and an action of *intensity* independent of quantity, capable of overcoming considerable resistance.*

In the same memoir however, Peltier took occasion to say that he considered "dynamic intensity" an inappropriate expression for electricity in movement; and that the term if retained should be used to designate not a modification of the electric current, but a particular disposition of the electro-motor. He discarded the idea that intensity represents a peculiar quality in the current itself; but considered the action as only the consequence of increased resistance offered by the pile to a backward movement or return of the electric flow: or in other words that intensity regarded as the power of overcoming obstacles in the external path, results from the greater obstacles presented by the battery to a neutralization by retrogradation.†

The designations under discussion have been largely superseded in modern authorities by the mathematical treatment of the subject, which takes cognizance alone of the ratio between electromotive force and resistance differences in the circuits. Thus Professor Jenkin, speaking of the two classes of batteries, remarks: "With a short circuit of small external resistance, we can increase the current by increasing the size of cells, or what is equivalent to this, by joining several cells in multiple arc. With a long circuit of great external resistance, large cells (or many of them joined in multiple

---

* *Annales de Chimie et de Physique*, 1836, vol. lxiii. pp. 245, 246.

† Same work, p. 253.

arc) will fail to give us strong currents, but we may increase the current by joining the same cells in series. - - - Cells joined *in series* are sometimes described as joined for 'intensity'; and cells joined *in multiple arc*, as joined for 'quantity.' These terms are remnants of an erroneous theory."*

Again, in speaking of galvanometers of long and fine coils, as distinguished from those of short and thick wire coils, he says: "In some writings these two classes of instruments are spoken of as adapted to two different classes of 'currents' instead of to two different classes of *circuits*. The instrument with numerous turns of fine wire is said to indicate 'intensity' currents, the other class to indicate 'quantity' currents. These two old names survive, although the fallacious theory which assumed that there were two kinds of *currents* is extinct: the term 'intensity galvanometer' is used to signify an instrument with thousands of turns of thin wire in its coil, and 'quantity galvanometer'—an instrument with few turns of thick wire. I shall name the two varieties 'long coil' and 'short coil' galvanometers."†

Admirable as the mathematical theory of galvanic circuits has proved itself in its fullness and precision, it does not supply us with any satisfactory physical conception of the palpable dynamic difference in the resultant galvanic *currents*. The old terms, whether accurate or not, are still convenient designations of the acknowledged differences when reference is had to effects rather than to arrangements.‡

No one has more clearly pointed out the almost constant antithesis between the actions of "static" and "dynamic" electricity, than Peltier himself. "Static electricity is duplex; each of its forms is collected, controlled, and maintained separately; being manifested only in the state of isolation and separation: these forms are only preserved thus separate by non-conducting substances, and their action endures as long as their insulation. Dynamic electricity is not double; it cannot be separately either collected, controlled, or maintained; being manifested only at the instant of its transmission through conductors insulated or not: for continuous effect it is necessary that the producing cause be continuous. The former collects only at the surface, being equally or unequally distributed thereon according to the form of the surface. The latter is propa-

---

* *Electricity and Magnetism.* By Fleeming Jenkin. 16mo. London and New York, 1873, chap. iv. sect. 7, p. 88.

† Same work, chap. xiii. sect. 3, p. 190.

‡ Peltier from experiments (the results of which he has detailed) controverted the universality of the law of Ohm and Gauss, that galvanic resistance is directly proportioned to the length of the conducting wire, and inversely proportional to the area of its cross-section. (*Comptes Rendus*, Oct. 12, 1835, vol. 1. pp. 203, 204.)

gated equally through the interior of conducting bodies, and in proportion to their mass quite irrespective of the form of their surfaces. Two bodies charged with the same kind of static electricity, exhibit mutual repulsion; while if charged with contrary kinds they exhibit mutual attraction: and by contact establish a complete neutralization. Two currents of dynamic electricity, in the same direction attract each other; in opposite directions repel each other: the contact of their conductors produces neither division nor neutralization; nor does any external communication disturb the current in a closed circuit. A body charged with either kind of static electricity exerts no action but attraction on a neutral body; it induces the opposite electrical state on the portion of a body approached, repelling its own kind to the further extremity. A current of dynamic electricity produces various inductive effects on neighboring bodies, as transverse magnetization, instantaneous impulses at the moment of any change, chemical actions, etc. The former finds an equilibrium of its two forms in very unequal degrees in different metals.* The latter finds only conducting differences between the metals; and is not affected by other currents. The former is feeble or intense according to the extent of surface on which it is accumulated; and manifests its *tension* by a greater or less attraction or repulsion. The latter exhibits the states of quantity—measured by the deflection of the galvanometer, and of intensity—measured by the power of overcoming resistance or of traversing poor conductors." †

Characteristically different as are the phenomena thus exhibited by mechanical and chemical electricities, (to distinguish which we have unfortunately no satisfactory expressions,) almost as marked — though in a much smaller degree, are the peculiarities of galvanism itself, in what must be called its varying states of tension. And for these striking differences, Ohm's celebrated law that "the strength of the current is proportional to the electro-motive force divided by the conducting resistance," affords no more intelligible explanation than it does for the peculiar deportment of so-called "static" electricity. Indeed Ohm's formula represents but a close

* Peltier first demonstrated that the electric capacity of the metals for the same kind from a constant source, is very unequal: thus zinc takes and retains more positive than negative electricity, while the contrary takes place with copper: so gold is more apt than silver or platina to become charged with positive electricity. (*Comptes Rendus*, 1835, vol. i. pp. 360 and 470.)

† *Annales de Chimie et de Physique*, 1838, vol. lxvii. pp. 426–428. The title of this memoir is "Experimental researches on the quantities of static and dynamic action produced by the oxidation of a milligramme of zinc:" and the author arrives at the conclusion that the static effects are as the squares of the dynamic effects; or conversely, the dynamic as the square roots of the static. (p. 446.)

approximation to the actual facts of electrical transmission; and gives us no account of the remarkable fact discovered by Henry that the magnetizing power of a current actually increases with the length of the conductor, up to a certain point: nor of his other discovery, the "extra current" or the induction of a current upon itself. Indeed it takes no cognizance of any of the numerous perturbations dependent on the mysterious re-actions of electrical "induction."

## Note C. (From p. 229.)

### THE ELECTRO-MAGNETIC TELEGRAPH.

From among living eye-witnesses of Henry's early telegraphic experiments in the years 1831 and 1832, the following may be cited:

Dr. Orlando Meads, a former student of the Albany Academy, in an anniversary discourse commemorating the fiftieth year of its existence, thus referred to the scenes he witnessed a third of a century before: "The older students of the Academy in the years 1830, 1831, and 1832, and others who witnessed his experiments which at that time excited so much interest in this city, will remember the long coils of wire which ran circuit upon circuit for more than a mile in length around one of the upper rooms in the Academy, for the purpose of illustrating the fact that a galvanic current could be transmitted through its whole length so as to excite a magnet at the farther end of the line, and thus move a steel bar which struck a bell. This in a scientific point of view, was the demonstration and accomplishment of all that was required for the magnetic telegraph. - - - Let us not forget that the click of the telegraph which is heard from every joint of those mystic wires which now link together every city, and village, and post, and camp, and station, all over this continent, is but the echo of that little bell which first sounded in that upper room of the Academy."*

On the same occasion, the Hon. Alexander W. Bradford, also a former pupil of the Academy, (who finished his course at the Institution and left it in 1832,) recalled the suspended lines of insulated copper wire through which his teacher had demonstrated "the magnetic power of the galvanic battery; and years before the invention of the telegraph, proclaimed to America and to Europe the means of communication by the electric fluid. I was an eye-

* "Historical Discourse": on the Celebration of the Semi-Centennial Anniversary of the Albany Academy, June 23, 1863. *Proceedings*, etc. pp. 25, 26.

witness to those experiments, and to their eventual demonstration and triumph." *

Professor James Hall, (in the same year in which he was President of the American Association at its Albany meeting,) in a letter addressed to Professor Henry, January 19, 1856, relates the circumstances of a visit to the Albany Academy in August, 1832, on which occasion he was shown a long circuit of wire about the walls of a larger upper room, "and at one termination of this, in the recess of a window, a bell was fixed, while the other extremity was connected with a galvanic apparatus. You showed us the manner in which the bell could be made to ring by a current of electricity transmitted through this wire; and you remarked that this method might be adopted for giving signals by the ringing of a bell at the distance of many miles from the point of its connection with the galvanic apparatus. All the circumstances attending this visit to Albany are fresh in my recollection; and during the past years while so much has been said respecting the invention of electric telegraphs, I have often had occasion to mention the exhibition of your electric telegraph in the Albany Academy, in 1832." †

Professor Morse, who states that the idea of an electric telegraph first occurred to him in October, 1832, commenced experimenting on this conception in the latter part of 1835. The following is his own account of his first experiments:

"In the year 1835, I was appointed a professor in the New York City University, and about the month of November of that year, I occupied rooms in the University buildings. There I immediately commenced with very limited means to experiment upon my invention. My first instrument was made up of an old picture or canvas frame fastened to a table, the wheels of an old wooden clock moved by a weight to carry the paper forward, three wooden drums upon one of which the paper was wound and passed over the other two, a wooden pendulum suspended to the top piece of the picture or stretching frame and vibrating across the paper as it passed over the center wooden drum, a pencil at the lower end of the pendulum in contact with the paper, an electro-magnet fastened to a shelf across the picture or stretching frame opposite to an armature made fast to the pendulum, a type-rule and type for breaking the circuit on an endless band (composed of carpet-binding) which passed over two wooden rollers moved by a wooden crank and carried forward by points projecting from the bottom of the rule downward into the carpet-binding, a lever with a small weight on the upper side and a

* "Commemorative Address": at Semi-Centennial Anniversary of Albany Academy, June 23, 1863. Proceedings, etc. p. 48.

4 Published in the Smithsonian Report for 1857, p. 96.

tooth projecting downward at one end operated on by the type, and a metallic fork also projecting downward over two mercury-cups and a short circuit of wire embracing the helices of the electro-magnet, connected with the positive and negative poles of the battery and terminating in the mercury-cups.  - - -  Early in 1836, I procured forty feet of wire, and putting it in the circuit I found that my battery of one cup was not sufficient to work my instrument."*

The last statement exhibits a singular unconsciousness of the real defect of his receiving apparatus, and of the fact that no number of galvanic cups would have sufficed "to work the instrument" as then constructed.  It is true (as first shown by Henry) that an "intensity" battery of many elements is required to operate a magnetic telegraph line; but (as also shown by him) a no less essential constituent, is an "intensity" magnet, if any use is to be made of the armature.  And on this point Professor Morse seems never to have understood the vital importance of Henry's discoveries to the success of his own invention.  Had he employed the most powerful of then existing magnets, (Henry's Yale College magnet of 1831, lifting 2,300 pounds, or Henry's Princeton College magnet of 1834, lifting 3,500 pounds,) he would still have found neither one cup nor one thousand cups "sufficient to work the instrument" through a circuit of fine wire, at the distance of a single mile.†  Although Professor Morse was enabled therefore to operate the armature of his Sturgeon magnet through a few yards of wire, it is certain that his experiments in 1836 were, for any *telegraphic* purpose, an absolute failure:—a failure as complete as were those undertaken by Barlow in 1825.  The relevancy of his incidental remark as in extenuation — "one cup was not sufficient to work my instrument," may therefore be appreciated.

As an artist of repute, Mr. Morse had been appointed professor of the "Arts of Design," in the newly established New York City University, in the autumn of 1835; but with any literature of science, he was remarkably unfamiliar.  He therefore very naturally had recourse to his colleague Professor Leonard D. Gale (of the chair of chemistry) for needed scientific assistance.  The following is Dr. Gale's account of Morse's original invention:

"In the winter of 1836–'37, Samuel F. B. Morse, who as well as myself was a professor in the New York University, city of

---

* Professor Morse's deposition in the "Bain case," 1850.

† "Electro-magnets of the greatest power, even when the most energetic batteries are employed, utterly cease to act when they are connected by considerable lengths of wire with the battery." (J. F. Daniell's *Introduction to the Study of Chemical Philosophy.* 2nd ed. 8vo. London, 1843, chap. xvi. sect. 850, p. 576.)

New York, came to my lecture room, and said he had a machine in his lecture room or studio which he wished to show me. I accompanied him to his room and there saw resting on a table a single-pair galvanic battery, an electro-magnet, an arrangement of pencil, a paper-covered roller, pinion wheels, levers, etc. for making letters and figures to be used for sending and receiving words and sentences through long distances. - - - It was evident to me that the one large cup-battery of Morse should be made into ten or fifteen smaller ones to make it a battery of intensity. - - - Accordingly I substituted the battery of many cups for the battery of one cup. The remaining defect in the Morse machine as first seen by me was that the coil of wire around the poles of the electro-magnet consisted of but a few turns only, while to give the greatest projectile power, the number of turns should be increased from tens to hundreds, as shown by Professor Henry in his paper published in the *American Journal of Science*, 1831. - - - After substituting the battery of twenty cups for that of a single cup, we added some hundred or more turns to the coil of wire around the poles of the magnet, and sent a message through 200 feet of conductors; then through 1,000 feet." *

After many trials at recording numbers by zig-zag markings counted in groups separated by a space, a continuous dispatch was for the first time effected on the 2d and 4th of September, 1837, in the form of V-shaped lines inscribed on the paper fillet, to the following effect: "215—36—2—58—112—04—01837:" which message as interpreted by a numbered vocabulary from which it was compiled, expressed the phrase "successful experiment with telegraph, September 4, 1837." †

About a month later, Professor Morse filed in the United States Patent Office a "Caveat," signed October 3d, 1837, comprising: "1st, a system of signs by which numbers and consequently words and sentences are signified; 2d, a set of type adapted to regulate and communicate the signs, with cases for convenient keeping of the type, and rules in which to set up the type; 3d, an apparatus called a port-rule for regulating the movement of the type-rules, which rules by means of the type in their turn regulate the times and intervals of the passage of electricity; 4th, a register which records the signs permanently; 5th, a dictionary or vocabulary of

---

* *Memorial of S. F. B. Morse.* 8vo. Washington, 1875, pp. 15-17.

† A fac-simile of this first "successful experiment" was published in the New York *Journal of Commerce*, for Thursday, Sept. 7th, 1837; and was reproduced in Vail's *American Electro-Magnetic Telegraph.* 8vo. Philadelphia, 1845, p. 75. The date, September, 1837, is accordingly that of the reduction of Morse's telegraph to a practical operation.

words numbered and adapted to this system of telegraph; **6th,** modes of laying **the conductors** to preserve them from injury."

A new and improved transmitting and recording apparatus was completed for Professor **Morse,** by his partner, Mr Alfred Vail, of the Speedwell Iron-works, near Morristown, N. J. at the close of the year 1837; **and early in** January, 1838, Professor Morse first discarded the numeral signs for words, and employed a true *alphabet* of "dots and dashes." The first exhibition of an alphabetic record of words and sentences took place in the New York City University, January 24th, 1838, through ten miles of wire wound on reels. The New York *Journal of Commerce*, in a notice of this performance, remarked: "Professor **Morse has recently improved** on his mode of marking, by which he **can dispense altogether with** the telegraphic dictionary, using letters instead of numbers." * The biographer of Morse **designates the dispatch** transmitted through the wires on this **occasion, "the first** *sentence* that was ever recorded by the telegraph." †

An application **for a patent** (signed by Professor Morse, April 7th, 1838,) was filed in the Patent Office; **and in** addition to the several parts **described** in the earlier Caveat, this application included **the new system of alphabetic symbols,** and the "relay" of successive **electro-magnetic circuits.** At his own request, the grant of the **patent was suspended** until he should have made a visit to Europe: **and it was not issued** till June 20th, 1840. On his return from his European **tour, Professor** Morse, in May, 1839, sought an **interview** with Henry at **Princeton,** from which he received much encouragement: having the differences between the "quantity" and "intensity" magnets fully explained to him, and learning from that cautious investigator that he was aware of no obstacle to the magnetization of soft iron "at the distance **of a** hundred miles or more" from the battery.‡

During the long **and** weary interval **in which Professor Morse** — with hope deferred — was unavailingly prosecuting his memorial **to** Congress for assistance, he received from Henry the following friendly and inspiriting letter:

"PRINCETON COLLEGE, **Feb. 24, 1842.**

"MY DEAR SIR: I am pleased to learn that you have again petitioned Congress in reference to your telegraph; and I most sincerely hope you will succeed in convincing our Representatives of the importance of the invention. - - - Science is now fully ripe

---

* New York *Journal of Commerce* of January 29th, 1838.

⸱ Prime's *Life of Morse*, 8vo. New York, 1875, p. 331.

‡ Prime's *Life of Morse*, chap. x. pp. 421, 422.

for this application, and I have not the least doubt, if proper means be afforded, of the perfect success of the invention. The idea of transmitting intelligence to a distance by means of electrical action has been suggested by various persons, from the time of Franklin to the present; but until within the last few years, or since the principal discoveries in electro-magnetism, all attempts to reduce it to practice were *necessarily unsuccessful*. The mere suggestion however of a scheme of this kind, is a matter for which little credit can be claimed, since it is one which would naturally arise in the mind of almost any person familiar with the phenomena of electricity: but the bringing it forward at the proper moment when the developments of science are able to furnish the means of certain success, and the devising a plan for carrying it into practical operation, are the grounds of a just claim to scientific reputation as well as to public patronage. About the same time with yourself, Professor Wheatstone of London, and Dr. Steinheil of Germany, proposed plans of the electro-magnetic telegraph; but these differ as much from yours as the nature of the common principle would well permit; and unless some essential improvements have lately been made in these European plans, I should prefer the one invented by yourself.

"With my best wishes for your success, I remain with much esteem,

"Yours, truly,

"Joseph Henry."

"This" says Morse's biographer, "was the most encouraging communication Professor Morse received during the dark ages between 1839 and 1843." * And appended to his memorial, it was undoubtedly influential in enlisting a more favorable attention to the unfamiliar project of an electro-magnetic telegraph. In December of the same year a bill appropriating thirty thousand dollars for testing the system invented by S. F. B. Morse, was reported in the House of Representatives by the Hon. C. G. Ferris of New York; passing that body February 23rd, and the Senate about a week later — March 3d, 1843, on the eve of the close of its session.

Under the appropriation thus secured, a line of four wires was extended from Washington to Baltimore, a distance of 40 miles; and on the 24th of May, 1844, the first message was satisfactorily transmitted between the two cities. The rapid success of the telegraph soon stimulated competition; and before many years elapsed, a series of resisting litigations was the natural consequence.

---

* ● Prime's Life of Morse, chap. x. p. 423.

Henry summoned to testify as to the condition of telegraphic science, as well as to his own experimental researches, previous to Morse's invention, was compelled to give evidence which did not sustain entirely the theory of the complainants, and therefore did not satisfy their very broad pretensions; though it did tend to establish Professor Morse's just claims to originality. This account can best be given in Henry's own statement:

"A series of controversies and lawsuits having arisen between rival claimants for telegraphic patents, I was repeatedly appealed to, to act as *expert* and witness in such cases. This I uniformly declined to do, not wishing to be in any manner involved in these litigations, but was finally compelled, under legal process, to return to Boston from Maine, whither I had gone on a visit, and to give evidence on the subject. My testimony was given with the statement that I was not a willing witness, and that I labored under the disadvantage of not having access to my notes and papers, which were in Washington. That testimony however I now reaffirm to be true in every essential particular. It was unimpeached before the court, and exercised an influence on the final decision of the question at issue. I was called upon on that occasion to state, not only what I had published, but what I had done, and what I had shown to others in regard to the telegraph. It was my wish, in every statement, to render Mr. Morse full and scrupulous justice. While I was constrained therefore to state that he had made no discoveries in science, I distinctly declared that he was entitled to the merit of combining and applying the discoveries of others, in the invention of the best practical form of the magnetic telegraph. My testimony tended to establish the fact that though not entitled to the exclusive use of the electro-magnet for telegraphic purposes, he was entitled to his particular machine, register, alphabet, &c. As this however did not meet the full requirements of Mr. Morse's comprehensive claim, I could not but be aware that, while aiming to depose nothing but truth and the whole truth, - - - I might expose myself to the possible, and as it has proved, the actual, danger of having my motives misconstrued and my testimony misrepresented. But I can truly aver that I had no desire to arrogate to myself undue merit, or to detract from the just claims of Mr. Morse." *

From this time, Professor Morse seemed to regard Henry with the jealous eye of a rival, as if holding him disposed for purposes of self-aggrandizement to detract from his own merit as projector of the telegraph. After years of preparation, he had completed

---

* *Smithsonian Report* for 1857, pp. 87, 88.

and signed in December, 1853, and in January of 1855, under the ill-advised promptings of interested supporters, caused to be published in a pamphlet of 96 pages, an elaborate and artfully contrived attack upon Henry's character as a scientific explorer, and as a trustworthy man; undertaking the hazardous task of exposing "the utter *non-reliability* of Henry's testimony." In this assault — so unfortunate for his own reputation, (if not for candor, at least for intelligence,) he announced:

"1st. I certainly shall show that I have not only manifested every disposition to give due credit to Professor Henry, but under the hasty impression that he deserved credit for discoveries in science bearing upon the telegraph, I did actually give him a degree of credit not only beyond what he had received at that time from the scientific world, but a degree of credit to which subsequent research has proved him not to be entitled. 2d. I shall show that I am not indebted to him for any discovery in science bearing on the telegraph, and that all discoveries of principles having this bearing were made not by Professor Henry, but by others and prior to any experiments of Professor Henry in the science of electro-magnetism. 3d. I shall further show that the claim set up for Professor Henry to the invention of an important part of my telegraph system, has no validity in fact." *

Neglecting entirely the first allegation, — as a sufficient answer to the second, Henry simply appealed to the unimpeachable testimony of Dr. Gale, who certainly had a much more precise knowledge of Professor Morse's early experiments and apparatus than the inventor himself. And in reply to the third allegation, driven in self-defence to the unusual step of self-assertion, Henry presented to the Regents for their adjudication, the evidences of his discoveries and of their respective dates of application and promulgation. †

Professor Gale, who still preserved a faithful friendship for his former colleague, yet in the interests of truth did not hesitate to renew his former testimony to the vital bearing of Henry's researches

---

* *A Defence against the injurious deductions drawn from the Deposition of Professor Henry.* New York, 1855, p. 8.

† A select committee appointed by the Board of Regents to investigate the imputations made by this remarkable assault — against the truthfulness of their Secretary, after a careful examination of all the evidences presented or accessible, submitted through its chairman, President Felton of Harvard University, a very able and exhaustive report, in which the tenor of the pamphlet is characterized as "a disingenuous piece of sophistical argument," and the conclusion is announced, "that Mr. Morse has failed to substantiate any one of the charges he has made against Professor Henry, although the burden of proof lay upon him; and that all the evidence — including the unbiased admissions of Mr. Morse himself, is on the other side. Mr. Morse's charges not only remain unproved, but they are positively disproved." (*Smithsonian Report* for 1857, pp. 88–98.)

on the success of the telegraph; and he frankly responded to Henry's inquiry in the following letter:

"WASHINGTON, D. C., April 7, 1856.

"SIR: In reply to your note of the 3d instant, respecting the Morse telegraph, asking me to state definitely the condition of the invention when I first saw the apparatus in the winter of 1836, I answer: This apparatus was Morse's original instrument, usually known as the type apparatus, in which the types, set up in a composing stick, were run through a circuit breaker, and in which the battery was the cylinder battery, with a single pair of plates. This arrangement also had another peculiarity, namely, it was the electro-magnet used by Moll,* and shown in drawings of the older works on that subject, having only a few turns of wire in the coil which surrounded the poles or arms of the magnet. The spareness of the wires in the magnet coils and the use of the single cup battery were to me, on the first look at the instrument, obvious marks of defect, and I accordingly suggested to the Professor, without giving my reasons for so doing, that a battery of many pairs should be substituted for that of a single pair, and that the coil on each arm of the magnet should be increased to many hundred turns each; which experiment, if I remember aright, was made on the same day with a battery and wire on hand, furnished I believe by myself, and it was found that while the original arrangement would only send the electric current through a few feet of wire, say 15 to 40, the modified arrangement would send it through as many hundred. Although I gave no reasons at the time to Professor Morse for the suggestions I had proposed in modifying the arrangement of the machine, I did so afterwards, and referred in my explanations to the paper of Professor Henry, in the 19th volume of the *American Journal of Science*, page 400 and onward.

"At the time I gave the suggestions above named, Professor Morse was not familiar with the then existing state of the science of electro-magnetism. Had he been so, or had he read and appreciated the paper of Henry, the suggestions made by me would naturally have occurred to his mind as they did to my own. But the principal part of Morse's great invention lay in the mechanical adaptation of a power to produce motion, and to increase or relax at will. It was only necessary for him to know that such a power existed for him to adapt mechanism to direct and control it. My suggestions were made to Professor Morse from inferences drawn by reading Professor Henry's paper above alluded to. Professor Morse

---

*[More correctly, the magnet of STURGEON.]

professed great surprise at the contents of the paper when I showed it to him, but especially at the remarks on Dr. Barlow's results respecting telegraphing, which were new to him, and he stated at the time that he was not aware that any one had even conceived the idea of using the magnet for such purposes.

 "With sentiments of esteem, I remain, yours truly,

"L. D. GALE.

"Prof. Jos. HENRY, *Secretary of the Smithsonian Institution.*"

A simple reference to published documents, abundantly established the indisputable originality and priority of Henry's successful researches; and conclusively exposed the falsity of Professor Morse's remaining allegations. The following summary from the historic evidence, as stated by Henry himself, is certainly (in the language of the committee of the Regents) "within what he might fairly have claimed :"

"From a careful investigation of the history of electro-magnetism in its connection with the telegraph, the following facts may be established :

"1. Previous to my investigations the means of developing magnetism in soft iron were imperfectly understood, and the electromagnet which then existed was inapplicable to the transmission of power to a distance.

"2. I was the first to prove by actual experiment that in order to develop magnetic power at a distance, a galvanic battery of intensity must be employed to project the current through the long conductor, and that a magnet surrounded by many turns of one long wire may be used to receive this current.

"3. I was the first actually to magnetize a piece of iron at a distance, and to call attention to the fact of the applicability of my experiments to the telegraph.

"4. I was the first to actually sound a bell at a distance by means of the electro-magnet.

"5. The principles I had developed were applied by Dr. Gale to render Morse's machine effective at a distance.

"The results here given were among my earliest experiments; in a scientific point of view I considered them of much less importance than what I subsequently accomplished; and had I not been called upon to give my testimony in regard to them, I would have suffered them to remain without calling public attention to them, a part of the history of science to be judged of by scientific men who are the best qualified to pronounce upon their merits." *

---

* *Smithsonian Report* for 1857, p. 106.

## Note D.   *(From p. 230.)*

### HENRY'S MUTIPLE-COIL MAGNET.

Professor M. Faraday, in the first series of his "Experimental Researches in Electricity," commencing in the latter part of 1831, employed for the magnet by which he made his most important discovery — that of magneto-electricity,—the multiple coil of Henry. He thus describes it: "A welded ring was made of soft round bar-iron, the metal being seven-eighths of an inch in thickness, and the ring six inches in external diameter.   Three helices were put around one part of this ring, each containing about twenty-four feet of copper wire one-twentieth of an inch thick: they were insulated from the iron and each other, and superposed in the manner before described.*   They could be used separately or arranged together. On the other part of the ring about sixty feet of similar copper wire in two pieces were applied in the same manner. - - - There is no doubt that arrangments like the magnets of Professors Moll, Henry, Ten-Eyck, and others, in which as many as 2,000 pounds have been lifted, may be used for these experiments."†

Henry's warm friend — Dr. Robert Hare of Philadelphia, (Professor of Chemistry in the University of Pennsylvania,) who early repeated his magnetic experiments, says in a letter to Mr. Sturgeon, dated April 5, 1832: "As soon as I heard of the wonderful magnet of Professor Henry, I repeated his experiments with copper wire varnished as above described; and I have recently made a magnet by means of copper wire, shellac varnish, and paper surrounding the iron,—which in proportion to its weight, holds more than his.   It weighs 17 pounds, and has held 783 pounds.   It is furnished with fourteen coils, of sixty feet each."‡

Professor N. J. Callan, of the College of Maynooth, Ireland, in 1836, giving an account of his "new galvanic battery" remarks

---

*[In his preceding electrical induction coils, Professor Faraday employed "twelve helices superposed, each containing an average length of wire of 27 feet, and all in the same direction." Of these, six were connected by their extremities with the battery — for the primary current, and the alternate six were gathered by their extremities, for testing the secondary or induced current.]

† *Phil. Trans. Roy. Soc.* Nov. 24, 1831, vol. cxxii. sects. 27 and 57; pp. 131, 138.—Also *Experimental Researches, etc.* 8vo. London, 1839, vol. i. pp. 7, 15.  At the time this was written, the only electro-magnet in existence—even approaching the lifting power stated, was the Yale College magnet of HENRY.  Nor had any other experimenter approximated within a *tenth* of this magnetic attraction.  And it is noteworthy that Professor Faraday adopted very precisely the character of coil originated and recommended by Henry, and did not adopt the single coil employed by Professor Moll.

‡ Sturgeon's *Annals of Electricity, etc.* Oct. 1836, vol. i. p. 10.

that "it rendered powerfully magnetic an electro-magnet on which were coiled 39 thick copper wires, each about 35 feet long." *

The only subsequent extension of Henry's results worthy of note, is that made by the ingenious English physicist Joule. It had been found that the maximum attractive force of the electro-magnet is exhibited near its surface, and that an enlargement of the iron does not correspondingly enhance its magnetic power.† If we adopt the conception of Coulomb and of Weber that the constituent molecules of the iron are each independent permanent magnets, this variation of magnetic force in a large iron bar, receives an easy explanation; since the middle portion of the bar is not only less coerced by the surrounding coil,‡ but is powerfully impressed by the opposite induction of the outer belt of polarized molecules. While therefore we should *a priori* expect the aggregate attractive force to increase with the size of the bar, (*i. e.* the cross-section or end-surface of the poles,) we find that this very extension occasions a large amount of neutralization by the interior opposite magnetism; such depolarization being obviously the condition of least constraint.§

Acting on the theory that the power of the magnet would depend on the extent of efficient polar surface, and at the same time on the propinquity of the electric coil, Joule's highest magnetic triumph consisted in giving a greatly increased *depth* to the horse-shoe, (as though a vast number of small horse-shoes were laid side to side and cemented together,) without an increase of its *width;* the former dimension exceeding the latter many times: so that the two poles presented a pair of long narrow parallel surfaces close together, bounding a long trough or gutter. And the addition of the oblong armature gave the whole the general appearance of a tube. The author thus describes its construction: "A piece of cylindrical wrought-iron, eight inches long, had a hole one inch in diameter bored the whole length of its axis; one side was then planed until

---

* *L. & E. Phil. Mag.* Dec. 1836, vol. ix. p. 475.

† Barlow had drawn the conclusion from his own experiments, that the magnetic power of iron resides entirely at the surface, and is irrespective of mass.

‡ The direct action of the electric circuit in the coil would probably not be sensibly less on the interior than on the exterior of a large iron core; but its polarizing energy must necessarily be largely expended in coercing the homologous direction of the nearest outer layers of molecules, leaving the interior mass more under the immediate inductive influence of its girdle of magnets.

§ Having this in view Joule (in imitation of Coulomb's faggot of thin magnets) employed with success a bundle of wires for the electro-magnetic core. (Sturgeon's *Annals,* etc. July, 1839, vol. iv. pp. 58–61.) It is evident also from the above, that the removal of the central portion of the inner core, in other words the employment of a tube of certain thickness, in place of the solid bar, would actually increase the resultant power of the magnet, with a diminished mass of iron.

the hole was exposed sufficiently to separate the 'poles' one-third of an inch. Another piece of iron also eight inches long was then planed, and being secured with its face in contact with the other planed surface, the whole was turned into a cylinder eight inches long, three inches and three-quarters in exterior—and one inch interior diameter. The larger piece was then covered with calico, and wound with four copper wires (covered with silk) each 23 feet long and one-eleventh of an inch in diameter;—a quantity which was just sufficient to hide the exterior surface, and entirely to fill the inside hole."* This magnet weighing without wire but 15 pounds, lifted 2,090 pounds.

Joule subsequently made another magnet still deeper, or longer in its tubular extent; the grooved iron with its closed armature being not unlike a gun-barrel. The length of this soft-iron cylinder was two feet; its external diameter about one inch and a half, and its internal diameter a half inch: the weight of the grooved magnet being 6 pounds 11 ounces, and that of its armature, 3 pounds 7 ounces. A copper rod three-eighths of an inch thick was bent once around each side of the tube, or elongated pole. With a battery of 8 cells of two square feet each (16 square feet) arranged as a single pair, a lifting power of 1,350 pounds was induced. The single thick copper rod having then been replaced with a bundle of 60 copper wires, each one-twenty-fifth of an inch thick, the magnet lifted 1,856 pounds. This remarkable success of the "multiple coil" led Joule to increase the number of coils in the former tube-like magnet. The four wires each one-eleventh of an inch thick were replaced by twenty-one wires of the same length, each one-twenty-fifth of an inch thick, the whole being bound together by cotton tape. "Sixteen cast-iron cells of the same size as those previously described, [each of two square feet,] were then arranged in a series of four, and connected by sufficiently good conductors to the electro-magnet. The power which was then necessary to break it from its armature, was 2,775 pounds, or nearly a ton and a quarter. An immense weight, when it is considered that the whole apparatus—magnet armature and coils—weighs less than 26 pounds."†

---

* Sturgeon's *Annals of Electricity*, etc. Sept. 1840, vol. v. pp. 190, 191. A second much smaller magnet of similar form, being 2.7 inches long, and half an inch in diameter, wrapped with 7 feet of insulated copper wire one-twentieth of an inch thick, and weighing 1,057 grains, (somewhat over two ounces,) lifted 49 pounds. A third magnet elliptical in form (0.37 inch broad and 0.15 inch thick) 0.7 inch long, covered with 19 inches of copper wire one-fortieth of an inch thick, and weighing 65.3 grains, lifted 12 pounds. And a fourth magnet one twenty-fifth of an inch thick and one-quarter of an inch long, with three turns of fine copper wire, weighing half a grain, lifted 1,417 grains.

† Sturgeon's *Annals of Electricity*, Dec. 1840, vol. v. pp. 471, 472.

Stimulated by Joule's successes, several attempts were made by others, embodying the same principle of narrow but greatly extended poles. Mr. Richard Roberts constructed what may be called a "disk" magnet, the square plate of iron being nearly two and a half inches thick, with a planed face six and five-eighths inches on the sides, and having a supporting eye formed on its back. Four equidistant parallel grooves each three-eighths of an inch wide and one inch and a quarter deep, divided the square face into five equal oblong "poles." A bundle of 36 copper wires (No. 18) was coiled in and out about these five poles, in three turns. The magnet with its coils weighed 35 pounds. The armature, a similar square plate one inch and a half thick, (without grooves,) weighed 23 pounds. With a battery of eight pairs, (each about 100 square inches, or five-sevenths of a square foot,) the magnet sustained 2,950 pounds; about one ton and a third.* This magnet is obviously equivalent to two or more of Joule's, placed side by side. Mr. Joseph Radford, about the same time, devised another form of "disk" magnet much more novel in construction. In this case a circular plate 9 inches in diameter and about an inch thick, (provided with a supporting eye at the middle of its back,) had a spiral groove cut in its planed face, one-quarter of an inch wide and three-eighths of an inch deep, making from the center about six turns, and leaving a spiral ridge of metal at the face about half an inch thick. Its weight (without wire) was 16 pounds 2 ounces, or with the wire coil 18 pounds 4 ounces. .The armature, a similar smooth disk of about two-thirds the thickness of the magnet, weighed 14 pounds 14 ounces. The coil, a bundle of 23 small copper wires entering from the back through a hole at the center of the disk and following the spiral groove, (which it filled,) passed out at the edge of. the disk. By this singular disposition of the coil, the single spiral "pole" or narrow ridge (half an inch in thickness) had a continuous north polarity on the one side and a continuous adjacent south polarity on its other side: being in the same condition as a long narrow bar of soft iron having a galvanic current passing longitudinally along its opposite sides in the same direction. With a battery of twelve pairs this spiral disk magnet sustained 2,500 pounds; about one ton and one-eighth. †

Another variety of the disk magnet devised by Joule, presented an annular face of about 12 inches exterior diameter and about 8 inches interior diameter, having 48 radial grooves separating 48 radial poles. A bundle of 16 copper wires bent alternately in and out about these 48 lateral ridges or face cogs, produced a series of

---

* Sturgeon's *Annals of Electricity*, Feb. 1841, vol. vi. pp. 167, 168.

† Sturgeon's *Annals of Electricity*, March, 1841, vol. vi. p. 231.

alternate poles. This was virtually an extension of the Roberts series of magnetic poles, equivalent to a series of 24 of Joule's narrow magnets placed side by side and arranged radially in a ring. This circular battery of magnets, excited by 16 cups arranged in a series of four, lifted 2,710 pounds.*

It will be noticed that in each of these interesting improvements on the simple horse-shoe "quantity" magnet, the highest efficiency was obtained by adopting Henry's system of "multiple coils."

This system has also been most successfully applied by Z. T. Gramme, of Paris, to the revolving annular inductor of his very ingenious and powerful form of magneto-electric machine.

---

### Note E.  (From p. 243.)

#### ABSTRACT OF PAPER ON SELF-INDUCTION.

Professor Bache, as a Secretary of the American Philosophical Society, (knowing that the "Transactions" of the Body, containing Henry's important Memoir, would not be formally published for a year or more,) with that energetic zeal of friendship so characteristic of the man, obtained permission to publish an abstract of the previous verbal communication; which he accordingly proceeded to have at once inserted in the forthcoming number of the Franklin Institute "Journal," with the following prefatory letter addressed "To the Committee of Publication" of that Journal:

GENTLEMEN:—The American Philosophical Society, at their last stated meeting, authorized the publication of the following abstract of a verbal communication made to the Society, by Professor Henry, on the 16th of January last. A memoir on this subject has been since submitted to the Society, containing an extension of the subject, the primary fact in relation to which was observed by Professor Henry as early as 1832, and announced by him in the *American Journal of Science*. Mr. Faraday having recently entered upon a similar train of observations, the immediate publication of the accompanying is important, that the prior claims of our fellow countryman may not be overlooked.

Very respectfully yours,

A. D. BACHE,
*One of the Secretaries Am. Philos. Soc.*
Philadelphia, Feb. 7th, 1835.

---

* Sturgeon's *Annals of Electricity*, June, 1841, vol. vi. p. 432.

" *Extract from the proceedings of the stated meeting of the* **American** *Philosophical Society,* **January 16,** *1835.*

"The following facts in reference to the spark, shock, &c. from a galvanic battery, when the poles are united by a long conductor, were communicated by Professor Joseph Henry, and those relating to the spark were illustrated experimentally:

"1. A long wire gives a more intense spark than a short one. There is, however, a length beyond which the effect is not increased; a wire of 120 feet gave about the same intensity of spark as one of 240 **feet.**

"2. A thick wire gives a larger spark than a smaller one of the same length.

"3. A wire coiled into a helix, gives a more vivid spark than the same wire when uncoiled.

"4. A ribbon of copper, coiled into a flat spiral, gives a more intense spark than any other arrangement yet tried.

"5. The effect is increased, by using a longer and wider ribbon, to an extent not yet determined. The greatest effect has been produced by a coil 96 feet long, and weighing 15 pounds; a larger conductor has not been received.

"6. A ribbon of copper, first doubled into two strands, and then coiled into a flat spiral, gives no spark, or a very feeble one.

"7. Large copper handles, soldered to the ends of the coil of 96 feet, and these both grasped, one by each hand, a shock is felt at the elbows, when the contact is broken in a battery with one and a half feet of zinc surface.

"8. A shock is also felt when the copper of the battery is grasped with one hand, and one of the handles with the other; the intensity however is not as great as in the last case. This method of receiving the shock may be called the direct method, the other the lateral one.

"9. The decomposition of a liquid is effected by the use of the coil from a single pair, by intermitting the current, and introducing a pair of decomposing wires.

"10. A mixture of oxygen and hydrogen is also exploded by using the coil, and breaking the contact, in a bladder containing the mixture.

"11. The property of producing an intense spark is induced, on a short wire, by introducing, at any point of a compound galvanic current, a large flat spiral.

"12. A spark is produced even when the plates of a single battery are separated by a foot or more of diluted acid.

"13. Little or no increase in the effect is produced by inserting a piece of soft iron into the center of a flat spiral.

"14. The effect produced by an electro-magnet, in giving the shock, is due principally to the coiling of the long wire which surrounds the soft iron." *

---

## Note F.   (From p. 255.)

### OSCILLATION OF ELECTRICAL DISCHARGE.

Sir William Thomson, in 1853, indicated the probability of an oscillatory character in the electrical discharge; remarking: "It appears to me not improbable that double, triple, and quadruple flashes of lightning which I have frequently seen on the continent of Europe, and sometimes though not so frequently in this country, (lasting generally long enough to allow an observer after his attention is drawn by the first light of the flash, to turn his head around and see distinctly the course of the lightning in the sky,) result from the discharge possessing this oscillatory character. - - - The decomposition of water by electricity from an ordinary electrical machine, in which, as has been shown by Faraday, more than the electro-chemical equivalent of the whole electricity that passes, appears in oxygen and hydrogen rising mixed from each pole, is probably due to electrical oscillations in the discharges consequent on the successive sparks." †

In a foot-note at this point of the paper, the eminent physicist adds: "This explanation occurred to me about a year and a half ago, in consequence of the conclusions regarding the oscillatory nature of the discharge in certain circumstances, drawn from mathematical investigation. I afterward found that it had been suggested as a conjecture by Helmholtz in his *Erhaltung der Kraft*, (Berlin, 1847,) in the following terms: 'It is easy to explain this law, if we assume that the discharge of a battery is not a simple motion of the electricity in one direction, but a backward and forward motion between the coatings, in oscillations which become continually smaller until the entire *vis viva* is destroyed by the sum of the resistances. The notion that the current of discharge consists of alternately opposed currents is favored by the alternately opposed magnetic actions of the same; and secondly by the phenomena observed by Wollaston while attempting to decompose

---

* *Journal of the Franklin Institute*, March, 1835, vol. xv. pp. 169, 170.

† *L. E. D. Phil. Mag.* June, 1853, vol. v. pp. 400, 401.

water by electric shocks, that both descriptions of gases are exhibited at both electrodes.' " *

Seventeen years after Henry's experimental determination, Mr. W. Feddersen, in 1859, observed the oscillatory nature of the electrical discharge, by employing the revolving mirror of Wheatstone, as first suggested by Sir William Thomson.†

It is remarkable however that very early in the century, the return discharge of electricity appears to have been distinctly noted. In Gilbert's *Annalen* for 1806, the phenomenon of a "back-stroke" is spoken of as being "not uncommon in thunder-storms." ‡ And twenty years before the conjecture by Helmholtz, or in 1827, the same suspicion or rather conviction of an oscillatory discharge was distinctly expressed by Felix Savary, who perplexed by the irregularity of magnetization in small needles, when effected by the Leyden jar, thus comments on the problem:

"An electrical discharge is a phenomenon of motion. Is this motion a translation of matter — continuous — in a fixed direction? If so, the alternations of opposite magnetisms observed at various distances from a rectilinear conductor, or in a helix for gradually increasing discharges, would be due solely to the mutual re-actions of the magnetic particles in the steel needles. The manner in which the behavior of a wire changes with its length, appears to me to exclude this supposition. Does the electric flow during a discharge consist on the contrary of a series of oscillations transmitted from the wire to the surrounding mediums, and speedily enfeebled by resistances which increase rapidly with the absolute velocity of the agitated particles? All the phenomena lead to this hypothesis; which assumes that not only the intensity, but the direction of the magnetism, depends on the laws according to which the minute motions die away in the wire, in the medium surrounding it, and in the substance which receives and preserves the magnetism. The oscillations in the wire would have an absolute velocity so much the less, and would subside so much the more rapidly, accordingly as the wire were longer, as it were finer, and as the resistance belonging to its constitution were greater. It may thus be explained how there is for a rectilinear conductor and a given discharge, a length of wire which will produce the strongest magnetization; if the

---

* Quoted from a memoir "On the Conservation of Force," by Dr. H. Helmholtz. Read before the Physical Society of Berlin, on the 23d of July, 1847. The memoir was translated by Dr. J. Tyndall, and published in his selection of "Scientific Memoirs," London, 1853, vol. i. p. 143. This interesting collection of foreign papers forms a continuation of Taylor's "Scientific Memoirs," in five volumes.

† Poggendorff's *Annalen der Physik*, 1859, vol. cviii. p. 499.

‡ Gilbert's *Annalen der Physik*, 1806, vol. xxiv. p. 351.

length is less, the minute motions diminish too **slowly**; if greater, their intensity is too much enfeebled."[*]

---

### Note G.  (*From p. 272.*)

#### WHEATSTONE'S CHRONOSCOPE.

For the purpose of measuring and registering extremely short intervals of time, Professor Charles Wheatstone, extending his earlier experiments of 1834, on the velocity of electricity by means of a revolving mirror, projected a "**chronoscope**" based on the automatic agency of electro-magnetism.  Among the applications in **view** were the determination **of the exact times** of falling bodies, **the duration of an explosion** of gunpowder, etc.  At what time **this** ingenious **device was** practically developed, it is difficult **to** say; but we learn **that** M. Konstantinoff, an accomplished Russian Artillery Officer, **visiting** England **in 1842**, had this **project** shown or explained **to him by** Professor **Wheatstone.**  Looking at the possibilities of **this suggestion from his professional** stand-point, M. Konstantinoff at once directed his attention to the contrivance **of a** modification of the arrangement, adapted to measure **the velocity** of a **projectile at various points of its flight.**  Invoking the well-known **electrical knowledge and skill of his** friend Mons. **L. Bre**guet of Paris in 1843, **the two commenced in June** of that year **the** construction of a machine which should **indicate and** record **30 or 40 successive observations within the few seconds of a** projectile's **flight.**  The apparatus was successfully completed May 29, 1844; and an account of it was read before the French Academy, January 20th, 1845.[†]  In this instrument, the various **records were** made on a timed revolving cylinder, by styles or pencils, actuated **by electro-**magnetic motions **at** the several moments of breaking successive circuits.  Wheatstone's reclamation, and account of his own invention, were published four **months later, through** the same channel.[‡]

The two chronoscopes **were undoubtedly the** same in principle, although Wheatstone's gave but **two** records;—an initial one by the falling or projected ball breaking **the galvanic circuit, and a** terminal one by a re-establishment of the circuit on the ball striking a horizontal or a vertical **spring plate and thus** causing a metallic contact to be made.  For measuring the interval, Wheatstone em-

---

[*] *Annales de Chimie et de Physique*, 1827, vol. xxxiv. pp. 51, 55.

[†] *Comptes Rendus*, Jan. 1845, vol. xx. pp. 157-162.

[‡] *Comptes Rendus*, May 26, 1845, vol. xx. pp. 1554-1561.

ployed a revolving time index on a dial, arrested by the armature of an electro-magnet. The arrangement adopted by Breguet and Konstantinoff in 1844, resembled much more closely that described and published by Henry in 1843, than that devised by Wheatstone and published in 1845; and both were really more complete for the specific purpose of measuring the velocity of projectiles, than the last-named, and first invented. Moreover, while the latter was a "chronoscope," the two former were really "chronographs."

Henry's second plan of registering by the induction spark, was far more delicate and exact than either; as it dispensed with the inertia of a moving galvanometer needle, or magnetic armature.

---

## Note II. (From p. 275.)

### HENRY'S "PROGRAMME OF ORGANIZATION."

The plan for the organization and conduct of the Smithsonian Institution, as more fully presented by the Secretary in his first annual report made December 8th, 1847, and adopted by the Board of Regents December 13th, 1847, is regarded as sufficiently interesting and important to be here given at length :

### "INTRODUCTION.

*General considerations which should serve as a guide in adopting a Plan of Organization.*

1. Will of Smithson. The property is bequeathed to the United States of America, "to found at Washington, under the name of the SMITHSONIAN INSTITUTION, an establishment for the increase and diffusion of knowledge among men."

2. The bequest is for the benefit of mankind. The Government of the United States is merely a trustee to carry out the design of the testator.

3. The Institution is not a national establishment, as is frequently supposed, but the establishment of an individual, and is to bear and perpetuate his name.

4. The objects of the Institution are, 1st, to increase, and 2d, to diffuse knowledge among men.

5. These two objects should not be confounded with one another. The first is to enlarge the existing stock of knowledge by the addition of new truths; and the second, to disseminate knowledge, thus increased, among men.

6. The will makes no restriction in favor of any particular kind of knowledge; hence all branches are entitled to a share of attention.

7. Knowledge can be increased by different methods of facilitating and promoting the discovery of new truths; and can be most extensively diffused among men by means of the press.

8: To effect the greatest amount of good, the organization should be such as to enable the Institution to produce results, in the way of increasing and diffusing knowledge, which cannot be produced either at all or so efficiently by the existing institutions in our country.

9. The organization should also be such as can be adopted provisionally; can be easily reduced to practice, receive modifications, or be abandoned, in whole or in part, without a sacrifice of the funds.

10. In order to compensate, in some measure, for the loss of time occasioned by the delay of eight years in establishing the Institution, a considerable portion of the interest which has accrued should be added to the principal.

11. In proportion to the wide field of knowledge to be cultivated, the funds are small. Economy should therefore be consulted in the construction of the building; and not only the first cost of the edifice should be considered, but also the continual expense of keeping it in repair, and of the support of the establishment necessarily connected with it. There should also be but few individuals permanently supported by the Institution.

12. The plan and dimensions of the building should be determined by the plan of the organization, and not the converse.

13. It should be recollected that mankind in general are to be benefitted by the bequest, and that therefore all unnecessary expenditure on local objects would be a perversion of the trust.

14. Besides the foregoing considerations, deduced immediately from the will of Smithson, regard must be had to certain requirements of the act of Congress establishing the Institution. These are, a library, a museum, and a gallery of art, with a building on a liberal scale to contain them.

## SECTION I.

*Plan of Organization of the Institution in accordance with the foregoing deductions from the Will of Smithson.*

To INCREASE KNOWLEDGE. It is proposed — 1. To stimulate men of talent to make original researches, by offering suitable rewards for memoirs containing new truths; and, — 2. To appropriate annually a portion of the income for particular researches, under the direction of suitable persons.

To DIFFUSE KNOWLEDGE. It is proposed — 1. To publish a series of periodical reports on the progress of the different branches of knowledge; and, — 2. To publish occasionally separate treatises on subjects of general interest.

### DETAILS OF THE PLAN TO INCREASE KNOWLEDGE.

I. *By stimulating researches.*—1. Facilities afforded for the production of original memoirs on all branches of knowledge. 2. The memoirs thus obtained to be published in a series of volumes, in a quarto form, and entitled Smithsonian Contributions to Knowledge. 3. No memoir on subjects of physical science to be accepted for publication which does not furnish a positive addition to human knowledge, resting on original research; and all unverified speculations to be rejected.* 4. Each memoir presented to the Institution to be submitted for examination to a commission of persons of reputation for learning in the branch to which the memoir pertains; and to be accepted for publication only in case the report of this commission is favorable. 5. The commission to be chosen by the officers of the Institution, and the name of the author (as far as practicable) concealed, unless a favorable decision be made. 6. The volumes of the memoirs to be exchanged for the Transactions of literary and scientific societies, and copies to be given to all the colleges and principal libraries in this country. One part of the remaining copies may be offered for sale; and the other carefully preserved, to form complete sets of the work, to supply the demand from new institutions. 7. An abstract or popular account of the contents of these memoirs to be given to the public through the annual report of the Regents to Congress.

II. *By appropriating a part of the income, annually, to special objects of research, under the direction of suitable persons.*—1. The objects and the amount appropriated, to be recommended by counsellors of the Institution. 2. Appropriations in different years to different objects; so that in course of time each branch of knowledge may receive a share. 3. The results obtained from these appropriations to be published, with the memoirs before mentioned, in the volumes of the Smithsonian Contributions to Knowledge. 4. Examples of objects for which appropriations may be made:

---

* "It has been supposed from the adoption of this proposition, that we are disposed to undervalue abstract speculation: on the contrary, we know that all the advances in true science, (namely a knowledge of the laws of phenomena,) are made by provisionally adopting well-conditioned hypotheses, the product of the imagination, and subsequently verifying them by an appeal to experiment and observation." (Explanations of the programme.)

26

(*a.*) System of extended meteorological observations **for** solving the problem of American storms.   (*b.*) Explorations in descriptive natural history, **and** geological, magnetical, and topographical surveys, to collect materials for the formation of a Physical Atlas **of** the United States.   (**c.**) Solution of experimental problems, such **as** a new determination **of** the weight **of** the earth, of the velocity **of** electricity, and of **light;** chemical analyses of soils and plants; **collection and** publication of scientific facts, accumulated in the **offices of** Government.   (*d.*) Institution of statistical inquiries with reference to physical, moral, **and** political subjects.   (*e.*) Historical researches, and accurate surveys of **places** celebrated **in American** history.   (*f.*) Ethnological researches, particularly **with reference** to the different races of men in North America; also, **explorations** and accurate **surveys of the** mounds and other remains of the ancient people of our country.

## DETAILS OF THE PLAN FOR DIFFUSING KNOWLEDGE.

I. *By the publication of a series of reports, giving an account of the new discoveries in science, and of the changes made from year to year in all branches of knowledge not strictly professional.\**— 1. These **reports** will diffuse a kind of knowledge generally interesting, **but which at present** is inaccessible to the public.   Some of **the** reports may be published annually, others at longer **intervals, as the** income **of** the Institution or **the** changes in the branches of knowledge may **indicate.**   2. The reports **are to be prepared by** collaborators eminent **in the** different branches of knowledge. 3. Each **collaborator to be** furnished with the journals and publications, **domestic and foreign,** necessary to the compilation of his report; **to be** paid a certain **sum for his labors, and to be** named on the title-page of the **report.**   **4. The reports to be** published **in** separate parts, so that persons interested in a particular branch **can** procure the parts relating **to it** without purchasing **the** whole. 5. These reports **may be** presented to Congress, **for** partial distribution, the remaining copies **to be given** to literary and scientific institutions, and sold to **individuals for** a moderate **price.†**

---

\* This part of the plan has been but partially carried out.

† The following are some of the subjects which may be embraced in the reports:
I. PHYSICAL CLASS.—1. Physics, including astronomy, natural philosophy, chemistry, and meteorology.  2. Natural history, including botany, zoology, geology, &c. 3. Agriculture.  4. Application of science to arts.

II. MORAL AND POLITICAL CLASS.—5. Ethnology, including particular history, comparative philology, antiquities, &c.  6. Statistics and political economy. 7. Mental and moral philosophy.  8. A survey of the political events of the world; penal reform, &c.

III. LITERATURE AND THE FINE ARTS.—9. Modern literature.  10. The fine arts, and their application to the useful arts.  11. Bibliography  12. Obituary notices of distinguished individuals.

II. *By the publication of separate treatises on subjects of general interest.*—1. These treatises may occasionally consist of valuable memoirs translated from foreign languages, or of articles prepared under the direction of the Institution, or procured by offering premiums for the best exposition of a given subject. 2. The treatises should in all cases be submitted to a commission of competent judges, previous to their publication. 3. As examples of these treatises, expositions may be obtained of the present state of the several branches of knowledge mentioned in the table of reports.

## SECTION II.

*Plan of Organization, in accordance with the terms of the resolutions of the Board of Regents providing for the two modes of increasing and diffusing knowledge.*

1. The act of Congress establishing the Institution contemplated the formation of a library and a museum; and the Board of Regents, including these objects in the plan of organization, resolved to divide the income * into two equal parts.

2. One part to be appropriated to increase and diffuse knowledge by means of publications and researches, agreeably to the scheme before given. The other part to be appropriated to the formation of a library and a collection of objects of nature and of art.

3. These two plans are not incompatible with one another.

4. To carry out the plan before described, a library will be required, consisting, 1st, of a complete collection of the transactions and proceedings of all the learned societies in the world; 2d, of the more important current periodical publications, and other works necessary in preparing the periodical reports.

5. The Institution should make special collections, particularly of objects to illustrate and verify its own publications.

6. Also, a collection of instruments of research in all branches of experimental science.

7. With reference to the collection of books, other than those mentioned above, catalogues of all the different libraries in the United States should be procured, in order that the valuable books first purchased may be such as are not to be found in the United States.

---

* The amount of the Smithsonian bequest received into the Treasury of the United States is_____ $515,169 00

Interest on the same to July 1, 1846, (devoted to the erection of the building)_____ 242,129 00

Annual income from the bequest_____ 30,910 14

[The expedient of devoting one-half the income to the Congressional programme, was by the urgency and influence of Henry, some years afterward revoked: though not without a violent opposition by the Library advocates.]

8. Also, catalogues of memoirs, and of books and other materials, should be collected for rendering the Institution a centre of bibliographical knowledge, whence the student may be directed to any work which he may require.

9. It is believed that the collections in natural history will increase by donation as rapidly as the income of the Institution can make provision for their reception, and therefore it will seldom be necessary to purchase articles of this kind.

10. Attempts should be made to procure for the gallery of art casts of the most celebrated articles of ancient and modern sculpture.

11. The arts may be encouraged by providing a room, free of expense, for the exhibition of the objects of the Art-Union and other similar societies.

12. A small appropriation should annually be made for models of antiquities, such as those of the remains of ancient temples, &c.

13. For the present, or until the building is fully completed, besides the Secretary, no permanent assistant will be required, except one, to act as librarian.

14. The Secretary, by the law of Congress, is alone responsible to the Regents. He shall take charge of the building and property, keep a record of proceedings, discharge the duties of librarian and keeper of the museum, and may, with the consent of the Regents, employ assistants.

15. The Secretary and his assistants (during the session of Congress) will be required to illustrate new discoveries in science, and to exhibit new objects of art. Distinguished individuals should also be invited to give lectures on subjects of general interest."

In his "Explanations and illustrations of the programme" presented to the Regents at the same time with the foregoing, Henry remarked: "The plan of increasing and diffusing knowledge, presented in the first section of the programme, will be found in strict accordance with the several propositions deduced from the Will of Smithson, and given in the introduction. It embraces—as a leading feature, the design of interesting the greatest number of individuals in the operations of the Institution, and of spreading its influence as widely as possible. It forms an active organization, exciting all to make original researches who are gifted with the necessary power, and diffusing a kind of knowledge now only accessible to the few, among all those who are willing to receive it. In this country, though many excel in the application of science to the practical arts of life, few devote themselves to the continued labor and patient thought necessary to the discovery and development of new truths. - - - The second section of the programme

gives — so far as they have been made out, the details of the part
of the plan of organization directed by the act of Congress establishing the Institution. The two plans, namely that of publication
and original research, and that of collections of objects of nature
and art, are not incompatible, and may be carried on harmoniously
with each other. The only effect which they will have on one
another is that of limiting the operation of each, on account of the
funds given to the other." *

That the fundamental assumption of this plan as to the true and
just interpretation of Smithson's Will, was not however peculiar to
Henry, is abundantly shown by many utterances of the thoughtful
and judicious.

In an appreciative memoir on the scientific work of Smithson,
written by Professor Walter R. Johnson of Philadelphia, in 1844,
he speaks in his introductory remarks of the gratitude due to the
public benefactor, "whether with Franklin he found a library, with
Maclure endow an academy for researches in natural science, or
with Smithson seek to stimulate into activity the spirit of philosophical research, to 'increase' by deepening the sources, and 'diffuse' by multiplying the channels of knowledge." And after
recounting the various investigations of Smithson, the writer concludes his review by asking: "What would have been the purposes
of an institution founded by Smithson in his life-time? To this
his *life-time* is a sufficient answer. Researches to 'increase' positive
knowledge, and publications to 'diffuse' and make that knowledge
available to mankind, — such were the great objects of his own constant praiseworthy and laborious efforts." †

The first Chancellor of the Institution — George M. Dallas,
(Vice-President of the United States,) in his address on the occasion of laying the corner-stone of the building, May 1, 1847,
remarked that the foundation was designed by Smithson to be
"an institution not merely for disseminating, spreading, teaching
knowledge, but also and *foremost* — for creating, originating, 'increasing' it."

A committee of the American Academy of Arts and Sciences,
appointed to examine the "programme of organization" submitted
by Henry to that body for its consideration, in a very full report
presented to — and unanimously adopted by — the Academy at Boston, December 7, 1847, expressed an entire concurrence in the views

---

* Programme, and Explanations. *Smithsonian Report* for 1847, pp. 128-139, of Sen.
ed. — pp. 120-131, of H. R. ed. Also *Smithsonian Report* for 1855, pp. 7-12.

† *A Memoir on the Scientific Character and Researches of James Smithson.* By
Professor Walter R. Johnson. Read before the National Institute, Washington,
April 6, 1844.

indicated, and a warm approval of the establishment proposed. After a recapitulation and analysis of the several details, the committee pronounced the opinion that "The most novel and important feature of the plan, is that which proposes to insure the publication of memoirs and treatises on important subjects of investigation, and to offer pecuniary encouragement to men of talent and attainment to engage in scientific research. It is believed that no institution in the country effects either of these objects to any great extent. The nearest approach to it is the practice of the Academy and other Philosophical Societies, of publishing the memoirs accepted by them. These however can rarely be works of great compass. No systematic plan of compensation for the preparation of works of scientific research, is known by the committee to have been attempted in this or any other country. It can scarcely be doubted that an important impulse would be given by the Institution in this way to the cultivation of scientific pursuits: while the extensive and widely ramified system of distribution and exchange by which the publications are to be distributed throughout the United States and the world, would secure them a circulation which works of science could scarcely attain in any other way. It is an obvious characteristic of this mode of applying the funds of the Institution, that its influence would operate most widely throughout the country; that locality would be of comparatively little importance as far as this influence is concerned; and that the Union would become (so to say) in this respect a great school of mutual instruction." *

---

## Note I. (*From p. 275.*)

### THE ELECTION OF THE FIRST "SECRETARY."

A special Committee of the Board of Regents appointed September 8th, 1846, "to digest a plan to carry out the provisions of the Act to establish the Smithsonian Institution," presented a somewhat elaborate report December 1st, 1846; in which they thus express themselves:

"Before concluding their report, your committee desire to add a few words touching the duty and qualifications of one of the officers of the Institution. Inasmuch as the Chancellor of the Smithsonian Institution being a regent, can receive no salary for his services, it results almost necessarily that the Secretary should become its chief

---

* This Report, dated Dec. 4, 1847, was signed by Edward Everett, Jared Sparks, Benjamin Pierce, Henry W. Longfellow, and Asa Gray. (*Smithsonian Report* for 1847, pp. 154, 155.—Sen. ed.)

executive officer. The charter seems to have intended that he should occupy a very responsible position. - .- - Your committee will not withhold their opinion that upon the choice of this single officer more probably than on any one other act of the Board, will depend the future good name and success and usefulness of the Smithsonian Institution."

The Board of Regents two days later proceeded to the election of this officer: and the result was announced in the *National Intelligencer* of the following day — December 4th. In the *Intelligencer* for Saturday, December 5th, 1846, the following editorial notice of this important proceeding was given:

"In a brief paragraph yesterday we announced that the Regents of the Smithsonian Institution had fixed their choice of Secretary, on Joseph Henry, LL. D. of Princeton College, New Jersey. The appointment of this officer was one of their most important and responsible duties. There has perhaps never been an occasion in the literary history of our country when so much depended upon the decision of so small a number of men. The success of one of the most liberal institutions in the world, depends much on the personal influence of the Secretary to be chosen by the Regents. Men of the highest literary distinction as well as personal merit in the nation were numbered among the candidates. It is no disparagement to their attainments to point out some of the circumstances which sanction the decision just made; for the statement of which, and the reference which it embraces to Professor Henry, we are indebted to the pen of a scientific friend.

"Foremost among American savans stands the name of FRANKLIN;—a name which belongs to the science of the world, and can hardly be said to have a locality. Second perhaps to Franklin only, stands the name of the philosopher of Princeton. It is not now the time nor place to enter into an enumeration of the extensive advances made in physical science by his researches. The brilliant discovery of Franklin of the identity of lightning and the electrical fluid, might have been supposed hardly to have left room for a gleaner in the field. Yet we venture the opinion that if Franklin's favorite aspiration could have been realized — if he could have been permitted to revisit after a lapse of half a century, the busy scenes of human life, he would have found himself a novice in his favorite science. A whole science — that of galvanism, (voltaic electricity,) electro-magnetism, magneto-electricity, thermo-electricity, etc. has been created since the time of Franklin. If the discovery of Franklin enables us to make the lightning harmless, that of the recent school of philosophers enables us to turn it in various ways to practical account in the business purposes of life. If we ask who gave to the electro-magnet of soft iron, now used for the telegraph, its present form, and discovered the laws by which its effective power could be made active, the answer is Joseph Henry. The discovery was first published in the proceedings of the Albany Institute. This was the earliest contribution to the progress of discovery made by the individual whom the choice of the Regents has elevated to the first literary station in the United States. Soon after this discovery Henry was called to the Chair of Experimental Philosophy at Princeton, where for the last fifteen years or more, he has filled the duties of his office in such a manner as to win for him the general esteem of the literary community of that time-honored seat of learning.

"With the relations between Professor Henry and his pupils we have no concern at present. It is of other relations in which he has stood toward the general cultivators of physical science throughout the world, that we propose to speak. One of the most important discoveries of recent date, that of the identity of the laws which regulate electric and magnetic, and electro-magnetic induction, was among the early fruits of his researches at Princeton. If Franklin discovered the identity between lightning and electricity, Henry has gone further, and reduced electric and magnetic action to the same laws. It is impossible in a short compass to do justice to the beauty and simplicity of Henry's laws of the action of the imponderable agents. Whoever will read the progress of his discoveries as published in the Transactions of the American Philosophical Society, will learn something of the spirit of inductive reasoning of which Henry's researches furnish one of the happiest illustrations. These discoveries are not confined in their sphere of utility to the limited circulation of the volumes of that Society. The student of physical science may read the reprints of them and the encomiums pronounced upon them in every language of civilized man throughout the globe. It was doubtless a knowledge of the extensive reputation which these and other discoveries have conferred on so young a man, which influenced the Regents in their selection of a Secretary. It is the man that gives dignity to the office, and not the office to the man. In his new sphere, Professor Henry will have advantages for the personal cultivation and advancement of science which the limited means of the Princeton College too frequently circumscribed. Men of science throughout the Union will find a central point for correspondence, and will pay to the individual that tribute of respect which among freemen would never be given to men of less attainments. We doubt not that the members of the republic of letters throughout the United States will applaud the choice, and give to the Regents their cordial support. It is not our purpose to enumerate all the claims which the Secretary elect has on the literary community. We have said enough to show that in discharging the responsible duty of this appointment, the Regents have looked with a single eye to the purposes of the munificent testator, the advancement of knowledge among men." *

## Note J.  (*From p. 276.*)

### HENRY'S PURPOSE OF ADMINISTRATION.

Perhaps no better inside view of Henry's primitive purpose can be obtained, than from the following private and unpublished letter to his personal friend President Nott, of Union College, Schenectady, N. Y. written during a visit to Princeton, very shortly after his election and removal to Washington:

"PRINCETON, December 26th, 1846.

"MY DEAR SIR: — Your favor of the 9th came to Princeton while I was at Washington, and I now answer it as soon as possible after my return. Please accept my thanks for your kind congratulations on my appointment to the office of Secretary of the Smithsonian Institution. I am not sure however that my appointment will prove a subject of congratulation. The office is one which I have by no means coveted, and which I have accepted at the earnest solicitation of some of the friends of science in our country, to prevent its falling into worse hands, and with the hope of saving the noble bequest of Smithson from being squandered on chimerical or unworthy projects. My first object is to urge on the Regents the adoption of a simple practical plan of carrying out the design of the Testator, viz: the "*increase* and *diffusion* of knowledge among men." For this purpose in my opinion the organization of the Institution should be such as to stimulate original research in all branches of knowledge, in every part of our country and throughout the world, and also to provide the means of diffusing at stated periods an account of the progress of general knowledge compiled from the Journals of all languages. To establish such an organization, I must endeavor to prevent expenditure of a large portion of the funds of the Smithsonian bequest on a pile of brick and mortar, filled with objects of curiosity, intended for the embellishment of Washington, and the amusement of those who visit that city. My object at present, is to prevent the adoption of plans

---

* *National Intelligencer*, Washington, Dec. 5, 1846, vol. xxxiv. no. 10,541.

which may tend to embarrass the future usefulness of **the Institution**, and for this purpose I do not intend to make any appointments unless expressly directed to do so by the Regents, until the organization **is** definitely settled.

"The **income of the** Institution is not sufficient **to** carry out a fourth part **of the plans** mentioned in the Act of Congress, and con**templated in the Report of the** Regents.   **For** example, to support **the expense of the Museum of** the Exploring Expedition presented **by Government to the** Smithsonian Institution, will require in **interest on building and expense of** attendance upward of 10,000 **dollars annually.   A corps** of Professors with necessary assistants **will amount** to **from 12,000 to 15,000** dollars.   From these **facts you will** readily **perceive that unless** the Institution is started with great caution there is danger of absorbing all the income in a few objects, which in themselves may not be the **best** means of carrying out the design of the **Testator.**   I have elaborated a simple plan of organization, **which I intend to** press with all my energy.   If this is adopted, **I am** confident the name **of** Smithson will **become** familiar to **every part of** the civilized **world.   If** I cannot succeed carrying **out** my plans—at least in **a** considerable degree, I shall **ithdraw** from the Institution.

"With **much respect and** esteem, **I** remain<br>"**Your** obedient servant,<br>"JOSEPH HENRY.

"Rev. Dr. ELIPHALET **NOTT,**
     "*President of Union College,* &c. &c."

* * *

*Note K.* ( *From p. 281.* )

STRUGGLE WITH THE LIBRARY SCHEME.

From **the first** organization **of the Smithsonian** Institution, or indeed from the still earlier times **of its** discussion **on the floors of** Congress, the great need **of a general library** of reference, on a scale comparable to that of **the** large **European** establishments, felt by **every** historical **and** literary student, naturally led such readers to **look** eagerly **to the** endowment of Smithson for the attainment of **this** desirable **end.   On December 15,** 1843, the Hon. Rufus **Choate**—chairman of the Senate committee on the library, obtained **the reference of the matter** of Smithson's **bequest** to his own com**mittee: and when on June 6, and again on December** 12, 1844, **Senator** Benjamin Tappan, a member of the same committee intro**duced** a bill establishing **on the Smithson fund, an agricultural** institution with a botanical garden, natural-history cabinet, library, laboratory, lecture-rooms and professorships, Mr. Choate in opposition to the plan, on **January** 8, 1845, contended that "we cannot do a safer, **surer,** more unexceptionable thing with the income, **or** with a portion of the income—(perhaps twenty thousand dollars a year for a few years,) than to expend it in accumulating a **grand** and **noble** public library; one which for variety, extent, and wealth, shall be confessed to be equal **to** any now in the world. Twenty thousand dollars a year for **twenty-five** years, are five hundred thousand dollars." And he offered as a substitute section, "that a **sum not** less than 20,000 dollars **be annually expended of** the interest of the fund aforesaid, in the **purchase of books."** \* This proposition however was not adopted.

In the House of Representatives, the Hon. Robert Dale Owen — chairman of a special committee on the subject, presented a bill February **28, and April 22, 1846,** establishing a normal educational institution; a feature strongly opposed by **Hon. John Q. Adams,** and on the **29th of April, 1846,** stricken out. On the same day, Hon. Bradford **R. Wood moved** as an amendment "that the sum of 20,000 dollars **of the interest** of said fund **be and is hereby** appropriated annually **for** the purchase or publication of **a library."** A substitute **bill presented** by Hon. William J. Hough on the same day, provided among various specifications, **for an** appropriation from the interest of the fund—"*not exceeding* an average of 25,000 dollars annually for the gradual formation of a library." Which bill was adopted. † This act passed the Senate, and **became a law,** August 10, 1846.

This **organic Act of** Congress **provided** (in sect. 3) a directorship for the **Institution, to** consist of **fifteen** Regents,—six of whom **should be members of** Congress, selected equally **from the two chambers; and** (in sect. 9) authorized the said managers "to make **such disposal as they** shall deem best **suited for the** promotion of the purposes of the testator,"—**of any** income not appropriated or required by **the** provisions of the act.

The Board of Regents, after **considerable** discussion, by resolution adopted January 26, 1847, apportioned one-half of the annual income (exclusive of building expenses) to the purpose of forming **a** library and museum, and one-half **for the** publication of original researches and for the support of **public lectures.** This compromise between contending parties, **by no means** satisfied the judgment of the Secretary. In his first **report to the Regents,** presented Decem-

\* *The Smithsonian Institution: Documents relative to its Origin and History.* Edited by William J. Rhees. (*Smith. Mis. Coll.* No.328,) pp. 262, 312, and 320.

† *The Smithsonian Institution.* By W. J. Rhees. Pp. 355, 396, 462-'4, 469-473.

ber 8, 1847, Henry strongly urged that "In carrying out the spirit of the plan adopted, namely that of affecting men in general by the operations of the Institution, it is evident that the principal means of 'diffusing knowledge' must be the *Press*."[*] In his second report he sets forth that "The Institution is not for a day, but is designed to endure as long as our Government shall exist; and it is therefore peculiarly important that in the beginning we should proceed carefully and not attempt to produce immediate effects at the expense of permanent usefulness. The process of 'increasing knowledge' is an extremely slow one, and the value of the results of this part of the plan, cannot be properly realized until some years have elapsed."[†] In his fourth report he recapitulates: "To carry out the design of the testator, various plans were proposed; but most of these were founded on an imperfect apprehension of the terms of the will. The great majority of them contemplated merely the 'diffusion' of popular information, and neglected the first and the most prominent requisition of the bequest, namely the 'increase of knowledge.' The only plan in strict conformity with the terms of the will, and which especially commended itself to men of science, a class to which Smithson himself belonged, was that of an active living organization, intended principally to promote the discovery and diffusion of new truths. - - - It was with the hope of being able to assist in the practical development of this plan that I was induced to accept the appointment of principal executive officer of the Institution. Many unforeseen obstacles however presented themselves to its full adoption; and its advocates soon found in contending with opposing views and adverse interests, a wide difference between what in their opinion ought to be done, and what they could actually accomplish. - - - After much discussion it was finally concluded to divide the income (after deducting the general expenses) into two equal parts, and to devote one part to the active operations set forth in the plan just described, and the other to the formation of a library, a museum, and a gallery of art. It was evident however that the small income of the original bequest — though in itself sufficient to do much good in the way of active operations, was inadequate to carry out this more extended plan. - - - Though one-half of the annual interest is to be expended on the library and the museum, the portion of the income which can be thus devoted to the former, will in my opinion never be sufficient without extraneous aid to collect and support a miscellaneous library of the first class. Indeed, all the income would

---

[*] *Smithsonian Report* for 1847, p. 133 (Sen. ed.)—p. 130 (H. R. ed.)

[†] *Smithsonian Report* for 1848, p. 156 (Sen. ed.)—p. 148 (H. R. ed.)

scarcely suffice for this purpose."[*]  In his fifth annual report he maintains that "the idea ought never to be entertained that the portion of the limited income of the Smithsonian fund which can be devoted to the purchase of books, will ever be sufficient to meet the wants of the American scholar."[†]  In his sixth annual report, exhibiting the valuable contributions to knowledge which the Institution had already effected in the few years of its existence, he remarks: "All the anticipations indulged with regard to it have been fully realized; and after an experience of six years, there can now be no doubt of the true policy of the Regents in regard to it. I am well aware however that the idea is entertained by some that the system of active operations though at present in a flourishing condition, cannot continue to be the prominent object of attention; and that under another set of directors other counsels will prevail and other measures be adopted, and what has been done in establishing this system will ultimately be undone."  He presents however the inspiriting and consoling reflection: "But if notwithstanding all this, the Institution is destined to a change of policy, what has been well done in the line we are advocating, can never be undone. The new truths developed by the researches originated by the Institution and recorded in its publications, the effect of its exchanges with foreign countries, and the results of its cataloguing system, can never be obliterated: they will endure through all coming time. Should the Government of the United States be dissolved, and the Smithsonian fund dissipated to the winds, — the 'Smithsonian Contributions to Knowledge' will still be found in the principal libraries of the world, a perpetual monument of the wisdom and liberality of the founder of the Institution, and of the faithfulness of those who first directed its affairs.  Whatever therefore may be the future condition of the Institution, the true policy for the present, is to devote its energies to the system of active operations.  All other objects should be subordinate to this, and in no wise be suffered to diminish the good which it is capable of producing.  It should be prosecuted with discretion, but with vigor: the *results* will be its vindication."[‡]  In his next annual report he reiterates: "A miscellaneous and general library, museum, and gallery of art, (though important in themselves,) have from the first been considered by those who have critically examined the Will of Smithson, to be too restricted in their operations and too local in their influence, to meet the comprehensive intentions of the testator; and the hope

---

[*] *Smithsonian Report* for 1850, pp. 186, 187, and 205 (Sen. ed.)—pp. 178, 179, and 197 (H. R. ed.)

[†] *Smithsonian Report* for 1851, p. 224 (Sen. ed.)—p. 216 (H. R. ed.)

[‡] *Smithsonian Report* for 1852, pp. 233, 234 (Sen. ed.)—pp. 225, 226 (H. R. ed.)

has been cherished that other means may ultimately be provided for the support of those objects, and that the whole income of the Smithsonian fund may be devoted to the more legitimate objects of the noble bequest." *

At a meeting of the Board of Regents held March 12, 1853, a committee of seven was appointed to consider and report upon "the subject of the distribution of the income of the Institution, in the manner contemplated by the original plan of organization." Hon. R. Choate, a member of this committee, being unable to attend its meetings, (having returned to Boston at the end of his Senatorial term in 1846,) Hon. James Meacham (of the House of Representatives) was appointed to take his place, February 18, 1854. At a meeting of the Regents held May 20, 1854, Hon. James A. Pearce, chairman of the committee, submitted its report, presenting a very full discussion of the legal questions — as to the discretionary power of the Regents, and the true policy of the Institution. On the first point, after showing how faithfully the specific requirements of the organic Act had been executed, the committee in referring to the clause that the annual expenditure for the library should not exceed 25,000 dollars in the average, maintained that "this is nothing but a *limitation* upon the discretion of the Regents, and can by no rule of construction be considered as intimating the desire of Congress that such sum should be annually appropriated. The limitation while it prevented the Regents from exceeding that sum, left them full discretion as to any amount within that limit." On the second point, the committee say: "What then are the considerations which should govern them in rejecting the plan which proposes a great library as the best and chief — if not the only means of executing the trust created by the Will of Smithson, and fulfilling their own duty under the law? The 'increase and diffusion of knowledge among men,' are the great purposes of this munificent trust. To increase knowledge implies research, or new and active investigation in some one or more of the departments of learning. To diffuse knowledge among men, implies active measures for its distribution so far as may be, among mankind. Neither of these purposes could be accomplished or materially advanced by the accumulation of a great library at the city of Washington. - - - The application of 25,000 dollars annually (five-sixths of the whole income at the date of the Act) to the purchase of books, would be inconsistent with and subversive of the whole tenor of all that precedes the 8th section.† - - - The committee need not repeat in detail all the

---

* *Smithsonian Report* for 1853, pp. 10, 11 (Sen. ed.)

[† The residue of the income would indeed have been wholly insufficient even for the necessary salaries and incidental expenses of the library itself,— to say nothing of the other interests specifically provided for by the 5th section of the act.]

parts of the plan of organization, but may mention that it included the exchange of the published transactions of the Institution with those of literary and scientific societies and establishments, and provided for a museum, and library, to consist of a complete collection of the transactions and proceedings of all the learned societies in the world, of the more important current periodical publications and other works necessary to scientific investigations; thus employing the instrumentalities pointed out in the law, as means of increasing and diffusing knowledge, entirely consistent with and necessary to the plan of research and publication. This plan is no longer experimental; it has been tested by experience; its success is acknowledged by all who are capable of forming a correct estimate of its results; and the Institution has every encouragement to pursue steadily its system of stimulating, assisting, and publishing research. - - - The committee submit to the Board the following resolutions: *Resolved*, That the seventh resolution passed by the Board of Regents on the 26th of January, 1847, requiring an equal division of the income between the active operations, and the museum and library, (when the buildings are completed,) be and it is hereby repealed. *Resolved*, That hereafter the annual appropriations shall be apportioned specifically among the different objects and operations of the Institution in such manner as may in the judgment of the Regents be necessary and proper for each, according to its intrinsic importance and a compliance in good faith with the law." * This report was signed by six of the committee: Mr. Meacham the last appointed member dissenting, and submitting an elaborate minority report, which comprised a very able and ingenious argument in defence of the library plan. † The resolutions offered by the committee were adopted by the Board of Regents January 15, 1855.

As six of the fifteen Regents were by law selected from senators and representatives, a very obvious resort for a member dissatisfied with the action of a majority, was a motion in Congress for the familiar "committee of inquiry." Accordingly Hon. James Meacham moved in the House, January 17, 1855, that a select committee of five be appointed, "and that said committee be directed to inquire and report to the House whether the Smithsonian Institution has been managed, and its funds expended in accordance with the law establishing the Institution; and whether any additional legislation be necessary to carry out the designs of its founders; and that said committee have power to send for persons and papers." The resolution was adopted by a vote of 93 to 91.‡

* *Smithsonian Report* for 1853, pp. 81-97 (Sen. ed.)
† *Smithsonian Report* for 1853, (appendix to H. R. ed.) pp. 247-296.
‡ *The Smithsonian Institution.* By W. J. Rhees, pp. 569-572.

On the 3d of March, 1855, Hon. Charles W. Upham, chairman of the select committee, submitted to the House what must be regarded as a minority report; declaring "No doubt we think can be entertained that the framers and enactors of the law expected that about 200,000 dollars would be expended 'for the formation of a library composed of valuable works pertaining to all departments of knowledge,' in eight years." After criticising the system approved by the Regents, of devoting a large portion of the Smithsonian income to the promotion of original research, the report states: "At the same time they do not cast blame or censure of any sort upon those who suggested and have labored to carry out that system. The design was in itself commendable and elevated. It has unquestionably been pursued with zeal, sincerity, integrity, and high motives and aims: but it is we think necessarily surrounded with very great difficulties. - - - But a few words are needed to do justice to the value of a great universal library at the metropolis of the Union:" &c. - - - The report concludes with the judgment that as a measure of mutual concession, "the compromise adopted at an early day by the Board of Regents, ought to be restored, and that all desirable ends may be ultimately secured by dividing the income equally between the library and museum on one part, and the active operations on the other." This report was signed by the chairman, Mr. Upham, alone;—two of the committee (Messrs. William H. Witte and Nathaniel G. Taylor) presenting a dissenting report, and the remaining two (Messrs. Richard C. Puryear and Daniel Wells) declining to sign either. The report submitted by Mr. Witte (no less elaborate than that by the chairman) concluded: "They believe that the Regents and the Secretary have managed the affairs of the Institution wisely, faithfully, and judiciously; that there is no necessity for further legislation on the subject; and that if the Institution be allowed to continue the plan which has been adopted and so far pursued with unquestionable success, it will satisfy all the requirements of the law, and the purposes of Smithson's Will, by 'increasing and diffusing knowledge among men.'" * Upon these conflicting and balanced reports no action was taken by the House.

Simultaneously in the Senate, Hon. John M. Clayton, January 17, 1855, introduced a resolution "that the Committee on the Judiciary inquire whether any, and if any — what action of the Senate is necessary and proper in regard to the Smithsonian Institution?" On the 6th of February, 1855, Hon. Andrew P. Butler, chairman of the Judiciary Committee, submitted to the Senate a report completely vindicating the course pursued by the Regents;

* *The Smithsonian Institution.* By W. J. Rhees, pp. 589–628.

in which it is maintained that "any increase of knowledge that might be acquired was not to be locked up in the Institution or preserved only for the citizens of Washington or persons who might visit the Institution. It was by the express terms of the trust, (which the United States was pledged to execute,) to be 'diffused among men.' This could be done in no other way than by publications at the expense of the Institution. Nor has Congress prescribed the sums which shall be appropriated to these different objects. It is left to the discretion and judgment of the Regents. - - - These operations appear to have been carried out by the Regents under the immediate superintendence of Professor Henry, with zeal, energy, and discretion, and with the strictest regard to economy in the expenditure of the funds. Nor does there seem to be any other mode which Congress could prescribe or the Regents adopt, which would better fulfill the high trust which the United States have undertaken to perform. - - - The committee see nothing therefore in their conduct which calls for any new legislation, or any change in the powers now exercised by the Regents." And the report concludes in "the language of the resolution, that 'no action of the Senate is necessary and proper in regard to the Smithsonian Institution:' and this is the unanimous opinion of the committee."*

And thus ended an earnest struggle of many years between Science and Literature for the possession of Smithson's endowment; and though the interest in the controversy has long since passed away in the permanent establishment of Henry's far-reaching policy, its history is suggestive and instructive. No better concluding summary can be presented, than by an extract from a quite recent judicious and dispassionate recapitulation of the discussion and its results, written for *The International Review*, by Mr. A. R. Spofford, the scholarly librarian of the Government Library at Washington:

"The net result of the protracted controversy was to leave the Regents to put their own interpretation upon the law, and every step since taken in the management of the Smithsonian bequest, has been in the direction of curtailing every expenditure for other objects than the procuring, publishing, and distributing of what were deemed valuable original contributions to human knowledge. In strict accordance with this theory, the library gathered by the purchases and exchanges of twenty years, was transferred to the Capitol in 1866, and became a part of the library of the Government. This large addition formed a most valuable complement to the collection already gathered at the Capitol. It embraced the largest assemblage of transactions and other publications of learned

---

* *Smithsonian Report* for 1855, pp. 83–86.—Rhees' *Smithsonian Institution*, pp. 562–567.

societies in all parts of the globe and in nearly all the modern languages, which is to be found in the country.  -  -  -  The Smithsonian deposit, kept up as it is from year to year by additions of new contributions in every department of scientific literature, supplies — in connection with the extensive Library of Congress, a larger collection of scientific books for use and reference, than is to be found in any one body elsewhere in the United States.  The waste of means incident to the duplication of two extensive libraries at the seat of Government is thus obviated, while the convenience and interests of scholars pursuing their researches, are in the highest degree promoted by the consolidation." *

### Note L.  (*From p. 285.*)

#### DISTRIBUTION OF SMITHSONIAN MATERIAL.

For the great organic purpose of furthering scientific research, not only have vast numbers of duplicate specimens been liberally distributed, but even reserved specimens of special interest or rarity have been loaned under proper conditions to original workers. Perhaps the review of a single year's application of such material, will best convey an idea of its general character:

"It has always been the policy of the Institution to furnish specimens for special study and investigation to naturalists of established reputation, either in this country or abroad.  The use of these specimens is granted under the express condition that they are to form the subject of investigation, the results of which are to be published by the Institution or some other establishment, and that in all cases full credit is to be given to the Institution for the assistance it has rendered.  Furthermore, in the case of the preparation of a monograph, a full set of the type specimens correctly labeled is to be put aside for the National Museum, and the remainder of the specimens made up into sets for distribution.  The following list presents the more important cases of the loan or assignment of materials during the past year.  Some of the specimens have already been returned, while the remainder are still in the hands of the parties to whom they were intrusted:

"Crania of the recent and fossil bison, musk-ox, &c. to Professor L. Agassiz, of Cambridge, Mass: — land shells of Central and South America to Thomas Bland, of New York: — land and fresh-water shells of North America to W. G. Binney, Burlington, N. J. — nests and eggs of North American birds to Dr. T. M. Brewer, Boston: —

birds of South America and Alaska to John Cassin, Philadelphia:—Alcadæ of North America to Dr. Elliott Coues, U. S. Army:—collections of American and foreign reptiles to Professor E. D. Cope, Philadelphia:—fungi from the Indian Territory to the Rev. M. A. Curtis, Hillsborough, N. C.—unfigured species of North American birds to D. G. Elliott, New York:—diatomaceous earths and deep-sea soundings to Arthur M. Edwards, New York:—Lepidoptera from various North American localities to W. H. Edwards, Coalburg, Va.—seeds of Boehmeria received from the Department of Agriculture, to Dr. Earl Flint, Nicaragua:—plants collected in Ecuador by the expedition under Professor Orton, to Dr. Asa Gray, Cambridge, Mass.—miscellaneous specimens of North American insects to Professor T. Glover, Department of Agriculture, Washington:—general collection of birds of Costa Rica and Yucatan to George N. Lawrence, New York:—American Unionidæ to Isaac Lea, Philadelphia:—series of North American salamanders to St. George Mivart, London:—American Diptera to Baron R. Osten-Sacken, New York:—Lepidoptera of Ecuador and Yucatan to Tryon Reakirt, Philadelphia:—plants collected in Alaska by various expeditions to Dr. J. T. Rothrock, McVeytown, Pa.—birds of Buenos Ayres received from W. H. Hudson, and a series of small American owls, to Dr. P. L. Sclater and Osbert Salvin, London:—miscellaneous collections of American Orthoptera to S. H. Scudder, Boston:—collections of American Hemiptera to P. R. Uhler, Baltimore:—American myriapods and spiders to Dr. H. C. Wood, Philadelphia:—human crania from northwestern America and the ancient mounds of Kentucky, also collections from the ancient shell-heaps of Massachusetts and New Brunswick, to Dr. Jeffreys Wyman, Cambridge, Mass.

"Few persons are aware of the great extent to which this Smithsonian material has been used by American and foreign naturalists, or the number of new facts and new species which have been contributed to natural history through its means."*

---

## Note M. (*From p. 285.*)

### OVERFLOWING CONDITION OF THE MUSEUM.

"It is a question whether any museum in the world is in receipt of so great an amount of material as the National Museum at Washington; and were the rule of the British Museum to prevail, it would be crushed by the weight of its own riches. The constant

---

* *Smithsonian Report* for 1868, pp. 36, 37.

effort however on the part of the Smithsonian Institution to utilize this material in the interest of science and education, tends to keep down the mass, though it is only at the expense of the incessant activity and constant labor of the Museum force that this object is in any measure accomplished. - - - It may be proper to state that for the exhibition of the full series of objects now in possession of the Institution, and not including any unnecessary duplicates, much ampler accommodations will be needed than can be had in the building; and if these are to be displayed as they should be, it will be necessary at no distant day to provide means for extending the space, either by a transfer of the entire collection to new buildings, or by making additions to that of the Smithsonian Institution. In illustration of this statement it may be remarked that of sixty-seven thousand specimens of birds entered in the catalogues of the museum, and of which more than forty thousand are on hand,— (the remainder having been distributed,) less than five thousand are mounted and on exhibition, these occupying fully two-fifths of the present hall: the rest are preserved as skins, in chests, drawers, and boxes, and of them fifteen thousand — or three times the number at present on exhibition, require to be displayed for the proper illustration of even American ornithology. The urgency for additional room is still greater for the mammals. Here, out of some five or six thousand specimens, less than so many hundred are exhibited, the remainder alone being almost sufficient to occupy half of the hall. Of many thousands of skeletons of mammals, birds, reptiles, and fishes, a very small percentage is shown to the public, while exhibition-room to the amount of thousands of square feet is required for specimens that now occupy drawers in side apartments. Of the very large collection of alcoholic specimens which constitute the most important material in every public museum, scarcely anything is on exhibition, although the selection of a single series for this purpose is very desirable." *

"The Museum portion of the Smithsonian edifice consists of two rooms of about 10,000 square feet area each, with a connecting range and gallery of about 5,000 square feet. The specimens in cases are at present very much crowded, while very many others are in boxes occupying the passages and intermediate spaces. The basement of the Institution, nearly 400 feet long, is a series of store-rooms for the reception of portions of the collection not yet exhibited in the upper halls, and thus without benefit to the general public. - - - An estimate of 25,000 square feet, or a space equal to that of the upper halls, is by no means extravagant for the proper display of the specimens thus excluded.

---

"Anticipating the necessity of increased accommodations for the Centennial collections and accessions, the Smithsonian Institution in 1875 made application to Congress for the use of the Armory building in the square between Sixth and Seventh streets,—an edifice 100 feet by 50, having four floors. This it was supposed would be adequate at the close of the Centennial, for the reception and exhibition of at least the fishery exhibit and that of economical mineralogy. So great however was the surplus of Centennial material to be provided for, that the building is now filled with boxed specimens, occupying for the most part the entire space from floor to ceiling of each room. The building is not fire-proof, and although the specimens in it represent some of the most valuable and important of the series, there is nothing to prevent their destruction by fire, or their injury from damp, vermin, or other causes;— a result which would constitute an irreparable loss. As the four floors of the Armory referred to, present 20,000 feet of area, an estimate of 50,000 feet for the proper display of the specimens now stored in them cannot be considered extravagant; thus making the entire additional space required,— 75,000 square feet. Only one-fourth of the specimens in charge of the Institution are at present on exhibition, the remainder being entirely withdrawn from public inspection; so that the necessity for prompt effort to secure the proper accommodations will be readily understood. - - - In view of the fact that the collections for which provision is needed represent a bulk of at least three times the present capacity of the Smithsonian building, it is evident that to accommodate these, and to make reasonable provision for probable increase in the future, a building of great magnitude will be required."*

---

## Note N. (*From p. 309.*)

### INVESTIGATION OF ILLUMINANTS.

"At the commencement of the operations of the Light-House Board in 1852, sperm oil was generally employed for the purpose of illumination. This was an excellent illuminant; but as its price continued to advance from year to year, it was thought proper to attempt the introduction of some other material. The first attempt of this kind was that of the introduction of colza oil, which was generally used in the light-houses of Europe, and is extracted from the seed of a species of wild cabbage — known in this country as *rape*, and in France as *colza*. For this purpose a quantity of rape-

---

seed was imported from France and distributed through the agricultural department of the Patent Office to different parts of the country, with the hope that our farmers would be induced to attempt its cultivation. Although the climate of the country appeared favorable to its growth, and special instructions were prepared and distributed by the Light-House Board for its culture and the means of producing oil from it, yet the enterprise was not undertaken with any approximation to success, except in Wisconsin, where a manufactory of rape-seed oil was established by Colonel C. S. Hamilton, formerly of the United States Army. To this manufactory the Light-House Board gave special encouragement and purchased at a liberal price all the oil that could be supplied. The quantity however which could be procured was but a small part of the illuminating material required for the annual consumption of the Light-House Establishment."

After referring to some investigations made for the Board by Professor J. H. Alexander, of Baltimore, the Report quoted proceeds: "The chairman of the committee on experiments commenced himself to investigate the qualities of different kinds of oil, and was soon led to direct his attention to the comparative value of sperm and lard oils. The experiments made by Mr. Alexander were with small lamps, and the comparison in this case (as will be shown) was much against the lard oil. The first experiment of the new series, consisted in charging two small conical lamps of the capacity of about a half pint, one with pure sperm oil and the other with lard oil. These lamps were of single-rope wicks each containing the same number of strands: they were lighted at the same time, and the photometrical power ascertained by the method of shadows. At first the two were nearly equal in brilliancy, but after burning about three hours, the flame of the lard had declined in photometric power to about one-fifth of that of the flame of the sperm. The question then occurred as to the cause of this decline, and it was suggested that it might be due — first, to a greater specific gravity in the lard oil, which would retard the ascent of it in the wick after the level of the oil had been reduced by burning in the lamp; or second, to a want of a sufficient attraction between the oil and the wick to furnish the requisite supply as the oil descended in the lamp; or third, it might be due in part to the imperfect liquidity of the oil, which would also militate against its use in mechanical lamps.

"The lard oil was subjected to experiments in regard to each of these points. It was found by the usual method of weighing equal quantities of the two fluids, that the specific gravity of the lard was greater than that of the sperm; and also by dipping two portions of the same wick into the two liquids and noting the height to which each ascended in a given time, that the surface attraction of the sperm was greater than that of the lard, or in other words that the ascensional power of sperm was much greater than that of lard at ordinary temperatures. This method was also employed in obtaining the relative surface attraction of various other liquids; we say surface attraction instead of capillarity, because it was found in the course of these investigations that substances which had less capillarity (that is less elevating power in a fine tube) had greater power in ascending in the meshes of a wick. The relative fluidity of the different oils was obtained by filling in succession a pear-shaped vessel with a narrow neck, of about the capacity of a pint, having a hole in the lowest part of the bottom, of about a tenth of an inch in diameter. Such a vessel filled with any number of perfect liquids, would be emptied in the same time — whatever their specific gravity. As at any given horizon, inertia is directly proportional to gravity, the heavier the liquid the greater would be the power required to move it; but the motive power would be in proportion to the pressure, or in other words to the weight, and therefore all perfect liquids should issue from the same orifice with the same velocity. To test this proposition, eight fluid ounces of clean mercury and then the same bulk of distilled water, were allowed to run out of the vessel above mentioned: the time observed was the same within the nearest second. It was found in repeating this experiment with sperm and lard oils that the rapidity of the flow of the former exceeded considerably that of the latter; the ratio of time being 100 to 167.

"The results thus far in these investigations were apparently against the use of lard oil: it was observed however that in the experiments on the flow of the two oils, a variation in the time occurred, which could only be attributed to a variation in the temperature at which the experiments were made. In relation to this point, the effect of an increase of the temperature above that of the atmosphere, on the flowing of the two oils was observed. By this means the important fact was elicited that as the temperature was increased, the liquidity of the lard increased in a more rapid degree than that of the sperm, and that at the temperature of about 250° F. the liquidity of the former exceeded that of the latter. A similar series of experiments was made in regard to the rapidity of ascent of the oil in the wick, and with a similar result. At about the temperature of that before mentioned, the ascensional power of the lard was greater than that of the sperm. These results were recognized as having an important bearing on the question of the application of lard oil as a light-house illuminant. It only required to be burned at a high temperature; and as this could be readily obtained in the case of larger lamps, there appeared to be no difficulty in its application.

"The previous trials had been with small lamps with single solid wicks instead of the Fresnel lamp with hollow burners. After these preliminary experiments, two light-houses of the first order, at Cape Ann, Massachusetts, separated by a distance of only 900 feet, were selected as affording excellent facilities for trying in actual burning, the correctness of the conclusions which had previously been arrived at. One of these light-houses was supplied with sperm and the other with lard oil, each lamp being so trimmed as to exhibit its greatest capacity. It was found by photometrical trial that the lamp supplied with lard, exceeded in intensity of light that of the one furnished with sperm. The experiment was continued for several months, and the relative volume of the two materials carefully observed. The quantity of sperm burned during the continuance of the experiment, was to that of the lard, as 100 is to 104." *

This remarkable success in elevating the disparaged lard oil to the highest rank as an illuminant, was of course very damaging to the new manufacture of colza oil; and no more characteristic tribute to the energetic skill of Henry could be offered, than that contained in the following frank and manly letter by Colonel C. S. Hamilton, the manufacturer, (who by special invitation had been present at several competitive photometric trials,) addressed to the Naval Secretary of the Light-House Board, Commodore Andrew A. Harwood:

"FOND DU LAC, WIS. May 16, 1868.

"DEAR COMMODORE: I must confess my great disappointment at the result of the experiments at Staten Island. It is however not really so much the failure of rape-seed oil, as the undeniable excellence of lard oil as a burner. I am satisfied now that for self-heating lamps there is no oil that will bear comparison with lard, but I am equally satisfied that no colza oil will yield a better result than ours, under exactly the same tests. We have but one more experiment to make with colza; it is its extraction by chemical displacement. If this fails we shall abandon the whole business.

"If all things are put together, I think the following statement will be allowed, to wit: Our colza oil of this year is equal to any foreign colza. It is better than any we have heretofore made. It is better than sperm, or any other burner, excepting only lard oil. Our failure then is owing to the superior excellence of lard oil, which under the persistent investigation of the Board, has been

---

* *Report of the Light-House Board* for 1875, pp. 86-88.

shown to be the best and cheapest safe illuminator available. The Board are entitled to great credit in producing this result. It will be remembered that but a few years since, lard oil was pronounced unsuitable for light-house purposes; but the perseverance of the Board has brought out the fact that it is much the best and cheapest oil, and that the expenses of lighting the coast and harbors have been thereby greatly reduced. Surely the country at large should acknowledge this, and give due credit to the Board. We have endeavored to do with colza what the Board have effected with lard oil, and we have been unsuccessful both for ourselves and the light-house interest. - - -

"We are grateful to each member of the Board for the interest they have always shown in our undertaking, and for their uniform kindness and courtesy. Accept, my dear Commodore, for yourself and your associates in the Board, my warmest thanks for your many kind expressions of interest, and believe me

"Truly and gratefully, yours,

"C. S. HAMILTON."

www.ingramcontent.com/pod-product-compliance
Lightning Source LLC
Chambersburg PA
CBHW030107030726
47498CB00007B/2281